SOLITUDE

DIMENSION SPACE BOOK ONE

DEAN M COLE

CANDTOR PRESS, LLC

Solitude: A Post-Apocalyptic Thriller (Dimension Space Book One)

Published by CANDTOR Press, LLC

Solitude: Dimension Space Book One is a work of fiction. Names, characters, places, and incidents are either the products of the author's imagination or are used fictitiously. Any resemblance to actual persons, living or dead, events, or locales is entirely coincidental.

Cover Art © 2019 Tor Øra

ISBN-10: 1541381653

ISBN-13: 978-1541381650

Another Great Series by Dean

The Complete *Sector 64* Series

1947 - *First Contact a Sector 64 Prequel Novella*
Today - *Ambush - Book One of the Sector 64 Duology*
Tomorrow - *Retribution - Book Two of the Sector 64 Duology*

(Read the sneak peak of *Ambush* at the end of this book.)

PART I

"We wrap up our violent and mysterious world in a pretense of understanding. We paper over the voids of our comprehension with science and religion and make believe that order has been imposed. And, for the most of it, the fiction works. We skim across the surfaces, heedless of the depths below. Dragonflies flitting over a lake, miles deep, pursuing erratic paths to pointless ends. Until that moment when something from the cold unknown reaches up to take us."

— James Howard Kunstler

CHAPTER 1

Angela looked down to see the familiar horseshoe shape of Hudson Bay glide beneath her white boots. She shifted her gaze to the south and spotted Canada's biggest annular lake. It ringed Manicouagan Crater—one of Earth's largest asteroidal scars and easily visible from space.

"Uh, Commander Brown, if you're done sightseeing, I could use a hand here."

Angela smiled. Mindful of the ever-watchful eye of Mission Control, she resisted the urge to, playfully, hoist her middle finger. Instead, she gave him her cheesiest smile and said, "How may I be of assistance, Major?"

Major Peterson did a double take. He floated a few feet across from Angela. Behind the visor of his helmet, a crooked grin spread across his ebony face. "Really, Commander Brown? Assistance? What happened to, 'What can Brown do for you?'?"

Angela sighed and rolled her eyes. "Don't you start, too." Inside her helmet, her head shook side-to-side. "Crack one public joke, and it follows you around for the rest of your life."

"That'll learn ya," Bill Peterson said with a smile.

Angela ignored him and continued. "That was 2018. It's been two years. I mean, really?!"

Paying no heed to her, the major wrapped his gauntleted hand around a coffee cup-sized white cylinder. His body writhed as he struggled with the stubborn electrical connector.

The pair of astronauts floated near the left or port end of the International Space Station's 300-foot-long solar array truss. The structure supported all sixteen of the station's main solar panels. To Angela, the long edifice looked like the mutated body of a dragonfly with way too many wings.

"This thing doesn't want to budge," he said with a grunt. The man's entire body lurched as he tried to force the electrical connector to turn.

"Is that Charlie Eight One Niner?" Angela said.

After giving the connector's three-inch-thick barrel a final fruitless twist, he released it with a frustrated growl. "The one and only!"

The two spacesuited figures floated in the shadow of the station's outermost solar panel, but sunlight reflected off the truss, illuminating the major's face. He looked from the cylindrical connector and winked at her. "Got a can of WD-40?"

Angela smiled and held up a large set of white pliers. "Nope. But I do have the convincer."

She tilted the joystick grasped in her right hand. The bracket under her feet vibrated, and the robotic manipulator arm attached to the bottom of her boots moved Angela toward Major Bill Peterson.

A moment later she released the controller. Now they floated face-to-face: Angela standing on the end of the long manipulator arm, Bill clipped to the array's hard points, the offending power coupling between them. A metal label riveted to its side read:

C819

Angela grasped its outer ring with the convincer—a tool specifically designed for stubborn connectors. In the zero-G environment, she relied on the stability of Canadarm2, the manipulator arm strapped to her feet, to give her the leverage that she needed to apply a twisting force to the wrench.

The sticky connector finally broke free on her third attempt.

With a crackle of breaking squelch, a new voice blared from the radio speaker. "Great job, Commander."

"Why, thank you, Houston," Angela said. "While I have my tools out, is there anything else … *I* can do for you?" She glared at Bill and silently mouthed, *Thanks, butt hole!*

In 2018, when UPS had brought back their old slogan, she'd asked a pesky reporter, "What can Brown do for you?" The S.O.B. had run with it. His editor had even made it the title of the front-page article. It had stuck, and now two years later, even she had almost uttered the damn thing!

"Actually, Commander Brown, there is something you can do for me."

Angela suddenly realized that the voice belonged to Randy McCree, the director of Mission Control.

"Oh … hello, Director. To what do we owe the pleasure?" Angela said, wincing inwardly. She resented the nervous feeling in her gut. The young physicist hadn't asked for this assignment, hadn't wanted it. In fact, Angela would've been happy if they'd left her to her experiments.

Ahead of the space station, Iceland appeared on the eastern horizon. Behind them, the inverted white triangle of Greenland's southern tip retreated, slowly sliding behind the curving line of the planet's western limb.

"Got something I'd like you to take a look at," McCree said.

Angela's head moved back and forth as she scanned the long solar array. Great! She had only been mission commander for a week, and on her first spacewalk, she'd already screwed up so badly that someone had summoned the director.

Apparently, NASA's ever-watchful eye was focused on her at that moment. Randy McCree chuckled. "It's nothing to do with your work. You'll need to look a little farther away to check this issue."

"Okay," Angela said, drawing out the word. "What do you have for us, Director?"

"Need you to take a look at Europe."

"Europe? Have you guys misplaced France … again?"

After a pregnant pause, the director's voice returned flat and humorless. "It seems we might have."

Angela and Major Peterson exchanged confused glances as their smiles faded.

Randy McCree didn't wait for her to reply. "A few minutes ago, several data centers went quiet. Our hackers can't get anything from them, either."

Angela knew that by hackers he meant Information Technologies, or I.T. for short.

"Did they lose power?" Major Peterson said.

"No. There just isn't any new or active data coming through them. Since then, the problem has only worsened."

"Um, Houston, I'm not sure what we can see or do for you from here. I mean, Teddy is pretty good with computers. But—"

"All the servers are in Central Europe," Randy said, cutting her off. His voice had acquired a frazzled edge. "But there's more. We can't raise anyone on the phone either. And all of the region's news networks went silent, too. There's a satellite looking at the area." He paused as if searching for words. "But what we're seeing … It doesn't make sense."

The cold blue waters of the North Atlantic scrolled beneath the ISS. Their current track across the planet would soon take them over Ireland, Britain, and indeed, France.

"I need human eyes on this thing," Randy McCree said.

Angela knitted her eyebrows. "Thing? What are you seeing, sir?"

"Well, it almost looks like an aurora."

She and Bill exchanged concerned glances. Exceptional auroras usually signaled the arrival of particularly energetic solar discharges—something that could prove fatal to astronauts not within the metal walls of the space station.

"Is it a coronal mass ejection, sir?" Angela said calmly, relieved that her concern hadn't crept into the words.

"No, no, no. We haven't had any CMEs in the last several days, and certainly, nothing pointing toward Earth. No, this is something else."

Angela started breathing again and opened a station-wide channel. "Teddy, I need you in the Cupola."

"What's up, Command-Oh?" the Russian crew member said, his mock SoCal surfer boy accent lilting each word.

Angela looked ahead. Beneath the aft end of the port or leftmost forward-pointing solar panel, she watched Ireland's rocky shoreline crest the blue horizon. Overhead and to her right, the long, articulated truss that connected all sixteen of the station's main solar arrays extended 150 feet to the structure's midway point. There it connected to the line of modules that formed the body of the ISS. Between her and the intersection, banks of solar arrays extended left and right like mirrored wings.

She looked forward again. As they continued eastward, Angela glimpsed an upside-down reflection of Ireland on the bottom of the outermost solar panel.

Movement to her right front drew her eye. In the faceted windows of the Cupola, a blond mane drifted into view. Even from 200 feet, she could see it filling a significant portion of the station's observatory.

"Jesus, Teddy! I told you to tie that back," Angela said and then reopened the connection with Houston.

"Hey, man. Don't be hating on the 'fro."

She cleared her throat. "Um, Mission Specialist Theodore Petrovich, we're on with Director McCree."

Teddy donned a navy blue baseball cap that sported the circled red chevron of Roscosmos, the Russian Federal Space Agency. The hat reined in his blond mane. Inside the observatory, the man held up his palms in a what-gives gesture. His mock Valley intonation morphed back into his almost clichéd Russian accent and dropped an octave. "Da, Commander. I'm in position." After a brief pause, he added, "Good morning, Director McCree. What can *Brown* do for you?"

Angela shot him an angry look that went unnoticed by all but Major Peterson who chuckled lightly by her side.

"Telemetry shows that you are about to pass over Ireland," the director said. "There's an atmospheric anomaly we'd like you to take a look at. It's over England now and approaching their west coast. So you should—"

"No way!" Teddy interrupted, the return of his Russianized SoCal accent drawing out the words. After uttering a few others in his native tongue, he said, "What in the *hell* is that?!"

To Angela's right, Bill twitched. "Son of a ...!" he said with a tone of shocked awe. After casting an embarrassed glance toward her, he pointed east.

She looked forward, and her eyes widened.

A curtain of white light was rising above the horizon.

"Oh my God," Angela said in a whisper. She could see why the director had compared it to an aurora. In the upper reaches of the atmosphere, its light faded to black in undulating feathery fingers.

Then the full height of the thing rolled into view, and the comparison collapsed. The colorful sheets of the aurora borealis usually ran in faint curving lines that never quite reached the planet's surface. However, this thing's light extended all the way from the edge of space down to the ground.

"That's no aurora," Bill said.

Angela nodded wordlessly, unable to speak. This was wrong, very wrong.

The curtain of white ... energy? ... appeared to run in a perfectly straight line left and right until it disappeared over the curve of the north and south horizons.

What the hell could create something like that? she wondered.

The director's voice snapped Angela from her reverie. "What are you seeing, Commander?"

"Houston, we've spotted the ... the anomaly." Breathlessly, she added, "It looks like a wall of light!" Her respiration rate had doubled. The astronaut swallowed, trying to rein it in. "But not like an aurora. The light reaches all the way to the surface. I-I can't see through it!"

The damn thing was high, too high!

"Houston, I'm not sure we'll clear it!" Bill Peterson said. "Looks like we're flying straight at it."

The ISS's ever-arcing orbital path sent them careening toward the white wall. Its upper reaches extended high above the planet. The opaque curtain concealed everything beyond it. It looked as if the space station was rushing toward the energetic rampart like a doomed moth on a collision course with a planet-sized windshield.

Angela's entire body tensed. Pain radiated from her clenched fists. Then the planet's eastern horizon slid into view over the energy curtain's upper reaches, and she relaxed a shade. If they could see the horizon beyond the anomaly, they must be above it. Right?

As their path carried them closer to the wave, Europe and then England and even the Isle of Man slid into view behind the wall. In the highest reaches of the ever-thinning atmosphere, the anomaly appeared to fade and then disappear completely. But she had no way to know if its effect—whatever that effect might be—extended above that point.

Angela's body began to tense again as the thought took root like a weed.

Inexorably, the ISS continued east, racing toward its date with the anomaly.

Looking down now, she watched the base of the wave move across the surface, advancing westward, moving in the opposite direction of the ISS. The wavefront raced across the Irish Sea. As the station passed over the Cliffs of Moher on Ireland's western shore, the curtain of light swallowed Dublin ahead to the east.

She held her breath as they sped toward the upper reaches of the anomaly.

"Here it comes!" Teddy shouted.

Angela crossed forearms in front of her helmet. To her right, Bill had the same involuntary response. "Oh God!" he yelled.

Head turned slightly, Angela watched through narrowed eyes as the wall rushed at them. North and south, its extremities appeared motionless, but the central section rushed at them with impossible speed, closing the gap in milliseconds.

Then the curtain of light vanished as it passed beneath the ISS. Below her boots, the plane of light disappeared completely!

"It's—"

Before she could announce the fact, the line returned. Edge on, the two-dimensional plane had become invisible, but as they continued along their eastward track, it reappeared.

Angela released her held breath and reopened the private ISS-wide channel. "Is everyone okay?"

"Dude!" Teddy said with a long exhalation that matched hers. "Da, I'm fine."

Angela looked over to Major Peterson. She saw a reflection of the white wave's undulating upper extremity painted across his curving visor. "Bill?"

Wide-eyed, the man looked up from the light. After a moment, he nodded and held up a thumb. "All good here." Then he shook his head. "But you're the physicist." Bill pointed beneath them. "Any idea what the *hell* that is?"

Angela shook her head as well. "Not a clue."

Director McCree's urgent voice broke into their conversation. "Commander Brown, are you okay? Come in, over."

Angela reconnected to the external radio. "Roger, Houston. I think we're okay." She paused, looking down, watching the wave cross the island's west coast and head out to sea. "It's moving west pretty fast. It just crossed Ireland in a few seconds."

"Roger. That's what we're seeing here," McCree said. "None of the station's radiation detectors spiked as you crossed the boundary. Now that you've had a ... uh, closer look, can you tell what it is?"

Angela shook her head. "No clue, Houston. But it's not an aurora, not like any I've ever seen, anyway. I just noticed something else. Now that we've passed it, I can see it has an arc."

As they glided past the English Channel and over the French countryside, she scanned north and south. "If I'm right, it's a ring. We should be seeing the other side of it in a few minutes."

"Yes, you will, Commander. The far side of it just reached the Black Sea." After a pause, his voice returned with renewed gravitas. "And we just lost contact with Moscow."

"Oh, my God," Angela whispered.

"Moscow?" Teddy said uneasily.

"Yes, Mr. Petrovich. We'll reestablish communications as soon as we can, but it might be a while. Our hackers still haven't figured out a workaround."

The director's words triggered an epiphany. "Houston," Angela said. "Has this thing lost any energy? Does it appear to have lost any of its intensity since you first detected it?"

"No, Commander," McCree said in a matter-of-fact tone that told her he'd already thought of the issue she was about to raise.

"Sir, we need to abandon the station," Angela said.

"What?!" Teddy said.

Angela held up a hand toward the Cupola and the Russian cosmonaut inside it. "We are already on minimal rations. Considering our logistical situation here, we can't afford to chance an extended break in communications."

"I concur, Commander Brown," the director said. "I want you guys on the ground before that wave hits Houston. At a minimum, it's knocking out communications. If it's also disrupting or frying computer networks, you could be stranded up there for a while."

Angela pointed at Bill and gestured toward the distant airlock. He nodded.

While the major began to unclip himself from the array's hard points, she actuated the robotic arm. Attached to her lower legs, it carried her away from the array, the arm's long length undulating as she demanded its top speed. Even at this rate, it would take three to four minutes for the arm to traverse its long tracks and deposit her at the airlock.

As the orbiter's great circle route now took them southeast over the Alps, Angela scanned the horizon. She couldn't see the wall of light. After reporting the fact to Houston, she said, "Has it dissipated?"

"No," McCree said. "It's still expanding. We've plotted the ring of energy on your orbital track. I have it up on the main display. You're crossing the epicenter now."

After a brief pause, the director's voice returned with an urgent tone. "I just received the reentry timing from Telemetry. You need to be aboard the Soyuz and heading earthward in the next five minutes. Otherwise, you're going to fly through the wall during your descent and come down in the affected zone."

"Holy shit," Angela whispered. She toggled the station-wide channel and yelled, "Teddy!"

"On it, Command-Oh!"

Angela's respiration rate redoubled. Jesus Christ! It normally took a half-hour just to run the escape module's pre-flight checklist. Teddy, the diminished crew's only civilian was a mission specialist, not a pilot, although, like every other crew member, he'd received extensive training on Soyuz operations for this very contingency.

She looked at Bill, their actual pilot. Over her head, the astronaut was moving hand-over-hand toward the distant airlock. He was falling behind her. The requirement to maintain a constant tether was slowing him down.

"Free flight it, Bill. You'll never make it at that rate."

"Roger, Commander."

He unclipped the tether. After a pause to judge the trajectory, Major Peterson launched himself toward the airlock.

"If you start to drift off course, use your jet pack."

"No need," Major Peterson said. "Looks like I nailed the vector on the first try. Just have to stick the landing."

Angela adjusted the robotic arm so that her back faced the planet and her helmet pointed toward the airlock. Now oriented toward the truss, she watched as the spacesuited body of Major Bill Peterson flew over its multiple structures. With his arms extended, he looked like Superman flying over an arcane angular construct. A moment later, he overtook her, his flight speed outstripping the manipulator arm's laggardly pace. As he reached the Quest airlock, Bill grasped the bar over the closed hatch and stopped his inertia with a grunt of exertion.

While closed for the safety of those inside the station, the lock was left depressurized during spacewalks. This permitted a rapid ingress in case of an EVA emergency.

Bill opened the door and slid into the airlock feet first and then looked back at her. Angela was still twenty feet away.

She waved a gauntlet at him. "Don't wait for me. Rapid cycle it, Major."

He nodded and then disappeared into the crew airlock, pulling the hatch closed.

"Hurry every chance you get, Bill. Once you're in, place the station in Assured Safe Crew Return. As soon as you toggle ASCR mode, get your ass in the Soyuz and help Teddy finish the pre-flight checks."

"I got this, Commander."

Angela felt her face flush. Major Peterson should have been named mission commander, not her. She knew he would have been if the focus of the current expedition hadn't been on her gravity wave experiment.

She checked the watch strapped to her left wrist. "How's it coming in there, Teddy?"

"Soyuz is online, but the damned gyros spooled down again. I have them spinning up now."

Angela nodded. "Good job." If the Soyuz departed with unstable gyros, the ship would likely enter the atmosphere on its head and burn up.

"Bill and I won't have time to don our Russian suits. We'll have to enter the descent modules in these. We'll ditch the jet packs. Every-thing else is coming along for the ride. It'll be cramped and uncom-fortable, but we'll have to make it work."

The bulky Simplified Aid for EVA Rescue (SAFER) backpack, barely fit through many of the station's passageways. While the jet pack was significantly smaller than previous versions, it would never fit into the Soyuz, especially with all three seats occupied.

"Hey, Command-Oh," Teddy said, his surfer boy persona back in full effect. "I guess that supply ship blowing up wasn't such a bad thing after all, eh?"

Angela smiled ruefully at his bastardization of her title. "Maybe so, Teddy."

Actually, she knew he was right. The catastrophic loss of last month's resupply mission had required an early return of three of the station's residents. Bob Everett, the expedition commander up to that point, had returned with a fever and abdominal pains that turned out to be the onset of appendicitis. He and the other two crew members still being aboard would have made this significantly more difficult.

Angela grabbed the airlock's external grab bar and toggled the manipulator arm's release button. She felt a click in the sole of her boots, and then they were free from the bindings. As she pulled away from the device and pointed her feet back toward the planet, the Black Sea rolled beneath them.

She looked southeast, and her eyes widened.

"Jesus Christ!"

"What is it, Commander?" Major Peterson said.

"We're approaching the other side of the light wave." Angela shook her head. "It hasn't faded one damn bit."

She consulted her watch.

Less than two minutes left until they had to be on their way.

Damn it!

"How's it coming in there, Bill?" As she asked the question, the airlock's external light tripped green.

"I've already dumped my SAFER and initiated ASCR mode. The airlock should finish cycling any sec—"

"It just did," Angela said as she opened the lock's outer door. "I'm going in now. You boys better be ready to go when I get in there. We're cutting it damn close."

"Yes, ma'am," they replied in unison.

In her own ears, the commands sounded paper-thin. Why should these two men bend to the will of a theoretical physicist high on her own power?

"Not now, Angela," she whispered, making sure not to transmit. "Not the time for self-doubts." Shaking her head, she closed the outer door and locked it. Then she slammed the side of a closed fist into the atmospheric cycler.

Nothing happened!

No rush of air.

The status segment remained unchanged.

She was still in hard vacuum.

Aiming precisely, she pressed the button again, this time using her glove's thumb to push the control's geometric center.

Nothing!

"Damn, damn, *damn!*"

"What is it, Command-Oh?" Teddy said.

"The lock won't cycle!"

"Uh-oh," Major Peterson said. He grunted with exertion. "I'm on my way."

Angela looked at her watch and shook her head. "Belay that, Major Peterson. You're in charge now. Lock the hatch and launch the Soyuz."

"I'm not leaving you behind, Commander. We can—"

"That's an order, Major!" she said, willing her voice to hold, to not crack. "Launch the capsule. You only have sixty seconds."

"But—"

"Listen, guys," Angela said, cutting off Teddy's protest. "I'll be fine. It'll take a few minutes, but I can manually cycle the lock. I'm the lucky one. I get to hang out up here for a while longer. But if you don't launch now, you'll fly into that wall of light, and we have no idea what that will do to the descent module."

"This is bullshit!" Teddy said.

"Major Peterson, this is Director McCree. Commander Brown is right. Because of this supply shortage, if we lose communications or the ability to bring you back for anything more than a couple of weeks, you'll run out of food and water. There aren't enough supplies to support all three of you for an extended time. But if there's just one person …" He left the sentence unfinished.

"Why don't we just stay with her and then descend after the light passes?" Teddy said plaintively.

"No!" Director McCree said. "Without communications, we can't coordinate the link-up. You could come down in a remote area or the open ocean. You'd be more likely to die from exposure than be found. You need to launch now, Major Peterson!"

Angela watched the sweep-second hand of her watch race toward the deadline. "Go, Bill!"

"Okay, Angela," the major whispered. "Houston, the hatch is closed. Blowing the locks in three, two, one."

"This is bullshit!" Teddy repeated.

As time ran out, Angela felt a slight tremor pass through the hand that rested on the airlock's skin.

"Houston," Major Peterson said somberly. "Soyuz is away."

CHAPTER 2

"**D**amn it, Vaughn. You sound like an asthmatic trying to crest Everest."

"Screw you, too," Army Captain Vaughn Singleton said between wheezes. Bent at the waist, hands on knees, he cast a sideward glance at Mark, his tormentor. Vaughn drew another wheezing breath and gave his old flight schoolmate the middle-finger salute. "You're number one with me, asshole."

"Wow!" Mark gestured to the large, cavernous room ahead of them. "So that's my thanks for getting you into the new vacuum chamber?"

Beginning to catch his breath, Vaughn stood upright. His space-suit's boots disappeared beneath the planetary body of his considerable abdomen. He gestured to the suit. "You didn't tell me these things weighed five hundred pounds. This is like doing a twenty-mile forced march with a VW Beetle strapped to my back."

Lieutenant Colonel Mark Hennessy made a show of looking over his shoulder and then back at Vaughn. Behind his visor, the astronaut cocked an eyebrow. "I've told you a *trillion* times not to exaggerate. You're lucky these are the lightweight suits." The man gestured over his shoulder. "Besides, it's only been a hundred yards."

Vaughn shrugged. After gulping down another breath, he said, "Feels more like a thousand."

"Jesus, Singleton, just think if you hadn't been breathing pure oxygen for the last seven hours."

"Yeah, but that was just sitting around, doing nothing, not walking around with a car strapped to my back."

Mark pointed at Vaughn's belly. "It ain't on your back, my friend. You wouldn't be breathing so hard if you didn't have to haul that around."

"Did I mention that you're still number one with me?" Vaughn said, not bothering to throw the unicorn this time.

Mark chuckled and patted him on the shoulder. "Come on. We're almost there."

As they walked, Vaughn stared up at the distant top of the fifty-foot-wide door that stood open ahead of the two spacesuited men. They were about to enter the new Space Power Annex, the first human-rated, large-scale vacuum chamber.

"It's like stepping into a giant beer can," Vaughn said.

Mark laughed and pointed to his abdomen again. "That's your tool shed talking."

Vaughn winced inwardly at the second reference but smiled and patted his beer belly. "Don't be hating on the shed." He pointed into the facility. "Whatever the hell it looks like, thanks for getting me in, Mark."

The astronaut gave a slight nod and smiled. "Just don't screw up."

Vaughn held up both hands, palms forward. "Hey, I'm just a sandbag on this one. What's to screw up?" As Vaughn said it, a bead of sweat trickled across his right eyebrow. The hand he diverted to dab the droplet ran into the helmet visor ... again. Mark apparently hadn't seen the foible. He appeared to be studying something inside the large chamber ahead. Feigning purpose, Vaughn shifted his errant hand and adjusted a knob on the side of his spacesuit's helmet and then lowered his arm. After a self-conscious glance at his old friend, he stared into the 150-foot-tall chamber beyond the square opening. Inside that *beer can*, they'd soon be in a hard vacuum.

Vaughn's eyes fell from the doorway to his ever-expanding gut. He really needed to start running. He'd been telling himself that ever since finishing flight school ten years ago but had never gotten around to it. And since the shit hit the fan last year, tomorrow always seemed like a better time to start.

As if reading his mind, Mark said, "Have you heard from Jill?"

"No, thank God." Vaughn shook his head. "She's the last person on earth I want to talk to right now."

"That's kind of harsh, isn't it? I mean, all things considered …"

"What the hell is that supposed to mean?" Vaughn stopped and turned to look at Mark.

The lieutenant colonel held up his hands in surrender. "Nothing, never mind."

Vaughn frowned at him for a moment, but then a grin eased across his face. "I know, I can be a bit of an asshole at times."

"At times?" Mark said with a chuckle as they resumed their labored stroll toward the vacuum chamber's massive door. "Damn entitled rich kid," he added, grinning as well.

Vaughn cocked an eyebrow and gave the tall man a sideways glance. "How's that spacesuit fitting, Chewy? Does your fur get matted in there?"

Chuckling as they finished trading well-worn barbs from their old flight school days, the two men passed through the wide opening and stepped into the chamber.

Vaughn looked up. A long cable hung from an overhead hoist that ran from the center of the domed ceiling. The hook at the bottom of its hundred-foot span supported today's experiment. Studying the attached object, he stared at the machine's arcane plumbing and electronics. Vaughn felt his pulse quicken again, but not from exertion. This was pure exhilaration.

"Now there's a shit-eating grin," Mark said.

"This is so cool!" Vaughn whispered. "I can't believe you get to work with it every day."

The shoulders of Mark's spacesuit rose and fell. "I guess it beats working for a living."

Vaughn heard a loud clunk. The cocooning helmet made it sound as if the noise had come from every direction.

Apparently seeing his confusion, Mark hitched a thumb over his shoulder, gesturing behind them. "They're closing the door."

Wide-eyed, the Army attack helicopter pilot turned and watched the narrowing gap through which they'd entered. Vaughn's wheezing returned as he began to hyperventilate, thoughts of the impending drop into vacuum evaporating his excitement.

"Oh, Jesus," Vaughn said between breaths. He pointed at his spacesuit. "I don't know, Mark. Are you sure about these? What if a seal fails?"

A nasal voice blared from the speaker in Vaughn's helmet. "Are you guys alright in there?"

Mark toggled the radio. "Yes, Sandusky Control. Captain Singleton is ... acclimating ... to his suit."

Vaughn started to bend over again, but Mark grabbed his right shoulder and helped him upright. The astronaut switched back to their private channel. "Come on, brother." Mark gave him a meaningful look and then nodded toward a wall-mounted camera. "I vouched for you."

The annoying voice returned. "Okay, Team Sigma, but I have to tell you, if Captain Singleton's heart rate gets much higher, I'll have to call it. Can't have the young man stroking out on us in the middle of the experiment."

Vaughn took a deep breath and then held it, willing himself to chill out.

Mark waved to the camera. "He'll be fine."

After a long pause, a sigh came over the radio. Finally, the man in Sandusky Control said, "Roger. We're a go at this end."

Vaughn released the held breath and then twitched when the massive door closed with a final clunk, sealing them inside the world's largest vacuum chamber.

Still looking into the camera, Mark patted Vaughn's shoulder with one gloved hand and held out the other, thumb extended. "Roger, Sandusky. We're a go in here as well."

~

Vaughn looked at the atmospheric pressure gauge embedded in his suit's left forearm. Except for the farthest right digit, it displayed a series of zeroes on both sides of a decimal point.

His focus shifted to the belly that supported his forearm like a shelf. *Jesus, Singleton! What are you doing? Gotta do something about that already.*

Ever since the divorce, he'd planned to join one of those twenty-four-hour gyms, but something else always popped up. He'd even thought about trying online dating. Looking down at his gut again, he rolled his eyes. But who would want to date his fat ass?

Vaughn had stayed fit for her, and look what that had gotten him.

Shaking his head, he shifted his focus back to the forearm display just as the final number rolled to zero.

Seated to his right, Mark extended a gloved thumb. "Okay, Sandusky," the astronaut said over the radio. "I'm showing hard vacuum here."

Vaughn's hand bounced off of his visor again. He furrowed his forehead in another vain attempt to get the sweatband to absorb the errant trickle. Blurred vision and the sensation of sweat burning an inconsolable eye rewarded his efforts.

"Damn it!" Vaughn said as he tried to blink away the moisture.

Mark laughed and shook his head. He activated their private suit-to-suit intercom. "Told you it was on wrong."

"How can you put a sweatband on wrong?" Vaughn said through another growl, still trying to blink the sweat from his eyes.

Mark pointed at Vaughn's helmet. "Like that." After a moment, the astronaut pursed his lips and then added, "You've always been a hard-headed son of a bitch, Vaughn, always had to do things your way."

Singleton hoisted an eyebrow. "Are you done, Colonel?" He waved a thick booklet in the airless air. "This checklist ain't gonna finish itself."

Mark gave him a hard look. "I'm serious, Vaughn." He paused and pointed at himself. "This could've just as easily been you."

"Sure, rub it in. You know I always wanted to be an astronaut."

Mark nodded. "Yeah, so what did you do about it?"

"Hey, it wasn't my fault—"

"Yes, it was!" the astronaut interrupted. Before Vaughn could protest, Mark held up a hand. "You're the best pilot I've ever known. Back in flight school, nobody could touch you. We did good just to hang in your wake. Hell, it's because of that fact that I was able to get you in here."

"Yeah, right," Vaughn said sardonically. "I'm sure you—"

"Shut the hell up and listen for a change, Vaughn. I saw the promotion board results. I know you got passed over again. And considering the bad officer eval you got during that last combat deployment, I know you're on your way out."

Vaughn's head rocked backward, his eyes narrowing. How the hell had Mark found that out? He wanted to glare at the man, wanted to yell at him, but all he could do was stare at the floor of the thruster module, gnashing his teeth.

"Listen to me, Vaughn."

Looking up, the Army captain raised his eyebrows and nodded toward the camera that monitored their progress.

"They're running checks," Mark said. "We have a couple of minutes to ourselves."

Vaughn waved the checklist again.

Mark shook his head. "We can't do the next item until they're done," the astronaut said.

Vaughn's shoulders slumped.

Mark smiled, but then it faded to a frown. "You are a hard-headed SOB. You always have to do things your own way."

"I think we've already covered that," Vaughn said.

Mark ignored him. "You're smart enough that it usually works, but not always. And it's made you lazy."

"What?"

"It led to the divorce and the bad eval."

Vaughn felt his face redden.

Mark held up his hand. "It's not the end of the world; it's a chance for you to start over. But you have to lose the chip."

"Chip? What do you mean?"

"I joke about it, but you've always been an entitled little shit, Vaughn. Hell, when we first met, that was one of the things I liked about you. I looked up to you. We all did. But ever since flight school ended, you've done nothing to further your career. It's like you found out you could succeed without trying, so you let that attitude creep into every part of your life. It cost you your marriage and is, ultimately, why you're on your way out of the military. And since Jill left, you've gotten even worse."

"Screw you, Mark. I busted my ass for her *and* for the Army."

Behind the visor, the astronaut's head shook side to side. "No, you didn't. You always did what you thought should be enough. And for some, that would have been enough. But people see your potential, Vaughn. They see what you're capable of."

"So you're saying they: Jill, the Army, and everyone else, wrote me off because I didn't live up to my *potential?*" Vaughn said, using air quotes to emphasize the last word.

Mark nodded. "Basically, yeah. You have incredible potential, but you haven't applied it in years." He gave Vaughn's belly a meaningful glance. "That's why you have that."

Suddenly self-conscious, Vaughn tried to suck in his gut. "What the hell are you talking about?"

"We were in our mid-twenties back in flight school," Mark said. "None of us had to work out to stay thin. But that was ten years ago." He pointed to his own thin abdomen and then to the rank insignia and NASA logo Velcroed to the center of his chestplate. "You think any of this came without a lot of work, think I could have attained any of it without applying myself?"

Vaughn opened his mouth to protest, but Mark cut him off.

"We only have a few more seconds, so listen, jackass."

He ground his teeth but nodded for Mark to continue.

"Like I said, you're the best pilot I ever met. No, the military thing isn't going to work out—that career is over. But you're only thirty-five. You have your whole life ahead of you. I have some contacts at Lockheed. They could use someone with your intelligence and ability. If you apply yourself, you can succeed there."

"If I'm so goddamned *good*, why in the hell didn't I get this assignment?" Vaughn said, raising his voice and pointing at Mark's NASA patch. "No, instead they sent me back to the fucking sandbox and ruined my marriage!"

The astronaut shook his head. "It's not always someone else's fault, Vaughn."

Through his visor, Vaughn glared at the man, but he couldn't hold onto the anger. The mix of pity and disappointment in his friend's eyes cut deeper than the words. Vaughn shook his head, but his gaze fell to the floor.

The thing was, Mark was right, but hearing his internal thoughts parroted by the astronaut had kicked Vaughn's well-worn defenses into high gear.

The radio crackled back to life. "Okay, Team Sigma. We're ready on this end," reported the mission controller.

Thankful for the interruption, Vaughn looked up at Mark and raised the checklist. "Thanks, Dad," he said flatly over their private channel. "I'm happier alone. I don't need anybody or anything. Now, if there's nothing else, I believe we have some work to do."

Mark pursed his lips again. "Just consider the Lockheed thing, it could be a fresh start, a chance to apply yourself," he said. After a sigh, he turned from Vaughn and toggled the external communication link. "Roger, Sandusky. We're ready on this end."

"All systems are a go," the controller said. "You're cleared for the first hover test."

Sitting in the capsule's right seat, Mark pointed to Vaughn. "Next checklist item, Captain."

Vaughn quashed the emotions dredged up by the discussion—a task with which he had years of experience. He smiled as his heart started racing. They were about to be the first humans to hover a reactionless thruster in untethered free flight!

NASA had been testing this new thruster technology for several years. Scientists at their Eagleworks Advanced Propulsion Physics Laboratory drew upon lessons learned on a previous, unrelated technology known as the EM Drive. It inspired them to take the idea in a whole new direction. They created the QG or Quantum Gravity Drive. Initially, most scientists had written off the QG Drive as a hoax, claiming it violated the laws of physics, but to their consternation, it worked. One experiment after another kept showing anomalous or unexpected thrust. The first tests had been at very low power settings, but this was the first test of the drive at full flight power.

Since its controversial inception, many questions had hovered over the thruster, not the least of which was whether or not the tech would work at higher, more useful power levels. If its power-to-thrust ratio proved scalable, if it could be used to move large objects with the same efficiency that it moved small objects in early tests, then the QG Drive would be humankind's ticket to the outer solar system and possibly to the stars beyond.

Considering the controversy and with so much on the line, NASA had clamped a lid of secrecy on this test.

Vaughn started wheezing again. His heart pounded in his ears. He swallowed and read the next item on the checklist. "Gear locks."

Lieutenant Colonel Mark Hennessy flipped a switch. Vaughn felt a soundless metallic clunk radiate through the module's seat.

"Unlatched," the astronaut said.

The module rested on the scaffolding. Only gravity held it in place. Overhead, the previously disconnected hoist hook finished retracting. Now a hundred feet of vacuum was all that separated the top of the skinless module's frame from the domed ceiling.

"Stand by for launch," the controller announced.

The two men exchanged excited glances.

For this top secret test, NASA had designed the module to operate in the vacuum of space, but in here, it only needed to hover. So the engineers had configured its controls like those of a helicopter. Mark held the cyclic stick in his right hand. That flight controller looked like a three-foot-long joystick attached to the floor between Mark's legs. The astronaut would use it to arrest any sideward or lateral drift and keep the craft centered in the chamber. The lever in his left hand looked like an oversized parking brake handle. It replicated a helicopter's collective control. Anchored at its base, the forward-tilted stick would increase the drive's thrust when raised, and reduce it when lowered.

Both men had started their military careers as Army helicopter pilots. After attending flight school together, the two of them had transferred to Fort Hood in Texas. They'd been assigned to the same unit and had flown together during multiple Middle East combat tours. However, in the years since, their careers had taken radically different paths. Mark's had led to NASA via a short stint as an instructor at the Navy's test pilot school.

Vaughn didn't want to think about his own career path.

Mark looked at him and winked. "Ready to make history?"

The Army captain tried to look nonchalant as he shrugged. "It's not like anyone will ever hear about this *super-secret* test anytime soon."

He had no idea how right he was.

"You're go for power-up," said the controller.

Mark nodded and toggled the radio. "Roger, Sandusky. Increasing power now."

The smile fell from the astronaut's face. With a look of concentration, he watched the module's instrumentation and lifted the stick in his left hand a fraction of an inch.

Through the seat, Vaughn felt a high-frequency vibration, like the physical manifestation of a hum.

"There's ten percent, Sandusky."

"Roger, Sigma. All systems nominal."

Mark's hand raised another notch and the vibrations intensified, creating a tingling sensation across the back of Vaughn's thighs.

The astronaut read off the displayed power. "Twenty percent. Thirty. Forty."

The vibrations faded and then disappeared.

"Fifty percent."

Something moved in Vaughn's peripheral vision. Through the

flight module's open architecture, he saw the chamber's near wall sliding down.

They were climbing!

The module had left the ground!

The weirdness of it slammed home. No beating rotor blades. No screaming jet engines. They weren't standing on a plume of roaring rocket flames. Without a visible means of propulsion, the module simply rose from the ground like a flying saucer in a sci-fi flick.

Grinning from ear to ear, Vaughn turned to Mark. "This is awesome!"

A smile cracked through the test pilot's serious façade. "Sandusky, we have liftoff! Ten feet. Twenty feet. Twenty-five, thirty."

The climb decelerated. As the vehicle ascended through forty feet, the radar altimeter's rate of change slowed, the value increasing in single digits. A moment later it stopped.

"Fifty feet. All systems nominal," Mark said.

Vaughn watched as Hennessy used the cyclic control to arrest a slight left drift, and then guided the module smoothly back to the center of the chamber.

"Sandusky, we're in a stable hover." The astronaut paused, scanning the craft's instruments. Then his smile brightened. "Power at fifty-three percent!" he said excitedly.

Clapping and loud cheers erupted over the connection with Control.

Vaughn toggled their private channel again. "What's significant about that number?"

"It's below the threshold."

"What threshold?"

"Jesus, Vaughn," Mark said, shaking his head. "You're always in your own little world. It means it's scalable! The QG-Thruster can reach space ... From the ground!"

Vaughn's eyes widened, and he pointed at the floor of the module. "This thing could reach orbit from here?"

Mark shook his head. "No, it only has batteries for power." He consulted the vehicle's instruments. "We've been going for less than a minute, and I've already used up half of our available power. If we took this thing outside, we'd probably rise a couple of hundred feet and then fall like homesick rocks." With his right boot, the astronaut tapped one of the module's external structural members: a two-inch pipe. "And even if we had unlimited power, its open frame isn't exactly aerodynamic." He looked up through the triangular collection of tubes that formed the conical roof of the module. "I wouldn't want to try to fly this bad boy through the atmosphere."

The cheers pouring from the link with Sandusky Control suddenly evaporated.

A female voice came over the radio. "Team Sigma … uh … Shut it down." The woman sounded distracted.

Mark gave Vaughn a confused look. Turning back to the instrument panel, he said, "Sandusky? Did you copy my last? We're hovering at *fifty feet*! And well below threshold!"

"Yeah … yeah … we copied you, Sigma," she said sounding completely preoccupied.

Over the connection, Vaughn heard someone yelling in the background.

Now exasperated, the woman said, "Something is happening down here."

Mark's apparent confusion deepened. He looked at Vaughn again and toggled their private link. "That's the local director."

The Army captain shrugged his ignorance.

Hennessy frowned. "The head of the Space Power Annex."

"Terminate the test, Mark!" the director said urgently. "We need to get you out of there."

"Okay, Sandusky," Mark said. He consulted the module's chronograph. "Terminating hover at zero seven thirty-eight."

"Roger, Sigma," she replied, still sounding distracted.

The colonel lowered the stick in his left hand. Vaughn looked through the craft's frame and saw the wall's aluminum surface begin to scroll past in the opposite direction.

"Forty-five feet," Mark called out. "Forty. Thirty. Twenty."

The stick raised a notch, and the rate of descent halved.

"Fifteen feet ... Ten—"

"What the hell is tha ...?" the director blurted over the radio, cutting off Mark, but the woman's words trailed off mid-sentence. Vaughn could hear her quickening breath. In the background, several voices raised, some screaming. Then the director's voice returned. "What the hell is it? Oh, God! No! ... No—!"

The transmission cut out.

Mark gave him a quick, confused glance.

Bewildered, Vaughn stared past the astronaut, looking over the man's head, watching the metal walls of the chamber as they scrolled upward and the ship descended.

The colonel continued his countdown. "Four ... three ... two—"

Suddenly, a visible wave passed across the wall.

Vaughn's eyes widened as the aluminum surface appeared to flex. Then he squinted and threw his hands in front of his face as the wall flashed brilliant white like burning phosphorus.

An instant later, the light faded, and the module touched down with a spine-jarring jolt.

CHAPTER 3

Having freed herself from the wayward airlock and slipped out of her spacesuit, Angela drifted into the Cupola. The station had never sounded or felt this empty. A chill ran through her. Wrapping arms around herself, Angela tried to stifle a shiver as she gazed through the multiple windows of the station's faceted observatory.

The ISS had just flown over the planetary boundary where day turned to night. The late-evening lights of India's southeast coastal communities passed beneath her.

At its current altitude, the ISS still basked in the sun's radiance. To all those millions of Indians and Sri Lankans below it, the ISS would look like a swiftly moving star drifting across their currently cloudless sky.

Angela looked northwest. She could no longer see the curtain of light. Looking down again, she whispered, "Something's coming, folks, something very weird."

With eye-jarring finality, the shimmering radiance of city lights gave way to the oceanic void, painting the jagged shoreline like a diamond-encrusted fractal dropped onto a canvas of black velvet.

Floating in the dark abyss between Heaven and Earth, the station silently glided out to sea, beginning its lonely journey across the Indian Ocean.

Angela stared into the deep. Looking down at its inky surface was like looking into a region of space where ships, not stars, formed the constellations.

Soon the ISS would cross the equator. Its great circle route would then take her over Australia and the South Pacific. Finally, reaching the southern point of its trip around the planet's tilted axis, the station would begin to track northeasterly, toward North America.

The last vestige of the coastal lights disappeared over the northwest horizon. Angela turned to the observatory's single computer monitor. Currently, the station's predicted orbital plot filled the screen. It featured the overlapping squiggly lines of the ISS's projected orbital track as it worked its way around a planet that spun on a tilted axis. The station's icon drifted southeast along a curving line that ran from India to Australia, but now a new line displayed the progress of her shipmates aboard the descent module. Their deorbit burn had placed them into a reentry track. The Soyuz now lagged behind and much lower than the ISS.

Angela touched the screen and said, "Bill and Ted's not-so-excellent adventure."

She cast a forlorn glance at her surroundings and then looked back to their icon. Angela didn't know whether to be worried for them or herself.

Having already passed over the day-night terminator, the station now flew into the planet's shadow, plunging the Cupola into darkness. Her eyes quickly adjusted to the change, but robbed of the sun's warming rays and still in her spacesuit's sweat-soaked undergarments, Angela shivered in the cold blue light that radiated from the computer monitor.

New sounds joined her dark, lonely universe. Long creaks and sharp pops echoed through the deserted station. No longer heated by the sun, its external surfaces began to cool and contract. Angela hugged herself tightly in a failed attempt to stave off another shiver.

The computer screen flickered. It refreshed, and new data

appeared. She floated closer, studying the details. Then light glinted in her peripheral vision. She looked up to see a pale blue reflection of her face in one of the observatory's thick windows.

Angela frowned. "First emergency on your watch, and you can't even complete a station evac," she said and then shook her head. Imitating Teddy's accented bastardization of her undeserved title, she added, "Nice move, Command-Oh."

She turned back to the screen. A loose strand of her tied-back auburn hair drifted into her eyes. Angela blew it out of the way and studied the computer display. Parallel concentric lines now arced across the image. After a moment, she realized that the arcs plotted the future position of the advancing wavefront. Each line had a discrete timestamp. On the screen's left half, the values increased in thirty-minute increments from east to west. Judging by the station's projected track, it appeared that she would recross the anomaly some-where near Colorado. The predicted touchdown point of the Soyuz descent module sat in Southern California's Mojave Desert. Their estimated time of arrival or ETA placed her fellow astronauts on the ground just before the wave crossed that region.

Running her finger across the Soyuz's symbol, she whispered, "Safe flying, boys."

A moment later, Angela plucked a headset out of the air and slipped it over her head. She pressed the transmit button. "Houston, this is Commander Brown. Come in, over."

"Roger, Commander," Randal McCree said wearily. "Tracking you on station video. See you in the Cupola now." The gravitas in his voice had somehow deepened. After a long pause, he said, "I'm so sorry, Angela. I—"

"No, sir," she said, cutting him off. "You made the right call. I just screwed it up."

Another long pause greeted her words. Angela was about to say more, but then he said, "I'm not so sure about that." His voice sounded strained. "Stand by for a video feed, Commander."

Several seconds later, the orbital plot disappeared from the Cupo-la's display, and she saw a shaky image of the director's face. He had opened a private video channel. It appeared the feed was coming from a handheld camera, likely his smartphone. Plaques and photos hung on the wall behind him. Randy had moved into his office. The man's normally tanned face looked ghostly white.

"Hey, Angela," he said somberly.

She looked into the small lens above the display. "What the hell is going on, Randy?"

His pallor shifted another shade whiter. The director shook his head. "I don't know if recalling your crew was the right thing to do," he said, speaking softly. "And you ... I-I don't know if I've saved you or doomed you."

Shocked by the man's reversal, Angela stared at him for a long, silent moment. Finally, she said, "You know something. What is it, Randy? What have you found out? Have you heard from someone inside the area?"

"No. I wish." He paused, shaking his head. "We still haven't been able to reach anyone in there." His eyes seemed to stare through her. Distractedly, he said, "It still isn't slowing or weakening. The damn thing has already passed over half of the world's population. *Half!*" Anguished eyes stared from the display. "That's billions of people!" he said, his voice cracking.

The raw emotions in the man's voice sent another shiver down her spine, but this one had nothing to do with the temperature of the air or the dampness of her clothes. Angela looked back at him for a long moment. Swallowing hard, she said, "What did you find out, Randy?"

He stared back at her wordlessly. A lone tear fell from his left eye.

"What did you see?" she whispered.

"They're ... all gone," he said. "All of them."

Angela blinked. "What do you mean: gone? Are they all dead?"

"No," Randy said, shaking his head. "Just ... gone."

"You're not making any sense."

"It doesn't *make* sense, Angela," he said. "At first, we only had a couple of commercial satellites over the area. The imagery wasn't very detailed. We couldn't make out anything smaller than a car." He paused, shaking his head. The director looked down for a moment.

When he looked up again, the haunted look in his eyes made Angela's blood run cold. He glimpsed off-camera as if to confirm no one was listening. Lowering his voice, he said, "A few minutes ago, a Keyhole spy satellite passed over the region."

Randy paused. The look in his eyes unnerved her more than had anything else in that strange day.

"What did you see?" Angela said again.

"They're all gone," he repeated. Before she could respond, he continued. "People, animals, even the dogs and cats as far as we can tell, all gone."

"Oh, my God," Angela said with widening eyes. "You *are* saying they're dead?"

Fear gripped her soul. Not for family, she'd been an only child, and her parents had both died years ago. Angela had no husband or love interest—she'd been married to her career since finishing her PhD in physics. No, not for herself. Angela's fear was for her friends. Like the one currently staring out of the display.

Then she realized that said friend was shaking his head.

"They're *gone*," the director repeated, emphasizing the second word. "No bodies in cars or on sidewalks, no dead cows in the field, no cats or dogs in the street." He paused, shaking his head again. "It's like every living creature just … vanished."

It was Angela's turn to stare silently. Her pulse pounded in her ears. She stared at the screen, trying to comprehend the unfathomable. She couldn't wrap her mind around what he was saying. It was too big. The scale of it … So many people just … gone? What was happening to them? What the hell could do that?

"Everything's gone? What's left? Just raw earth?"

"No," the director whispered with apparent confusion. "It looks like plant life was left untouched." His eyes took on that distant look. He shook his head again and said, "What could take one and leave the other?"

She shook her head. "No, Randy. I refuse to accept that. It's simply not possible. There must be something wrong with that satellite."

The director closed his eyes. "That's what we thought, too." He sighed. "But then we saw it happen live, watched an airplane full of people disappear! In real time!"

Angela's eyes widened. She pulled back from the monitor. "What?! Where'd they go?" She knew it was a stupid question. Randy couldn't know the answer.

Still looking mystified, he shook his head. "We have no idea."

After a moment, his eyes focused. "The President retreated to his bunker. Key personnel from the White House and the Pentagon went underground an hour ago." He gave her a meaningful look and added, "I advised the President and the Joint Chiefs of your situation. They assured me they'll do everything they can to recover you."

Angela swallowed again, nodding somberly. Then her eyes widened. "What about you, Randy?"

The director smiled mirthlessly. "We've moved all non-essential personnel into the facility's utility tunnels, although I'm not sure it will help. Considering this thing's apparent power, I doubt a few feet or even a few hundred feet of dirt will diminish its effect, here or in D.C."

Randy's face wavered as tears muddled Angela's vision. In micro-gravity, they didn't fall; they just piled up in her eyes. "Your family ...?" she started to say, but her voice cracked. She couldn't finish the question. Angela dabbed the puddled tears from her eyes with her sleeve.

Randy nodded. "Betty and the twins are on their way here." He looked down. The back of his hand batted away another tear. The director took a deep breath. "Everyone will head into the tunnels before the wave gets here, but I'm not going until my family arrives."

Suddenly, the look in his eyes changed. "But we haven't given up, Commander. There's a plan in the works."

"A plan?" Angela said dubiously. She'd seen the immensity of the light wave. The scale of it was beyond comprehension. "What can we possibly do against something that powerful?"

"You turn off its source," Randy said. "We can't figure out what in the hell could do this." He looked up with raised eyebrows. "But we think we know where it came from."

Angela blinked, but then she nodded and said, "It has to be the

Super Collider. I don't think it's a coincidence that CERN sits right in the middle of this thing's starting point."

The thought had first occurred to Angela when the director had told her that she was over the wave's epicenter, back when the ISS had crossed over the border between France and Switzerland. The underground complex known as the Large Hadron Collider, or CERN when referred to by its French acronym, sat under the border region west of Geneva.

On the screen, the director nodded again. "The Joint Chiefs came to the same conclusion an hour ago."

As a theoretical physicist, Angela hadn't wanted to believe that her colleagues had somehow caused this, but since she'd made the association, the thought had taken root. There was another reason to make the link. Last week, the scientists operating the seventeen-mile-wide collider had initiated a new experimental run. Dubbed the High Luminosity LHC, the major upgrade to the Large Hadron Collider had increased the strength and quantity of atomic collisions by an order of magnitude. Around the world, theoretical physicists—like Angela—anxiously awaited the anticipated tenfold increase in data.

Angela chewed her lip for a moment. Finally, she nodded. "What's in the works?"

Randy checked his surroundings again and then, speaking softly, said, "The President authorized a full-scale nuclear attack."

"Holy shit," Angela said in a whisper. Then she raised her voice. "We're going to nuke Europe?!"

Randy gave a curt nod.

Anger coupled with a wave of nausea passed over Angela. "That's crazy!" she screamed. "How can they fire nuclear weapons at France and Switzerland?"

"We don't have a choice, Commander," Randy said. "Every minute that wave continues its march across the planet, we're losing millions of people."

Angela shook her head so vigorously she lost her grip and started floating away from the monitor. She grabbed onto a bar and pulled herself back to the screen. Glaring into the camera lens, she said,

"What if we're wrong? What if it's some kind of glitch with the satellite? We'd be killing millions of people ourselves."

Randy shook his head. "It's not a glitch, Angela."

"How can you know—?"

The director held up a hand. "This wasn't the President's first choice. He ordered a quick reaction force into the area. They were to go in and shut down CERN, kill its power." McCree's face darkened. "The commandos were flying through a mountain range. The pilots timed it so that the airplane passed through a canyon when they hit the wave. But when their aircraft flew through it, everyone on-board disappeared. The plane continued on a straight line for a mile or two, but then it slammed into a mountain."

Angela shook her head. "No, no, no. They can't do this! Listen, Randy. That's tragic. I'm sorry that we lost the commandos, but just because the plane crashed doesn't mean the people inside disappeared."

"Remember the video I mentioned? The President and the Joint Chiefs were watching a live feed from inside the plane, Angela. When they hit the line, everyone just vanished."

"Oh, my God," she whispered as her indignation boiled away. She looked outside to see the lights of Australia's northwest coast glide into view. She chewed her lip for a moment, thinking of all the people sleeping under those lights, likely unaware of the coming wave.

Angela closed her eyes and took a deep breath. Finally, she let it out in a long exhalation and then looked at the director. "When do they launch?"

Randy moved the camera closer. Now his face filled the display. "They already did," he said softly.

"But the collider is five hundred feet underground," Angela said.

The director nodded. "The President is taking no chances. There are enough nukes headed that way to crack the planet's crust. They'll have no trouble punching through."

As Angela absorbed the information, Randy glanced at his watch. Then his face disappeared from the display. The image of his office rocked and spun. When the background stabilized, she was looking at the director from his side. A flat plane of swirled, dark brown wood-grain filled the lower third of the image. Randy had propped up the smartphone on his desk with its camera pointed at his left side. With both hands freed, he began typing commands into his computer. Seen from an oblique angle, a new image popped up on his monitor.

"Satellite feed?" Angela guessed.

Without turning toward her, the director nodded. "Yeah, we have one passing over the area right now. It doesn't have the acuity of a spy satellite. We won't even be able to see the missiles, but that won't matter. This light show should be visible from the Moon."

Angela swallowed. Her dry throat clicked audibly. Then her eyes widened. "Is that the countdown?"

A series of numbers occupied the near corner of the display. The leftmost digits already sat on zero, but those on the right still streamed through descending values.

Randy pointed to them. "Yeah. First impacts in fifteen seconds."

"Oh, my God," Angela whispered as a mixture of hope and dread gripped her. In spite of her disgust with the idea, she now found herself almost rooting for the nukes, but at the same time she couldn't help but worry for her friends that worked on the project. Many of her classmates and professors from MIT frequented CERN.

Were they about to die? Were they already dead?

Emotionally hollowed-out and speechless, Angela clung to one of the observatory's grab bars. Floating weightlessly, she looked at her bloodless nail beds. The underlying fingers dug into the padded bar.

Movement drew her eyes back to the monitor. Randy had picked up the camera and turned it so that the satellite image and its count-down to destruction dominated the video feed.

A moment later, the last seconds, and possibly the lives of millions, drained from the timer.

Nothing happened.

The zeroed-out string of numbers sat motionlessly at the bottom corner of the underlying image. No flashes of light blossomed over the European countryside. Angela began to think the video had frozen, that it was buffering, but then the silvery surface of Lake

Geneva drifted into view. Further proving the video's live nature, the director's quickened breaths rasped from the speakers, and the entire scene quivered slightly as the man's unsteady hand kept the smartphone trained on the display.

"What the hell?" he whispered between gasps.

The image swirled and spun again. It stabilized with a clunk. The director had laid the phone down this time. Ceiling tiles now filled the image. Randy leaned into the field of view. Angela saw him hold a handset to his ear. "What happened?"

As Randy listened to the person on the other end, the color drained from his face again. The ghostly pallor returned, washing back across his visage. Finally, he nodded and wordlessly dropped the handset back into its cradle.

Ash-white, he stared mutely ahead.

Angela's throat clicked in her ears. In a hoarse whisper, she said, "What is it, Randy? What happened?"

His head slowly shook from side to side. "We lost them."

Angela opened her mouth to ask what he meant, but the director continued.

"They had telemetry on over a hundred missiles, but each of them disappeared an instant before their programmed detonation."

"Did they lose power?" Angela asked.

On the display, she saw the director shake his head again.

"No. They just ... disappeared." He picked up the smartphone and looked at her with confused, haunted eyes. "They were tracking the missiles with radar. When the telemetry died, so did their radar returns."

In the background, the now receding French-Swiss border region still filled the director's computer screen. Somewhere down there, things had gone catastrophically wrong. What had the scientists done? Angela shook her head. She was at a loss, couldn't imagine any scenario where their actions could generate a globe-spanning effect. If they had produced a micro black hole, it would have quickly evaporated in a flash of Hawking radiation—an event they'd actually hoped to capture in the coming weeks, given the LHC's new capabilities. But even at those upgraded power levels, the force of the proton collisions paled when compared to the energy levels of the cosmic rays that constantly bombarded our atmosphere. Mother Nature had been running these experiments for billions of years, yet here we were, unfazed.

Until today.

A disembodied voice came through the connection. McCree looked off-screen. "What?"

The unintelligible feminine voice spoke again.

McCree's eyes widened. "Who?!" he asked with a fresh tinge of excitement. He stood and shouted, "Where?!"

After receiving an equally excited yet still unintelligible reply, Randy, now running, looked back into the camera. "I have to go, Angela. We've heard from some people inside the zone! I'll call you back!"

She threw up a hand. "Wait!"

The connection died.

"No," Angela whispered through a constricting throat. Her fingers touched the suddenly black screen.

"Come back."

CHAPTER 4

Vaughn tried to blink the blue spots from his vision. He looked at Mark. Barely discernible through the flash's after-image, the astronaut appeared to suffer from the same affliction. Blinking and squinting, the two men stared at one another in shocked silence.

"What the hell was that?!" Vaughn said. He swallowed hard. "Did the thruster explode?"

Mark shook his head. "No. That was new," he said distractedly. "I think something shorted out." He paused, appearing to consider his own words. Then he nodded. "Yeah. Maybe they had an electrical fire in Control ... a cascading failure that burned out a circuit in here." With raised eyebrows, he added, "That could've been what they were yelling about."

The astronaut toggled the radio. "Sandusky, this is Team Sigma." Still blinking, he scanned the instrument panel. Finally spotting his quarry, Mark leaned closer to the console and squinted his eyes. "We landed at ... uh ... zero seven-forty."

No response.

He keyed the radio again. "Sandusky, everything alright in there?"

Still no response.

Mark shook his head again. "What the hell?!"

"You're asking me?" Vaughn said.

Mark grinned and cocked an eyebrow. "Yeah, you're right. Don't know what I was thinking." He paused and then added, "Whatever the problem is, I'm sure they'll get it worked out in a minute."

The after-image of the fluorescing wall's brilliance still obscured most of Vaughn's field of view. Trying to discern his surroundings was like trying to see the world while looking through the holes of an electric blue sieve. Blinking his eyes furiously, Vaughn started wheezing again. "I can't clear these spots from my eyes!"

"Calm down. They'll clear."

Panting and blinking, Singleton scanned the room, testing his vision against varying backgrounds. He was about to ask Mark how the hell he could know his sight would return if this were new, but the next time Vaughn looked at the hovercraft's instrument panel, he saw more detail. He looked at Mark. Blue spots no longer obscured large portions of the man's face.

Vaughn pointed at the walls and raised an eyebrow. "You think that light came from a short circuit?" he said skeptically.

Mark smiled reassuringly and started climbing out of his seat. "Yeah, my money is on it being an electrical overload that even fried some of the systems in here." He paused and looked around. Then he turned back to Vaughn and shrugged. "I don't see how it could've been anything else."

The astronaut finished climbing out of the seat and stepped down from the module. In spite of the madness of the moment, the ex-helicopter pilot had landed the module almost exactly where it had started. The nearby gantry deck was inches from the side of the module. The man inspected the outside of the vehicle—probably searching for the source of the electrical arc.

Vaughn raised his eyebrow again and looked at the chamber's walls. "Any sign of what short-circuited?"

Now standing outside of the module on the gantry's upper deck and looking at Vaughn through the craft's open architecture, the astronaut shook his head. "No. Everything up here looks normal." He tapped the side of his helmet. "Whatever caused that flash probably fried the vehicle's communications link. Our commo is routed through it." Mark pointed a thumb over his shoulder. "Let's head down. I can reconfigure the links on the radio racks downstairs."

Vaughn nodded and unbuckled his restraints. He began to stand but knocked his helmet into an unseen obstacle, falling back into the seat with teeth-jarring force. For a panicked moment, he sat there listening for the hiss of a cracked helmet. It was hard to hear anything over the rasp of his breathing and the pounding of his heart.

"You didn't crack it," Mark said with a chuckle. He extended a hand through the module's open architecture. "Come on."

Vaughn batted away the glove. "I got this."

"Suit yourself."

On the second attempt, Vaughn cleared the obstacle and exited the vehicle.

Finally out of the thruster module and wheezing again, he followed Mark down the gantry ladder. When they reached the bottom, the astronaut started studying the underside of the vehicle. Breathing heavily, Vaughn looked over Mark's shoulder. "What are you looking for?"

The colonel shrugged and then pointed into the shadowed interstices of the thruster's undercarriage. "I thought the light might have come from beneath us."

Vaughn shook his head. "Sorry, buddy. I have to call bullshit on that one. If the light came from under here, there would've been long shadows running up the walls and overhead. I was looking up. The ceiling glowed just as brightly as the walls."

Mark stared at him for a long moment. In spite of his outward calm, the look on the man's face reflected Vaughn's unease. Finally, the astronaut nodded and walked toward the chamber wall.

After glancing back into the arcane plumbing that crowded the module's belly, the Army aviator chased after his friend.

When they reached the perimeter, the colonel slowly extended a gloved hand toward the inner surface of the aluminum wall.

Vaughn's eyes widened. "What the hell are you doing, Mark? Did you see how bright that metal got? It could be hot!"

Ignoring Vaughn's protestations, the astronaut touched the metal tentatively and then inspected the fingertips of his spacesuit's glove.

"You crazy son of a bitch!" Vaughn said.

The astronaut held out the glove. "Nothing."

Vaughn shook his head and then pointed at the wall. "Did you stop to consider the consequences of failure? What if that had melted a hole through one of your fingertips?"

Mark shrugged. "Duct tape."

Vaughn smiled and shook his head. "Oh, I see. Uh, you're Mark Watney, and this is the fucking *Martian*. Can I be Venkat Kapoor?"

The colonel laughed and then touched the wall again, this time sliding the gauntlet's palm across the silver surface. "It's not hot. Like I said, I think we just saw an electric arc."

There was something about the way that wall had appeared to flex that had Vaughn's short hairs standing on end. Had he just imagined it? He must have, right? The amount of energy required to make the entire wall flex like plastic exceeded anything he could imagine.

Well, there was one: a nuke detonated next door would probably do it, but if that had happened, they were likely dead men walking. Vaughn didn't want to contemplate that possibility. And he sure as hell didn't want to think what would be waiting for them outside these walls if that had happened.

Singleton looked from the wall to see Mark staring at him with raised eyebrows. "Earth to Captain Singleton."

Vaughn blinked. "What?"

"I said, if it wasn't an arc, what was it?"

Vaughn glanced back at the wall, and then shook his head. "I-I don't know, but if something shorted out or arced under the module, why weren't there any shadows?"

Mark pointed at the wall again. "Shiny metal walls. Lots of reflective surfaces. They could've spread the light around."

"I don't know," Vaughn said, shaking his head. He couldn't purge the image of the walls bowing in like a sheet flapping in the breeze. Could it have been an illusion created by the light?

44

The colonel looked about the chamber. Then he pointed off to the side. "Let's try the radios."

Vaughn gave the wall one last wary look and then followed the astronaut to a nearby rack of electronics.

Mark flipped a few of its switches and then said, "This will bypass the module's radios and route them directly to our suits."

Vaughn nodded. "At this point, I'd take a couple of cans and a goddamned string."

The astronaut smiled behind his visor. "I might be able to do better than that."

A few flipped switches later, the astronaut toggled his suit's radio. "Sandusky, this is Team Sigma, over."

Nothing. Long seconds ticked by, but the radio remained stubbornly quiet.

"Control, This is Colonel Hennessy. Come in, please."

Still nothing.

Vaughn glanced back to the wall. Something was very wrong here.

"Damn it," Mark whispered. He selected a new intercom channel. "Space Power Operations, this is Team Sigma," he said, a nervous edge clipping his words. "Sorry to bother you guys, but we've lost commo with Sandusky Control. Can someone over there try to raise them on a landline?"

Deafening silence greeted even this new effort.

A knot began to twist in Vaughn's gut. "What kind of screwed-up operation are y'all running?" he said.

Mark looked at him and shook his head. "Nothing like this has ever happened. Ever!"

Vaughn pointed at the rack of electronics. "Maybe the power surge cooked the radio stack, too." That knot in his gut said this was bullshit, but Vaughn didn't know what else to say.

The astronaut shook his head. "They're all live connections." He pointed at the rack. "All of the lights are green. The radios are transmitting and receiving, both over the air to our suits and through their hardwired connections to the outside world. Nothing's fried, and it's not a power failure," he said.

"Guess that rules out World War Three," Singleton said with a relieved chuckle.

"What?"

Vaughn waved him off. "Nothing. Just my imagination getting the better of me."

Mark cocked an eyebrow but nodded his understanding. He switched to a third line. "Glenn Research Center Operations, this is Lieutenant Colonel Mark Hennessy in the vacuum chamber. Is anyone there?"

Vaughn's hand went to his right rear pocket. Of course, his spacesuit didn't have one, so his questing glove came up empty. It didn't matter. A cellphone was useless in the chamber. The room's metal walls blocked all radio signals. A mobile phone could neither send nor receive calls or the internet. Previously, Mark had told him that the communications cables, as well as the power wires, ran through a heavily sealed conduit that penetrated the chamber's aluminum and concrete walls. The only way they were going to talk to anyone was through those wires.

When the third call to Glenn Ops went unanswered, Mark toggled the fourth line. "Plum Brook Station, this is Lieutenant Colonel Mark Hennessy in the Space Power Annex. Please come in!"

Silently, the two men exchanged worried looks.

Vaughn felt a fresh bead of sweat trying to breach his improperly donned headband.

Frustrating minutes later, they had worked their way through NASA's complete local organizational chart. Mark had tried to contact every echelon. Each unanswered radio call had tightened the knot in Vaughn's gut another notch. From the upper management at Sandusky Mission Control—the space center's main operations command—to the tech reps that should be standing just outside of the vacuum chamber's massive door, each call had apparently fallen on deaf ears. That last attempt had been through an old-school telephone. The red handset hung from an antique phone base that had no buttons. Big white letters spelled out EMERGENCY across its spine. Because of the room's lack of atmosphere, the astronaut had pressed the phone's mouthpiece to his helmet and yelled for someone to pick up. He told Vaughn that the visor's vibrations would transmit into the device's chassis and therefore into the microphone, and vice versa from the phone's speaker into his helmet.

Several attempts later, Mark looked at Vaughn with evident confusion. "They're not answering either." He hung up the phone and shook his head. "What the hell?"

"What about the main conduit?" Vaughn said, thinking about the bundle of cables that, in the chamber's radio-free interior, formed their only link to the outside world. "Maybe the power surge fried all our communication wires."

Mark shook his head again. "No. Like I said, all the connections are live."

Vaughn's eyes widened, and he pointed to the metal walls. "Or maybe that was an electromagnetic pulse, an EMP."

Mark fell silent. He chewed a lip as he considered Vaughn's words.

The Army aviator continued, giving voice to his thoughts as they formed. Pointing up, he said, "If someone popped a nuke in the upper atmosphere, the EMP would have fried every unshielded circuit between Chicago and the East Coast. The wires might be intact, but with its computer chips fried, the radio wouldn't be transmitting or receiving, regardless of what those green lights tell you."

"Holy shit ..." the astronaut whispered. "That could be it." Then doubt twisted his face. "But why do we still have power? That's all computer controlled as well."

Vaughn shook his head. "Hell if I know." He pointed toward the fifty-foot-tall door. "Let's get out of here, and then we can ask them in person."

"It's not that easy," Mark said. "The external crew has to start the atmospheric cycle. Otherwise ..." His words tapered off. He frowned and shook his head. "Trust me: you don't wanna go down that path."

Mark turned back and stared at the radio rack for a long moment. Then he shrugged his shoulders. "Screw it," he said and then reached into the electronics and started disconnecting wires. A moment later, the colonel went back to the EMERGENCY phone. He ripped the cord out of the handset and dropped it. The red, dog bone-shaped plastic piece fell to the metallic floor, bouncing away noiselessly in the vacuum. Then he pulled the phone's base off the wall.

The astronaut returned to the radio rack. Severed cords hung from the boxy red telephone like torn entrails. He placed the unit on a shelf. Grabbing a nearby implement, Mark pried off the phone's top cover, exposing a hidden and long disused rotary dial.

"Jesus!" Vaughn said. "How did that museum piece get in here?"

The astronaut shrugged. "Probably came from the old chamber in Sandusky."

Bent over his work, Mark struggled with gloved fingers to connect the frayed wires that extended from the end of the coiled red cord.

Vaughn looked around. Again his eyes returned to the chamber's silvery walls. He felt nauseous. If that had been an EMP, if those aluminum panels had in fact flexed, then it had been a damned close explosion. But they couldn't have flexed. Six-foot-thick concrete walls backed them.

He looked from the wall to the hunched-over astronaut. "Hey, Mark. Just before that flash, did you see—?"

"That should do it," the Colonel said, cutting him off.

"Do what?" Vaughn said.

The astronaut didn't respond. Instead, he stepped back and nodded. Then he flicked a switch on one of the components bolted to the electronics rack. Across its front, the series of green lights sprang back to life.

Suddenly a dial tone streamed into Vaughn's ears.

Mark looked at him triumphantly. "I tied the radio into the land-line." He paused and then turned raised eyebrows toward Vaughn. "Now we know it wasn't an EMP. An electromagnetic pulse would have fried the phone lines, too."

"I don't know," Vaughn said.

"What were you saying?"

Vaughn glanced at the wall and then shook his head. "N-Nothing." He gestured to the antique phone. "What's next?"

Mark shrugged. "Let's make a call."

With a gauntleted hand, he attempted to turn the old dial, but the glove's fingertip wouldn't fit in the hole. He grabbed the small screwdriver he'd used to pry off the phone's false front and jabbed it into the first number hole.

"I'm calling the duty officer's station. That phone is manned twenty-four/seven."

Several arcing strokes later, he finished dialing.

A moment later, a warbling ringtone blared from their radio speakers.

"Great job, Colonel!" Vaughn said as the smiling men bumped gloved fists.

Then an automated voice answered the call.

Their grins vaporized. Raised fists fell.

The knot in Vaughn's stomach returned with a vengeance.

"What the hell?" he whispered. Vaughn worried he would soon vomit in his helmet. Just thinking about the possibility almost made it a self-fulfilling prophecy. Through a force of will, he pushed the thought aside.

The men exchanged nervous glances. Then shaking his head, the colonel disconnected the call and began the laborious act of dialing another number.

No one answered that one either.

Mark cursed as he reset the phone and then dialed a third number.

Vaughn felt the acid churning in his stomach as call after call fell on apparently deaf ears.

When yet another attempt went unanswered, Mark stared at the radio for a long moment. Finally, he gave a short nod and then dialed a new number with a different area code.

One ring.

No answer.

Second ring.

Still no answer. Mark turned an ash-white face toward Vaughn. "That's Houston," he whispered.

Third ring.

Vaughn felt like Mark looked. What the hell was going on? What had happened?

Fourth—

A loud click interrupted the growling tone mid-ring.

An out of breath female voice said, "Johnson Space Center Mission Control." She paused for breath and then added, "Director McCree's office." The woman sounded nervous, harried. "Who's calling?"

"Yes!" Vaughn said with a spreading grin.

Mark held up a hand and then toggled his radio connection. "This is Lieutenant Colonel Mark Hennessy calling from the Space Power Annex at Glenn Research Center."

"I'm sorry, Colonel, but as you can imagine, Director McCree is extremely busy … Wait!" the woman shouted with a start. "Did you say *Glenn Research?!*"

Mark looked at Vaughn and shrugged his shoulders. Then he toggled the radio. "Uh, yes, ma'am."

"You're in Ohio?!" the woman asked incredulously.

"Yes, I am in Ohio," Mark said. "Last time I checked, that's where we keep the Space Power Annex."

"Oh, thank goodness," the woman said excitedly, apparently unscathed by Mark's sarcasm. "Hold for the director." A loud clunk followed by a rocking noise came over the connection. She had apparently dropped the handset onto the desk, rather than placing them on hold.

Vaughn's grin faltered. He looked at Mark. "What in the hell is going on?"

The astronaut shook his head again. "I guess something's happened. Something big."

Singleton laughed mirthlessly. "Thank you, Captain Obvious," he said as he cast another uneasy glance at the chamber's walls. Then Vaughn nodded at the jury-rigged telephone. "Guess we're about to find out how big."

Vaughn heard rapid-fire footsteps over the telephonic connection. With another clunk of a jostled handset, a winded male voice said,

"This is Director McCree. Who the hell is this?! Better not be a goddamned prank call!"

"Director McCree, this is Lieutenant Colonel Mark Henne—"

"Mark!" McCree interrupted excitedly. "Where are you, Colonel?"

"We're in the new vacuum chamber, sir. In the Space Power Annex."

"In Ohio?"

Mark gave Vaughn another confused look. "Yes, sir. In Ohio," he said, omitting the sarcasm this time.

"Oh, thank you!" the director said with evident relief. "Maybe it's losing power."

"What are you talking about, sir? What the hell is going on?"

"Wait," the director said, ignoring Mark's question. "What were you doing in the chamber, Colonel?"

"I'm with Team Sigma. We were testing the Q-G thruster module, sir."

"Shit," McCree said, his excitement evaporating. "You were in hard vacuum when it happened, weren't you?"

"When what happened, sir?"

"Oh shit," McCree whispered. "You don't know."

"Actually, sir, there was … something," Mark said. "We saw a flash. That's when we lost commo with Glenn Mission Control."

"Colonel, listen, I don't have much time. It's almost here."

"What is, sir?"

"The same light you saw, Mark," the director said impatiently. "It's about to hit Houston. I need to know what you were doing the exact moment you saw that light."

"We were hovering the module."

"Were you still tethered?"

"No, sir."

"So you were in a vacuum and untethered," the director said with a defeated sigh. The man's voice sounded distant, suddenly detached, as if the handset had drifted from his lips and he was no longer talking to Mark. "It hasn't weakened. They were disconnected from the planet, even at the molecular level. That must be what saved them."

Vaughn heard a feminine voice in the background say, "I can't reach your wife, sir." He could hear tears in the woman's voice. "I can't reach anyone. All the cell networks have crashed. They must be overloaded."

"She's all alone out there," McCree said in choked words. "Her and the twins ... Oh, Betsy ..."

The woman's voice returned. "Oh, God! Through the window ... I see it! It's coming so fast!"

The abject terror in the woman's voice along with the ache evident in the director's choked words dug a hole in Vaughn's gut.

"Get out of here, Ellen," the director said. "Go on down to the tunnel. I'll be right behind you."

Vaughn and Mark exchanged horrified, pained glances. Vaughn reached again for his back pocket, wanting, no, needing to call his mom. He had no idea what the hell was happening, but hearing these people worrying about their families had him doing the same.

Through the connection, he heard the director say, "Betsy ... Oh, my Betsy ..."

"Director?" Mark said, almost whispering.

"Oh shit!" McCree shouted with sudden clarity. The handset returned to his mouth. Between heavy breaths, he said, "Colonel Hennessy ... Mark! Listen! You ... you have to rescue Commander Brown! You have to—"

The director's voice died mid-sentence.

A loud clunk followed by the rumbling and rocking sound of a dropped phone shot from the speaker.

Wide-eyed, Vaughn stared mutely at Mark.

Maddening moments later, the distant handset finally came to rest, and nothing but deafening silence oozed from the connection.

CHAPTER 5

Vaughn couldn't speak. The fear, no, the abject horror that had poured from the connection threatened to make him physically ill.

"Hello?" Mark yelled for the third time. Again no one answered. Nothing but silence came from the apparently live connection.

It was all Vaughn could do to hold down the morning's breakfast. His own raspy breaths echoed within his helmet again, but this time, they had nothing to do with his poor physical fitness. Bent over, hands on knees, he closed his eyes and swallowed back the bile that threatened to burst through his defenses. From his bent-over position, the Army captain cast a wary eye toward the makeshift telephone but shook his head. He was almost thankful that he didn't have his phone. Even if he had the nerve to risk the emotional consequences of an unanswered call to his mother, he couldn't place it. Nobody memorized numbers these days, and Vaughn was no exception.

"What in the *hell* is going on?!" Mark said, yanking Vaughn from his reverie. The astronaut's words had a panicked edge. "What the *fuck* is happening to everyone?!"

Vaughn shook his head. "Hell if I know!" he shouted between

breaths. Fearing he was starting to hyperventilate, he took one last deep breath and held it. When stars began to fill his vision, he released the air in a long, slow exhalation.

Mark shook his head. "This doesn't make sense!" He paused. Then looking at Vaughn, he said, "I mean, what was all that talk about being disconnected from the planet?"

Vaughn stood upright. "I don't know." He swept a hand toward the wall. "But we sure as hell aren't going to figure it out in here!"

Wide-eyed, Hennessy gave a quick nod. "You're right." The man looked around, scanning the room. Apparently spotting his quarry, he started walking around the base of the gantry, toward the far wall.

"What are you doing?" Vaughn said as he followed him.

The astronaut pointed ahead. "Over here. It's the manual pressure release, an emergency fail-safe." He walked up to a red box that sported a transparent front panel. Evenly spaced white chevrons covered the three-foot-tall, vertically oriented glass rectangle. A network of pipes protruded from the top and bottom of the fixture. A small tool hung from a chain on its right side.

Mark grabbed the bronze hammer and struck the clear panel. In surreal silence, the safety glass shattered into thousands of pebble-sized shards and fell to the floor. Not wanting to risk a torn glove in the room's vacuum, Hennessy cautiously reached through the opening and pulled a metal pipe out of the enclosure. He stuck one end of it into a metal sleeve that protruded from arcane plumbing within the box. After twisting the tube a quarter turn, Mark grabbed the protruding end of it and began to pump the apparent handle up and down like a man trying to jack up a car.

"It's a hydraulic pump?"

"Yeah," Mark said. "We'll have to take turns. I've never had to do this, but I've heard it takes about a million pumps."

Vaughn ignored the exaggeration. "What do you think happened to the director?" He paused and then pointed through the large door. "To everybody out there?"

The astronaut kept jacking the lever. Between breaths, he said, "I don't know. Maybe you were right, and that light was from an EMP."

"No, I couldn't have been right," Vaughn said, shaking his head. "The phone lines and apparently every telecom facility between here and Houston are still online. Besides, an EMP wouldn't affect people. It doesn't have enough power ..."

Vaughn paused. His eyes widened. "Oh shit! Mark! What if something happened to the sun?"

The astronaut's arm froze mid-stroke. His head slowly turned toward Vaughn. "Shit ..." He stared through him. "If it did, if there's a massive solar flare going on, opening this door is the last thing we should do."

"How long can we stay in here?"

Mark frowned and shook his head. "Not long." He looked at his watch. "We've already been in here significantly longer than planned. Our CO2 scrubbers will max out soon." He shrugged. After a pause, the astronaut pointed to his suit's environmental controls and then hitched a thumb at the chamber door. "Pick your poison, Captain."

"Screw that," Vaughn said. "I'm not going silently into the night. If we're going to die anyway, I'd rather have an answer, to know what the hell happened."

Mark raised his eyebrows. "Even if that answer comes as a flare of lethal radiation?"

Vaughn nodded soberly. "Yes, even if."

The astronaut nodded slowly. "I agree, friend."

He grabbed the end of the lever and started to stroke it up and down again.

After a few minutes, Mark's pace fell off. Over their intercom, the man's breaths rasped in his ears. Vaughn held out his hand. "Let me."

Mark backed away from the wall. Bending at the waist and resting a hand on a knee, he extended the other toward the lever. "Be my guest."

Vaughn began cranking the handle up and down. After a few strokes, his wheezes returned. Moisture started to collect on the inside of his visor. For what felt like hours, Vaughn's universe condensed down to an oscillating silver pipe and the sound of his rasping breath—that and the mounting pain in his side. He mused that perhaps Mark hadn't exaggerated the required number of pumps.

Some time later, an insistent hand pressed on his shoulder, snapping Vaughn out of his trance.

"Give me that before you stroke out," Mark said as he gently shoved him aside.

"All … yours," Vaughn said between pants. "How long did I go?"

The astronaut grabbed the pipe and started pumping it at a significantly higher rate than had Vaughn. Hennessy consulted the watch strapped to his suit's forearm. "About three minutes."

"Bullsh—" Vaughn began to protest, but then a hissing sound stopped him mid-word. His eyes widened. "Did you hear that?"

Behind his fogged visor, the astronaut's head nodded. He paused and pointed to the digital display on his wrist. "We finished opening the valve in the first few minutes. Pressure's been building since. The air is still pretty thin, but it's finally thick enough to carry sound."

"If the valve is open, why the hell are you still pumping?"

The astronaut stopped and bent over again, breathing heavily. He pointed at the lever. "This door wasn't designed to be opened from the inside, not electronically, anyway." He paused. After a deep breath, Mark stood and resumed pumping. "The backup system is entirely hydromechanical. The designers assumed it would only be used in case of a total electrical failure. So we'll have to keep pumping until the door opens enough for us to get out." He gave Vaughn a meaningful look. "Or until we get that answering flash of light."

Inside Vaughn's helmet, a red light started pulsing above the top right corner of his visor. His eyes widened. Feeling like an insistent child, Vaughn patted Mark's shoulder again. When the man looked at him, Singleton pointed toward the flashing light. "What the hell does this mean?"

Still pumping the lever up and down, the astronaut nodded. "Figured that was coming. Mine will start flashing soon, too."

As if on cue, the right side of Mark's forehead began to intermittently glow red as the same light started flashing within his helmet.

"What the hell is wrong now?"

Still jacking the lever, Mark said, "Our CO2 scrubbers are falling behind."

A loud metallic report reverberated through the chamber's atmosphere and aluminum floor.

Both men flinched and looked toward the door. Mark stopped pumping. He turned back to Vaughn. "That was the first lock."

Singleton raised his eyebrows. "No sign of a solar flare yet."

"There's still a lot of latches to go."

The astronaut checked his atmospheric gauges. After a quick nod, he started working on his helmet's locking ring.

"Pressure's up to normal."

"It's about time," Vaughn said as he began to grope blindly for his helmet's lock as well. Condensed moisture now covered the inner surface of his visor, obscuring much of his vision. He fumbled with the latch, but his fat, glove-encumbered fingers found no purchase.

Through the haze, he saw Mark twist his helmet ninety degrees and then remove it. He placed it on a nearby workbench and then turned to Vaughn. The astronaut extended a hand. "Here, let me."

Vaughn wanted to bat the hand away, but even before the CO2 alarm, he'd been more than ready to have the damned fishbowl off of his head.

A moment later, Hennessy twisted the helmet and lifted it away from Vaughn's suit. Refreshing cold air flowed down the now open neck. He looked at Mark, shocked to see roiling torrents of steam rising from the top of the man's spacesuit, his head barely visible in the tumultuous column.

Vaughn grinned. "You look like a dryer vent in midwinter."

Just as he uttered the words, the trickle of vapors rising around his own head escalated into a torrent as steam began to boil out of his spacesuit as well. A chill ran down his spine as a fresh wave of frigid air plunged down the crack of his ass.

"Holy shit!" Vaughn shivered and looked wide-eyed at Mark. "It's *freezing* in here!"

The astronaut nodded. "Thermodynamics at work, my friend. NASA doesn't dump regular air back into the chamber. They compress the room's original atmosphere and store it in large tanks. When the engineers are ready to flood the space with air, they normally run it over a heater to compensate for expansion cooling, but the mechanical backup doesn't have that feature."

Vaughn saw ice already forming on his discarded helmet. He could feel condensation freezing on his nose hairs as well.

The astronaut shivered and said, "Hopefully, we can finish this before we freeze to death."

"Jesus," Vaughn said. He pushed aside Mark and stepped to the pump. In his mind's eye, he saw the series of mechanical locks that ringed the massive chamber door. "That was just the first lock we heard?"

Mark nodded. "Yep. We have about thirty more to go. And when the last one unlatches, the pump will start turning the gears that move the door."

Vaughn shivered again as another chill wracked his body. Remembering how slowly the door had moved when it closed, he started pumping the lever furiously.

Icicles now hung from Vaughn's nostrils. In front of him, Mark continued to pump the handle. The same wintry decorations adorned the astronaut's nose.

"I think that was the last latch," the man said between breaths.

Suddenly, blinding light flooded the chamber. Both men flinched and threw up their arms as they turned toward the source.

Vaughn squinted into the glare. White light now framed the massive metal door.

"Is that …?" Vaughn started.

Mark shook his head. "I don't think so. My eyes are already adjusting to the light. It always looks this bright when the door cracks open."

The astronaut stepped tentatively toward the door. Vaughn reached out and grabbed his shoulder. "Are you sure about this?"

Hennessy nodded. "I'm sure I want to get a closer look before we open it any farther."

He shrugged off Vaughn's hand and continued walking toward the door.

Vaughn watched him for a moment. The light was eye-burningly bright, but it didn't seem lethal. He walked after the astronaut. Mark had already reached the near edge of the door.

Vaughn gasped as the man, haloed in the golden light that streamed through the crack, appeared to catch on fire, but the illusion faded quickly. It was just backlit steam rising from the frost in the astronaut's hair.

Colonel Hennessy peered through the half-inch crack for a long moment. Then he turned from the light and looked at Vaughn with evident confusion. "Everything looks ... normal."

"Let me see." He pushed aside the astronaut and stepped to the edge of the door and into the pleasant warmth that flowed through the crevice. He positioned his left eye in front of the narrow opening. It quickly adjusted to the light beyond. In the bay that lay on the other side of the door, a forklift sat with its tines halfway inserted into a pallet. Vaughn couldn't see much more than that through the opening's narrow aperture. From the angle of the shadows, it appeared that the room's outer door was still open, but the light looked normal, no brighter than he would've expected on a regular day.

"You're right," Vaughn said.

Mark patted his shoulder. "Come on. Let's get this thing opened enough so that we can get the hell out of here."

Several minutes later, two frost-covered spacesuits fell through the narrow slit of the vacuum chamber's now partially retracted door.

"Get the hell off me!" Mark said.

After the tall, thin astronaut had squeezed through the narrow opening, he'd had to pull and tug to get Vaughn and his belly out of the chamber. When he'd popped free, they'd fallen into a heap.

Vaughn rolled off of him. Laying his head on the warm concrete floor, he panted for a few seconds. Cold air still poured through the opening, sweeping away the steam of their breaths.

Mark stood and then helped Vaughn to his feet.

They looked around. The previously busy facility sat devoid of movement or noise.

Vaughn looked at Mark and shook his head. "Where is everybody? I mean, worst-case scenario, I thought we might find crispy bodies. But ..." He paused, waving a hand toward the empty facility. "But not this. Nothing! Nobody. No *bodies*, even!"

Hennessy nodded. "I know. This just keeps getting weirder and weirder." He pointed a thumb over his shoulder. "Let's go check the equipment room."

Vaughn nodded. "Yeah," he said distractedly as he looked around trying to spot somebody.

"You're not going to need that."

"What?" Vaughn said, turning back to the astronaut.

"The helmet. I don't think you'll need it."

Vaughn looked down to see it still in his left hand. He released the helmet, and it bounced off the concrete floor with a loud crack.

"What the hell?!" Mark yelled. "Do you know how much that thing costs?"

Vaughn's eyes focused, and he looked at the astronaut. "I think we have way bigger problems than a broken helmet."

Mark glared at him for a moment. Then his eyes widened, and he said, "Do you smell that?"

Vaughn nodded as the odor wafted over him. He recognized the stench as it generated a wave of nausea. "Oh shit. It smells like ... burned meat."

"Yeah, it does," Mark said. He looked behind himself. "Smells like it's coming from this way. Let's check it out."

The astronaut turned and started walking toward the building's administrative section.

Vaughn stood frozen in place. Unbidden, his hand drifted to his nonexistent back pocket, muscle memory seeking the phone in its usual location. Of course, it still wasn't there. He didn't know if its absence was a blessing or a curse. Whatever had happened here had also happened in Houston, so it had probably reached Colorado as well. A simple phone call might answer the question. If she didn't answer, well, absence of evidence wasn't proof of absence. That's what he'd try to tell himself. But if she did answer, he'd know she was okay. Staring at the floor, Vaughn shook his head. If she didn't—

"What are you doing?" Mark asked sharply.

Vaughn looked up. Hennessy had stopped short of the door to the facility's inner offices and turned back toward him with an impatient look.

Yanked from his thoughts, Vaughn stared back at him mutely. Then he said, "Shouldn't we try to call someone else?"

"We will, but right now, someone right here might need our help."

Vaughn nodded. "Yeah … yeah, you're right." Uprooting his spacesuit's boots, he walked toward Mark and then followed him into the facility.

A few minutes later, they stepped into a foul-smelling break room. Vaughn and Mark had wandered through the entire building, seeking the source of the stench. They still hadn't seen anyone. The equipment room, as well as every office they'd passed, had been completely devoid of life. Their noses had finally led them to this room and its smoky kitchen.

Along the way, they'd seen plenty of evidence of sudden disappearance. Here in the break room, it looked like people had run out mid-meal. On the table, a spoon rested in a small puddle of oats next to a half-filled bowl of the same.

The smell of burned popcorn filled the room. Vaughn opened the microwave to find a puffed-up bag of the stuff still sitting on the oven's glass carousel.

Charred embers sat in a small skillet.

He pointed into the pan. "Scrambled eggs?"

Mark nodded. "Charcoal now."

Adding to the room's stench, the skillet's melted plastic handle sat on the stove top, the portion closest to the still glowing burner bubbling and smoking.

Vaughn rotated the stove's knob and clicked it into the off position.

He looked at Mark. "Where did they all—?"

A loud explosion—felt as much as heard—rocked the building.

After exchanging shocked looks, the two men, still in their helmetless spacesuits, ran toward the exit. Moments later, they stood under a surreally normal blue sky.

Panting, trying to purge the smells and images from his head, Vaughn looked around. They had emerged into a central courtyard. He could hear the rumble of a far-off fire, but the buildings and trees that ringed the quadrangle made it difficult to see very far. Distant columns of smoke dotted the bits of horizon visible through a couple of the gaps.

Singleton shook his head. "What the hell?"

Mark pointed over Vaughn's shoulder. "Over there!"

He looked in the indicated direction. From behind the building they'd just exited, a black column of smoke stretched high into the sky. Then a roiling churning tumor of orange fire climbed into view above the roof of the Space Power Annex. It raced heavenward, following the black column's path.

Vaughn looked at Hennessy. "That's Cleveland Airport, isn't it?"

Mark nodded. "Must've been an accident."

Vaughn's eyes widened. "Maybe that's where everyone went."

"You're right," Mark said. He started to jog toward the corner of the facility. "Let's see if we can help."

Vaughn followed him, struggling to keep up with the man. As they neared the building's edge, the faint whisper of a distant fire rose into a deep roar that sounded like continuous thunder.

A moment later, he rounded the corner and plowed into Hennessy. The man had stopped dead in his tracks.

"Jesus, Mark! What in the …?"

The words died in his mouth. The devastation before them defied logic.

Across the expansive field, it looked as if giants had started a bonfire using broken aircraft hulls as kindling.

"What in the hell?" Vaughn croaked.

"Come on," Mark said. "We need to help them." He pointed toward the burning mass of heaped airplanes. "I don't see any fire trucks. Crash rescue hasn't responded."

Mark jogged toward a nearby gate in the fence that ran along their shared property line. He punched in a code, and it opened.

They were still a mile from the crash site, but a couple of hundred yards into the airport property, they found an idling truck. It sat in a low drainage easement. The pickup's right front wheel had dropped into the shallow concrete culvert at the ditch's center. Mark jumped behind the wheel and quickly backed the truck out of the jam. Vaughn hopped into the passenger seat and soon the two men were racing across the grass field. He braced his forearm against the ceiling to stop from slamming into it as the truck lurched across low mounds hidden in the knee-deep grass.

Braking hard, Mark brought the truck to a sliding stop on the sod adjacent to the west end of the airport's main runway.

They jumped out of the vehicle. Vaughn raised an arm to shield his face from the heat that radiated from the tremendous fire and scanned the area. They stood in knee-deep grass, but ten feet in front of the truck, nothing remained of the sod but smoldering embers. A burning pile of ruptured airplane hulls covered the ground a quarter-mile ahead of the two men, but their spilled contents littered the intervening earth. Busted suitcases and mangled metal lay strewn across the tortured field. Closer to the colossal Boeing-fed bonfire, scattered clumps of luggage burned. Under the smoke-darkened sky, they looked like surreal campfires, but not one body, alive or dead, stoked these untended flames.

This didn't make any sense. As a pilot, Vaughn had seen crash scene photos. In them, bodies had littered the ground. But here, he couldn't see a single one.

Vaughn looked at his old friend and then down at his own grass-stained spacesuit. The two men looked like lost spacemen as they stood stupefied before the hellish altar of piled fuselages and shattered flight surfaces. Broken wings and tail sections protruded from the mass at odd angles. Squinting and using raised forearms to shield their faces from the heat, the two men exchanged confused glances.

Vaughn scanned his surroundings again. They couldn't move any closer. The flames were too intense. He could already feel the inner half of the suit that faced the fire starting to warm. But it didn't matter.

"There's no one to save, Mark. They're all gone."

"How can that be?" the astronaut shouted over the din of burning airplanes. "How could everyone just ... disappear?"

Vaughn shook his head. "That light we saw. It ... it must have—"

Suddenly, a new noise rose above the roar of the burning airplanes, an odd metallic scraping noise. The sound had come from behind them.

The men looked over their shoulders.

Two miles to their east, a wide-bodied jet had just landed on the approach end of the runway they were standing next to. The airplane's pilots had failed to extend the landing gear. They'd belly-landed the Boeing 777.

"Why in the hell would they land on this runway?" Vaughn said. He stared incredulously at the rapidly approaching passenger jet. "And why aren't they using their reverse thrusters?"

Something knocked into him. Vaughn lunged sideways. His feet pumped, just managing to stay under him.

"Run!" Mark screamed into his face.

Shocked into action, Singleton chased after his fleeing friend. Running away from the runway perpendicularly, they ran for their lives.

Looking over his right shoulder, Vaughn watched the plane as it bore down on them. In spreading fans, twin streams of phosphorescent white sparks flew from its belly, but even with all that drag, the triple seven wasn't slowing fast enough. It would soon pass right behind them! Then the right wing dropped a few feet, and the bottom of its engine ground into the tarmac. Fresh gouts of white-hot sparks spewed out from the contact point. The additional drag pulled the Boeing off of the runway centerline.

Now the plane was heading straight toward Vaughn!

The dragging right engine suddenly snapped off of the wing.

Earth and sod sprayed up into the air, and the massive turbofan started tumbling across the field. No longer being pulled right by the now departed engine, the wide-bodied fuselage stopped its right turn and tracked straight, but it still looked determined to run him down.

"Shit, shit, *shit!*" Vaughn shouted.

Mark was just ahead of him. "Come on!" he screamed. "Run faster!"

Vaughn stopped looking at the onrushing plane and focused on the ground in front of him, running as fast as he could muster in the heavy spacesuit.

Now twenty feet ahead of him, Mark dove for cover.

The nose of the huge airplane passed just behind Vaughn. Then a blast of wind shoved him in the back, flinging him to the ground face first just as the wing flashed over him.

Pulling his face out of the dirt, Vaughn looked left, watching as the plane rushed to join its burning friends.

Mark stood up a few feet in front of him. After watching the retreating jet for a moment, he turned an astonished face to Vaughn. "Can you believe tha—?"

The ground shook as if a mine had detonated, and Mark disappeared mid-word. Where he had been standing, a geyser of dirt spewed into the air.

Having obliterated Vaughn's friend, the still tumbling engine—the same one that had broken off the wing earlier—chased after the careening airplane.

"Mark!"

Then as if someone had opened a blast furnace door, a wave of heat washed over Vaughn as the Boeing Triple Seven slammed into the pile of demolished planes and erupted.

Numbing shock wrapped Vaughn in its cold embrace. He took a hesitant step toward the place where his friend had been standing just moments before. "No, no, no," he whispered as he stopped, pulling up short. "No!"

His friend … There was nothing left of him!

Falling to his knees, Vaughn stared into the small crater, unable to wrap his mind around what had happened to his buddy.

After a few minutes, the blossoming heat of fresh explosions shook him out of his trance.

Like a zombie, he climbed to his feet and trudged to the miraculously untouched pickup truck. Now covered in mud and grass, Vaughn sat behind the steering wheel of the still idling vehicle. Looking through the passenger window, he stared across the field, unable to pull his eyes from the small, red-ringed crater: all that remained of his flight schoolmate, his friend, his only friend.

"No, no, no," he said over and over again. Like a chanting monk, Vaughn continued the incantation until a new sound came from behind him.

Again the squealing protest of metal sliding across pavement rose above the roar of the jet-fueled fire.

In the truck's rearview mirror, Vaughn watched another empty passenger jet slide down the runway, directly at him.

CHAPTER 6

B eneath the space station, tall cumulous clouds reached into the atmosphere above the Pacific Ocean. Like fingers extended into a river of golden light, they cut long shadows that flowed into the darkness of the planet's ever-advancing day-night terminator.

The world wavered as if globe-spanning earthquakes had liquefied entire continents. Angela tried to blink the distorting moisture from her vision, but in the station's zero-G environment, the tears only piled up on the surface of her eyes. She dabbed them and then watched as the ISS and the US West Coast crossed into the night as one. The day that might have seen the end of humankind along with most, if not all, of the planet's animal life ended with a surreally beautiful sunset.

Could every person Angela had ever known be ... gone? She didn't want to say dead, couldn't even think it. Like Randy had said: They were gone. But where? And could it have affected everyone? Surely someone had been far enough underground to remain. The last thing the director had told her was that they'd heard from people in the zone. But she still hadn't heard back from Houston. That radio had remained stubbornly quiet.

In the meantime, Angela had watched the wave of light burn its way across the entire planet. At its widest, the white wall of energy had girdled the Earth like a globe-spanning gimbal. Then the ring had begun to contract as it continued its path of annihilation across the second hemisphere. On one orbit, the shrinking circle of light had been closing on a point in the South Pacific. When the next circuit returned her to that side of the planet, the white curtain had vanished. Having swept across the entire Earth, the miles-high wall of light had just … disappeared.

As far as Angela could tell, the wave never lost any of its energy. As it crossed New Zealand, one of the last places to fall, it looked just as bright and reached just as high into the atmosphere as it had the first time she'd crossed its boundary.

That had been five orbits ago. She'd spent most of the intervening hours in the Cupola, looking down on the scrolling surface.

She knew that Teddy and Bill had landed in the desert Southwest, somewhere beneath the station's current position. Their reentry track should've deposited them in the Mojave Desert. They had probably come down just before the light wave had swept across this part of North America. By the time they'd touched down, Houston had … gone. After Texas, the arid states of the desert Southwest had fallen like dominoes.

Angela believed that somewhere below her rested an empty Soyuz capsule, the only marker her two friends would likely ever have. Looking down on that portion of the night-drowned continent, she placed a hand against the cold glass panel. Again, massive, continent-displacing waves crowded her vision. Angela dabbed the tears from her eyes.

She grabbed the headset floating next to the window on her right. After pulling it over her tied-back brown hair, she fished its cable out of the air. Angela toggled its midspan switch, activating the transmitter.

"To any station, this is Commander Angela Brown aboard the International Space Station. Please, please, please, come in."

She released the transmit key. A burst of static provided the only reply. After several additional fruitless attempts, Angela adjusted a knob. Then she began transmitting anew on the next frequency. She'd been at this for the last several hours.

After losing contact with NASA, Angela had dragged the two-meter packet radio into the Cupola. Over the last three months, she had used it to communicate with amateur radio operators around the globe. It had been part of her daily routine since arriving on the station.

Her interest in radios dated back to her childhood. Angela's mom had given her a walkie-talkie as a kid. Even as a thirteen-year-old, she'd been fascinated by the space program. The young girl would track the location of the ISS. When it was overhead, she would run outside and try to call them on that little handheld radio. Of course, the only replies she ever got were from other kids and weirdos. But the magic of the idea had never left her.

Angela had first heard about the station's ham radio set during her astronaut training. She had immediately taken a course and received her radio license. The investment had paid off shortly after she'd arrived on the ISS. She had dusted off the equipment and turned it on. Soon she was talking with all manner of people. Angela smiled wistfully as she recalled all of the times that radio operators had asked, "What can Brown do for you?"

She shook her head. Right now, Angela would give anything to hear that annoying greeting just one more time.

Anyway, the payoff had come during her second day aboard the ISS. She'd had a conversation with a young African girl in Equatorial Guinea. Her name was Afia, and Angela had heard the magic and wonder in the little girl's voice. It was her most poignant moment as an astronaut, but now the memory drove fresh daggers into her heart.

Today, as she'd followed the light's path across the surface, Angela had spoken with several people. She'd tried to reach Afia, but her calls had gone unanswered. The terror in the voices of those she had reached had torn at Angela's heart. In each instance, she'd told them to seek shelter, to get as far underground as possible. She doubted it would help, but Angela wouldn't accept that it was hopeless.

Station after station had fallen silent. The last had been an older gentleman in New Zealand. He'd seemed resigned to his fate, even cracking a few jokes. Then he, too, had gone quiet … or just gone. Since then, Angela had been unable to raise anyone.

Now, after another fruitless attempt to make contact, she tried the final listed ISS frequency. "To any station, this is Commander Angela Brown aboard the ISS. Please respond."

As empty static filled her ears, fresh tears threatened to flood her vision. "Anybody. God, please!" She sniffed and then in barely audible words said, "Somebody, please answer."

A soft object bounced into Angela's face again.

"Stop it, Teddy," she mumbled. "Five more minutes. Just a little more sleep."

Another gentle bump.

"Stop."

Angela's eyes opened to half-mast.

Something yellow and out of focus flickered through her vision. Angela blinked, and the yellow smudge resolved as a floating ration bag. A lanyard prevented it from drifting too far. A moment later, it floated in front of a vent. The current of air tossed the bag into her face again.

Reality crashed down around Angela. Teddy was gone, and Bill, too, along with the whole damned world.

She angrily batted away the ration bag. Its lanyard snapped, and the pouch ricocheted off of the module's far wall and disappeared down a dark passageway.

The dim lighting of the station's sleeping quarters matched her mood. She felt hollowed out, but at the same time, there was a part of her that kept saying it wasn't real, like it all had been nothing but a bad dream.

Angela shook her head. She knew better. Before seeking the refuge of sleep, she'd already seen signs of humanity's disappearance.

Our cities were burning.

Even from the altitude of the space station, she had already seen massive columns of smoke streaming from a few major metropolitan areas. At first, the sight had confused her, but then Angela pictured all of the ignition sources present in everyday life: everything from a suddenly empty car careening into a gas station to an airplane crashing into a refinery. Even something as mundane as a kitchen grease fire left unchecked could wipe out an entire community. Without the taming hand of man, fire had run rampant. It was as if the planet was in a hurry to purge the stench of humanity from its surface.

And she was lonely. Not that she was unused to being alone. After her father's death, she'd been a loner as a latchkey kid. She'd nurtured the trait at MIT, often holing up in her dorm room for an entire weekend of study.

But this was different. As far as she knew, no person had ever been this alone in the entire universe. That knowledge alone served to deepen the sense of loneliness.

A deep gurgling rumble rose from her abdomen.

Angela was starving.

She shook her head. What was the use? Starvation was likely going to kill her. She might as well get used to the sensation. It wasn't like she had an endless reserve of food, especially considering the loss of the last resupply mission.

Angela shook her head. No, she couldn't think that way. There had to be somebody. Surely some coal miners deep underground had survived. Not that they could help Angela in her current predicament. But maybe the President and the Joint Chiefs had survived deep in their bunkers. They would know what to do.

Freeing herself from the sleeping restraints, Angela pushed off the near wall. Practiced maneuvers and small trajectory adjustments guided her floating body through the hatch and into the passageway. There she snatched the yellow pouch and tore it open. Soon the sound of smacking peanut butter echoed through the empty module.

She departed Zvezda, the Russian module that served as the station's primary sleeping quarters, and glided deeper into the ISS.

A few moments later, Angela floated into the Japanese Experiment Module. Stopping herself in the JEM, she squirted a glob of raspberry jam into the air, careful not to launch it across the round room. The managers of the Japanese space program might get upset if she soiled the inside of their module. A hysterical laugh escaped her lips as she considered the absurdity of the thought.

First sleep, now laughter. Angela felt another cry coming. She punched a padded wall. The impact sent her and the jam tumbling across the module. Both hit the far wall. The jam stuck to the JEM.

"JEM jam!" she said with a snort.

Then Angela ricocheted off the same wall and floated back across the room, dissolving into a laughing mess.

It might have been hysteria, but Angela didn't care. The laughter felt good. Even the tears had. The raw emotions felt cleansing. Whatever had happened on the surface was another world away, literally. It seemed illusory, but this was *real*, JEM jam and all. She was alive! And she'd be damned if she would give up on that. Director McCree had heard from someone in the zone. She had to believe that it hadn't been a mistake, that someone would come for her.

Besides, if somebody was alive down there on that unreal world, likely they were going to risk a not insignificant percentage of humanity's remaining population just to come rescue her. They would need to know that she was worth the risk, worth saving.

She wiped tears from her eyes, and took a deep breath. After blowing that ever-loose strand of hair out of her vision, she nodded.

"You've got some work to do, Commander Brown. Time to earn that title."

CHAPTER 7

V aughn put the airport maintenance truck in park. He stepped out of the vehicle, leaving the door open and the engine running. Still numb and in shock, the spacesuited man stared at the piled-up smoking hulks that clogged the big intersection. Pointed in every direction, crumpled vehicles of all sizes filled the crossroads, every one of them driverless. As far as he could see, not a single body occupied any of the vehicles.

Vaughn cupped his hands around his mouth. "Hello! Anyone, please! I need help. My friend … He's … He …" His shoulders slumped. What was the use? His friend was dead, and the scene here was no different than what he'd found at the airport after he'd lost Mark. The thought brought the horrible images rushing back. For a long moment, he just stood there, staring at the intersection's apocalyptic milieu but not seeing any of it.

A shudder ran down his spine.

Vaughn had watched that second airplane in the pickup's rearview mirror, but his focus had kept shifting to the red-rimmed crater. It lay along the same line of sight, a dark smudge visible just beneath the mirror's plastic rim.

Vaughn's bloodshot eyes had flicked up to the rearview. The

onrushing airliner loomed largely. As its reflected nose swelled, the wingtips scrolled out of view to the left and right. The screech loosed by the metal structures of the Boeing's tortured belly sounded like the battle cries of the Devil's own legion.

"I'll be back," Vaughn promised as he focused back on the point of Mark's demise.

He dropped the truck into gear and punched the accelerator, cutting the wheel hard right and racing the pickup away from the runway perpendicularly. The small crater passed to his left. It felt like a betrayal to just leave, but Vaughn had no choice. He had to find help. Had to find someone who could help him with Mark's … remains.

The pickup bounced its way across the airfield's hidden mounds. The passenger jet slid through the rearview mirror's field of view, passing directly over the spot where Vaughn and the truck had been sitting only moments before. Then, on his left, it disappeared in a brilliant orange fireball as it joined its friends in the wide-body bonfire. Vaughn was thankful to see that Mark's final resting place had not been disturbed.

After getting clear of the runway environment, Vaughn had searched the airport grounds. He'd still found no sign of life or even bodies. Afterward, he had returned to Glenn Research Center. The gate between the two facilities refused to open. The security detail was nowhere to be seen, so now a broken red and white-striped plank rested on the pavement just inside the checkpoint, and the truck was down one headlight.

He drove through the entire compound without seeing anyone. Eventually, Vaughn found an open maintenance shed. After grabbing a roll of black plastic sheeting and a shovel, he returned to the airfield.

Vaughn draped a plastic sheet across the small crater that contained his friend's pulverized remains. He couldn't stand the thought of buzzards gnawing on Mark's shattered body. Not that he'd seen any birds. Vaughn supposed they were keeping their distance from the still burning airplanes … Unless they'd gone the way of everyone else. He piled enough dirt around the plastic's perimeter and its center to ensure the visqueen wouldn't blow away. Afterward,

Vaughn fashioned a cross from aircraft wires and two aluminum struts scavenged from strewn wreckage. He pounded it into the ground adjacent to the plastic and then saluted.

"You deserve better than this, Colonel Hennessy." Breathing heavily, he added, "As soon as I can find some help, we'll come back for you, Mark."

Then he'd climbed back into the truck and crossed the airport grounds, driving through Glenn Research Center without stopping or slowing down. Heading northwest, he'd passed through the heavily wooded area north of the compound without spotting people or birds or even so much as a damned squirrel.

What the *fuck* had happened? How in the hell could people and animals just ... disappear?

He hadn't stopped the truck until he'd come upon this clogged intersection.

Now Vaughn walked toward it, weaving between the crashed and crumpled empty cars that littered the street as well as the sidewalks.

Reaching an impasse, he climbed onto the top of a three-foot-long clump of metal that looked more like an accordion than a car.

In his grass- and mud-stained spacesuit, Vaughn unsteadily stood upright and cupped his hands around his mouth again. "Hello?!"

He stretched his neck, turning his head side to side, desperately seeking the sound of a reply over the roar of distant fires.

Nothing, not a goddamned peep!

He scanned the intersecting roads. In all four directions, to the limit of his vision, nothing moved on the ground or in the air, save the pervasive smoke.

Vaughn did a double take, his eyes returning to a flat-sided UPS truck. It sat in front of a store a hundred feet from the intersection. The driver had probably been making a delivery when *it* happened— whatever the hell *it* was. Just to the right of the vehicle, an SUV protruded from the store's shattered display window.

Like an island of civility, the brown panel truck stood unblemished despite the near miss with the careening SUV as well as the demolition derby-like destruction that crowded the road and sidewalks for hundreds of feet in every direction.

For some reason, Vaughn's eyes kept going to the yellow words inscribed on the side of the truck:

WHAT CAN BROWN DO FOR YOU?

He had seen the same question written across the flank of a UPS cargo jet parked on the ramp at the airport. They'd drawn his eyes then, too. It was a popular slogan from over a decade ago, but the shipping company had recently rebooted it. For some reason, the words seemed to hold special meaning today. He could feel something there, something tickling the back of his mind, but the harder he tried to bring it forward, the more elusive it became.

Vaughn shook his head and dragged his eyes from the UPS truck. He scanned the streets that fed into the intersection. It appeared that, after their occupants had vanished, all of the cars and trucks had simply continued until they'd hit something or been hit.

Beyond the intersection, on the outside radius of an elevated curving portion of Interstate 480, piled vehicles still burned. As with the crossing roads, the cars and trucks up there had piled up when they ran out of clear, straight road.

Vaughn flinched as an explosion rattled the ubiquitous pebbles of shattered safety glass. A fresh plume of black smoke rose from behind the building fronted by the UPS truck. It looked like the fire was coming from the next block over. Probably another vehicle's gas tank had cooked off. It was the third one he'd heard since arriving at the intersection.

Columns of smoke still littered the city's skyline, but some of them now appeared much larger. About a half-mile away, raging flames engulfed an entire condominium complex.

Singleton looked at his smartphone again. The data network was still down. He couldn't access any sites. He'd grabbed the phone upon returning to the NASA facility in search of plastic. He had already called all but one number in his contact list. Even the pharmacy outside of Fort Drum, New York. On that call, Vaughn had navigated through their telephonic maze until it finally gave him the option to speak with a real live pharmacist. He didn't need one, but he'd take anyone he could get at this point. After six rings, a recorded voice told him that no one was available to take his call. Vaughn elected not to leave his name, number, and date of birth. Instead, he jabbed a finger into the screen, ending the call.

A moment later, he stared at the new name he'd selected, the one number he'd yet to try, unable to bring himself to it.

A trembling finger hovered over the contact's name.

What if she didn't answer?

But if she did…

He closed his eyes.

After a long sigh, Vaughn touched the glowing name. The smiling face of a gray-haired woman beamed at him from the screen.

The warbling tone of the first ring blared from the speakerphone. It echoed off the nearby buildings.

Then another.

And then a third.

Vaughn tilted his head back and stared at the smoke-hazed blue sky.

Fourth ring.

He closed his eyes and whispered, "Please, Mom. Please answer."

The fifth ring cut out mid-tone.

Vaughn's eyes flew open.

"Hello, this is Vera Singleton. Please leave a message after the beep thingy. God bless you."

Vaughn attempted to swallow down the lump in his throat. He batted away a tear that tried to leak from his right eye.

"She's probably at her yoga class," Vaughn lied to himself as he ended the call.

But what if she wasn't, what if…?

No! She was all Vaughn had. The events that had driven them to Boulder during his adolescence had strengthened their bond. Even before this screwed-up year had taken so much, so many others from him, Vaughn had always been close to his mother.

And now...

After a long moment, Vaughn shook his head. "To hell with this."

He stepped off the crumpled car, almost slipping in the mud that had sloughed off of the spacesuit. Following his muddy trail, he walked back to the airport truck and climbed in. Vaughn slammed the door hard enough to make the rolled down window rattle in its frame. Starting the engine and dropping the pickup into drive, he punched the throttle. Tires squealed their protest. The powder blue and white truck swapped ends enshrouded in the blue smoke of burning rubber. Having reversed directions, the truck fishtailed down the street, racing back toward the NASA facility.

The truck eased to a stop. Vaughn placed it in park and killed the ignition. He sat there looking through the windshield. He still couldn't grasp what had happened, but it was time to leave Cleveland, to broaden his search.

But first, there was something he needed to take care of.

Vaughn stepped out of the vehicle and closed the door. Looking behind the truck, he gazed down the length of the runway. Judging by the wreckage, it had been a while since another plane had belly-landed here. By now, any aircraft that had had its flight director preprogrammed to fly to Cleveland had either arrived or crashed somewhere else.

Vaughn grabbed a shovel from the back of the truck and walked toward the waiting task. He shook his head. No, this wasn't a task, it was his duty. Mark had been the best friend he'd ever had, and he wasn't about to leave him like this. Obviously, he hadn't found help. He supposed he could've gotten a backhoe for this, but that seemed too industrial, too impersonal. Lieutenant Colonel Mark Hennessy deserved a hell of a lot better than that.

A few feet from the plastic-covered crater, Vaughn jabbed the blade of the shovel into the ground. On the way there, he'd stopped by the facility's locker room and changed back into his camouflaged Army flight suit. Instead of a spacesuit, tan combat boots now adorned his feet. The beige neoprene sole of the right one slammed into the top lip of the shovel, driving it deeper into the scoured, raw earth. Vaughn wrenched the handle and pried up a wedge-shaped chunk of soil.

He slung the dirt aside and then speared the earth anew with his pitiful implement. Already, he was starting to breathe heavily.

An hour and a half later, his uniform soaked with sweat, Vaughn jabbed the shovel into the ground next to the hole. He'd taken several breaks but had finally reached a depth that he judged to be respectfully deep and adequate for the solemn task.

Leaning against the shovel and panting, he cast a forlorn glance toward the nearest edge of the black visqueen. Vaughn shook his head. "It should've been me!" Pausing, he swept his arm in a long, arcing gesture. "I shouldn't be the one to survive this fucking mess." Leaving the shovel, he walked to the edge of the small crater left by the tumbling turbojet engine. Looking down through tear-muddled eyes, he said, "You should've left me, goddammit! You would've gotten clear if you hadn't waited for my slow ass to start running."

With the side of his boot, Vaughn shoved the nearest portion of the ringing mound of dirt off of the plastic sheet. Bending over, he grabbed the edge of the visqueen and began to pull it back. The soil he'd put on top of it sloughed off, and the plastic peeled away from the ground wetly, leaving a red stippled surface in its wake. As Vaughn continued the morbid reveal, recognizable parts of his friend came into view.

"Oh shit," he croaked through his constricting larynx. Gnashing his teeth together, he made a sharp head shake. "Pull it together, Singleton!" he said with a growl.

Another hour later, he tamped down the last of the earth over Colonel Hennessy's grave. He trudged back to the impact crater in boots that seemed to weigh a ton. Vaughn wrestled the makeshift cross out of the ground. Returning to the mounded earth, he pounded it into place at the head of the gravesite.

Standing back, Vaughn saluted again. "You were a good man, Mark, a better friend than I deserved, and you deserve better than this."

Sweat dripped from his face as he lowered the salute. Vaughn wanted to say more, felt like he should say a lot more, but none of this felt real. Vaughn half-expected to see Mark come strolling across the field and tell him that it was all just a big joke.

Ha ha…

He knew better, knew it was all too real, but it was just too much for one man to absorb.

Singleton stared at the sweat that dripped from the hat in his wringing hands. Dragging his eyes from the camouflaged cap, he looked at the provisional cross.

In choked words, Vaughn said, "I'm sorry, friend."

The truck came to a sliding stop in front of a large NASA hangar. Vaughn stepped out of the pickup. Standing in the parking lot, he looked to the left of the large blue building. Faint smoke wafted lazily from the heap of broken and burned-out airplane hulls on the far side of the airport.

Vaughn closed his eyes. A mental image of Mark filled the visual void. The man stood in knee-deep grass. In his spacesuit, he looked like a surreally misplaced astronaut. He still bore the amazed smile generated by their close call with the careening airplane. Then the man's grinning visage disappeared in the blink of his mind's eye. In his wake, a dirt geyser shot into the sky.

Vaughn's eyes flew open. He turned from the field, and another of the day's mysteries scrolled into view. His brows furrowed as he stared at the cargo plane he'd seen earlier. Now it stood just across the fence from him, parked in front of the UPS package processing facility.

Again, his eyes went to the yellow lettering.

"WHAT CAN BROWN DO FOR YOU?"

He felt that nagging realization trying to percolate up from the shadowed depths of his subconscious.

"Why in the hell does that mean something to me?"

After staring for several long seconds, he shook his head. It wouldn't come.

Whatever it was, it could wait.

The Army aviator walked to the small office door at the front right of the hangar. As he'd suspected, it was unlocked. Vaughn glanced over his shoulder. After looking at the recently reincarnated UPS slogan, he shook his head, unable to make the connection. Finally, he turned and entered the hangar.

Banal elevator music echoed through the labyrinth corridors of the building's front offices. The smell of burned coffee wafted through its white halls and cubicles. He pushed through a set of double doors and entered the main hangar bay. Here the familiar scents of hydraulic oil and cleaning solvent purged the acrid odors from his sinuses.

Vaughn walked to the far side of the facility and then pressed a green button. As if announcing a retreating truck, a beeping alert echoed through the hangar, and the hundred-foot-tall steel doors began to roll open on their tracks.

A few minutes later, an ancient aircraft tug backed out of the hangar. It chased the billowing blue smoke produced by its old engine. The vehicle passed between the fully opened doors with a yellow tow bar hooked to its retreating front end. Then, rolling backward, the tailwheel and tilted tail rotor of a Black Hawk helicopter emerged from the opening. Finally, the rest of the glossy black and gold fuselage of the US Customs and Border Protection UH-60L slid into view.

The tug's engine roared, and another cloud of blue smoke billowed across the sea of concrete. The boxy metal vehicle's low-geared transmission whined as it attained its top speed of ten miles per hour.

When the helicopter reached the center of the tarmac, Vaughn brought the coupled crafts to a stop and then stepped down from the tug's top-mounted seat.

He squatted next to the helicopter's tailwheel. His knees barked with pain. Vaughn grabbed the tow bar's release pin and pulled. It wouldn't budge. "Damnit!" He felt his face flush with the exertion. He yanked on the handle. His fat jiggled with each pull. Then the pin released with a loud pop.

Vaughn fell hard on his ass, his teeth clicking together. The coppery taste of blood filled his mouth. He spit a wad of the red stuff onto the white pavement.

"Shit!"

Singleton sat there cross-legged for a long moment, exploring his mouth with a grease-stained finger. Looking under the Black Hawk's tail, he stared across the airport grounds, trying to understand the apocalyptic panorama painted across its expanse.

Shaking his head, Vaughn wiped the red finger against the tan leg of his desert-camouflaged flight suit. He spit another bloody glob onto the pavement. It wasn't as much this time. He shook his head again and then grabbed the helicopter's whale tail of a horizontal stabilizer and pulled himself upright.

Wheezing, Vaughn walked to the tug and climbed onto its top-mounted tractor seat. After pausing to catch his breath, he dropped the vehicle into reverse and released the handbrake. He guided the tug with its still connected tow bar away from the helicopter and parked it on the far side of the square section of tarmac.

Vaughn had already checked the Black Hawk's logbook. It was clean with no open maintenance issues. A quick pre-flight inspection told him everything else that he needed to know. The helicopter was flight-ready, and someone had been good enough to leave it topped off with fuel.

Vaughn was traveling light. He'd flown in from New York yesterday and had left his bag in his hotel room when Mark picked him up that morning. Due to the road conditions, that bag would be waiting there until he could return with help. Until then, he would make do with the clothes on his back. He supposed he could land in a Walmart parking lot or maybe even that of his hotel and get supplies. But sooner rather than later, Vaughn wanted, no, he needed to find someone and find out what had happened, and he sure as hell wasn't going to find either here in Cleveland.

Without so much as a traveling toothbrush, the Army pilot climbed into the Black Hawk's primary pilot seat. Vaughn flipped switches and twisted knobs as he went through memorized pre-start checklist items. Arcane pieces of unknown electronics that appeared to relate to the helicopter's Border Patrol mission created a couple of hitches in his normal flow. Finally, he powered up the aircraft's on-board auxiliary power unit, or APU. Its small turbine engine fired to life, creating a high-pitched whine that echoed off of the hangar. Using the power supplied by the APU, he finished testing the Black Hawk's systems and then donned a borrowed flight helmet.

Vaughn looked up at the helicopter's throttles and fuel levers. The moment of truth had arrived.

Would it start?

Vaughn had never flown the civilian edition of the Black Hawk. However, he had a couple of thousand hours flying the Army's version of this aircraft in Afghanistan and Iraq. If the damn thing would start, he had no doubt that he could fly it. Hell, as a helicopter pilot, he could likely fly just about any aircraft in the world. It might not be pretty, but he knew he could keep the greasy side down and make survivable takeoffs and landings. Vaughn had considered taking one of the intact airplanes that sat on the Cleveland aviation ramp. He looked at the crashed jets that littered the airport's runways and shook his head. Even if he could find a runway clear enough to permit a takeoff, there'd be no guarantee that he'd find a suitable landing strip at the other end.

No, a helicopter was his best bet, at least until he could find the edge of the devastation. There had to be an end to it, right?

Shaking off that last unsettling thought, Vaughn reached up for the throttle quadrant. His thumb hovered over the starter button. "Here goes nothing," he said and pressed the switch.

And received exactly that: nothing.

"What the hell?"

He pressed it again.

Still it refused to respond.

"Shit!"

He scanned the helicopter's instruments and switches but couldn't find anything wrong or out of place. Then he bent over and looked at the side of the center console.

"Crap! Really?"

An empty key slot frowned at him from the edge of the control panel. A few decades ago, some military flight school flunky had taken an Army helicopter on a joyride. It had ended with the young man in Fort Leavenworth's military prison, but not before he'd landed the Huey on the White House lawn. Afterward, the government had installed an ignition switch in all military airplanes and helicopters—and apparently in all government-owned civil aircraft as well. Once you started the engines, you could pull the key out with no ill effects—you wouldn't want a plane to fall out of the sky just because a ten-dollar switch had failed—but without that key, you couldn't start the helicopter.

"Smooth move, dumbass!" he said, shaking his head.

Vaughn climbed out of the aircraft. He walked a few steps and then paused, looking back at the Sikorsky and its still running APU. Military procedures—and likely US Customs, as well—dictated that you never walked away from a running turbine engine. He scanned the visible portions of the airport and then shrugged his shoulders. Screw it! It wasn't like someone was going to steal the damned thing.

Not without a key, anyway.

Oh, were that your only concern, Captain, he thought wryly.

Vaughn shook his head and jogged back into the hangar.

After a ten-minute search, he gave up on the key. Wheezing again, he dug through a mechanic's toolbox. He found the necessary implements and stuffed them into the leg pockets of his flight suit. Then he trotted back to the helicopter.

A couple of minutes and a bloody knuckle later, he had the barrel of the ignition switch pulled from its inch-wide hole. Like multicolored entrails, four wires ran from the back of the small silver cylinder and into the opening, disappearing into the shadowed interior of the center console. He disconnected two of the wires and then connected them to the same lugs as their opposite member. This bypassed the keyed switch, taking it out of the loop. Vaughn reinstalled the device back into its hole and stuffed the tools into a pouch attached to the inside of the pilot's door.

A quick scan of the airport grounds showed that he was still alone. Vaughn climbed back into the pilot's seat. After a silent prayer, he took a deep breath and then pressed the start button again. The whoosh of compressed air blowing through the number one engine's starter rewarded his efforts.

He pumped his free hand. "Yes!"

A few minutes later, Vaughn had both engines running and all of the helicopter's systems online. He taxied the Black Hawk up to the rolling gate that separated NASA's aviation ramp from the taxiways of Cleveland Hopkins International Airport.

Vaughn looked at the radio control head and frowned. "Might as well give it a try." He tuned the radio and then squeezed the transmit trigger. "Hopkins Tower, this is November Two Three Four Six Five," he said, using the aircraft's tail number as his call sign.

Of course, no one answered. Vaughn could have tried several other air traffic control frequencies, but he'd already placed enough unanswered calls for one day.

As he listened to the silent radio, six words came to mind:

What can Brown do for you?

He looked left. The giant vertical fin of the parked wide-bodied MD-11 cargo plane protruded above the roof of the United Parcel Service facility. Why did their slogan keep bouncing around inside his noggin?

Vaughn shook his head. Turning, he looked across the field and stared at the silent control tower.

"Screw it!"

He brought the helicopter to a high hover. To his far right, the pile of broken and burned fuselages still smoked. Vaughn could just make out the crossed aluminum struts that he'd driven into the ground. A tear leaked from his left eye. He released the collective control for a moment and brusquely batted away the moisture with the back of his left hand.

Where to go?

Vaughn knew that Cleveland and Houston and likely everything in between had fallen to whatever had caused all of this. With its timing, the light must have swept from north to south or east to west, or a combination of the two. Vaughn didn't know what the light had been or where it had originated, but he reasoned that it must've run out of steam somewhere south and west of Houston.

Considering his mother's location in Boulder, Vaughn prayed that it hadn't made it much farther west at all.

Finally, he nodded and said, "Colorado it is."

Vaughn squinted into the low sun. Hovering a hundred feet above the ground, the aircraft turned toward the golden orb. He lowered the nose of the helicopter and increased power. The Black Hawk quickly accelerated as it climbed into the orange sky.

As he flew past Mark's shallow grave, Vaughn glanced down and shook his head. Then he looked forward and lowered the helmet's smoked visor.

"I'll come back for you, Mark."

CHAPTER 8

"This is Commander Angela Brown broadcasting from the International Space Station. I am alone and stranded on the ISS with no descent module, no way to get to the surface. Please reply on this frequency at twelve hundred Zulu or twenty-four hundred Zulu. That's noon and midnight Greenwich Mean Time. I will monitor the frequency both times each day." Two seconds later, the message repeated. "This is Commander—"

Angela turned down the radio. She plucked the floating clipboard out of the air and placed a check mark adjacent to the item on her improvised list. After reading the next line, she looked around the JEM. It was the station's largest module. The Japanese Experiment Module even had its own manipulator arm. Through the port cone's window, she looked out on the Terrace. It was the informal but descriptive name of the Exposed Facility. Currently, it hosted several power-hungry experiments that ran in hard vacuum.

Angela didn't have unlimited resources. Primarily, she needed to conserve food, water, and oxygen. While she had plenty of electricity, there was no sense in placing unnecessary loads on circuits that also powered limited lifespan components upon which her very life depended. So Angela started turning off each experiment.

After finishing with the Terrace, Angela shifted to the projects running inside the module. After shutting down a crystal processing test and one that studied thermal dynamics in microgravity, she moved to a life sciences experiment. Her hand hovered over its kill switch. If allowed to continue long-term, this one would definitely consume some of her most precious resources. The project's enclosure had a dedicated heater and an independent environmental control system, but more importantly, it required a constant supply of water and nutrients.

It had to go.

But Angela's hand refused the order to terminate the experiment. Instead, it dug in her pouch and extracted a tool. A few minutes later, the implement along with several metal screws went back into the bag. The enclosure's glass front broke free from a black seal after a bit of prying. Angela peered expectantly into the dimly lit confines of the now open self-contained unit.

Twitching whiskers emerged from the gloom. Then beady red eyes manifested behind them. Finally, the two white mice swam into the JEM's bright interior.

Mabel and Nate mastered microgravity aerial navigation shortly after arriving on the ISS aboard Angela's flight. Initially, the two rodents had floated around their enclosure, bouncing off the walls between unproductive spasming fits of twitching legs. They soon learned to propel themselves and maneuver using a combination of purposeful wall kicks followed by something that approximated swimming. It was slow, but the little boogers could get to the reward of cheese that awaited proper navigation.

Angela held out a small yellow cube of Cheddar. Mabel spotted it first. Soon she was kicking and stroking her way through the module's cool air. A moment later, the cute little fart wrapped all four of her legs around Angela's outstretched fingers.

Nate floated a half-meter in front of them. Framed by long, white whiskers, his twitching pink nose sniffed the air. He looked at her as if to say, "Hey, where's mine?"

Angela smiled. With her other hand, she sent a cube slowly tumbling toward him. "There you go, Nate. Bon appétit, little guy."

It might be a waste of resources, but Angela didn't care.

She would rather have a couple of mice for company than converse with a Wilson volleyball. Besides, for all she knew, these might be the last two animals on—or above—the planet.

Nate showed his appreciation for the treat by peeing and pooping all the way to the floating cheese.

Angela cocked an eyebrow. "We'll have to do something about that."

Having placed Nate and Mabel into their new home—a Tupperware bowl with holes cut into the lid for air circulation—Angela headed to her assigned workstation. There was one additional, power-hungry experiment that she needed to terminate. She had saved this one for last as it was her favorite.

When the loss of the resupply flight had forced the halving of the station's crew, this experiment's importance had directly led to her assignment as Expedition Commander. As the station's sole theoretical physicist, Angela was the only person on-board that understood the inner workings of its electronics and sensors. Hell, she'd been part of the MIT team that had built the damn thing: the first space-based gravity wave detector.

The Modified NASA Laser Interferometer Space Antenna (MONA-LISA) looked for gravity waves in a particular frequency range. Building on the success of previous land-based experiments and employing recent technological advances, MONA-LISA was significantly smaller than its proposed but never deployed predecessors. It maintained a laser link with two mirrors that flew in formation with the space station. Between the laser's power demands and the detector's required operating temperature being near absolute zero, the experiment would hog her limited resources.

Twenty-four hours ago, Angela had first seen the mysterious light.

Now she watched Europe pass beneath the ISS once again, this time on the live external video feed piped to her workstation monitor. After seeing a wave of energy wipe humankind from the planet, gravitational-wave astronomy no longer seemed important.

Her finger hovered over the module's power switch. Then she saw movement on the device's display. A small gravity wave signal sent a tremor through all three graph lines. Somewhere in the universe, likely millions if not billions of years ago, two black holes were in the throes of merger, spinning about their common point at incredible speed and carving their wakes across space-time.

Out of curiosity, Angela asked the computer to calculate the distance to source. These events happened at a known rate. Therefore, just as with electromagnetic astronomy, one could measure distance to the point of origin by the amount of frequency loss or Doppler effect red shifting.

A moment later, the computed distance to source popped up on the screen. Angela stared at it, unable to believe the number.

"What the hell?" She shook her head. "That must be a mistake."

She entered the command again.

A few moments later, the same report popped up:

< 1 Light-Second to Source

That didn't make any sense. They had always expected to be measuring distances in light years, so a light-second was the smallest unit the gravity wave detector could specify. The Moon was more than a light-second from Earth. So that would mean the gravity waves were coming from somewhere near the planet.

Angela's eyes widened. Theoretical physicists had long hypothesized the existence of miniature black holes, singularities left over from the Big Bang. Unlike the micro black holes that they had hoped to create and sense with the Super Collider, miniature singularities could have the mass of Mount Everest. They wouldn't evaporate in a puff of Hawking radiation. Theoretically, they could still exist today.

In spite of the day's tragic events and her precarious predicament,

Angela's pulse raced as she contemplated the exciting possibilities. Had her detector just found the first evidence of a primordial black hole? And not just one but two? She looked at the waveform again. The signal was the unmistakable footprint of a binary, a pair of black holes rapidly orbiting about a common point.

Her eyes returned to the displayed distance to source. The range of less than one light-second meant that the binary was within 186,000 miles.

"Let's narrow that down."

Angela floated over to the detector's keyboard. Her fingers became a blur of activity. The programmers at MIT had set the distance to display in increments of light years, but she knew that the underlying data had much finer detail than that. Light travels at 186,000 miles per second, so she only needed to change the formula to display the distance to source in miles.

She hit the enter key and then closed the page. The gravity wave display returned. Its signal filled the screen again, even stronger now. Angela looked at the distance to source. Her brows knitted together as a confused look took over her visage.

"What the hell?"

The number rapidly counted down through three hundred miles.

"Oh shit!"

Was the station about to disappear into a black hole?

Just as she had the thought, the rate of closure slowed precipitously. Angela's suddenly tensed shoulders relaxed a shade. The numbers continued to count down like the points of an algebraic curve as it neared its closest pass to the horizontal axis. It appeared that the station would soon fly parallel to the binary pair at which point their paths would begin to diverge or separate.

Then the distance to source began to settle on an all-too-familiar value of 250 miles.

"That's the altitude of the ISS," Angela said with fresh confusion.

Her eyes slowly moved to the live video feed that streamed from the station's external camera. She watched as the lowlands of Eastern

France gave way to the mountains of Switzerland. The Super Collider, CERN, lay beneath that border.

As did the epicenter of the life-stealing light wave.

And it was the region where dozens of nukes had disappeared, vanishing in an instant.

As if swallowed by a singularity, Angela realized.

And at that moment, all of it was exactly 249 miles beneath her.

The station passed over Switzerland's Lake Geneva and continued its easterly course, its orbital path now carrying it away from the region.

As the ISS raced away from CERN, the gravity wave detector's distance to source began an accelerating count up from the lowest value it had reached.

249 miles!

"The source is the Super Collider?!"

That didn't make sense! Primordial black holes or PBHs likely contained the mass of a mountain but should be smaller than an atom. Even if a pair of PBHs had impacted Earth, they would have quickly passed through the entire planet, leaving nothing but a microscopic trail of radiation. On the other hand, if a slow-moving pair of singularities had merged with the surface, they would have fallen into the planet's gravity well. They wouldn't hang around CERN.

Not without an external force keeping them in check.

Angela's eyes drifted back to the image of the surface as it scrolled beneath the station.

"What the hell is going on down there?" she whispered. Her eyes narrowed. "And *who* is controlling it?"

PART II

"He walked out in the gray light and stood and he saw for a brief moment the absolute truth of the world. The cold relentless circling of the intestate earth. Darkness implacable. The blind dogs of the sun in their running. The crushing black vacuum of the universe. And somewhere two hunted animals trembling like ground-foxes in their cover. Borrowed time and borrowed world and borrowed eyes with which to sorrow it."

— Cormac McCarthy, The Road

CHAPTER 9

Vaughn woke to the sound of rolling thunder. Blinking sleep-clouded eyes, he stared up at water-stained, sagging ceiling tiles. The thunder continued unabated, sounding like an unrelenting artillery barrage.

"What the hell is that?"

He struggled out of the clutches of the overstuffed couch that had served as his bed for the night. Finally free of it, Vaughn stood, panting already.

Yesterday, before the universe had changed, he'd resolved to get back in shape. Now Vaughn looked at his exposed belly and shook his head.

"What's the use?"

His thoughts returned to his mother. He needed to find her, to know, one way or the other, if she was okay.

The deep, distant rumble continued its roaring report.

He'd ended up here in Gary, Indiana, last night.

Originally, Vaughn had planned to stop at Chicago O'Hare Airport. However, a huge column of black smoke had obscured the setting sun, accelerating the onset of night. It pierced the upper atmosphere ahead of his appropriated helicopter. He'd first seen the dark cloud as he closed to within a hundred miles of Chicago. Then, from the outskirts of the city, the rising black pillar's base of orange fire and its churning intensity had made it look as if a volcano had sprouted from Lake Michigan's southwestern shore.

At ten miles away, the massive black column blotted out half of the sky. Just then, another airport had scrolled beneath his helicopter. Vaughn checked the moving map and then nodded. "Gary, Indiana, it is."

With the reincarnation of Krakatoa blowing its top dead ahead, Vaughn opted for the relatively clear-aired and fire-free environs of Gary-Chicago International. A strong easterly breeze had kept the area's air fairly clear. He reasoned that it should keep the worst of the fires at bay as well.

The two-hour flight from Glenn Research Center had drained the helicopter's fuel tanks and filled the pilot's bladder. En route, Vaughn had tried multiple air traffic control frequencies, all to no avail.

The situation on the ground in Gary had looked the same as it had in Cleveland. Before landing, he'd circled the airport. Crashed airplanes littered its main runways. The terminal had burned down, and the tail section of a large passenger jet protruded from the airport's still-burning jet fuel tank farm. Sporadic fires dotted the surrounding suburbs, but nothing like the firestorm to the west.

After scanning the rest of the airfield, Vaughn had landed on the general aviation ramp, next to its fortunately unscathed fuel pumps. Numb and probably in shock, he had stumbled from the helicopter and walked into the nearest building. The offices of the airport's Fixed Base Operator or FBO featured an opulent pilot lounge with a comfortable-looking couch. Vaughn had broken the glass front of their vending machine. After downing a soda and two bags of Funyuns, he'd collapsed into the waiting sofa.

Singleton barely remembered lying down. He'd fallen asleep the instant his head had hit the black leather armrest.

Images from the day's apocalyptic events had haunted his dreams. Again and again, he watched Mark's astonished face disappear behind a brown and red geyser of gory dirt. Between those horrible visions,

Vaughn had wandered an empty street. In his spacesuit again, he would clamber to the end of the block. There, the road made a hard left, and then the street, identical to the last, continued for another block before turning left yet again. The roads formed a loop that he couldn't escape.

In every version of the dream, a UPS truck stood alone on one of the four streets. Each time he'd seen the vehicle, Vaughn's eyes had gravitated to the slogan emblazoned across its side, but as in the waking world, its significance remained a mystery.

Now awake but exhausted and bone-weary, he walked to the door of the windowless room. It opened, and bright light assaulted his dark-adapted eyes. Blinking against the amber brilliance, Vaughn stared open-mouthed at the hellish panorama that filled the portion of the world visible through the next room's glass wall. From the window's left extremity to its right, coruscating orange fire tumbled through churning black shadows.

Across the river from the airport, a wall of roaring fire boiled up from a residential subdivision. Vaughn stepped forward on unsteady legs. The eastern edge of the conflagration came into view on his left as he neared the twenty-foot-wide window.

While Vaughn had slept, the firestorm had burned its way into East Chicago, somehow swimming upstream against the protection of the opposing wind.

Vaughn remembered the massive tank farm that occupied the industrial district. He leaned forward and looked right. To the west, fire lined much of the horizon. The white metal tanks stood as black silhouettes against its orange brilliance. Vaughn could see fumes rising from some of them.

He flinched as one of the storage tanks erupted in a blinding flash.

Vaughn registered the onrushing pressure wave in time to throw up his arms. The ear-splitting explosion struck the building. The glass wall shattered and blew inward, pelting Vaughn's exposed skin with pebble-sized glass shards. With ringing ears, the dazed man stared at dozens of small cuts on his belly and legs.

Another tank cooked off. Its shock wave knocked Vaughn into

action. He ran across broken glass in socked feet. In the pilot lounge, he threw on his pants and jabbed already bloodstained socks into the waiting boots, not bothering with the laces. Then Vaughn grabbed the rest of his clothes and ran back out of the building, exiting through the blown-out glass wall.

As he sprinted across the tarmac, a third tank exploded. The shock wave knocked him sideways, but Vaughn kept his footing. Radiant heat from the massive fires soaked into his bloodied bare skin. Squinting, he held up the top half of his flight suit, using the flame-retardant garment to shield his face from the heat.

"Good thing I refueled you last night," Vaughn said between wheezing breaths. He threw open the pilot door and tossed his clothes onto the left seat. Then he flung himself into the right one. The heat assaulting his exposed skin halved as soon as he passed behind the protection of the windshield. Even though the glass blocked most of the radiant heat, the cockpit's interior already felt hot.

Vaughn would cook in here if he didn't get moving.

A fourth tank detonated. The pressure wave's sonic vapor cloud raced toward the helicopter. Its passage shook the aircraft and caused the still stationary rotor blades to heave. Even though the Black Hawk's nose pointed straight at the exploding tanks, its windshields held.

Vaughn raced through the aircraft start procedure. He soon had both engines at flight speed. Just as he began to take off, three more storage tanks exploded in a rapid-fire cascade. The shock wave shoved the hovering helicopter a few feet across the tarmac. Then a smoking, curled-up chunk of metal slammed into the concrete where the Black Hawk had been only a moment before.

"Son of a bitch!"

Vaughn jammed in right pedal. The aircraft pivoted about its mast. Now facing east, away from the worst of the fire, he pulled an armload of collective and shoved the cyclic stick forward. The helicopter quickly accelerated toward the only portion of the horizon not blotted out by smoke and flames.

The aircraft leveled off at a thousand feet—about the height of a skyscraper. At this altitude, Vaughn could see narrow, but easily navigable paths between the columns of roiling smoke. He turned the Black Hawk toward downtown, giving the exploding tank farm a wide berth.

Vaughn wanted to see what had happened to the city. As he approached Chicago proper, the few remaining low clouds dried up completely. Apparently, the atmosphere had grown too hot to support them.

The helicopter passed between two massive columns of smoke, and a scene from Hell revealed itself. Entire residential blocks burned. Multiple pillars of towering flames tilted to and fro in unison, whipped about like tall grass in a windstorm by the relatively cool air that rushed in from Lake Michigan.

Then he saw downtown.

"Jesus Christ!"

In the incredible panorama revealed across the helicopter's windshield, halos of fire burned from the roofs of skyscrapers like candles of the gods.

"How in hell did all these fires get started?"

But then he remembered a thought he'd had over the suburbs. The light wave had passed through this region during breakfast. The image of the charred eggs in the NASA break room swam into his mind's eye. Ahead of him now lay the evidence of what happened when you multiplied that problem a millionfold.

The entire city of Chicago was burning again, but an old lady and her cow had nothing to do with it this time.

A few minutes later, O'Hare Airport emerged from the smoke. Fire fully engulfed its expansive jet fuel tank farm. Above it, a roiling column of orange flame and churning black smoke disappeared into the dark sky. The overhanging cloud of the stuff turned day into night. In the surrounding area, only sporadic fires and patches of still functioning city lights illuminated the hellish scene. Barely visible in the darkness, a macabre line of burned-out Boeing and Airbus wide-bodied jets filled the south end of all four north-south runways.

It was as if God had swept humankind from the planet, and now he was in the process of scouring its residue from the surface as well.

Vaughn shook his head.

"Enough of this shit!"

He banked the helicopter and departed Chicago, heading southwest—toward Colorado.

Dense unending smog reduced Vaughn's flight visibility. That and strong headwinds turned what should have been a six-hour flight to Denver into a two-day ordeal. After leaving Chicago, he overnighted in Lincoln, Nebraska, landing there completely exhausted and distraught.

Along the way, he had gazed upon each new horizon with renewed hope, sure this would be the edge of the devastation. But in every instance, the short-lived wave of hope died as it crashed against the rocks of burned-out cities, piled-up vehicles, and crashed airplanes. Mile after agonizing mile, Vaughn stitched together a chain of dashed hopes that extended into the desolate Plains States. Just as a watched pot never boils, apparently, a watched apocalypse never ends: the constant vigil seemed to pack six extra hours into the day. By the time he reached Lincoln, the dejected man could barely pull himself from the cockpit of the quieted helicopter.

Twice during the eternal day, he'd worked up the nerve to try his mother's number again. Both attempts went unanswered.

After another night of pilot lounge couch surfing and vending machine cuisine, Vaughn refueled the helicopter and departed west. Again, he hadn't bothered with supplies. A towel bath in the airport's bathroom had alleviated his case of swamp ass, but Vaughn's flight suit was rank. By now, it could probably stand on its own. He didn't care about any of that. The need to find the edge of the destruction drove him to continue. It afforded no opportunity for detours or respite.

An hour into the flight, the first lightning bolt lit up the murky morning sky. Then another followed by two more struck off the nose of the Black Hawk. Gray skies gave way to charcoal and then black.

Vaughn guided the helicopter closer to the rolling wheat-covered plains. Soon he drew level with the tops of the region's few trees. In the diminishing daylight, he had trouble discerning the lay of the land ahead of the Black Hawk.

The bottom fell out of the storm. Rain pelted the low-flying helicopter, further degrading his forward visibility. Vaughn slowed the aircraft to thirty knots and brought it down so low that its tires dragged through the tops of the manic waves of grain.

The helicopter shuddered. Its indicated airspeed shot up to ninety knots, but the GPS's ground speed held firm at thirty. The needle of the Black Hawk's round outside air temperature gauge turned like an unwinding clock hand, dropping thirty degrees in seconds.

Vaughn realized that he'd just plowed into the leading edge of a powerful cold front.

Horizontal rain crashed into the Black Hawk, rendering the windshield completely opaque, even with the wipers on high. Vaughn kept the helicopter level by looking out the side window, but that, too, proved difficult. Wind-driven ripples raced through the straw-colored fields. The ephemeral waves of grain lashed at the helicopter's tires without effect, but the visual illusion created by the rushing undulations made sideways surface navigation all but impossible.

"This is too much!"

Vaughn slowed the copter to ten knots and then drove it onto the ground. The four-foot-tall stalks of spring wheat parted, yielding to the insistent nose of the onrushing helicopter. Vaughn bounced up and down as the main landing gear skipped over the furrowed ground. Then the vertical movement stopped.

For a moment, he thought the helicopter must have left the ground and lifted back into the air. The yellow field appeared to rush past his door. He tried to push the collective control, but it was all the way down. Then he saw that the ground speed had fallen to zero.

The helicopter had stopped.

Vaughn reached up for the throttles, intent on shutting down the engines. Then he saw the surging airspeed needle. The winds were blowing it better than eighty miles an hour.

Since when do cold fronts have winds this high? Vaughn wondered, but then his eyes widened. He yanked his hand from the throttles.

"Tornado Alley!"

He'd landed in the heart of it!

After squinting through the windshield, Vaughn eyed the throttles again. Taking off wasn't an option, not in this storm. He could kill the engines, but in high winds, helicopter blades could flap dangerously, especially during coast down. They'd been known to cut through cockpits. At full speed, the rotor blades were more stable, but if he kept running and a tornado did come—

Suddenly, a violent gust rocked the helicopter.

Vaughn froze.

The wind had shifted. Now it blew across the aircraft, racing in from its left.

He growled and shook his head. "Stupid move, Singleton." He could have at least tried to check the weather before he'd departed Lincoln. Vaughn doubted he would have found a current forecast, but he hadn't even bothered to check the airport's pilot planning room. Who knows? He might have found some leftover prog charts– weather maps that plot regional conditions for days in advance.

No, he'd been too goddamned single-minded.

Vaughn could almost see Mark shaking his head.

Then surging winds howled, eclipsing the roaring engines and pulsing rotor blades. The helicopter leaned right. Vaughn pressed the stick left, tilting the rotors into the screaming hurricane-force winds. Something dark flew across the field ahead of him. Then amber straws and dark earth sprayed the windshield. The still beating wipers smeared the mess across the glass.

"Shit! Tornado!"

Then Vaughn glimpsed it as a charcoal smudge against the back-drop of black clouds. Through the mud-streaked windshield, he tried to judge the distance. The vortex looked huge. He couldn't tell for sure, but it looked as if the tornado was crossing from left to right. It didn't appear to be growing closer.

The pitch of the wind rose another notch. The Black Hawk leaned precariously. If it got any stronger, the helicopter would roll over and beat itself to death.

He didn't dare move the collective control. That would only make things worse, but he did have another option.

Vaughn eased in a little left pedal, and the nose shifted a few degrees in that direction. He applied additional pedal, and it continued the yawing turn. The back of the copter jumped a few times as the tailwheel skated across furrowed ground, but it finally came to a stop with the nose facing back into the wind.

The turn had placed the funnel cloud on the helicopter's right side. Looking through the right window, Vaughn now had an unsullied and literally front-seat view of the tornado.

Something dark flew over the Black Hawk. Vaughn looked up and suddenly understood why he'd seen so few trees. A small, uprooted oak tumbled overhead and then disappeared behind the helicopter.

For an insane moment, he considered trying to fly away from the tornado. He looked at it with wide eyes.

Still no closer.

Vaughn would sit still, for now, take his chances with flying debris. If he launched into this storm, he'd likely lose sight of the ground or lose control of the helicopter or both.

Through slitted eyes, Vaughn watched the swirling cloud. He gripped the sticks with two white-knuckled fists, feeling like a loaded spring trap, ready to snap the flight controls up the instant the funnel cloud moved toward the helicopter.

Suddenly, the tornado appeared to turn away from him. Its apparent width rapidly diminished and then it drew up, away from the ground. A moment later, it disappeared into the base of the black clouds.

Before Vaughn could relax, another bolt of lightning struck, this one so close the sound arrived in unison with the light. Then the sky opened up again. Rain crashed down. The helicopter shuddered violently as a fresh blast of wind raked across it.

Between the sideways rain, blowing wheat, and flying mud, Vaughn couldn't see more than a hundred yards in any direction, even less in some. The helicopter was stable for now, but he knew there were likely more tornados out there. If one hit the Black Hawk, it would toss the aircraft around like a toy, an event he'd probably not survive.

He could just leave the helicopter running and try to find cover, but then he'd be completely exposed to the elements and flying debris. Vaughn eyed the external temperature and shook his head. Out in the frigid driving rain, he'd be just as likely to die of exposure as find shelter.

"Screw that. I'll take my chances in here."

Vaughn cranked up the Black Hawk's heater. Staring into the storm, he cinched the neck of his flight suit against the cold air leaking into the cockpit.

Thinking of Mark, Vaughn recalled the conversation they had just before the vacuum chamber flight. His friend had told him he could start over, could do better if he'd just *apply* himself.

Vaughn shook his head as he stared into the raging storm. "Well, Colonel Hennessy, I'm batting a thousand on your whole fresh start thing," he said sarcastically. "Not that it matters now."

CHAPTER 10

An hour later, the storm relented. No other tornados had emerged from the black clouds. Dark, bulbous cumulus gave way to a smooth layer of low, gray clouds, restoring a measure of light to the world as they glided overhead. The wind dropped to a manageable level, and the temperature hung just above freezing.

In the still running Black Hawk, Vaughn started adjusting the controls for takeoff, but then, in his mind's eye, he saw Mark's shaking head again.

"Goddammit!"

Frowning, Vaughn shoved the collective control back down to the stop and shut down the helicopter, cursing under his breath through the entire process.

A moment later, he stepped from the cockpit of the now silent aircraft. Shivering in the cold, brisk air, he stared across the destroyed field of matted wheat. The uprooted oak had landed a hundred yards behind the Black Hawk. The upside-down tree's earth covered roots scratched at the steel-gray sky. Vaughn started to walk toward the back of the helicopter. Looking up, he inspected the aircraft and its rotors for damage. Aside from the brown mud splattered across its side and the yellow wheat stalks jammed into its every nook and cranny, the helicopter looked miraculously unblemished.

Vaughn gave the inverted tree a final bewildered glance as he rounded the back of the Black Hawk. Then he walked along its left side, inspecting the other half of the main rotors. He stumbled as something snagged his right boot. Vaughn looked down to see a strand of barbed wire wrapped around it. Visually, he followed the path of the wire as it stretched across patches of earth and toppled wheat. It led straight to the helicopter's left wheel. To his shock, Vaughn saw that it had hooked around the main landing gear's large vertical strut, catching it just above the big, black tire.

"Son of a …" he whispered.

Turning left, he followed the wire away from the Black Hawk. About twenty feet out, he found the first of a line of laid-over posts.

Apparently, the helicopter had plowed through a fence during its short landing roll. Vaughn peered under its belly and saw that the wire had completely wrapped around the hub of the right tire, trapping it between the wheel and the strut. That must have happened when he'd turned the copter into the wind. If he'd tried to take off with that wire wrapped around the main gear, Vaughn would have likely crashed, flipping ass over teakettle when the twisted steel strands yanked the bottom of the helicopter out from under him.

In his mind's eye, he saw Mark nodding.

"I hear you, buddy."

Vaughn dug a pair of cutters from the tools he'd stashed in the pocket at the bottom of the pilot's door. A few minutes later, he had the wire cut free from the helicopter. He dragged it well clear and wrapped the loose ends around a branch of the inverted oak tree.

Then he climbed back into the pilot's seat. He soon had both engines running. After a final check of the aircraft's flight systems, he pulled power and guided the helicopter into a stable hover, pivoting it left and right to ensure nothing else had latched onto the Hawk.

Now confident that the aircraft was clear and flyable, Vaughn turned its nose to the west.

"Thanks, Mark. I owe you one," he said somberly. Then Vaughn remembered Mark's shove, the one that had snapped him out of the trance induced by the onrushing jet, and he added, "Again."

Vaughn adjusted the controls and the helicopter accelerated across the ground and then climbed away from the tortured field. The Black Hawk leveled off beneath a leaden mantle of low clouds. Vaughn wasn't surprised to see a meandering trail of scoured earth. Coming in from his left side, the wandering brown path approached from the southwest. Beneath Vaughn, the trail faded into a spiral of twisted wheat stalks where it had broken from the ground and returned to the cloud that had birthed it.

Three hours later—at the end of yet another chain of dashed hopes —the Black Hawk finally emerged from the back of the cold front, breaking into clear air. On the western horizon ahead of the helicopter, snow-covered mountains buttressed a surreally beautiful azure sky.

The clear, smog-free atmosphere stoked hopes that he'd finally found the edge of the light wave's effect. But then he swept in over Denver's eastern suburbs and saw the truth of the situation. The same scenes of sudden disappearance that he'd encountered innumerable times in Cleveland and everywhere along his journey now scrolled beneath his helicopter.

Isolated areas had burned, but it appeared that the vast majority of this city stood unblemished. However, its few remaining fires, along with the town's still accident-clogged intersections, told him that the dearth of devastation wasn't the result of human intervention. A fresh coating of snow covered Denver and the mountains beyond. With a sinking heart, Vaughn realized that the city's saving grace must have been the rain and snow. The moisture had tamped down the fires that would have otherwise obliterated it.

Tears clouded Vaughn's vision. He wiped them away with the back of a glove.

He had all but known this outcome awaited him when the first phone call had gone unanswered. His mother never missed a call, especially when her only son was on the other end of it. But having the proof of the fact staring him in the face made the news no easier to digest.

Vaughn felt hollowed out. Since his wife had skipped out on him, he had withdrawn from so much in life, but not from his mother. As an only child, he'd become the man of the family at the ripe old age of 13, when his father had died in a car crash. He could still remember hearing the knock on the door, the hushed words from the foyer. A stifled wail. The look on his mother's face when she'd returned to the living room.

The death had hit both of them hard. Vaughn's father had been a good man and a better father.

And he'd been a good provider.

Mark had been wrong about one thing: Vaughn hadn't been a rich kid, not always, anyway.

His mother never had to work. As a stay-at-home mom, she had home-schooled her young son. The settlement they'd received from the trucking company responsible for the accident hadn't changed that arrangement.

She'd moved them from Houston to Boulder. Even through Vaughn's high school years, she'd continued to serve as his teacher. When most of his contemporaries were rebelling against their parents and chasing girls, Vaughn had spent his teens at his mother's side. They had served one another as emotional crutches through those years, she as the parent and teacher, he as the budding man of the house.

In hindsight, Vaughn now knew that the combination of home-schooling coupled with the symbiotic relationship with his mother had emotionally stunted him, forever making him socially awkward. It was a fact that his ex had been all too happy to point out on many occasions.

Now his first instinct was to fly the Black Hawk up to Boulder on Denver's west side, to visit his mother's home, but with all of the snow on the ground, an off-airport landing wasn't the best idea. And if he ended up needing the helicopter again and if it required servicing, he'd be a long way from the tools and parts necessary for the job.

Besides, in his mother's upscale community, he wasn't likely to find a vehicle capable of circumnavigating the city's many choked roads.

So Vaughn turned the helicopter toward a place that contained all of those things.

White powder blasted from the Hummer's grill as it crashed through another drift. For a whited-out moment, snow obscured the windshield. Then wipers swept the surreally blue sky back into view.

Vaughn had found the ride not long after landing. The big military four-by-four had already gotten him through several snowdrifts. The Hummer had successfully negotiated numerous pileups, and where burning neighborhoods had blocked all roads, the vehicle had made easy work of the area's rugged terrain.

Even with the truck's assistance, the normally forty-five-minute drive from Denver to Boulder took two hours. Ice, mud, and soot caked the Hummer's exterior by the time he arrived at his mother's hillside villa on Sunshine Canyon Drive. He parked the dirty vehicle in the street, not wanting to sully her driveway.

The unlocked front door offered no resistance. It opened, and the conflicting smells of redolent flowers and burned coffee swept over him.

Vaughn deposited his dirty boots in the foyer and walked hesitantly into the house. Lights shone from the kitchen. Like the rest of the neighborhood, the home still had electricity.

He peered into the room but saw nothing out of place. Vaughn flinched as an air-raid siren blared from deeper inside the home. Then he heard the accompanying guitar riff and recognized the song. His mother, a metalhead since the seventies, had apparently left her collection of heavy metal music set on loop. Two days after the Disappearance—as Vaughn now thought of it—Ozzy Osbourne's warbling voice belted out the lyrics to Black Sabbath's *War Pigs*.

After turning off the coffee maker, Vaughn searched the rest of the bottom floor. Upstairs he found the source of the music, her laptop. It sat open and still powered up. Colorful lines danced across the screen. He tapped the display, and the screensaver vanished, replaced by a large headline.

"It's the End of the World!"

Vaughn stared at the words for a long moment. Seeing his worst fears—thoughts which he hadn't dared to voice—emblazoned across his mother's computer screen hit him like a sledgehammer.

Vaughn's knees buckled. He collapsed into the desk chair.

According to the article, the wave of light had first appeared somewhere in Eurasia. At the time of the posting, the curtain of energy had already swept through all of Europe and much of Asia along with the eastern half of North America. Vaughn skipped over the reports that chronicled the light wave's effect—he'd seen enough of that first-hand. Instead, he focused on the statements given by scientists and observers from around the globe. None of them knew what the light was or what had caused it, but every one of them said that they'd seen no reduction in the anomaly. According to the sources, it hadn't attenuated in any detectable way. Ground- and space-based observations still showed a feature that reached from the surface to the outer edge of the atmosphere, just as bright and tall as it had been when it first crossed Europe.

Now Singleton thought he understood why Director McCree had lost hope, why the man had sounded so dejected when he discovered that the two of them had been disconnected from the planet's molecular field. Until then, all of the evidence at his disposal must have pointed to the loss of *everyone* behind the wall of light, even those underground. That's why he initially mistook their survival as a sign that the wave was losing strength. Otherwise, he'd have simply reasoned that the chamber's thick walls had shielded them from the light's effect. However, the hope had died when he realized that the wave hadn't weakened, that Mark and Vaughn's unique isolation had saved them.

This thought slammed home another, more ominous realization.

In the entirety of humankind's history, no person on the planet had ever been as disconnected from it as Mark and Vaughn had been when the light swept through their part of it.

He now faced a horrible possibility. Taking the article as fact, believing that the wave had continued its path across the planet unabated, without weakening, left him with one inescapable conclusion:

Vaughn was almost certainly the last being on Earth.

Unfortunately, the realization pushed out all other thoughts. Later, Vaughn would regret not fully accounting for the last part of that epiphany, not considering what it meant for a person not *on* the planet.

At that moment, one sentence kept repeating in his mind:

I don't need anybody or anything.

Vaughn shook his head. He'd felt righteous when he had said that to Mark, but now it sounded like a moronic protestation issued by a clueless jackass.

After a long moment, another thought did burn its way into his shocked mind. The article's presence on this computer removed any hope that his mother had passed in the blissful ignorance of sleep.

He slammed the computer's lid closed. "Damnit!" The motion disturbed the curtains behind the desk. Through them, Vaughn glimpsed something out of place. He stood and pushed one of the cloth panels aside and peered down into the backyard.

"What the hell is that?"

A minute later, he stepped onto the snow-covered lawn. Forty feet away, the two items he'd seen from upstairs still didn't resolve. They sat under the low-hanging branches of a ponderosa pine. Only a light dusting of snow had reached the ground under those limbs. A few steps later, he stood between the two items. A face-down open hardback novel rested on its crumpled pages. A toppled coffee cup lay two feet from it.

Bending over, Vaughn reached for the second item with a trembling hand. After a pause, he snatched up the mug. Standing, he held it at eye level. A crescent-shaped rouge smudge adorned one side of the cup's rim.

His mother's favorite lipstick color.

He lowered the mug and gazed east. From this vantage point, one could see all the way across Denver. Vaughn knew that two days earlier, it had offered his mother the no doubt fearful sight of her impending death.

The skyline began to waver in his vision. The cup dropped next to the book. A moment later, he dropped as well, landing hard on his ass.

For the first time since the Disappearance, Vaughn wept openly.

CHAPTER 11

Her dad stood before the grill, making her favorite dinner. The little girl who had known the man watched with rapt attention. The aroma of the meat set her mouth to watering. Steak always smelled *so* good. Angela's stomach didn't growl, it roared. She clapped her hands together.

"Daddy! When will it be ready?"

Her excitement faltered as did her smile.

Something was wrong.

Her dad looked gaunt, drawn, older than he'd ever looked in life.

And the smell. The little girl wrinkled her nose. A sickly sweet odor had suddenly mixed with the aroma of cooking meat.

The overly aged version of her father waved his tongs over the grill. Its top was too high. Even on her tippy toes, little Angela couldn't see the meat.

"It's ready, pumpkin," the man said in a gravelly voice.

The long ends of the utensil again disappeared as her dad reached for their dinner.

Angela looked pensively from the grill to her father's deteriorating face.

Turning to his daughter, the now corpse-like man presented the smoldering carcass of a previously white mouse. Bubbling fat protruded through patches of charred fur.

The little girl screamed and yanked her head back, striking a hard surface. Then a flash of white light washed across the yard, and her father vanished, but the burned rodent remained, hanging weightlessly in the air.

Angela blinked sleepy eyes and rubbed the back of her head. The reality of the space station's interior chased out the last vestige of that long-ago backyard, but the dream shifted into waking nightmare as the scorched mouse remained. Staring at the very real manifestation, Angela gasped.

She continued to blink eyes that now burned and watered.

Suddenly, her lungs were burning as well.

"Oh shit!" Angela screamed between coughs. "Mabel?! What the hell happened?" But Mabel was dead. The carcass's ruptured, empty eye sockets stared unblinkingly as its smoking body slowly tumbled past her face.

Suddenly, a blaring klaxon echoed across the station. Then Angela saw flickering yellow and orange light coming from one of the passageways that led from the module.

"Fire!" she screamed.

The sight sent a pulse of adrenaline coursing through her veins. Pushing off the wall, Angela shot across the module, somersaulting mid-flight so that she landed feet first next to the room's fire extinguisher. She placed her feet on either side of the cylinder and with one hand she pried the extinguisher from its mount. The Velcro released with the sound of tearing paper. With her other hand, Angela freed the adjacent respirator.

As coughs continued to wrack her body, she released the extinguisher. The red bottle tumbled slowly next to her as she donned the oxygen mask. She cleared the device and took several deep breaths.

As her coughs began to subside, Angela swatted two switches. The first shut down the station's ventilation system, stopping it from feeding fresh air into the fire. The second one deactivated the smoke alarm. Its blaring horn finally fell silent.

Angela reoriented her body, snatched up the tumbling extinguisher, and pushed off the wall on a trajectory that sent her flying toward the flickering corridor. As she floated across the module, Angela stared warily into the passageway's white-walled confines.

The station's lights began to flicker. For a moment, they appeared to pulse in unison with the yellow strobing of the unseen fire, but then the module's lights died, plunging Angela into a surreal kaleidoscope of glimmering amber radiance. Ahead of her, black shadows and orange light danced in the aimless smoke.

On Earth, the fire's heat would travel upward, away from the source, but here, the fumes had nowhere to go in the corridor's zero-G environment. The smoke just stacked up on itself.

Angela's passage into the tube pushed a wave of clear air ahead of her. Through the respite, she caught a glimpse of glowing wires and flaming insulation. With her left hand, she grabbed a conduit that ran along the opposing wall, trying to arrest her flight and brace herself for the thrust that the discharging fire extinguisher would impart.

A scream of agony burst through Angela's pursed lips as she yanked her hand from the hot metal pipe. Unchecked inertia sent her body tumbling deeper into the smoke-filled corridor.

Pain exploded across her right forearm as a blazing jet of burning insulation strafed it. The fire-retardant cloth of the sleeping garment proved to be anything but, as flames began to spread up its sleeve.

"Son of a ...!" Angela yelled as she aimed the extinguisher's nozzle at her arm and squeezed the trigger.

Nothing happened. It didn't activate. The lever wouldn't even depress.

She hadn't pulled the goddamned pin!

Still drifting, Angela held the extinguisher in her burned hand. She tried to snatch the pin with the hand that protruded from the end of the flaming sleeve, but it slipped from her fingers. She frantically batted at the damned thing again and finally yanked it free, snapping its lanyard and sending both pieces tumbling into the smoke.

Angela aimed at the burning arm and squeezed the trigger again. This time it worked, extinguishing her sleeve. But its thrust accelerated her body's tumble, sending her careening blindly into the next module. For a brief moment, alternating periods of black void and orange light filled her universe.

Then something punched her in the face.

For a disoriented, dazed moment, Angela just floated, shaking her head, trying to clear it.

The world no longer tumbled around her. She'd flown face first into the module's far wall. The blow had arrested her spin. Fortunately, the mask had absorbed much of the impact.

Stabilizing herself, Angela grabbed a nearby structure and turned her body back toward the flickering light and smoke.

Finally, the module's emergency lights snapped on, flooding the smoke-filled room with their amber glow. That should've happened as soon as the module lost electricity. Something must be pumping enough voltage through the station to spoof the circuits into thinking they're still powered.

On this end of the smoke-filled passage, she spotted an electrical junction box connected to the bundle of conduits. Smoke radiated from the hot surfaces of several of the pipes that led from the box into the corridor. As she watched, one gained an orange hue. The junction box had a large, untripped circuit-breaker. Angela kicked off the far wall and glided to it. Nearing her target, she felt heat radiating from the spider web of cables and conduits. She raised the extinguisher and then slammed its bottom into the top of the breaker. It snapped open with a loud pop.

Immediately, the crackle of burning insulation within the connected conduits began to diminish, falling away like the sound of a whistling teakettle pulled from a hot burner.

"Oh, thank goodness," she whispered, the respirator muffling her words.

Yellow light flickered with diminishing intensity within the smoky corridor. Angela eased into the tube. She tested the temperature of a thankfully cool structural member and then braced herself against it. She aimed the extinguisher into the base of the flames and squeezed the trigger.

116

~

Now that she'd extinguished the fire, Angela went around the Zvezda Crew Module, manually switching off all of the components connected to the fried wires. Then she tried to reset the Power Management and Distribution computer, but the PMAD refused to respond. It was dead, a six million-dollar paperweight.

Through the respirator's hazed visor, Angela checked her O2 bottle.

Its gauge hovered near zero!

She toggled the PMAD's switch a third time. Still nothing happened. "Shit!" she said, smacking its now dingy white metallic surface.

If Angela didn't restore power and get the crew module's air going soon, she'd have to abandon this section. Thanks to recent modifications, the environmental control computer had automatically closed all of the ISS's hatches to stop smoke from filling the entire station. Now she needed to retreat to that smoke-free region before her oxygen supply depleted.

Frustrated, shaking her head, Angela pushed off the wall and drifted toward the nearest hatch. She pulled up short at the sight of a three-quarters closed door.

"Why didn't you close?!" she whispered. The hatches usually took a few seconds to close. The power must have failed before they could seal!

Angela pulled the door fully open and stared into another smoke-hazed module.

"Shit, shit, *shit!*"

The steady hiss of her oxygen supply faded and then fell silent. She tried to draw a breath but the mask's one-way valves prevented external air from entering, so it just sucked down onto her face. Angela pulled it off. It peeled away from her sweaty skin with a wet slurp. Caustic smoke instantly assaulted her eyes and lungs. Her vision muddled as zero-G tears piled up in burning eyes. Angela started coughing as every breath of the station's heated atmosphere scraped at the inside of her chest.

Blinking furiously and rubbing soot-grimed hands against her eyes, Angela aimed for the next module and pushed off the wall. She drifted into the room as another spasm of coughs wracked her body. Between hacks, she spotted her quarry through the haze.

Angela redirected her drift, angling for the safe haven. She grabbed a structural member and flipped over so that her feet slid into its lower torso assembly. A moment later and still coughing, she pulled the hard-shelled upper torso of the spacesuit over her head, snaking her hands into its arms. Angela struggled to connect the two halves, but the hacking spasms made it impossible.

"Damnit!" Angela screamed, abandoning the effort.

She grabbed the helmet from its mount and pulled it over her head, locking it into place. With her watering eyes squeezed shut, she activated the suit's environmental controls. Finally, cool, fresh air began to flow around her face. Angela inhaled it, but the movement of her chest drew smoke up from the suit's open waist. She tried again to latch it, but her resumed body-wracking coughs made it impossible.

Angela felt her mind beginning to fuzz.

With a force of will, she tamped down the spasms, concentrating on sipping the stream of air that flowed through the helmet. She closed her eyes. Using slow methodic movements, Angela finally sealed the suit. The latch clicked home just as her spasming diaphragm won its battle, and the held breath exploded from her lips.

A cough-filled minute later, the suit's systems gained the upper hand, finally clearing the last of the caustic fumes from its internal environment.

Floating in the middle of the module's hazy atmosphere and breathing heavily, Angela stared into the yellow glare of the nearest emergency light. She'd initially thought that the loss of electricity had been limited to the Zvezda Service Module. Now she wondered how the rest of the station had fared. With the complete loss of power, the smoke had likely reached every corner of the ISS. Other than the few empty spacesuits that haunted the station's interior like silent sentries, she probably had no safe haven.

Angela's eyes widened. "Nate!"

Mabel was dead, her burned corpse had been all too real, but Angela hadn't seen Nate or their makeshift habitat. Apparently, poor Mabel had escaped it, again.

A shadow drifted past a nearby external port.

Angela's eyes widened. "What the hell?" She kicked off a wall and glided toward the window. "Oh, thank you! I can't believe it. They've come for me! They're …!"

The words and short-lived hope died along with a piece of her soul.

"No, no, no …" Angela whispered as she stared disbelievingly at the scene outside. How could this have happened? A debris field, a cloud of multicolored, twisted material cluttered the narrow portion of space visible through the small window.

"What happened?"

Suddenly, the shadow returned as a large, dark mass blotted out the scene. A moment later, it disappeared, its broad flat end flying out of sight like an undulating tapeworm. Angela glimpsed its black surface long enough to recognize it as one of the station's giant solar panels.

She inched closer to the port until the helmet's curved visor clinked against the thick clear panel. Through narrowed eyes she looked past the tumbling bits of debris, focusing on the nearest portion of the solar array truss.

"What the hell?"

Bare wires now ran the length of the structure. But there shouldn't have been any exposed cables. In the areas where they touched the truss, the wires had twisted and deformed. It appeared that they had partially melted, spot-welding themselves to the adjacent metal bars.

Angela released a string of curse words that would have made a pro football coach blush.

Somehow, all of the wires that carried high-voltage electricity from the solar arrays to the station had superheated.

At first, she'd assumed that Mabel had chewed through some electrical insulation and been cooked by the resultant short circuit, but there's nothing the mouse could've done to cause this level of destruction.

Angela's heart sank as she considered just what could have poured that much power into the arrays, enough to fry the entire system.

It must have been a massive solar flare! The Sun must've launched a coronal mass ejection or CME straight at the Earth. The powerful pulse of energy had slammed into the station.

Now Angela wondered how many millisieverts of radiation she had absorbed. A CME of this magnitude had never struck the station. She'd have to check a dosimeter later.

Normally, the team at Mission Control in Houston alerted the crew of incoming flares. But considering her looped plea for help had gone unanswered for two weeks now, she doubted anyone had known it was coming.

If there is anyone left.

Angela shook her head, vigorously, as if doing so could quash the thought.

"Concentrate, Brown!" she said with a growl.

She needed more information than this limited field of view could provide.

Where's Nate?

Can't think of him right now. Bigger fish to fry.

The thought brought back the radiation concern which raised the ugly specter of why she hadn't been warned.

The vicious mental loop threatened to end her.

"Move it, Commander!"

Angela banished the thoughts as best she could and kicked off a wall.

A few moments later, she floated into the Cupola.

Angela felt ill as she stared open-mouthed through the faceted windows of the observatory. Like a slow-motion video of a Rocky Mountain blizzard, thousands of twisted chunks of foam and melted plastic tumbled lazily across a surreal panorama of destruction.

Beyond the storm, the few solar panels visible from the Cupola writhed, their now untethered inboard ends oscillating to and fro like black cobras dancing to the warbling whistle of a snake charmer's pungi.

"Aw, shit," Angela whispered.

CHAPTER 12

Angela opened the external airlock door. A moment later, she floated out into a slow-motion debris storm that twinkled with the radiance of a million diamonds. Light scintillated and flickered all around her as she moved out of the station's shadow. Angela squinted against its radiance. Even with the sun behind her, its reflected light felt as if it could burn through the back of her eyes and drill into her brain. She slid the helmet's tinted visor into place, and the pain relented.

Angela reached out and tried to grab one of the clear flakes. The first one crumbled between the fingers of her glove and floated away like sugar. Sunlight flared anew within each granule, imparting them with an internal brilliance that fluoresced like the fire of a microscopic nuclear furnace.

"There's a cloud of glass shards around the entire station," Angela said. She'd left a voice recorder pinned to the helmet speaker of one of the station's spacesuits. Angela had left both the radio and the recorder turned on so that she could leave a running narrative of her spacewalk in case … Well, just in case.

Another, larger flake drifted inches from her visor. Angela felt her eyes cross as she focused on the chip of glass. She reached out for it.

Being careful not to crush or bump it, she gently pinched the flat crystal between thumb and forefinger. In spite of her best efforts, the shard fractured. Part of it floated away, but she still held the largest fragment. Angela turned it over, studying its opposing surfaces. One side was perfectly flat, but on the crystal's opposite surface, light reflected off of grooves that formed a recognizable pattern.

"It's the glass coating from the arrays. Somehow the stuff's been blasted from the surface of one of the solar panels."

Angela unclipped her lanyard from the airlock's hard point and worked her way hand-over-hand along the outside of the station.

"Can't quite see them from here, so I'm transferring to the truss structure."

Angela passed back into the station's shadow. She retracted the tinted visor and studied the snow-like storm of debris that surrounded her spacesuit.

"There are bits of melted and twisted white insulation floating along with the glass shards."

A couple of pieces ricocheted off her helmet with audible clicks. Angela waved her free hand in front of the visor. "It's pretty cluttered out here."

She heard a faint squeak.

"Are you alright in there, Nate?"

She neither expected nor received an answer. In spite of the shit storm that floated around her, Angela grinned at the mental image of his twitching pink nose sniffing at the helmet's speaker. She'd found the fat little mouse hiding in the part of the station farthest from the Zvezda module. But even there, the air must have still been pretty caustic. Nate had been lethargic. Little spasms and squeaks—mouse coughs, Angela guessed—had rocked the pudgy guy. She'd placed him inside the same spare spacesuit that now also hosted the voice recorder. After purging all of the bad air, she'd shut off the flow of oxygen. Nate didn't need a constant supply of O2, and Angela didn't want to use her finite supply of CO_2 scrubbing lithium hydroxide for the purpose. He could last a day or more on the air in the suit's relatively cavernous interior.

Angela checked the sensor wrapped around her left forearm. "The dosimeter is still green. Radiation levels appear nominal."

Had anyone still been in Houston, she was sure that, out of an abundance of caution, the team at Johnson Space Center would have ordered her to remain in the shielded portion of the Russian Orbital Segment, or ROS, for the next few days. And while her time up here might feel rather unlimited, she didn't exactly have unlimited electrical resources. If she didn't get power restored soon, things were going to get bad in a hurry.

"You better not pee on that mic boom, Nate. I may have to use that suit someday."

Angela wasn't too concerned about the chance that he might start chewing on components. She'd clipped Nate's favorite chew toy to the inner surface of the suit's neck ring. When she'd left, the little rascal had been hard at work on the small nylon bone.

Angela brushed aside some floating insulation and then latched onto the truss structure. A few handholds later, her helmet rose above the plane of the station and out of its shadow. She squinted as thousands of swarming shards shined their reflected light into her eyes, making it impossible to see beyond a few feet.

"I mean it, Nate," she said as her hand fumbled for the sunshield. Finally finding it, Angela slid the tinted lens over her helmet's visor. Its polarized filter cut the glare, revealing the greater universe. "And you better not poop in …" The words died in her mouth, and the grin fell away.

"Oh shit!"

Angela stared across the length of the truss.

"All of the port side solar panels are toast," she said dejectedly.

The array support arms continued their ninety-minute rotation, but every one of the long solar panels in that direction had somehow disconnected from its inboard mount. Anchored to their outboard ends, all eight of the arrays on the port or left side of the station waved slowly to and fro like the tentacles of a giant sea anemone. Each slow undulation launched another cloud of sparkling glass shards.

It was simultaneously the most beautiful and singularly horrible thing she'd ever seen. It looked as if she'd been transported to some extraterrestrial world where space-based anemone released crystalline eggs in orgasmic waves.

"They're all flapping like seagrass."

Angela's eyes widened. She checked her dosimeter again.

It still showed normal radiation levels.

"The flare hasn't returned, so why are they still moving?"

She had expected to see the support arms still rotating, but out here in the vacuum of space, the panels shouldn't be flapping like that. Their internal friction should've slowed them by now.

A fresh wave began to propagate down the ribbon of black material. The movement released another cloud of crystals.

As Angela watched its terrible beauty, she suddenly understood. Each time a portion of the panel flaked away, it exposed the raw substrate to excess ultraviolet radiation. Under the sun's hot glare, the unprotected black surface must be expanding, causing it to flex like a synthetic muscle.

It wasn't a giant leap in logic. Angela had reason to think this. NASA and Roscosmos, the Russian space agency, had recently upgraded all of the station's solar panels. The new material converted light to electricity more efficiently than had the previous generation. In early development, the new substrate had suffered from heat expansion-related defects. However, the contractor reported that they had engineered the problem out of the final flight-ready panels.

"Bullshit you did," Angela said with a growl. "You lying sacks of shit!" She shook her head. "That low-bid contractor didn't fix the expansion problem," she reported to Nate and the recorder. "I don't know how it got past NASA's quality control people, but these panels were ticking time bombs. The solar flare must've released enough UV radiation to penetrate their glass coating. As soon as the substrate got exposed, it started expanding, fracturing the rest of the glass in a slow-motion cascading failure. Once the first part of it cracked, the rest was doomed to follow suit."

Reluctantly, Angela turned to inspect the other half of the station's solar panels, the eight arrays attached to the opposite end of the truss. Fresh anger washed over her as she watched the same surreal, alien-like release of glass shards burst from the other eight gently surging panels.

"Damnit! I've lost all sixteen of them!"

The main solar arrays weren't the only ones on the station. Angela craned her neck, trying to look aft.

"I can't quite see the Russian panels from here. Hang on."

She latched her tether to the truss's outermost hard point. Then Angela released her grip on the truss structure.

"I'll be able to see them from a higher vantage point."

A gentle nudge of her hand induced a slow, flat spin and sent her drifting upward, away from the station. As she ascended, Angela played out her tether's slack. The slow rotation gave her an ever-increasing field of vision. Soon she could see the entire station. When she reached the end of the lanyard, a light jolt reversed her direction, but she'd already seen enough.

Too much, actually.

Tears flowed.

Angela didn't try to stop them.

Why bother?

She was a dead woman.

From inside the station, she'd seen that one of the power wires still had its covering of white insulation. The sight of the undamaged cable had elicited the hope that she would find some intact arrays and would be able to configure the station to operate on reduced power—even now she could see that a second cable had survived on the other half of the assembly as well—but this wasn't a reduction.

It was a complete loss!

"They're all gone," Angela said, shaking her head.

She felt as if she were narrating her own death, because, without an electrical supply, she wasn't long for this world. Unlike the Space Shuttles and the Apollo ships before them, the station didn't have fuel cells. She had plenty of water and liquid O2, but without electricity, she couldn't even convert it into breathable oxygen in a manner sufficient to extend her life beyond a few days.

"Nate, we are well and truly—!"

A grunt exploded from her lips as her rebounding spacesuit collided with the truss structure. Angela arched her body and snapped her head back, narrowly avoiding smacking her visor into a piece of shiny metal. She grabbed a structural member and reined in her inertia, preventing a second trip out to the end of the tether.

The tears had started to dry under the gentle flow of the suit's conditioned air, but now they returned.

"Shit, shit, *shit!*" she screamed.

Her visor clicked as it came to rest against the bright cable. Angela blinked several times, trying to clear the moisture. The piled-up tears made the shiny metal look like flowing mercury.

Suddenly, she froze. Releasing the adjacent structural member, Angela touched her gloved hand to the bare, quarter-inch-thick cable.

"Could it?"

A moment later, she finally blinked the last of the water from her vision. A slowly undulating teardrop floated inside her visor. Beyond it, her gloved fingers traced the braided strands of wire. She nodded. The hint of a grin parted her lips. "Yes, it sure the hell can."

"Houston," she said to Nate and the voice recorder, "We have a *solution* … maybe."

CHAPTER 13

"Shit, shit, *shit!*" Vaughn screamed through a throat constricted by sheer terror.

Beneath his hands and their white-knuckled death grip on the thick cable, Vaughn's body swung like a 250-pound pendulum. Nothing but a thousand feet of empty air separated the bottom of his shoes from the rushing river at the base of the canyon.

The red-faced man shook his head. How the hell had it come to this?

After finding his mother's dropped coffee mug, Vaughn had spent hours on her computer, searching the internet for information. The networks had crashed in the early hours of the Disappearance, but apparently, as an ever-increasing portion of the world's population vanished, the interwebs had come back online. In the closing hours, the remnants of humanity had chronicled the advance of the wave as it finished its sweep of the planet.

The last report had come from an individual in New Zealand. After that, all active communications and uploads had fallen silent.

Having the carpet of hope yanked out from under him had plunged Vaughn down a dark well. One he'd wallowed in for the two weeks since his arrival in the mile-high city.

After finding his mother's lipstick-lined coffee mug and following the all-too-enlightening internet search, Vaughn had departed her house to the hard rocking sounds of AC/DC's *Have a Drink on Me*.

"Sounds like a goddamned good idea to me!"

Over the next two weeks, Vaughn had worked his way down Boulder's bar-lined Pearl Street. On more than one occasion, he'd awoken face down on a bar floor, often in a puddle of bile and booze. It was a miracle that he hadn't drowned in the pooled vomit.

That morning he'd woken with the words of Stephen King's Andy Dufresne echoing in his throbbing head: "Get busy living, or get busy dying."

After a couple of weeks' worth of leisurely trying to kill himself, Vaughn had decided to take a more proactive tack.

It was time to get busy dying.

First Singleton had returned to his mother's home. He'd walked through the house and into the backyard. Lying down on his side, he propped his head up on a hand, the supporting elbow resting on brown grass now sprinkled with green blades. The haunting, lipstick-lined coffee cup sat atop the now closed hardback book like a small, makeshift memorial.

Vaughn clinked his twenty-four-ounce can of liquid courage against the cup. "You always supported me, Mom, even when I was a screw-up—which was pretty much all the time." He raised the can in a toast. "Nothing's changed about that."

"Happier alone?" He shook his head. "Don't need anybody or anyone? What a crock of shit. As the saying goes, I've lived to regret that one."

He took a long draw from the beer, then wiped his lips with his shirtsleeve.

"But I have a remedy for that. I'll be with you soon. Gonna take a drive down to Colorado Springs, pay a visit to the Royal." It was the name they'd always used for the Royal Gorge suspension bridge, the world's tallest. "No way for me to screw that up. I jump from there," he said and then waved the beer in the air, "and it's bye-bye, Vaughn."

He took another pull from the tall boy.

"So, like I said, I'll be joining you soon, Mom." He paused, and a confused look took over his features. "Or will I? Where *did* you go?"

Vaughn shook his head.

The question had rattled around his polluted mind for weeks now. Where in the hell had everyone gone? Had they been vaporized? If so, why hadn't their clothes been left behind? In the days since the Disappearance, Vaughn hadn't seen so much as a mosquito.

Had all of the planet's animal life been ...

What?

Vaporized?

Cooked off?

Elevated to a higher dimension?

"Is it that, Mom? Are you kicking back on some higher plane? Have I been left behind? Am I a ghost, the boogeyman in some kid's closet?"

He hoisted the can again. "I'll drink to that."

And so, he did.

After a long, wet belch, Vaughn said, "At least I don't have to worry about something eating me." He winced. "Sorry. TMI?" But apparently, he wasn't too sorry, because he expanded on the thought. "You see, I don't think I'll even rot. Probably just end up as a broken mummy at the bottom of the canyon."

He paused and then pursed his lips. "I know, definitely too much information that time."

He poured the last of the beer into his mother's cup, then stood. "I love you, Mom."

Three hours later, he stood again, this time with his back to the bridge, his heels lit upon the angle iron ledge and nothing but a thousand feet of air between his boot-clad toes and the railroad-lined river below. To either side, his hands had a death grip on the handrail that dug into his back.

Of course, Vaughn couldn't see said boots. Looking down, he

peered over his ample belly—the indulgences of the past two weeks had only worsened that problem.

The sound of his pounding heart surged in his ears, eclipsing even the wind. The rest of the universe seemed to dissolve. His world became a tunnel of space devoid of all but a circle of canyon floor and the 1053 feet of empty air between him and it.

Hyperventilating, Vaughn had closed his eyes. For the third time, he had subvocalized a ten count, and also for the third time, his hands had refused to let go. They wouldn't release the rail.

He had decided that the imagery was causing the balking, so Singleton had turned to face the bridge. That way he wouldn't have the ice-inducing vision of his final resting place staring him in the face. But as his toes perched on the angle iron ledge, Vaughn had lost hold of the rail. His hands had slipped, their death grip failing him. At first, they had refused every order to release, and now the traitorous sons of bitches seemed to want to force the issue.

Vaughn should have been happy, should've been pleased that he'd been relieved of the responsibility for pulling this particularly sticky trigger. But instead, only one thought had entered his mind:

He wanted to live!

As if in slow motion, his arms had windmilled like Michael Phelps swimming while baked out of his gourd. Each time a hand touched the rail, its fingers had bounced off, finding no purchase.

Then his upper body had tilted earthward.

He was going to fall!

The rail was no longer within reach!

Vaughn had searched desperately for something he could grab. Under the bridge, a complex network of wires spanned the canyon. One of the thickest cables crossed six feet beneath him.

Careful not to push off, Vaughn had given up on his battle to grasp the handrail. He'd allowed his knees to slacken. The toes of his boots slipped from their steel perch. Gravity made its claim and took him. The bottom of the bridge flashed through Vaughn's peripheral vision, but his eyes remained locked on the rapidly approaching complex of cables. Just as his feet struck the main one, his hands grasped the two nearest vertical wires. The hard rubber soles of his boots squeaked on the shiny metal. His right hand got hold of its targeted cable, but the left—apparently still bent on destruction—flailed fruitlessly.

His inertia carried him out, away from the wires. Then, with another squeak, his left foot slipped off of the main cable, but his right hand had apparently decided it, too, wanted to live.

It held fast.

For an eternal second, Vaughn teetered on one foot. Then that boot had slipped off of the cable. His hand had slid down the vertical wire until it reached the bottom intersection. At the same moment, the other hand had finally rejoined the team. It grasped the main cable and stopped the fall, leaving Vaughn hanging with nothing but a thousand feet of air between the soles of his boots and the river below.

Presently, Vaughn screamed, "Shit, shit, *shit!*" again as he stared at the distant river.

He closed his eyes. Through a force of will, Vaughn reined in his wheezing breath. The muscles in his overtaxed hands burned. He wouldn't be able to hold on much longer.

On his left, the cable arched downward, toward its anchor on that side of the canyon. Vaughn redirected the pendulous swinging of his legs from fore and aft to sideways. He tried to hook a heel over the wire. It slipped off with another rubbery squeak. Then with an echoing grunt, he thrust his left leg over the cable, successfully hooking a calf over it on the second desperate attempt.

He spent the next minute wrestling the rest of his body onto the perch. After catching his breath, he shimmied hand-over-hand toward the left anchor, always sure to maintain three points of contact. A fall this close to the edge would be much shorter, but just as fatal, with the likely addition of a long, agonizing death.

Yay! Vaughn thought wryly.

A few nervous and shaky interchanges later, he finally reached the catwalk. Not trusting his balance, Vaughn crossed the horizontal truss on hands and knees until he reached the point where it passed over the canyon's treed ledge. He swung his lower limbs over the edge and then dropped six feet to the ground. His exhausted legs gave out, crumpling under him. Vaughn collapsed into a laughing, crying mass of jiggling flesh. The laughter and even the tears felt cleansing.

After a few minutes, he rolled onto his back and stared at the drifting cotton ball clouds.

Vaughn held two extended middle fingers to the sky.

"I'm alive! I'm fucking *alive!*"

His arms dropped to the ground. As he lay there spread-eagle, tears rolled from the corners of his eyes.

Vaughn sighed. In a whisper, he added, "And it's not my fault, goddamn it."

Finally, he sat up and drew in a deep breath. Then he let it out in a long exhalation.

"Well, Captain Singleton, it's time to get busy living."

CHAPTER 14

Angela latched herself to the array arm's outermost structural member. At the outboard end of the support arm, the angular momentum of its slow, ninety-minute rotation generated just enough artificial gravity to cause the four-foot-wide roll of wire attached to her hip to hang feather-light by her boots.

The microgravity created an up reference, making the distant truss appear to be above her. Heart racing in response to the fresh dose of adrenaline pumping through her, Angela looked down and watched a universe worth of stars scroll beneath her hanging feet.

The rotating support arms were still making their once-per-orbit revolution. The minuscule friction produced at the truss's pivot point hadn't appreciably slowed them. Actually, from the sun's perspective, the arms weren't turning. To it, the station flipped end over end once per trip around the planet, while the solar array support arms always faced the sun. But that was an illusion of perspective. Here at the outboard end of that arm, Angela could barely feel it, but she knew that moving farther out from that center of rotation would increase the effect of that angular momentum. She was counting on it, actually. She reasoned that the angular momentum coupled with the differential gravity exerted across the length of the spooled out wire would keep it taut.

Now the horizon slid under her boots as the array arm's sedate rotation brought it parallel to the planet's surface.

"What do you think, Nate?" Angela said. "Is this going to work?"

Refusing to reveal his opinion, the little mouse remained mute—as he did on all subjects, save cheese.

"Blah, blah, blah, Nate. Do you ever shut up?"

An errant lock of hair drifted into Angela's right eye ... again. She blew it out of the way. Then she unclipped the thick bundle of looped wire from her hip.

"Better hope this works, little buddy."

Angela looked at the four-foot-wide ring and nodded.

"I got the idea from an experiment NASA did back in ninety-six," she said to the voice recorder in Nate's spacesuit habitat. "During a Shuttle flight, astronauts deployed a long cable from the cargo bay to see if the wire would generate electricity as it cut through Earth's magnetic field, but it snapped before they finished spooling it out, so they thought it had failed. Most of the cable was lost to space, but when the scientists examined the frayed end that had returned with the Shuttle, they discovered that it had melted."

"The experiment hadn't failed, really. It had exceeded expectations. The wire created too much electricity, so it should work for the station, too."

She'd spent the last two days scavenging all of the recently bared wire from the station's truss, working long hours in her spacesuit. Now it was time to spool it out.

Initially, Angela had planned to brace herself against the array arm and sling the counterweight into space. However, the cable would likely get tangled, pull up short and then rebound right at her. Plus, she didn't know how much force the fully extended wire would exert. Angela had clamped the cable to the strut using some pretty robust hardware, but she worried that if she threw the line, and it didn't get tangled, it would hit the end of its reach with enough inertia to rip that cable out of its mount and send the whole bundle off on its own new orbit.

Then she and Nate would get to experience a slow, agonizing death.

No, she needed to modulate the spooling out of the cable.

"Here goes nothing."

Angela released the massive wrench that she'd attached to the end to act as a counterweight. The wrench slowly drifted away from her. Without much effect, she tried to help the cable along with her gloved hand. It was like trying to push a wet noodle. The wire and its makeshift counterweight lazily unwound its way toward the west, behind the station.

As the array support arm continued to turn like the minute hand of a crazy ninety-minute clock, the cable's far end slowly inched below the horizon. In three-quarters of an hour, it would finish the earthward half of its turn, and this end of the structure would rise above the opposite horizon ahead of the station.

As she watched the slow, almost nonexistent progress of the wire, Angela began to worry that it wasn't going to work. It looked as if it had stopped, like it was just hanging there idly. Then her body twitched as she reached the end of her personal tether.

"Oh shit!" Angela screamed as she twisted around. Accustomed to weightlessness, she'd forgotten to hold onto her hard point. Now twisting on the end of the lanyard, Angela fought to hold the looped cable in her right hand while she tried and failed to reach the crossbar with the other.

She kept swinging back and forth like a slow-motion pendulum.

Angela glanced down toward the planet. For the first time in her career, she gained a sudden fear of heights. If the tether failed now, she would be thrown clear of the station.

Angela thought her jet pack had sufficient compressed gas to return her to the ISS. Likely, the SAFER module could arrest the outbound velocity and fly her back, but considering the dire consequences of failure, she sure as hell didn't want to find out.

She had latched the tether to the spacesuit's left hip. Now Angela hung from it, teeter-tottering like a human see-saw. She held the large loop of cable in her right hand. As she oscillated back and forth, she tried to latch onto the end of the array arm with the closest available limb, alternating between her hands and feet. The glove bounced off of the white metal bar, knocking her upper body away from it, so she tried to hook a heel over it. On the fourth iteration of this insane see-sawing motion, she finally hooked a calf over the nearest structural member. A moment later, she draped her other leg over the bar as well.

Angela panted heavily, trying to catch her breath.

Now hanging upside down from the back of her knees, Angela looked like the world's highest trapeze artist. Heart racing, she peered overhead, looking down on the planet below. The cable had started to move in earnest. Loop after loop of wire fell from her right hand, each a little faster than the previous.

She had to slow it down. Otherwise, the line might snap when it reached the end.

Angela looked at the palm of her suit's left glove, eyeing the insulation and the white duct tape that held the extra padding that she had added. Fortunately, her frantic attempts to grab the end of the array arm hadn't dislodged any of it.

"NASA engineering at its finest."

She grabbed the cable. As the fingers of the glove closed around the wire, the thick padding made it feel like she was holding a vibrating softball. The tremors manifested as noise in her suit. Its pitch raised an octave as the cable continued to pick up speed. She squeezed her hand and the frequency of the vibrations leveled and then began to fall off a bit.

"It's working, Nate!"

She felt a soft tug, and then a puff of insulation and tape sprayed from her glove. At the same time, she heard a hiccup in the whine of the sliding cable.

"Shit!" she yelled. "Have to watch for those splices, Commander."

She shook her head. The spacesuit's gloves were very durable, but if she'd been stupid enough to try to brake the cable's momentum against the glove's unprotected palms, that cable splice might have torn out a chunk of it and exposed Angela to the vacuum of space.

"The glove's makeshift padding just paid off," she reported to the voice recorder.

"I sure as hell hope nobody ever hears this, because if you're listening to my stupid ramblings, it means you've arrived to find the station empty but for a mouse carcass and this damned smartphone filled with my babbling voice."

"Here comes another splice." Angela released the wire and let it pass.

"Damnit!" she shouted. "The wire took off the instant I released it."

Angela grabbed the rapidly accelerating cable.

"That whine you're likely hearing is the braided line rubbing against the glove's added padding."

Angela bore down on the wire, squeezing it. The droning dropped an octave as she managed to slow the line. Being stretched between it and the station, she started to feel like a torture victim on the rack.

"Hang on," she said with a grunt. "It's really starting to pull now, and there's another splice coming."

The whining continued to ramp up. Heat began building in the glove. Then a fine spray started to radiate from the padding.

"Crap! It's melting the insulation."

Angela grunted with exertion as she fought to keep the wire's acceleration in check.

"Feels like my damn knees are going to pop out of socket. I don't think I can hold it much—" Then a scream burst through her lips as the next splice tore at the padding, launching a fresh gout of insulation and tape. "Damn it! I didn't let go quick enough! Another splice nicked me."

A whistle rang out, and her ears popped as the suit's internal atmospheric pressure dropped.

"Shit! Got a hole in my glove!"

Angela checked the suit's gauges.

"Not too bad. It's small. I'll tape it in a minute." She paused, grunting as she fought to rein in the cable's inertia. "Have to stop this damned thing from snapping off."

The last loop fell away.

The muscles in her hand cramped painfully. She screamed through gnashed teeth. Angela could feel the veins in her neck bulging with exertion.

Suddenly, the glove's insulation burst into flames. The escaping mix of oxygen and melted foam burned like a tiny rocket plume, spewing from her glove like Iron Man in flight.

"Shit! Hand's on fire!"

The wire snapped taut and then went slack.

"Please, don't tell me the damned counterweight broke off!" Angela said as she snatched a roll of duct tape from her utility belt. With her flame-free hand, she wrapped up the glove. The fire extinguished, and the leak sealed.

Angela looked up. To the limit of her vision, the cable looked loose, its long, wavering curls disappearing toward the scrolling ocean below.

She squinted her eyes, trying to make out the wire's distant end, but it was too far away to discern. Then she saw the angle of the cable's curls starting to diminish.

A moment later, the line went taut again.

Watching its slow bounce, Angela nodded triumphantly.

"We're good! It held!"

A few moments later, Angela returned to the base of the support arm. She inspected the insulated clamps she'd used to secure the cable to the structure. She'd left the wire disconnected from the station's electrical system, so that a partial slip of the cable wouldn't destroy one of only two still functioning connectors.

With her well-insulated hand, she grabbed the barrel of the connector's live end. A frown pursed her lips as she looked at the label riveted to its side:

C819

It was the same connector that she and Bill had been working on when all this had started.

Thinking about the first experiment's melted wire, Angela closed her eyes and uttered a silent prayer. Then she said, "I'm about to connect the cable, so if this is the last recording and you've been trying to figure out what the hell caused that big burn mark on the port end of the array truss ... Well, now you know."

Angela turned her head sideways and squinted her eyes as she looked askance at connector C819, slowly inching the two pieces together. Just before they made contact, the connectors glowed as a blindingly bright arc vaporized a splinter of conductive material that floated between the two halves. Then the connector clicked home, and the light died.

"Still here," she reported. "We're definitely making electricity. Got a flash during the connection. Good thing I'm wearing Depends," she said with a relieved chuckle.

"Now that it's bonded to the system, everything looks good ... so far. Won't know until I try to fire up the power management computer."

Angela took a deep breath and then let it out in a long, exhausted sigh.

"But that's going to have to wait a little longer. According to my calculations, that first cable will only generate half of the electricity I need."

She looked at the second spool. Three hundred feet from her current location, the other half of her tether experiment waited at the opposite end of the array truss structure. The spool floated lazily, attached to the only other support arm that still had a functional power connector.

Now that she'd finished attaching the first tether, it was time to do the second one.

She checked her gauges. Even factoring in the air lost during the leak, she should have enough.

Just.

Angela sighed again. "One down, one to go."

~

An hour later and now with partially melted insulation and scorched duct tape wrapped around both of her gloves, Angela floated out of the airlock and back into the dark station. The suit's pulsing red warning light intermittently illuminated her blue-tinged face as she struggled for breath.

She tried and failed to release the helmet visor, but all of the padding wrapped around her gloves made it impossible.

Trapped in her spacesuit, Angela felt the tenuous thread of consciousness threatening to snap—an event that would certainly lead to her death.

The sweat-soaked loose strand of hair floated into her right eye again, but Angela didn't have the breath to blow it out of the way.

Weak light streamed from her tumbling flashlight, sweeping its yellow beam through the dark interior of the station. Writhing and fighting with the layers of duct tape that were fouling the right glove's locking cuff, she ricocheted against the far wall. Angela would happily tear off the tape with her teeth, but if she could do that, she wouldn't be in the throes of suffocation induced by a depleted O2 supply.

Angela had to get a hand free! She frantically beat the gloves against one another. Finally, a piece of insulation flew away. She tore at the freshly exposed edge. Then the left glove twisted off. Angela slung it aside. The sticky mess adhered to a nearby bulkhead.

She opened the visor.

Steam boiled out of the helmet.

Angela took a deep, gasping breath of the station's cold air.

"Thank you," she croaked.

For long minutes, Angela floated motionlessly in the middle of the station, her fogged breath gouging steam-filled columns into its icy atmosphere.

Gradually, color returned to her grayed-out peripheral vision.

With slow, lethargic movements, Angela twisted off the other glove. Finally, she unlatched the helmet and lifted it clear.

The ISS's atmosphere had gotten pretty rank since the battery bank had died yesterday, but cold, smelly oxygen was better than none.

"I'm back in the station," she said with steamed breath, updating the ever-listening recorder.

Angela made a sour face. "I'm not sure which smells worse, me or the inside of this station."

She sniffed the steam rising from the collar of her spacesuit. "Yep, I win. Serious case of monkey butt here."

Angela grabbed the tumbling flashlight and floated over to Nate's spacesuit habitat and slid the visor open. His pink nose and white whiskers emerged out of the helmet's shadowed interior.

Angela smiled weakly as the rest of the fat little mouse floated into view. "There's my buddy. How do you keep gaining weight? I have you on strict rations, mister. Got a little stash you're keeping to yourself?"

Utterly exhausted, Angela shivered as she rubbed her neck, rocking her head side to side. The vertebrae popped audibly. She took another deep breath and then crinkled her nose. "Love what you've done with the place. What a wonderful smell you've created, Nate."

Angela finished wriggling out of her spacesuit.

She plucked the white rodent from the air and placed him on her right shoulder. He seemed to enjoy riding along with her when she moved around the station. If she didn't bring him, he'd often squeak incessantly.

Angela tucked the iPhone under the waistband of her pants. The voice recorder app was still running. Nate gripped the wet fabric of her steaming hoodie as they glided down the tube toward the electrical controls. Once there, Angela plucked the mouse from her shoulder. He floated next to her as she stared at the power management and distribution computer.

"I left the PMAD's main breakers off. Even though it is used to dealing with the fluctuating electricity supplied by the solar arrays, I wanted to be here when it started to receive the feed from the two tethers. That way, if something went really wrong, I *might* have a chance to shut it off before the whole damn thing melts."

She extended a trembling hand toward the breaker. "Well, if this works and it doesn't kill me, I'll have the world's first tether-powered space station."

Angela swallowed and then said, "Here goes." She flipped the lever. It snapped into the on position with a loud click.

And nothing happened.

"Please," she whispered.

Suddenly, an amber LED on the panel flashed to life. Then another group of them lit up as well, these all green!

"Houston, we have power!"

After clapping her hands and giving Nate a miniature high-five, she moved to the distribution panel. First, she turned on the station's lighting circuit.

Angela squinted as beautiful, glorious light flooded the module. A moment later, she reached for environmental control, but before she could activate it, a loud click echoed through the module, and the lights died. Angela yanked her hand back, but the sound had come from the PMAD. Its amber LED now flashed furiously. A message popped up next to the light:

"Insufficient electricity for current demand."

"Shit!"

Angela checked the power levels. Her improvised dynamo was generating usable electricity, but not enough to run the whole ISS. She would have to shut down and close off most of the station.

"Well, Nate, I don't think it'll matter much to you, but our living space is about to get a *lot* smaller."

CHAPTER 15

A skinny man ran down Boulder's Main Street. Silver hairs highlighted his red and brown beard. The man reached up and pressed the side of one of the Bluetooth earbuds.

"Tell me another joke, Siri."

A few seconds later, the jogger began laughing. "Good one."

Vaughn long-pressed the headset's button again. After the short chime, he said, "Siri, what's on my calendar for the day?"

"Sky Captain, you have lunch with the President at eleven. I also see dinner with Marilyn Monroe scheduled for five PM."

"Thank you, Siri."

Another voice chimed up. "Three miles completed. Total time: twenty-six minutes, thirty-nine seconds. Average pace: eight fifty-three per mile."

"Enough of that shit," Vaughn said. He slowed to a walk, two fingers pressed to his carotid. "Yep, still ticking." He lowered his hand and checked his watch. "Holy shit! I'm late."

Picking up the pace, he jogged another block.

"There it is!"

Having lost its cargo unknown miles before arriving at this desti-nation, a long passenger train had come to a stop in the middle of

Boulder. Ahead of Vaughn, its silver railcar straddled Main Street. The purring sound of a well-muffled, top-of-the-line generator came from the far side of the train.

Vaughn stepped onto the stairs at the near end of the railcar. He pressed a red button, and the 1950s-styled diner car's glass door slid open with a rude-sounding burp of compressed air.

He stepped into the air-conditioned space and raised a hand. "Hey, Jack. Sorry I'm late." He looked beyond the row of booths. Spotting his goal, Vaughn walked briskly through the railcar. He waved dismissively. "Don't get up. I'll be right back."

Reaching the car's far end, Singleton opened the large refrigerator. Cool, fogged air poured out, chilling his sweat-covered body. His arm disappeared into the appliance's dark interior and then emerged with a ceramic-capped green bottle. After a moment's consideration, he reached in and dug out a second one.

Vaughn stepped up to the brightly colored jukebox. He grabbed a coin from the stack on top of the machine and dropped it into the slot. It fell through arcane innards sounding like a gambling token bouncing through a Pachinko machine. Vaughn selected a song completely at odds with the diner's 1950s motif.

Bouncing his head to the hard rocking beats of Metallica's *Fuel*, Vaughn walked back to the diner's only inhabited booth. He plopped down onto the bench opposite its celebrity occupant. Vaughn placed the two beers on the table, then grabbed the closest one and opened it. The bottle's rubber-lined ceramic cap lifted with a satisfying *pop*.

Singleton raised the pint to his lips and took a long draw from the ice-cold beer.

His eyes widened, and he lowered the bottle. "Sorry. How rude of me." He slid the second beer across the table's white Formica top. "There you go, Jack."

The life-sized cardboard silhouette of President John F. Kennedy didn't move. It just continued staring blankly over Singleton's head.

Vaughn frowned. He reached over the table and grabbed the shoulder of the cardboard man. After a little coaxing, the half-folded likeness of JFK now smiled right at Vaughn.

"That's better, Jack. Always important to maintain eye contact." He gestured with the beer bottle. "Drink up."

Vaughn took another long swallow. "Ahh," he said, then burped loudly and rubbed his flattened abs.

The day after the aborted suicide attempt, Vaughn had woken in a comfortable bed and with a clear head for the first time in weeks. He'd started running then. In the subsequent six weeks, he'd lost sixty pounds. Fortunately, the Disappearance had only taken living animals. There was plenty of canned meat and, in the areas where electricity still worked, lots of the frozen variety as well. His diet consisted solely of lean meats and canned veggies. Sore muscles and sugar cravings filled those first days, but since then, things had gotten better. Even his outlook had improved. He'd struck up this friendship with the dead president.

Vaughn raised both eyebrows and gave the head of state a knowing grin. "Did I mention I'm having dinner with an old friend of yours?"

Suddenly, the ceiling's indirect lighting flickered. Outside, the purring generator sputtered and then backfired. The lights continued to strobe, and the music from the jukebox got louder.

"Goddamn it!"

Vaughn slammed the beer bottle down hard enough to send a gout of it spraying across the cardboard cut-out. An undignified rivulet of the bubbling yellow liquid ran down the President's face.

Then flickering yellow light flared up outside, backlighting the curtains at the end of the booth.

"What the hell?"

Singleton brusquely swept aside the ruffled cloth. Through the window, he saw flames crawling across the generator he'd placed behind the railcar. Then the fire jumped to a puddle under the small machine. The flames tumbled and hopped their way up a rivulet. Vaughn's wide eyes traced the liquid to its source. Ten feet away, it connected to a much larger puddle beneath the 5000-gallon gasoline tanker that he had jury-rigged to the generator.

"Oh shit!"

Vaughn jumped from the booth and sprinted toward the exit. Just as he reached for the red button to open the glass door, he heard a loud whoosh.

Suddenly, a wall of flame filled the gap between the two cars.

Vaughn snatched his hand back. Now bright yellow light flickered through all of the curtains on that end of the railcar.

James Hetfield's voice blared from the jukebox, singing about his need for fuel and fire and it being that which he desired.

"No, no! I don't desire that at all!" Vaughn said as he ran through the dining car.

Reaching the far end, he found fire now filling that gap as well. In mere seconds, burning fuel had engulfed all but one side of the diner. And considering that the street sloped toward the flame-free side of the railcar, Vaughn knew it wouldn't be long before the leaking fuel worked its way to that side as well. Judging by the smell of gasoline fumes, it probably already had.

The temperature began rising in the long, metal box.

Each of the panoramic windows on the flame-free side of the car stood roughly four feet wide by four feet tall, offering a view down Main Street. He ran to the nearest one and slammed his elbow into the glass. It bounced off painfully but with no effect.

Vaughn could hear Mark chiding him about the jury-rigged plumbing he'd used to connect the tanker truck to the generator. Two months after his death, the man still haunted Vaughn's thoughts, lending his voice to Singleton's every inner doubt.

"Not now, Hennessy!" Vaughn yelled.

He looked around, desperate to find something with which to hit the glass.

Singleton ran back to the center of the diner and snatched up the President's beer. He reared back and then whipped the bottle at the window like a major league pitcher throwing high heat. It slammed into the glass with a satisfying crack. However, it was the bottle that broke, not the window.

"Son of a bitch!"

Remembering something he'd seen behind the bar, Vaughn ran back to that end of the diner car. A metal meat-tenderizing hammer sat behind the counter. He snatched it up and ran back to the nearest window. He struck the glass with the tool and still it didn't give.

Outside, flames began to lick up from beneath the railcar.

"Really?!"

He had to get out right now! If the gasoline beneath the train didn't cook him first, the few thousand gallons of it sitting in that tanker would soon blow him and this diner to smithereens.

In sync with the rapid-fire beat of the unfortunately named song, Vaughn pounded the window with the faceted face of the mallet like a manic bass drum player on speed, but the glass stubbornly refused to shatter.

He wiped sweat from his forehead. Remembering something he'd read online, Vaughn pushed the tapered point of the mallet's metal handle into the glass.

Suddenly, the window shattered into thousands of pebble-sized shards. Then he saw a red handle on its now empty frame. It read: EMERGENCY EXIT - PULL TO JETTISON.

Vaughn shook his head. "Idiot!"

From underneath the railcar, flames began licking at the bottom of the opening.

He took a step back and then jumped through the window. Vaughn landed hard on the road surface, tripping and falling to his hands and knees.

Wanting to get away from the 5000-gallon tanker, he leaped to his feet and began running down Main, sprinting between its twinned line of parallel parked cars.

Brilliant light washed out the scene and reality seemed to skip forward a beat.

Vaughn found himself lying upside down between the plastic bumpers of two vehicles. He had no idea how he'd gotten there. One moment he'd been running, the next he was looking up at an upside-down Colorado license plate, a ringing sound filling his ears.

Vaughn rolled onto his side. Finally, he got his feet under him and stood. The world began to spin. His knees buckled, dropping Vaughn onto the car. He felt its hood crumple under his now bony butt.

Dazed, he scanned the scene with blinking eyes. Shattered glass glittered under most of the cars that lined Main. Behind them, all of the storefronts had blown in.

Farther up the street, the jagged metal edge of the dining car's roof pointed skyward, its top opened like a treasure chest. The explosion of the tanker had finished the job started by Vaughn. All of the rail-car's stubborn glass now decorated the street.

A tattered and partially burned effigy of President Kennedy lay in the middle of the road between Singleton and the wrecked railcar.

Behind the train, the 5000-gallon tanker continued to burn. A roiling column of orange fire and black smoke raced into the sky under a spreading mushroom cloud.

Vaughn felt something wet on his neck. Probing the area below his ears, his hand came away bloody. Not too much, probably nothing worse than a couple of ruptured eardrums. Over the ringing, he could hear the inferno's roar, so at least he wasn't deaf.

Standing unsteadily, Vaughn started walking up the street, away from the blast zone. A minute later, he entered the drugstore at the near right corner of the next block. Inside, Singleton secured some gauze and cotton balls along with some antiseptic ointment. After tending to his bloodied knees and wiping the same from his ears and neck, he walked to the cooler, steering clear of the dark freezer. He'd learned the hard way not to open those. The smell of rotted meat would chase him out of the building. Instead, he opened the beverage cooler and grabbed a beer.

In his best Forrest Gump impression, he said, "Momma always said warm beer is better than no beer." He no longer drank as heavily as he had after arriving in Denver. Since the aborted suicide, he'd narrowed it down to a couple of beers a day, but it wasn't every day that you survived a brush with an exploding tanker truck.

Vaughn raised the bottle an inch. "I'll drink to that."

Smiling, he sauntered between the shadowed rows of product shelves. As he neared the cash register, he held up a quarter—his tender for all things—and tossed it onto the countertop. It ricocheted and bounced off of a newspaper. The age-yellowed USA Today fell open, exposing a back-page article.

Vaughn froze with the bottle raised to his mouth. Warm fluid ran down his shirt, but he didn't notice. The article's headline was all he could see. Its words released a cascading epiphany two months in the making.

Printed in small black letters, a familiar slogan served as the article's headline:

"What Can Brown Do For You?"

Beneath that, the subtitle read:

"Commander Angela Brown to Perform Marathon Spacewalk Today."

The forgotten beer fell to the floor and shattered. Vaughn stared open-mouthed at the name as he recalled Director McCree's no longer cryptic final words: *You have to rescue Commander Brown!*

"Oh, *fuck!*"

CHAPTER 16

Her mother used to call Angela's morning hair a rat's nest.

"If you could only see me now, Mom."

She'd left her hair untied that morning. Already two inches longer than on Day Zero, it floated around her head in a giant halo like a reddish-brown, straight-haired Afro.

Clad in tiny blue and pink diapers made from towelettes, four pink mice clambered through her hair. Shortly after birth, the little tykes had taken to nesting in Angela's auburn locks.

She looked across to their mother. "Really, Nadine? First, you fool me into calling you Nate. Then you leave me with your kids. Are you sure you aren't a man?"

In response, Nadine hiked up her right rear leg and started scratching behind her ear. The twitching strokes sent the furry white mother of four tumbling across the JEM.

An alarm began its warbling wail.

"Already?" Angela said.

Running fingers through her hair, she picked out the little stowaways and held them gingerly in her hand. Pushing off the nearest surface, she floated across the module and grabbed the clear plastic box that floated near the far corner.

Angela pried off the lid and placed the tiny pink mice into it.

The siren continued to wail.

She spotted Nadine. The little fart was swimming away from her with all her might.

"Oh no, you don't, missy."

In dingy sweatpants and a hoodie stuffed with scavenged makeshift insulation, Angela pushed off a piece of equipment. She quickly closed the gap, overtaking the fleeing mouse. Angela grabbed its wriggling tail and pulled the squealing rodent toward the box. A moment later the mouse floated inside the transparent enclosure. Nadine's twitching pink nose protruded from one of the box's many air holes.

"It's for your own good, Nadine. Remember what happened to Mabel—sorry, I mean Mack. A Mabel couldn't very well have gotten you pregnant, now, could she?" Angela pointed toward the closed hatch at the far side of the JEM. "I have to go in there, and I can't bring you. It's way too cold." She shook her head. "I can't have you, Nate Junior, or one of his siblings chewing into another power coupling."

Nadine didn't reply, just kept sniffing the air.

"I don't want to do another space burial." She also didn't want to think about how her stomach rumbled and her mouth watered every time she remembered the smell of cooked mouse meat.

Angela gave Nadine's plump little body a longing glance.

No, she didn't want to think about that at all.

Angela turned away from Nadine and her brood. A shiver that had nothing to do with the room's chilly temperature ran down her spine. She opened the hatch, and the cold air that poured from the opening deepened the chill. She passed into the darkness and closed the hatch behind her. Angela pulled the hoodie over her head. As she cinched its drawstrings, her puffed hair left a nice cushion of warmth around her head. She'd fashioned a scarf from a pair of white towels. Seeing her breath fog, Angela pulled the scarf over her face. Next, she donned mittens made from multiple layers of Teddy's athletic socks. From the smell of them, Teddy had worn each pair more than once.

Two months ago, on Day Zero, they'd been running short on food and other goods. NASA had slated a resupply mission for the following week, but of course, it had never come. Over the six weeks since Mabel or Mack had met his end, Angela had often regretted giving the mouse a space burial, especially so after she ran out of protein supplements.

Her mouth began to water.

She pushed the thought from her mind and opened the far hatch. Passing into the Tranquility module, she closed the door. Angela pulled off the hoodie as she drifted into the Cupola's sun-warmed interior.

She pressed a button, and the alarm finally stopped. Then she reset it for 1200 Zulu. She reached for the ham radio volume knob and then, seeing her reflection, pulled up short.

"Oh, God ..."

Angela felt a lump trying to form in her throat. Through tear-muddled eyes, she stared at her all-too-skinny arm. No longer hidden beneath the camouflaging bulk of the hoodie, its bulbous elbow and bony forearm looked like something out of a World War II concentration camp photo.

The ever-present unending pang of hunger excoriated the lining of her stomach as if digging at it with a melon baller. The memory of the smell of cooked mouse swam to the surface once more.

In spite of the warm sunlight falling on her sallow cheeks, Angela shivered again. Shaking it off, she grasped the radio's volume knob and turned it up.

"... from the International Space Station," her recorded voice said. "Please reply on this frequency at twelve hundred Zulu or twenty-four hundred Zulu. That's noon and midnight Greenwich Mean Time. I will monitor the frequency both times each day."

Angela hit the switch that stopped the looped audio. Then she released the transmit button. Crackling static began to stream through the speakers of the headphones. She plucked the thin headset out of the air and slid it over her matted, greasy hair.

Through the Cupola's main window, Angela watched a snow-capped range slide under the space station. Then mountains gave way to plains. Denver sat nestled between them. It was only in the last couple of weeks that the atmosphere had cleared enough to get this good of a view.

In the Cupola's main window, Angela glimpsed the reflection of her gaunt, emaciated face superimposed over the planet. The entire image wavered as tears began to stack up in her vision.

"Why do you keep going to the same dry well?"

Angela shifted her eyes to the radio. "Why bother?" she said, but then she sighed and positioned the end of the headset's mic boom in front of her dry, cracked lips. Shaking her head, she pressed the transmit key.

"This is Angela Brown. Is anybody out there?"

CHAPTER 17

The vehicle's big tires squealed and barked in protest of the sliding stop. Vaughn had crested a small rise to find another cluttered intersection blocking his path.

After a brief pause, the front tires turned right, and the Hummer crept over the curb. The big military four-by-four crushed a cactus and then dropped onto the parking lot of Boulder Pawn.

As Vaughn negotiated the obstacles, the director's final words ran through his mind in a constant loop.

You have to rescue Commander Brown!

Vaughn shook his head. He didn't remember seeing anything about the ISS on his mother's computer, but of course, he hadn't been looking for news of that sort then or anytime since. The newspaper article he'd seen today had been on the back page, but still…

He gnashed his teeth. "Damnit, Vaughn!" he said with a growl. "You should've figured it out!"

He raised his eyebrows. "Why *only* Commander Brown? She was up there with other astronauts."

Vaughn pursed his lips as he considered the possibility. The woman was the station's commander. Maybe the director had meant that she would need their help getting the entire crew down.

"But why? Why would they need help." Vaughn paused, looking down at the steering wheel. "Why would they need ... me?"

The truck eased over the far curb and then dropped back onto the road. Vaughn pursed his lips and punched the accelerator.

"Maybe they don't. They could already be on the ground!" He smiled. "Either way, I'm not alone!"

Vaughn frowned. "But if they landed ... Where? When? How in the hell will I find them?"

Along with the director's final words, these questions had been bouncing around his mind since he'd spotted the article.

Vaughn shook his head again. "One step at a time, Singleton. Contact the space station, and then go from there."

Fortunately, there happened to be a place suitable for the task right there in Denver.

If Vaughn couldn't get answers from the ISS, he'd have to broaden his search. Houston? Florida ... Russia?

He sighed. "One step at a time," he repeated. "Make the call first. If that doesn't work ..." He frowned as the questions tried to resume their manic loop. "Stop it, jackass!"

Vaughn smiled self-consciously. Then he patted the steering wheel. "Not alone, after all!"

Several excursions later, he zoomed past a green sign that read: Buckley Air Force Base 1 Mile. Vaughn reached the exit and guided the truck onto the base. A few blocks after that, he brought the Hummer to a screeching halt in front of a complex of buildings.

Vaughn had noticed this fenced-off facility after he'd parked the helicopter in the adjacent Colorado National Guard hangar. The main building sat inside its own security cordon with the words Aerospace Data Facility scrolled across its façade.

He knew that the US National Reconnaissance Office controlled America's complement of spy satellites from this facility and two other locations, so he had reasoned that NASA must have an office here, too.

Armed with a crowbar and a flashlight, Vaughn worked his way into the labyrinth building. He soon found an entire section of it dedicated to NASA. Then he located a communications console that sported a three-ring binder that listed several frequencies for the International Space Station.

"Bingo!"

The electricity had failed, but Vaughn had come prepared for that. He set up a portable generator in a remote office that had an external window. Then he ran a power cable up to the console. Vaughn removed the cabinet's back panel. Several minutes later, he finished connecting the power.

Vaughn jumped to his feet and then flipped on the panel's dedicated breaker switch. Cooling fans whirred to life. He craned his neck to see the front of the control panel. Lights now shone from the radio's face.

He pumped his fist in the air. "Yes!"

Vaughn donned the console's headset and dialed in the first listed frequency. He didn't hear anything. The headset sounded completely dead. After verifying that it was indeed fully plugged into the console, he tried the next frequency.

Still nothing.

The headphones shouldn't be completely silent. They should emit something. He scanned the console's myriad knobs and then shook his head. "Jeez, Vaughn."

He twisted the volume knob up from zero. Faint, intermittent static suddenly tickled his ears. He turned the knob farther right and the sound grew louder.

Vaughn rolled his eyes. "Shut it, Hennessy. Not now."

After a deep breath and a hard swallow, he pressed the transmit button.

"ISS, this is Army Captain Vaughn Singleton. Come in, over."

Only clicks, ticks, and another short burst of static answered him.

Vaughn tried three more times with the same results. Then he decided to go back to the first frequency. He hadn't had the volume up when he'd tried that one.

Through squinted eyes, he watched as the last of the tiny digits rolled into place. Suddenly a roaring, ear-splitting voice exploded from the radio. Vaughn batted off the headset before he even registered that he was swiping at it.

The thing crashed onto the console with an echoing thud, and the female voice stopped.

"Oh shit!"

The woman started talking again. Vaughn scooped up the headset and slid it back on. He couldn't understand her distorted words. The high volume rendered them indiscernible. She stopped talking just as Vaughn turned it down.

He mashed the transmit key. "Is this Commander Brown?"

"This is Commander Angela Brown broadcasting from the International Space Station."

As soon as she'd said her name, Vaughn started pumping his fist in the air again. He reached for the transmit key again, but the commander wasn't finished.

"I am alone and stranded on the ISS with no descent module, no way to get to the surface. Please reply on this frequency at twelve hundred Zulu or twenty-four hundred Zulu. That's noon and midnight Greenwich Mean Time. I will monitor the frequency both times each day."

Vaughn's shoulders slumped, but the grin stayed on his face. "I can't believe it! She's alive."

He pulled out his phone and checked the time. The last cell tower had dropped offline a month ago, but he imagined the smartphone's clock was still pretty accurate. According to its display, the current local time was eleven AM, which meant it was 1800 Zulu.

Or was it?

Had his phone automatically sprung forward? Had it shifted to Mountain Daylight Saving Time? Vaughn didn't know. If the time was eleven MDT, then it was currently 1700 Zulu. The commander would listen for a reply in six or seven hours.

There wasn't enough fuel for the generator to run that long.

If … No, *when* the commander came on line, even if it was sooner, Vaughn wanted to be monitoring this radio. And now that he had it powered up, he was loath to shut down the radio.

"Shit!"

After a final forlorn glance at the console, Vaughn held up a finger. Employing his best Schwarzenegger impression, he said, "I'll be back."

An hour later, the Hummer skidded back into its parking spot. Vaughn dragged a couple of gas cans into the makeshift generator room down the hall from NASA. He topped off the machine's fuel tank and then returned to the radio room. He dropped back into the console's chair and slid the headset over his ears.

The commander's recorded voice repeated its message. Vaughn smiled and sighed. He thought about his cardboard friends. "No offense, Jack and Marilyn, but recorded or not, it's good to hear the voice of a real, living human being."

Vaughn leaned back in the comfortable armchair and opened the newspaper he'd taken from the drugstore. Apparently, on the day of the Disappearance, Commander Angela Brown and Major Bill Peterson were scheduled to do a historic EVA. The spacewalk's anticipated duration would smash the current record for an EVA completed by a female astronaut.

At the end of the page, USA Today invited Vaughn to continue reading the article on page B-12.

He turned to the specified page and then his eyebrows raised.

"Wow! Who knew?"

Beautiful dark eyes—probably brown, but impossible to tell from the black and white image—stared out from a smiling face. The caption above it said, "What Can Brown Do For You?"

"Me," Vaughn said. Then he looked around self-consciously. After a moment, he shook his head and laughed.

For the last two months, only Siri had answered his questions. And without a data connection, her responses were frustratingly limited. However, Vaughn had reasoned that talking to her was a damn sight better than conversing with a green-haired volleyball or even a well-dressed mannequin, although in a lingerie store, Vaughn had seen a few of the latter that elicited a disturbing desire to do more than talk. He'd also started to worry that, eventually, Jack and Marilyn would start answering him. Fortunately, he hadn't slipped that far … yet.

With a quick head shake, Vaughn pushed out the thoughts. He looked into the eyes at the center of the black and white image. "Hello, Commander Brown. Pleased to meet you." He nodded. "Captain Vaughn Singleton at your service. How may I help?"

"Oh, that's right. You need saving," he said with exaggerated understanding. "That's what the director told me." Then Vaughn's eyes dropped, as did his shoulders. "I was just too stupid to understand, too damned self-absorbed." He shook his head. "Sorry."

After a long moment, his face brightened. Vaughn looked up with a smile. "But I think I know how to help, how to rescue you! When you hear it, you'll probably think I'm crazy, but it's actually something I've thought about doing just for fun."

Vaughn's smile faltered as the commander's message repeated. He tilted his head. "But why don't you have a way down? What happened to your descent module?"

He sat up in his chair. "And for that matter, why are you alone?"

Then a possibility occurred to him. "The rest of the crew must have abandoned station, taken the module." He nodded slowly, his eyes becoming unfocused. "She got left behind."

Vaughn frowned. He knew how that felt.

"But why did any of them evacuate? NASA had to know that everyone hit by the light had vanished. The director had said as much."

Another realization slammed into Vaughn.

The presence of a looped recording was not proof of life. The woman could have succumbed to any number of maladies in the two months since the Disappearance. Vaughn knew all too well that suicide sat high up on that grim list. He was a self-centered loner who generally disliked people—at least that was what he'd always told himself. On the face of it, he was the ideal candidate for this solo act. However, suicide had almost claimed him.

After a long moment, Vaughn shook his head and leaned back in the chair. He checked his watch. In a few hours, he'd know the answer to that and more.

He hoped.

Oh, how he hoped.

~

Vaughn rubbed his eyes. Then he blinked them in the silent darkness, trying to remember where he was. He shifted his weight, and a faint metallic squeak came from beneath him. Groping in the dark, he discovered he was sitting in an office chair.

Vaughn shot to his feet.

"Oh shit!"

He'd fallen asleep!

Too quiet...

"The generator!"

NASA's part of the building had no outside windows. However, a modicum of light shone under its main entry door.

Vaughn started to run toward the luminous sliver, but in the darkness, he tripped over a linear shadow that he belatedly recognized as the generator's power cord. He sprawled head first into the door, knocking it open.

Golden rays of a setting sun shone through the windows of an adjacent room. Rubbing his head, Vaughn squinted aching eyes. Finally, he surged out of the dust-filled radiant beams and into the dark hallway beyond.

Probing with his hands, he followed the power cable to the generator room. He pulled open its door, and another solar blast burned into his eyes.

Vaughn squinted against the glare and ran to the west-facing windows. He grabbed one of the deposited fuel cans. After a quick refill and several yanks on a reluctant cord, he finally had the generator running again.

When Vaughn trotted back into NASA's office, he saw light shining from the radio. He stepped to the console and then slid the headset over his ears.

The woman's voice had died.

Vaughn frantically checked all of the knobs.

The volume was up. He should be able to hear her!

"Shit!"

Vaughn stared at the radio's glowing face, unsure of what to do.

Had the electricity surged when the generator died?

Had he fried the receiver?!

"No, no, no," he whispered. "Please, no."

Vaughn swung his body around to the back of the console.

Lying on the floor, he stared into the cabinet's dark interior, trying to see any signs that some component had burned out or if a breaker had tripped.

Suddenly, a crackling pop came from the top of the console.

Vaughn froze.

"This is Angela Brown," said a frail, raspy feminine voice. "Is anybody out there?"

CHAPTER 18

Angela released the transmit key and shook her head. Who the hell was she fooling? Nobody was ever going to answer the call.

Tears flowed freely now. Pooled liquid completely covered her eyes, making it look as if water had flooded the entire Cupola. Angela didn't bother batting away the moisture.

"Enough already."

Through the murk, she watched her wavering hand reach for the radio's power button.

Just as Angela's extended index finger touched the round switch, a short burst of static crackled in her ears.

"Commander Brown?" a male voice said tentatively. "Can you hear me?"

Angela yanked her hand from the radio so quickly that the movement sent her tumbling. The rolling motion of her body ripped the headset from her ears. A panicked thrashing moment later, she snatched it out of the air and slid them back on.

"Hello?" she said softly, worried she'd imagined the voice, wished it into existence.

"Yes!" the man yelled. "Thank you!"

His shouted words escaped the headset's small ear cups and echoed harshly within the confines of the Cupola. She heard him laugh and bang on something.

Wide-eyed and shocked into silence, Angela stared at the now quiet radio.

Had she just imagined all that?

Had she snapped?

The radio crackled again.

"Oh shit … Hello? Are you there?" The panicked edge in the man's voice pulled Angela out of her trance.

"You're real?" she whispered, as if talking too loud might break the connection.

"What?" the man said in American-accented English.

"Are you real?" Angela said louder, her voice cracking.

"Oh! Sorry. Yes, I'm real. Scout's honor."

Angela shuddered, and then she felt a knot unravel within her. Pent-up breath released in a long sigh.

"Thank you," she said, whispering again. "Thank you, thank you, th-thank you."

Angela began to cry uncontrollably as two months of unrealized emotions poured from her tortured mind and body.

Finally, she took a deep, hitching breath and then sighed.

The man's voice returned, now thick with emotion. "Don't thank me, Commander." He paused and then added, "I should have figured this out a long time ago."

Angela thought she heard tears in the man's words. She dabbed her eyes and then pressed the transmit button. "Who is this?"

"Sorry. Army Captain Vaughn Singleton … uh, at your service … At least, I hope I can be."

"Oh, you already have been, Captain." Angela sniffed and dabbed her eyes and nose. "I can't tell you how *good* it is just to hear another voice."

"You don't have to, Commander," Captain Singleton said. After a long, wet sniff, he added, "I know exactly what you mean."

Angela blinked. The man couldn't be alone, could he?

"Are you there, ma'am?"

She smiled. "Please, call me Angela."

"Okay, Angela." His voice reflected her smile. "Call me Vaughn."

"Hello, Vaughn. Pleased to meet you, sir."

"Pleased to meet you as well, Commander ... I mean, Angela."

She laughed. It felt good—wonderful, actually. Then she heard him laugh, too, and her heart glowed with it.

For a long moment, they laughed together. It was a beautiful sound, the prettiest thing she'd ever heard.

Finally, an awkward silence fell across them. Angela wiped moisture from her eyes—tears of joy this time.

"If you don't mind me asking, Angela, why are you still up there? ... And why alone?"

She had a million questions for Vaughn, but she answered his. Angela explained the evacuation. Told him how the director discovered too late that he should've ordered all of them to remain aboard the ISS. Then she told Vaughn what she'd seen, how the wave had swept across the entire planet.

"So," Angela said. "Where are you, Vaughn? D.C.?"

"D.C.?"

"Yeah, were you in the President's bunker?"

"No ... No ... I'm sorry, Angela, but I don't think anybody on the planet survived." A fresh wave of emotions washed through the man's words. "Everybody died ... Well, other than Mark and I." His voice fell to a whisper. "But now, he's dead, too. It's just me."

Angela floated silently for a long moment. She felt her face flush. Then she shook her head vigorously.

"No! You can't know that! I refuse to accept it, Vaughn. You were on the planet. If you survived, so could others!"

"Actually, I wasn't."

"What? What do you mean?"

"I ... We were in space."

"No," Angela said. "My crew were the only people in orbit that day. After last year's mishap, even the Chinese didn't have anyone up."

"Mark and I weren't in orbit."

165

"That doesn't make sense, Vaughn."

The radio fell silent. Through knitted eyebrows, Angela watched the planet scroll across the Cupola's window.

Finally, the man's voice returned. "It's not my fault."

"What? ... You need to tell me what—"

"I'm trying, Angela! ... Sorry ... Listen, Mark and I were at the Space Power Annex. You probably know him. He was an astronaut, like you. Lieutenant Colonel Mark Hennessy."

Angela nodded. "Yeah. I know ... I knew Mark, but nobody goes up from Glenn Research. It's not a launch facility. It's in the center of Cleveland."

"We didn't go up, not far anyway." After a brief pause, the man told her about a thruster test that they'd performed in NASA's vacuum chamber, about seeing the light and losing touch with everyone. Then he told her about their conversation with Director McCree and how they'd then lost contact with him as well.

Angela's eyes widened. "It was you," she said with dawning realization.

"What?"

"All this time, I've been thinking some people had survived the light because that's the last thing the director told me." She paused, struggling to rein in the emotions that were trying to breach her weakened defenses. Finally, she managed to say, "I'm so sorry I snapped at you, Vaughn. You were the one who saved me."

"Okay," Vaughn said, drawing out the word. "You've lost me, Angela."

"The director was talking with me when he got a call from someone inside the affected zone. I never heard back from him, but that call gave me hope." Angela paused, thinking about the electrical fire and the destroyed solar arrays. "Without that hope, that reason to believe rescue was possible, I never would have made it this long. I would have packed it in six weeks ago, Vaughn."

She dabbed moisture from her eyes.

The man remained silent.

"Don't you see, Captain? You gave me reason to live ... You saved me."

Singleton's voice returned thick with emotion. "It wasn't me, Angela. You have Mark to thank for that."

Something in the man's tone startled her. It didn't sound like just grief for the loss of a friend. It sounded like some deeper issue lay beneath the words, almost like ... self-loathing.

Angela remembered her mental state from a few minutes ago and shook her head. "No, Captain. It's you that survived, regardless of the why or the how. The *idea* of you kept me going, the thought that someone down there would find me." She wiped a dingy, damp sleeve across her eyes. "And *you* did, Vaughn! *You* found me!" She smiled with trembling lips. "Regardless of what happens now, you've already saved me. You, Captain."

After a long silence, his voice returned, this time without the underlying negative tone. "Thank you, Angela." He took a deep breath and then let it out in a long sigh. "I wish I could say that the director had spoken with someone else, that there might be other survivors, but I think you're right. It had to be us. He seemed pretty certain that the light had erased everyone connected to the planet."

"Yeah," Angela said, nodding. "And for all practical purposes, you were in space." As she said the words, a thought occurred to her. "It's like something changed the nature of matter, as if a cascading quantum shift worked its way through the entire planet."

The sound of light chuckling pulled Angela from her thoughts. "Okay ... Uh, sure," Captain Singleton said. "Guess you really are a theoretical physicist."

She blushed. "Pretty much."

Chewing her lower lip, she considered her next question. In spite of her proclamation that the man had already saved her, Angela really did want to get the hell off of this station.

"So, Vaughn. I take it you're not an astronaut?"

A long silence greeted her words. Finally, the man said, "No ... And I already know your next question."

After another pause, his voice returned, this time with a new air of confidence.

"But I think I know how to get you home."

Angela hoisted her eyebrows. "You have my undivided attention, Captain."

He took a deep breath and then said, "Since humankind just … vanished, all of its toys are still lying around, just waiting to be played with."

"Yeah," Angela said in a tone that said 'Go ahead.'

"Well, there's one in particular that I've been thinking about taking for a test spin. And now I have the best reason in the world to do it."

"Okay … and what might that be?"

"Aurora."

"The city? Aren't you close to there now?"

"No, the plane."

"*The* Aurora? You think the spaceplane is real?"

"Yes, Angela. Yes, I do. And I think I know just where to find it."

After Vaughn had told her of his admittedly crazy plan—a plan that Angela thought just might work—she'd told him of her predicament, about her basically nonexistent food supply.

For the last couple of weeks, ketchup seasoned with salt and sugar had provided the majority of her sustenance.

She hadn't wanted to pile on with news of her emaciation, but she was worried that, should preparations take too long, a stroke might debilitate her before the man could get to her.

As he absorbed the news of her situation, Vaughn's words became choked.

"It's not that bad," Angela lied. Then she smiled. "Just wanted you to know not to lollygag. Help me, Obi-Wan Kenobi; you're my only hope."

Vaughn's wonderful laugh echoed in the Cupola. "Okay, Princess Leia. I'll hurry every chance I get."

A few minutes later, Angela floated in a now silent Cupola. She had signed off the radio only moments before, but she already missed the sound of Vaughn's voice.

Smiling, she pulled the hoodie over her head and left the Cupola, its radio idle for the first time in months. She would return tomorrow at their agreed-upon check-in time. For now, she wanted to get back to the JEM. Angela couldn't wait to share the news with Nadine as well as Nate Junior and his siblings.

Hopefully, she wouldn't lick her lips.

CHAPTER 19

Vaughn threw the last bundle into the Hummer's back seat and closed the door before the whole mess could come tumbling out. Then he turned and stared up at his hilltop house. He'd adopted the mansion shortly after his aborted suicide. The big, east-facing home overlooked Boulder from its perch atop a Rocky Mountain foothill. During the last six weeks, Vaughn had grown to love the home, but now he was leaving it all behind.

And that was just fine with him.

Vaughn felt alive!

The conversation with Angela had cleansed him somehow. The sound of her voice, the words and the laughter that they'd shared had lifted two months of dread and loneliness. But Vaughn could still feel it all there, hovering over him like a guillotine held up by an unraveling rope.

Thanks to Vaughn's failure to connect the dots, the woman's very life now hung from that thin, unwinding thread. In Angela's weakened condition, another space station system failure or even something as simple as a minor bacterial infection would snap the line.

Vaughn turned from the house and climbed behind the wheel of the heavily provisioned Hummer. Its engine roared to life. He mashed the accelerator.

He had almost gone straight to the helicopter after sharing his plan with Angela, but his trek across the Plains and its tornadic storm had taught him the value of preparation. The house held all of the hard-to-find provisions that he would need for the trip across the mountains.

As Vaughn guided the vehicle through Boulder's and then Denver's choked streets and highways, he thought over his plan.

He had always wanted to be an astronaut, but as Mark had so adroitly pointed out, Vaughn had never proactively pursued the dream. Well now, astronaut or not, he needed to get into space, and he was pretty sure that he'd find something that would get him there at the Air Force's not-so-secret military base in Southern Nevada, the one popularly known as Area Fifty-One.

Aurora—the spaceplane, not the city—was supposedly a single-stage-to-orbit or SSTO vehicle. If it existed—and Vaughn had several reasons to believe that it did—the plane would be able to take off from a runway and fly into space using nothing but its on-board engines.

Finally, Vaughn guided the military four-by-four through Aurora —the city—and back on to Buckley Air Force Base.

An hour after that, he had transferred the truck's contents into the Black Hawk and topped it off with jet fuel. After putting the helicopter through a thorough pre-flight inspection, Vaughn strapped himself into the pilot's seat. A few minutes later, the Black Hawk climbed into the blue sky.

He turned it west, toward the Rockies.

As the helicopter rolled level, Vaughn stared at the mountain range, shaking his head.

"Shit!"

A miles-thick gray blanket of dark clouds now obscured its upper reaches. The hoary mantle flowed from draws and valleys, pouring out of the mountain range and streaming into the foothills like an ethereal glacier.

Sometime during the day, a late-season snowstorm had spilled over Colorado's back range.

"Wonderful!" Vaughn said, meaning anything but. How in the hell was he going to get around that?

He wasn't. A storm like that might extend a thousand miles north, south, or both. Without satellite or weather radar, he had no idea which way to deviate or how far he might have to go to get around it. He couldn't get over the weather either. The helicopter wasn't pressurized, and it didn't have an oxygen system.

Normally, Vaughn would plot an instrument route through the mountains. However, in the last couple of weeks, all of the electrical grids had finally kicked the bucket. That eliminated land-based navigational aids, leaving only space-based GPS. However, that navigational system required constant updates and tweaking to maintain accurate positional data. The current margin of error was just as likely to guide him into a mountaintop as it was to accurately navigate him through a mountain pass. He didn't want his last words to be, "What's that tree doing in a cloud?" said cloud being of the cumulogranite variety.

Even if he climbed into the storm, trusting the helicopter's de-icing and anti-icing equipment to keep it flyable, he'd still have to maintain an altitude greater than 15,000 feet just to safely clear all of the mountains between Denver and the state's western border. Again, not a good idea without O2.

Vaughn would have to fly through the storm, but he'd have to do it at an altitude that allowed him to see the ground. He would be flying IFR alright, but not Instrument Flight Rules, more like: I Follow Roads. He'd have to keep it low and at a pace that didn't outfly his visibility.

The Black Hawk descended until it was flying just a few hundred feet above Interstate 70. In front of the helicopter, the highway disappeared where it passed into Mount Vernon Canyon.

Vaughn shook his head as he looked at the looming gunmetal clouds and the spreading fan of snow that poured through the canyon's rocky cleft.

"Fuck me."

～

The first flakes began to race around his windshield. Up to this point, Vaughn had been able to maintain better than five hundred feet, but as he entered the falling snow, he guided the helicopter lower, flying ever closer to the surface of Interstate 70.

Visibility continued to degrade.

Vaughn shook his head. "Really?!"

The slopes of the mountains to his left and right began to disappear. Everything above his spinning rotor blades was gone.

A dark horizontal rectangle emerged ahead. Vaughn narrowed his eyes as he tried to make it out, but the object refused to resolve. In the storm's reduced visibility, he couldn't even discern its distance. "What the hell is—?"

The rectangle rapidly expanded in apparent size and shifted from charcoal to green, "Interstate 70 West" emblazoned across its surface.

"Shit!" Vaughn screamed as he yanked back on the stick. The broad sign passed mere inches beneath the chin bubble of his helicopter. In an instant, it was gone along with the rest of the world as the aircraft flew up into the storm clouds.

"Oh shit! Not good!"

Vaughn shoved the stick forward, arresting the climb. Then he initiated a slow descent, his hand taut on the control, ready to stop the downward motion as soon as he could see again.

Normally, he wouldn't even think of trying to reacquire visual contact with the ground while buried in a storm …

In the mountains!

Any other time, he would have climbed away from the surface and turned back toward clear air and Denver.

"Shit," he said through a growl, stretching the word into two syllables. Every muscle in his body tensed in anticipation of the coming ground. Breathing heavily, Vaughn clenched so tightly it felt as if half a yard of seat canvas had climbed up his colon.

Fortunately, the Black Hawk's stability augmentation and attitude hold would keep the helicopter level and on a steady track. Vaughn knew the area. No turns interrupted this stretch of I-70. He just had to hope that he hadn't drifted too far left or right during his panicked climb.

The radar altimeter counted down from two hundred feet.

Vaughn shook his head. "Should've taken the Lear."

He'd seen the jet at Buckley, but that really wasn't an option. Any plane capable of climbing above this storm needed to have a long runway waiting at the other end of the journey. Angela didn't have time for him to make a Nevadan dress rehearsal. He had to get there.

The Area Fifty-One airfield sat on a dry lake bed, 'dry' being the operative word. If this storm had crossed that area, it was likely to be a wet lake bed or just a lake.

"You're a helicopter pilot, Captain Singleton," he said through clenched teeth. "Make it work!"

Vaughn cast another glance at the digital radar altimeter.

Less than a hundred feet!

Nothing but white!

The GPS's ground speed was only twenty knots. Even if another sign presented itself, he should have adequate response time to avoid it without rocketing up, back into the storm.

Vaughn's heart raced.

Maybe he should have turned back.

Just as he had the thought, a treetop emerged from the storm and brushed his door. Then a line of them came into view to his front right. Vaughn eased the stick to the left, narrowly avoiding the next tree. He could see more of them on his far left. Looking between his feet, through the helicopter's chin bubble, Vaughn saw a ribbon of white cut between them.

"The road!"

He guided the helicopter back over the center of Interstate 70.

Another gray rectangle emerged ahead. Vaughn slowed the helicopter. Finally, the sign resolved.

Eisenhower Tunnel Two Miles
All Hazardous Material Exit US 6 Loveland Pass

Vaughn ground his teeth together again. He'd known this was coming, but it didn't make the news any more palatable.

He eased the stick forward as the white-out induced by the helicopter's rotor wash threatened to overtake the aircraft. Two stressful miles later, the sign for Loveland Pass emerged from the storm, and the Black Hawk followed the exit.

His body tensed—as did his rectal sphincter. Vaughn feared he'd likely sucked up a whole yard of the seat canvas by now.

He smiled self-consciously. "Definitely getting my fiber today."

The road narrowed as Highway 69 started its mountainous traverse in earnest. Like the interstate before it, 69 wasn't so much a road in this weather as a stream of snow.

The helicopter bucked and swayed as mountain winds started buffeting it. Fortunately, the path cut through the trees was much wider than his rotor diameter, so Vaughn could fly low enough to maintain adequate surface reference during the ascent.

He steered the Black Hawk around yet another bend in the highway. Blowing snow started to make it difficult for him to see its border.

Vaughn eased the helicopter right. The pines to his left rapidly diminished and then disappeared completely, but the trunks of the towering trees on the near side resolved from the storm like the rough legs of unseen giants.

With each new mile, he fought between keeping the pines close enough to see and his speed slow enough to avoid obstacles, all countered by the need to stay ahead of the rotor wash-induced white-out that constantly chased his helicopter.

As he ascended higher, the snow seemed to deepen. Here, the treetops barely protruded above it. A mile farther up the mountain, they disappeared completely. Now only periodic rock outcroppings and cliffs marked the path of the winding highway.

Vaughn shook his head. "It wasn't the snow getting deeper, jackass. It was the trees getting shorter."

He was now flying above the tree line—the point where air grew too thin to support large plants.

The worsening conditions had Vaughn's ass cutting fresh donut holes into the seat bottom.

He scanned the instruments and saw his knees trembling. Vaughn *was* scared, but that had nothing to do with the tremors.

It was freezing in here!

He reluctantly relaxed the death grip he had on the collective control and then released the stick just long enough to turn up the cabin heat.

When Vaughn looked back up, his mouth fell open. His arms and hands locked on the controls.

It looked as if he had flown into a white pillowcase.

He couldn't see a damned thing!

Suddenly, the main wheels bounced. Once. Twice!

"Oh shit! Ground!"

The helicopter tilted, threatening to roll. It must have started drifting right.

Instinct told Vaughn to apply left cyclic, but his training told him that would only accelerate the craft's rotation about the pivot point.

He dumped the collective, eliminating the lift vector.

The helicopter teetered on its right wheel for a long moment as it skidded forward. Then it dropped, slamming the left main gear into the snow as it slid to a stop.

"Son of a bitch!" Vaughn screamed as he pounded the top of the instrument panel. "That was too damned close!"

He looked around. Vaughn still couldn't see outside. Even with the helicopter's rotor blades at flat pitch, he was completely whited out. The aircraft had come to rest on a slope.

A hard gust rocked the Black Hawk and blasted the top off of a large snowdrift that sat just ahead of Vaughn's cockpit. Suddenly, he saw dark letters that appeared to float in the snow. They formed words. Through narrowed eyes, he tried to discern them, but then they started to march across his window. As the levitating letters neared his helicopter, the top of a sign resolved from the snow. Then the entire guidepost came into view and began to slide to the right. As the brown lettering scrolled past his right window, Vaughn finally registered the words.

"Loveland Pass," he said. "Elevation eleven thousand nine hundred and ninety feet."

Then his eyes widened. It wasn't the damned sign moving. It was the helicopter!

Suddenly, the aircraft bucked beneath him, tilted forward, and then, in a whirling cloud of snow, raced down the mountainside.

Then, dead ahead, a cliff wall emerged from the storm and towered above the helicopter.

"Fuck!"

Vaughn pulled the stick back as far as he dared and grabbed an armload of collective.

The twin turbine engines screamed as they raced to supply the demanded power.

The helicopter broke free of the white powder.

Cliff wall now filled the forward half of Vaughn's universe, but as he continued to pull back on the stick, the aircraft's nose pitched up. He didn't have enough airspeed to maintain this attitude for more than a second or two, but the maneuver finally arrested his forward velocity. With its nose pointing straight up, the helicopter slammed into the cliff's rocky surface. Vaughn felt its sheet metal belly and wheeled landing gear crunch into the rocks.

Then it hung on the wall!

Finally, the helicopter surrendered to the laws of physics and began to slide backward like an airplane doing a hammerhead stall.

Vaughn kicked in right pedal. The aircraft responded by pivoting about its mast.

Now he was rushing at the ground nose first!

With max power applied, the Black Hawk quickly accelerated. He eased the cyclic aft, balancing the need to arrest the helicopter's descent against the requirement to build enough airspeed to fly the aircraft away from the ground.

The digital altimeter's numbers rapidly counted down as the unseen mountainside rushed up to greet him. Then the countdown slowed and finally stopped as the Black Hawk leveled off.

Vaughn transitioned to his flight instruments, but just as he surrendered to the clouds, they disappeared.

The helicopter emerged into clear air under a gray sky.

Vaughn blinked in surprise as he watched the Pacific side of Loveland Pass scroll beneath him.

The back of the storm had crossed the Continental Divide and continued east!

Vaughn sighed and relaxed his cramping hands.

"Thank you!"

Southern Nevada lay a few hundred miles to his west. In that direction, he had unlimited visibility. The tallest mountain peaks disappeared into the flat ceiling of clouds, but now with the highest pass and the worst of the weather behind him, Vaughn could easily navigate their valleys and lesser passes.

He plugged KXTA—the airport identifier for Area Fifty-One's Groom Lake facility—into the navigation computer.

He gazed up into the sky.

"See you soon, Angela. See you soon."

CHAPTER 20

V aughn stepped out of the hangar, slamming the metal door behind him.

Another wild goose chase! Only a ten-year-old F-16 had occupied this one.

He shook his head. Area Fifty-One was turning into one damned big disappointment. Conspiracy theorists would be surprised by the base's banality. So far, Vaughn had entered several hangars. Aside from an F-35 fighter jet that sported some unrecognizable, arcane electronics, he'd seen nothing he wouldn't expect to find at any military airfield.

It didn't help his disposition that a combination of deteriorating weather, exhaustion, and fuel starvation had forced him to overnight in Utah's Canyonlands Airport. He'd finally arrived at the Groom Lake facility that morning.

Vaughn had found the field thankfully intact. No fires had broken out, and the lights were still on, although he'd soon deduced that the place was just as empty as the rest of the world.

As a military pilot, Vaughn had never heard anything to make him believe that Area Fifty-One housed either aliens or UFOs, but he had heard whisperings that the Air Force kept a spaceplane here. Named the Aurora, the plane was supposed to be a single-stage-to-orbit hybrid. Vaughn had even seen evidence of its development in images from Google Earth. He had spotted a pair of long, curving monorails that crossed a large swath of the adjacent dry lake bed. Those discrete rails continued their ever-flattening trajectories until, finally running straight, they joined the centerlines of the airfield's two longest runways.

Vaughn had read that the Aurora's hypersonic scramjet wouldn't even light until it reached supersonic speeds. For several years now, NASA had been testing the engine type in a long, sleek experimental airplane dubbed the X-43. Its scramjet had to be accelerated by a rocket motor and wouldn't provide thrust until it reached those high speeds.

So when Vaughn had seen the monorails, he'd reasoned that the Air Force or the CIA must have used rockets to accelerate a scramjet-equipped spaceplane along that rail until it reached a velocity conducive to its use. However, voids now dotted the curving lines like broken links in a chain, so the spaceplane's technology must have progressed beyond the need for rails.

Vaughn believed that the Aurora was the realization of that improvement and that he would find it here at the Groom Lake facility.

But every building that Vaughn had entered had looked just like all of the military hangars he'd visited throughout his career.

When he'd seen the electricity still working, Vaughn had worried about the base's electronic security systems, but so far, he hadn't found any locked doors. Just as the thought occurred to him, the knob in his hand refused to turn. He leaned a shoulder into the door, but it wouldn't budge.

Vaughn smiled and raised hopeful eyebrows.

A touchpad and lens adorned the wall to the right of the door.

"Hmmm …"

He nodded and then turned and jogged two hangars back.

A couple of minutes later, Vaughn returned wearing gloves and a heavy apron and towing the wheeled twin tanks and hose of an oxyacetylene cutting torch. He had noticed the set-up earlier and mentally marked its location.

Vaughn donned the goggles and then fired up the torch. He experimented with the knobs on each tank until he had what he guessed to be a proper flame. This was his first attempt at oxy-fuel cutting, but he didn't think it would be too hard.

An hour later—and with a newfound appreciation for the finer intricacies of cutting torch usage—Vaughn finally entered the smoke-hazed facility. Inside, a highly non-standard aircraft occupied the center of the large hangar.

He'd found the Aurora!

Vaughn stared open-mouthed at its dark, glistening skin. Then he jumped as a metallic clatter echoed off of the building's walls.

Vaughn looked down.

"Oh shit!"

He had dropped the still burning torch, and the damn thing had landed with its flames licking at the twinned hoses.

Vaughn kicked it, removing the immediate threat of a dubious, flaming end to the day. Then he walked back outside and shut off the oxyacetylene tank's main valves before he could find some other way to blow up himself and the spaceplane.

Reentering the hangar, Vaughn stared at the long, sleek craft. It looked like something out of a science fiction movie, like someone had mated a supersonic SR-71 Blackbird with NASA's hypersonic X-43. The drooped ends of the black plane's swept back wings hung only a few inches above the polished concrete floor.

Vaughn walked to the aircraft, studying its lines. The spaceplane's canopy sported clear panels, but unlike typical fighters, the glass didn't protrude above the flowing lines of the craft's top skin. The pilot would have unobstructed views up, left, and right, but a video feed must provide the forward field of view.

He climbed up the access ladder. Looking down into the cockpit, he was pleased to see familiar flight controls. Also, large rectangular computer screens, similar to those in his Black Hawk, filled the instrument panel.

Vaughn didn't have a lot of fixed-wing experience, but he'd never met an aircraft he couldn't fly. The few times he'd flown an airplane, he had quickly mastered its controls. Most rotary-wing pilots found fixed-wing aircraft to be an easy transition. In forward flight, they flew much like a helicopter, natural and intuitive, just faster—significantly so in this case.

Of course, things would get complicated in a hurry if malfunctions occurred. That was when experience and knowledge showed their true worth. Vaughn would have to maximize the little time available to learn as much as he could about the spaceplane and its systems. Fortunately, modern aircraft had a great deal of built-in automation and redundancy. Beyond that, Vaughn would need a certain amount of luck.

In a compartment on the right side of the spaceplane's spacious cockpit, he found its operator's manual. A few minutes later, he connected a ground power unit to the craft and energized its electrical systems.

Vaughn climbed into the cockpit. To prepare for the coming spacewalk, he started pre-breathing pure oxygen from an O2 bottle he'd found earlier. This would purge excess nitrogen from his body and, hopefully, prevent decompression sickness or 'the bends,' as most people called it.

Seated with the book open in his lap, he spent the next two hours studying the plane's displays and electronics. Fortunately, it shared lots of commonality with other aircraft. The computer-generated flight instruments mirrored those in his Black Hawk. The autopilots of the two diametrical aircraft even shared many of the same features.

Finally satisfied that he had a working knowledge of the spaceplane's systems, Vaughn shut down the bird and climbed out of its cockpit.

After a systematic search of the area, he found the ship's specialized fuel stored in a cryogenic cell. Vaughn donned the foil-lined protective garments. He had already tried to blow himself up once today, so he closed the valve of his oxygen bottle before he started the refueling operation. Several minutes later, he had the Aurora topped off.

Vaughn started up the O2 again and then went in search of the spacesuits. In the back of the hangar, he found a locker room. Long, thin-walled suits with silvery neck rings hung behind several of the narrow metal doors. The third one looked like it would fit.

Before trying it on, Vaughn checked his watch.

"Shit!"

He ran out of the locker room and through the hangar beyond. A moment later, Vaughn emerged under a midday sun and trotted over to his recently acquired truck and its stashed gear.

Soon the generator purred to life. The antenna he'd brought for the purpose pointed skyward. After another glance up, Vaughn pulled the oxygen mask aside and depressed the transmit key.

"Commander Brown, this is Army Captain …"

Vaughn shook his head and smiled.

"Hey, Angela, you there?"

CHAPTER 21

At the designated time, the radio speaker crackled to life. "Commander Brown, this is Army Captain ..." The man's voice stopped mid-sentence. Angela's heart skipped a beat, but then he returned. She could hear the smile in his words, could almost see it on the smoothly shaved face she'd pictured for him. "Hey, Angela, you there?"

She returned the imagined smile. "Hi, Vaughn. Yes, I'm here."

"I found it!"

Angela's eyes widened. "You found the Aurora?!"

"Sure did!"

After a long pause, Angela said, "Is it flyable?"

"Yep!"

She clapped her hands. "Oh, my God! You might really rescue me!"

"Might?" Vaughn said with feigned indignation. "Pshaw." Then he chuckled. "It'll be easier than flying through that damned storm."

"Storm? What happened?"

Over the next few minutes, the captain told her about a frightful trip through the mountains.

"Talk about pucker factor! When I finally made it to the other side and landed at Moab's Canyonlands Field for fuel, there was a donut hole cut in my seat. Think I got all the fiber I'll need for the next week or two."

Angela guffawed, bursting into laughter.

"Did you just snort, Commander Brown?"

This elicited a fresh batch of spasming giggles along with a few of the aforementioned snorts. "Guilty as charged," she finally managed.

"Well I'm glad you find my rectal distress so amusing," he said without malice.

Angela pictured that smooth-faced smile again. Then she caught a glimpse of her image in one of the Cupola's large glass panels. The reflected grin morphed into a frown on her hollow cheeks. Her gaunt appearance shook Angela to the core. She might be on the cusp of meeting, literally, the last man on Earth, and she looked like death warmed over.

Angela shook her head angrily.

Screw that!

She'd never needed anybody, much less a man. Now she was worried about how she'd look to her would-be rescuer.

No, she was better than that.

Angela pursed her lips and keyed the mic. "When can you launch, Captain?"

She winced. The words had come out harsher than intended.

After a long pause, Singleton returned, sounding confused. "Uh ... It's fueled and ready."

"Already?!"

"Yeah!"

"Are you sure? Did you check everything?"

The smile evaporated from the man's voice. "I got this, Commander."

Angela nodded. "Okay." Her voice softened. "Sorry. I really do appreciate everything you're doing, Vaughn."

His voice dropped, matching her tone. "No need to apologize, Angela."

An uncomfortable silence fell over them.

Finally, Vaughn spoke up. "From what I saw in the spaceplane's performance charts, it can climb and accelerate at the rate you esti-mated yesterday. Did you confirm those preliminary numbers? Is eighteen hundred Zulu still good?"

During their previous conversation, Angela had worked out the orbital intercept timing and trajectory for a ship launching from Southern Nevada. Over the subsequent twenty-four hours, she'd double- and triple-checked the timing. It turned out her initial, off-the-cuff estimate had been pretty close.

"Actually, you have another hour to work with, Captain. A departure time of nineteen hundred Zulu will work."

"Wow, that was a pretty impressive guesstimate, Commander."

Angela blushed. Not because of his praise, but because of the way she'd snapped at him earlier. She keyed the mic again. "I told you to make it Angela, Vaughn."

"Angela-Vaughn?" he said, the smile back in full force. "That's an odd name … but if you insist, I'll talk to you sometime after nineteen hundred, Angela-Vaughn."

Angela grinned. With a chuckle, she said, "I'll be listening, smart-ass."

PART III

"If it happens that the human race doesn't make it, then the fact that we were here once will not be altered, that once upon a time we peopled this astonishing blue planet, and wondered intelligently at everything about it and the other things who lived here with us on it, and that we celebrated the beauty of it in music and art, architecture, literature, and dance, and that there were times when we approached something godlike in our abilities and aspirations. We emerged out of depthless mystery, and back into mystery we returned, and in the end the mystery is all there is."

— James Howard Kunstler

CHAPTER 22

V aughn closed his eyes. "Try not to screw this up, Captain
Singleton."

The sleek black spaceplane now stood at the west end of a Groom
Lake runway. Sitting in its cockpit, the spacesuited man opened his
eyes and took a deep breath. He focused on the top half of the instrument panel. The clarity of the ultra-high-definition video painted
across its screen created the illusion that he was looking through an
actual canopy. Ahead of the spaceplane, the black concrete strips that
marked the runway's border stretched toward the east end of the lake
bed. In the distance, the parallel lines appeared to converge like the
rails of a train track.

The base's longest concrete runway would have sufficed, but a
broken-up Boeing 737 sat in the middle of its long expanse.
Conversely, the lake bed runway had no obstacles, and if Vaughn
inadvertently veered off of it during the takeoff roll, he was less likely
to wreck the spaceplane.

He took a deep breath and then toggled the starters. The hybrid jet
engines ignited with a whine. As they reached idle speed, the noise
grew into a thrumming roar. The entire ship vibrated with pent-up
power, like an angry bull pressing at the gate.

Using the spaceplane's on-board auxiliary power unit, Vaughn had already activated the Aurora's electronics, including the ship's space tracking computer interface. Its display showed several orbital targets. Most had arcane titles and icons. However, one image, imaginatively titled ISS, featured the station's familiar solar arrays. Programming an intercept had proven relatively straightforward. The computer-generated time until launch matched the countdown timer on his watch. Angela's calculations had been dead on.

The numbers of both clocks counted down through ten seconds.

Vaughn placed a trembling left hand on the ship's dual power levers. His heart felt as if it might burst. The adrenaline dumping into Vaughn's system had it beating so hard he could hear the pulse echoing inside the spacesuit's helmet.

"Don't screw up," he said again.

The countdowns hit zero.

Vaughn shoved both power levers forward.

Nothing happened.

"What the he—"

A sledgehammer slammed into the back of his seat. A tremendous shock wave rocked the spaceplane. Around it, the floor of the dry lake bed flared bright white. Then its luminosity appeared to fade as acceleration G-forces grayed out Vaughn's peripheral vision.

As he rocketed across the lake bed, it felt as if an elephant had sat on his chest. His universe shrank until he could only see a speed-blurred patch of runway ahead of the rushing spaceplane.

Tremendous vibrations rattled the rapidly accelerating ship. Vaughn eased the stick back. The tremors faded as the Aurora rotated and then rocketed away from Groom Lake's sandy surface.

Suddenly, red lights flashed and multiple warning horns bleated!

Overwhelmed by the sheer number of alerts, Vaughn stared motionlessly for a long moment. They all seem to have something to do with the ship having excess power applied. He started to pull back throttles, but then he saw the autopilot flashing for his attention.

Out of ideas, Vaughn pressed the pulsing buttons.

The nose abruptly lurched skyward, and the autothrottles halved the applied power.

It malfunctioned! The ship was going to stall!

Vaughn reached for the autopilot disconnect button, but then he saw the airspeed and yanked his hand away. It was still building, accelerating and gaining altitude at a prodigious rate.

He shook his head. "Damn it, Singleton! So much for not screwing up."

Vaughn had triggered the alarms. The relatively shallow climb that he'd initiated with full power applied had allowed the spaceplane to rocket through its maximum airspeed for that altitude. Likely, if he hadn't engaged the autopilot, the dynamic forces would have soon ripped off the wings.

When he'd reviewed the Operator's Manual, Vaughn had focused on the engine starting procedures as well as those for orbital maneuvering and docking, but feeling short on time, he'd rushed through the sections that covered takeoff and flight, deciding he could wing it.

Mark would have loved that, he thought wryly.

Now flying straight up, the apparently homesick spaceplane rocketed through 50,000 feet. Azure sky shifted to indigo. Stars became visible as a few points emerged from the darkening violet sky. Then a universe worth of stars blossomed across the canopy.

As it crested one hundred thousand feet, the plane's nose tilted from vertical, gradually nosing over. A few minutes later, the ship's hybrid thruster shut down, plunging Vaughn into sustained weightlessness for the first time in his life.

But he didn't get to enjoy it for long.

Multiple alarms suddenly rang across the cockpit. An amber message pulsed on the main display.

INSUFFICIENT FUEL
(Press For More Information)

Vaughn felt sick to his stomach, but the nausea had nothing to do with the sensation of free fall. He reached for the message with a reluctant trembling finger. Finally, he touched it. The audio alarm ceased, and a subtext popped up:

INSUFFICIENT FUEL TO RENDEZVOUS WITH TARGET: ISS

"Son of a bitch!"

His high-throttle burn through the lower atmosphere had used up his margin.

"Shit!"

On the real-time orbital display, the icon for the ISS was directly overhead. The original flight plan called for him to spend the next ninety-minute orbit matching speeds with the station. However, he could already see that wasn't going to happen. The ISS was quickly leaving him behind.

Some fuel remained in the tank. Vaughn tried to fire up the thrusters, but the computer refused to accept the command. A new rectangular "Insufficient Fuel" amber caution segment began pulsing on the screen. Vaughn pressed it again, but this time a different subtext popped up:

ADDITIONAL THRUSTING WILL LEAVE INSUFFICIENT FUEL
TO DEORBIT
OVERRIDE? YES NO

Vaughn's finger hovered over the green "YES" for several seconds. Finally, he shifted it over and jabbed the red "NO."

"Fuck!"

He slammed his head back. In the zero-G environment, it ricocheted painfully inside the helmet.

The radio sparked to life. "Vaughn, are you there? I see your transponder."

Blinking, he looked up. Vaughn saw the distant International Space Station as a brilliant point of light. As he watched it leave him behind, he shook his head.

"You're such a jackass, Vaughn."

"Come in, Captain Singleton. Are you there?"

Closing his eyes, he toggled the radio. "Hey, Angela."

"What's wrong?"

"I screwed up!" He grimaced and then softened his tone. "I'm sorry, Angela."

"What happened?"

"Burned too much fuel during the launch." He hesitated and then sighed. "I'll have to return to Groom Lake."

After a pregnant pause, the radio sparked back to life. "That's okay, Vaughn." The commander spoke in a non-judgmental tone that only deepened his feelings of guilt. "I've waited this long. Another day won't kill me ... probably."

Vaughn laughed in spite of himself. "Thanks for that, Angela. Wanna give the knife another twist?"

"No, that should be good enough." Her tone turned serious. "I'll calculate the next intercept window."

Vaughn nodded and took a deep breath. "Okay. As soon as the plane is in the right position, I'll deorbit and head back to Area Fifty-One."

Still shaking his head, Vaughn started entering the necessary information into the flight director.

The radio crackled. "Great job getting that thing into space on your first try. Pretty impressive for an Army helicopter pilot."

Vaughn grinned. "Wow! And the hits just keep coming."

Angela snorted again.

It was a beautiful sound. He had seen pictures of the smile that came with that snort. Vaughn truly hoped he hadn't lost his chance to see it in person.

"I know you'll do better tomorrow."

"Tomorrow?!"

"Yep. Orbital mechanics can be a bitch."

Vaughn watched the station race toward the eastern horizon like a speeding star. "I'm so sorry, Angela."

"Stop saying that, Captain. You're already my hero." After a pause, her voice returned, softly singing a ballad from the eighties about needing a hero, about him being larger than life. Then she laughed and snorted.

And Vaughn felt himself falling in love.

A lump formed in his throat.

Her fading chuckles elicited a final snort.

After a hard swallow, Vaughn keyed the mic. "I didn't know that old eighties song could sound so pretty."

"Why, thank you, sir."

"I'll try to live up to all that, although I'm not sure about the whole larger than life thing."

"You already are, Captain," she said softly. Then her tone turned serious. "We'll lose line of sight communication in a moment, so after you land, call me on the ham radio, and I'll give you the takeoff time for tomorrow. In the meantime, be careful, fly boy."

Vaughn smiled and nodded. "Yes, my princess."

An hour later, as the ship flew over the South Pacific, he activated the descent program. The autopilot brought the engines online and used the small thrusters embedded in the ship's skin to turn the craft one hundred eighty degrees. With the nose facing backward, Vaughn watched the countdown. This time he kept his hands away from the power levers.

When the countdown timer reached zero, the levers moved of their own accord. Instead of a sledgehammer to the back, Vaughn felt a gradual acceleration as his inertia pressed him into the seat. Firing its thrusters while flying backward caused the spaceplane to decelerate. He'd soon start to fall into the atmosphere. Before that happened, the aircraft would need to turn the nose forward.

Vaughn wondered about that. He hadn't seen any heat-absorbing tiles on its smooth bottom surface. Unlike the Space Shuttle, the Aurora appeared to have an all-metal skin. He supposed it might be a carbon composite, but either way, Vaughn didn't see how the skin could stand the extreme heat of reentry.

Suddenly the thruster cut out.

Vaughn looked around with wide eyes. The plane was still flying backward, and the Earth's surface, and therefore its atmosphere, already looked much closer.

He looked over his right shoulder and watched the distinctive shape of Mexico's Baja Peninsula slide into view behind the ship. Then he saw the right wingtip had started to glow. A faint tremor began to creep through the fuselage.

The plane was still facing the wrong direction!

Vaughn disengaged the autopilot and pressed the right pedal. A small thruster in the nose started pushing it in that direction.

Urgent alarms suddenly erupted. Multiple red lights began to strobe on the spaceplane's computer screen. The biggest one was a message announcing that the plane had improper alignment for scramjet reverse thrusting.

A devastating epiphany struck Vaughn like a Mack truck.

The plane had been waiting until it had sufficient opposite-flow ram air pressure to permit reverse thrusting. He'd forgotten that a scramjet equipped with a thrust diverter could do that.

"Fix it, Singleton!"

Vaughn applied full left pedal, desperately trying to reverse his mistake. The rotation had already turned the Aurora sideways! The jet of white gas that streamed from the nose thruster redoubled, but the turn didn't stop!

Hell, it didn't even slow!

The plane was too deep into the atmosphere. Its thruster didn't have a hope in hell of overriding the massive aerodynamic forces.

The spaceplane weathervaned, snapping the nose into the direction of flight.

Additional alarms rang out, and a fresh batch of warning lights illuminated.

Both wingtips now glowed white-hot.

A klaxon added its ringing endorsement to the cacophony blaring in Vaughn's ears. He didn't need to read any of the new alerts screaming their all caps messages across the computer screen.

Vaughn knew he was well and truly fucked.

On his left, the wing's entire surface now glowed white-hot.

Suddenly, it snapped off, departing the spaceplane in a flash!

The horizon tumbled.

And Vaughn fell into a black void.

CHAPTER 23

"A re you there, Vaughn?"

As it had on the previous three attempts, the radio remained silent. Angela's stomach knotted with worry. Multitudinous questions haunted her every moment.

Did something go wrong with the reentry? Had Vaughn died in a fiery crash?

Was she alone again?

Then there was the darkest thought of all.

Had the wrong man survived Day Zero?

Angela shook her head angrily.

No! She couldn't think that. Vaughn had risked his life for her.

She tried to shove out the thoughts, but they kept worming their way back, gnawing deeper into her mind with every passing hour of radio silence.

A warbling alarm trumpeted through the module. Angela grabbed her smartphone and canceled the alert. She gave the radio a final glance and then pushed off the bulkhead. A moment later, she glided into her old workstation and placed the phone in its cradle.

To keep track of the strange readings emanating from the Super

Collider, Angela had left the gravity wave detector running in spite of the station's reduced electrical supply.

She activated the phone's voice recorder.

"Still waiting for word from Captain Singleton." Angela paused and took a deep breath. "On the bright side, this gives me a chance to follow up on the situation around the Super Collider." She gnawed her lip and then said, "Still haven't told Vaughn about that. Figured he had enough on his plate … Guess I was right …"

Angela shook her head. "Sorry." She blew a loose strand of hair out of her eyes and then continued. "Anyway! The ISS is about to pass over Switzerland. If it's as clear as I hope, I'll get to see Geneva for the first time since Day Zero. As I mentioned previously, the anomalous gravitational waves have continued, but smoke and clouds have obscured the area. The fires burned themselves out a couple of weeks ago. Since then, spring rains have swept most of the crap out of the air."

She checked the gravimetric display. The first time she'd seen the anomaly, it had the recognizable spiraling pattern of merging black holes, but over the subsequent weeks, they'd taken on a completely different look. Now the rendered lines radiated out from a central point like petals of a daisy.

"Still seeing the gravity flower on the display. Not sure what the hell to make of it, but hopefully, we'll know something in a couple of minutes."

Thoughts of Vaughn briefly took a back seat as Angela stared intently at the live external video feed. She watched the burned-out husk of Paris drift silently across the display. As the station continued its easterly track, the French countryside glided into view. Angela chewed her lip nervously as she waited for the Swiss border region to slide into frame.

"Almost there."

A ray of noon sunlight glinted off of something on the surface.

"Just caught a reflection."

Her eyes narrowed as she drew closer to the monitor.

"Is that a river? It must be huge!"

Angela shook her head. She knew there hadn't been a big one there before.

"Guess it could be a combination of snow melt and spring rain. Maybe a dam burst somewhere upriver."

As the station progressed farther east, the waterway broadened, and additional streams slid into view. Then a massive silver surface edged into the image.

Angela's eyes widened, and she pulled away from the monitor. "What the heck is that?!" She leaned back in. "It looks like Lake Geneva grew tenfold! It's covering the whole area!"

Her wide eyes darted left and right as she scanned the image, searching for a recognizable point of reference. The lake had flooded the entire city as well as the French border.

Finally, she nodded. "It looks like the collider is right under the center of it."

Angela tilted her head. "But that doesn't make sense. The ground there slopes down, out of the Alps. Water shouldn't be able to collect like that." She paused and then raised her eyebrows. "Unless the land changed."

The large, glistening river she'd seen coming in from the west merged with its neighbors and connected with the mercurial lake. Then Angela saw several other rivers streaming into the reflective body from every direction.

Sunlight bounced off of the center of the lake, washing out the feed. The video camera adjusted to the change. In the now-dimmed image, the lake and its tributaries resolved as a silver daisy drawn against a black background.

Wide-eyed, Angela looked from the video feed to the identical pattern drawn across the gravimetric display.

"Oh, my God! It's the ... the gravity flower!"

CHAPTER 24

Something knocked Vaughn's head. Then it happened again.

He opened his eyes and tried to blink the world into focus.

Strobing white light circled him.

Gravity kept shifting.

In spite of his struggles to stop it, Vaughn's head lolled to and fro.

Finally, a grimy window came into focus. Through it, he watched an endless stream of undulating horizon sweep from left to right.

Vaughn swayed back and forth. He reached out to touch the … What? Canopy?

Canopy!

He was in a spaceplane!

Or … he had been … until …

Vaughn tried to sit up, but a harness and the wildly fluctuating G-forces threw him back into the seat.

He could remember seeing the wing glowing, but after that …

Nothing.

The world continued to revolve around the cockpit.

The spacesuit's helmet slammed back into the headrest.

"Flat spin! I'm in a flat spin!"

Vaughn reached for the flight controls, but there were none. Fighting against the oscillating forces, he looked left and right.

Both wings were gone!

"Shit!"

Staring wide-eyed through the dirty canopy, Vaughn couldn't see any part of the plane!

It was gone.

He leaned forward, trying to look up. Just before the G-forces slammed him back into the seat, Vaughn saw a small drogue chute fluttering in the dark sky above what he now realized was a capsule. Instead of an ejection seat, the spaceplane had an escape pod.

Under the stabilizing effect of the drogue, the capsule's rotation finally slowed. Vaughn leaned forward, looking at the canopy. He ran his fingers along its inner face. That wasn't dirt. The heat of an uncontrolled reentry had charred and scoured its outer surface. He could see that the superheated atmosphere had eroded the hardened canopy. The worst spots looked paper-thin. Fiery plasma had come within millimeters of flooding the cockpit.

Vaughn was damned lucky to be alive.

A new realization hit him like a punch to the gut.

He didn't have another spaceplane. He'd seen enough evidence in the Aurora's hangar to know that this craft had been the latest in a line of scramjets. Not only was it the only one in operation, it was the only one that had ever made orbit.

And now it was toast. Hell, with the exception of this capsule, it no longer existed.

How in the hell was he going to rescue Angela?

"Damn it!" Vaughn yelled as he slammed a fist into the ceiling.

He flinched as a loud bang rang through the capsule. Suddenly weightless, Vaughn floated off of the seat back. Only the harness held him in place. He jumped again as two sharp reports shook the pod. Outside, a hemispherical clamshell floated away, and a bundle of white and red cloth tumbled from the roof.

Then the capsule lurched as if it had bounced off the world's largest trampoline.

When the oscillations settled, Vaughn looked up to see a huge parachute.

For a couple of minutes, the capsule wound and then unwound beneath the flexing chute, causing it to undulate like a lethargic jellyfish pulsing its way across a cobalt sea.

A moment later, the pod finally stopped spinning. Vaughn leaned toward the hazed canopy and peered down. He was still above 10,000 feet. Beneath the slowly rotating capsule, a finger of sandy land snaked into a blue ocean. Vaughn recognized the thin strip of ground as Mexico's Baja Peninsula.

He stared wide-eyed at the line where tan desert met blue ocean, trying to judge which side of that boundary his capsule would land. It looked like he was headed toward the western shore. For a moment, upper-level winds carried the capsule inland, over the desert, but as it descended through 3000 feet, the pod began to drift toward the beach and the ocean beyond it.

"Oh shit!" Vaughn croaked.

The capsule's sideways drift slowed.

A minute later, the ground rushed up to greet him.

At the last moment, Vaughn thought to press his back and head into the seat.

Then a Mack truck seemed to slam into him.

His stream of consciousness skipped forward like a poorly spliced video.

Dazed and confused, Vaughn tried again to blink the world into focus. He was lying on his side. Actually, the entire capsule was. The sounds of metal grinding across sand and rocks rumbled through his helmet.

He started hyperventilating. The inside of his visor fogged.

An enormous crashing impact knocked the sliding capsule back into the air. Then the pod slammed into the ground again.

Vaughn's visor shattered. Hot air flooded into his helmet.

Blinking and panting, he looked through the canopy. The still inflated parachute was dragging him across the desert. Vaughn's eyes widened as it disappeared over a large, jagged outcropping of tombstone-shaped rocks. Unfortunately, the parachute's cords passed unmolested through a gap in the stones.

As the capsule rushed toward certain impalement, Vaughn saw a red- and yellow-striped handle in the pod's ceiling. Seeing its label, he grabbed the parachute jettison handle and yanked. It popped out of the recess trailing a thin cable.

Another loud bang echoed through the capsule as the racing parachute finally separated from it. The pod slid for a few more feet and then finally stopped with a jolting metallic crunch. The abrupt halt threw Vaughn into the harness hard enough to knock the air out of his lungs.

He lay there for a long moment, open-mouthed, struggling to breathe. When he finally did draw a breath, it exited him in a wheezing, spasming cough.

Vaughn grabbed the canopy jettison handle and gave it a twisting push.

A multitude of simultaneous blasts set his ears to ringing as a shock wave rocked the entire metal capsule, but the canopy remained in place. Then he looked through the top of the charred window and saw only rock.

The escape pod had come to rest with its exit jammed against one of the tombstone-shaped boulders.

"Shit! Really?!"

Acrid smoke that smelled like ignited gunpowder filled the module, burning Vaughn's eyes and lungs.

He started coughing again.

Thin rays of sunlight burned through the pod's smoke-filled atmosphere like white laser beams. With his gloved finger, Vaughn traced them to their source. Small gaps had appeared along the line where canopy met capsule. The explosive bolts had moved it some, opening up a small gap.

A bead of sweat trickled into his eyes.

It was getting damned hot in here.

Vaughn shook his head, then released the seat belt. After a few seconds of squirming into position, he placed his boots against the underside of the canopy. He took a few deep breaths and then shoved his hunched shoulders into the seat bottom, trying to slide the pod away from the pinned canopy.

Nothing happened!

It wouldn't budge!

The exertion popped fresh sweat from his brow. Vaughn swiped at it, but the suit's non-absorbent skin only smeared dust into the moisture. The back of the glove came away covered in the muddy mix.

The temperature was rising precipitously. The heat now pouring through the shattered visor made it feel as if Vaughn had stuck his face in an oven.

"Shit!"

He closed his eyes and took a deep breath. Looking around, he reevaluated his situation. Then, squirming around again in the confined space, Vaughn braced his back against the bottom of the canopy this time. He took another quick breath and then shoved his boots into the seat bottom.

Squealing its protest, the capsule finally budged. Vaughn took another breath and then shoved with all the might his skinny trembling runner's legs could generate. The metallic pod slid across the rocky sand with a loud squawk.

For a few seconds, he just lay there panting, relishing the relatively cool air that now poured through his shattered visor.

Finally, Vaughn squinted into the cloudless sky, then shook his head.

"Way to go, jackass."

Vaughn walked toward the top of an apparent cliff. The rock outcropping that had almost killed him had saved his life. Now twenty feet from the precipice, Vaughn still couldn't see land beneath the escarpment, only sparkling blue ocean. To either side of him, thin rock slabs, similar to the one that had stopped his pod, probed the cobalt sky like thirty-foot-tall praying hands.

As he drew closer to the cliff's edge, structures and developed land slid into view below. He stood on the precipice and studied the palm tree-lined walks and pools of a beach resort.

Vaughn began to shed the sweltering spacesuit. He soon had doffed the top half and started working on removing the lower portion. Now in nothing but socks, underwear, and t-shirt, Vaughn dug a multitool out of one of the suit's pouches. He sat on a nearby rock and started cutting and hacking the feet from the undoubtedly expensive spacesuit. He tossed aside the unneeded portion and then slipped the makeshift boots over his socked feet.

Vaughn stood. He looked back to the dented, burned, and now abraded capsule. Shaking his head, he turned and walked to a trail cut into the face of the cliff. He followed its zigzag path down and soon crossed onto the resort's property.

As Vaughn walked down the retreat's curving stone-lined side-walk, the shuffling sound of the loose-fitting, mangled spacesuit boots echoed off stucco walls.

Miraculously, the resort still had electricity. Water sprayed from several of the property's fountains, rising and falling in burbling vertical streams. It appeared that the lawn's sprinkler system had failed about a month after the world had ended. The overgrown and now very brown lawn had breached its confines before succumbing to the desert clime. It protruded from the concrete's cracks and expansion joints. Questing tan fingers of desiccated grass covered the walk's rock border and concealed its curving edges.

The pool was still full of welcoming blue water.

The inside of Vaughn's mouth felt like a sun-dried leather shammy.

He walked to the pool's edge and unceremoniously dropped into its cool embrace. The boots filled with water and fell from his kicking feet. Vaughn took a deep swallow then erupted into a spasm of coughs that ended with him vomiting up unwelcome salt water.

"Damn it!" He punched the water. Looking up into the surreally tranquil sky, Vaughn shook his head.

"Fuck, fuck, *fuck!*"

His legs went limp. His head slipped beneath the surface as he released his held breath in a long exhalation. The sound of the rising bubbles rang loud in his ears. Vaughn's ass hit the pool floor, and he just sat there shaking his head, silent tears of shame and frustration mixing freely with the pool's salt water.

When burning lungs forced Vaughn to the surface, he took in a long breath. Finally, he walked to the near edge, head hanging, saline tears flowing into the saltwater rivulets that ran from his matted hair and beard. Vaughn climbed from the pool and headed to an adjacent bar. He plucked a green bottle from a not-so-cool cooler and hoisted it into the air.

"Yeah, Houston. We've got a problem alright."

He downed the golden liquid in three long gulps. The empty bottle shattered at his feet. Vaughn cracked open another beer and held it up to the sky as well.

"Thanks to yours truly, we got one helluva cock-up!"

A moment later, the second empty bottle burst across the concrete.

Vaughn woke soaked in sweat. Each heartbeat brought a fresh wave of skull-splitting pain. The front door must have closed while he'd been asleep. He flipped on the bedside lamp and then rolled off the bed's flower-festooned polyester cover. He threw open the door.

Cool night air flowed around him. Vaughn stood there for a long moment, kneading his temples with his thumbs.

Head hanging, he sauntered back into the suite. He bounced off of the doorjamb as he stepped into the bathroom. Vaughn turned on the water. One solitary drop fell from the faucet.

Probably for the best.

Yesterday's beer binge had only worsened his thirst. His mouth had gone from desiccated shammy to Sahara desert. Had water flowed from the tap, Vaughn wouldn't have stopped with washing his face. He would have taken long slurping draws of the wet stuff. As much as he hated himself at the moment, he didn't think drinking Mexican tap water of unknown vintage constituted a good plan.

Vaughn found clear, safe bottled water in the room's small, inoperable refrigerator. He stood in the open front door, running fingers through greasy brown hair as he drank the warm water.

Aside from yesterday's salty dip, he hadn't bathed since before his ill-fated lunch with JFK. And judging by the odor rising from him, sleeping in a hot box hadn't improved the situation.

After his beer binge, Vaughn had discovered that the resort's air conditioners didn't work. Every room he'd stumbled into had been sweltering. Finally, Vaughn had settled on one in a deeply shaded corner. Before passing out, he'd propped open the door, giving the room a modicum of ventilation.

Apparently, the spacesuit boot had been about as effective of a doorstop as it had been a sneaker.

Vaughn kicked the shoe. It slid across the concrete and dropped into the pool. Seeing the splash, he thought of the single drop issued by the bathroom sink. After giving himself another appraising sniff, he stepped back into the room. A moment later, he emerged with a tiny bar of soap and an equally small bottle of shampoo.

Vaughn tossed a couple of musty white towels onto the pool's coping and then followed the space boot into the water.

Several minutes later, he emerged from the now cloudy and soap-scummed pool feeling cleaner on the outside, but his head and heart still ached.

He took another long draw from the bottle. The headache had ramped down. The pulse-induced throbbing in his noggin had dwindled from an overwhelming chain of tactical nuclear detonations to a manageable rhythmic series of hand grenade explosions. However, as his head cleared, the knowledge of his failure and its ramifications floated closer to the surface.

Vaughn threw aside the water.

"Too much blood in my alcohol system."

He'd drained the pool bar yesterday, so he walked up to the nearby lobby. He'd spotted a large cooler up there earlier.

Vaughn grabbed a warm beer and stepped back outside. He opened the brown bottle with the church key he'd stolen from the bar.

As he raised the beer, the naked man studied the eclectic collection of cars adorning the adjacent parking lot. Rental cars and SUVs filled most of the spots, but one vehicle, in particular, drew his eye. A dune buggy sat in a parking space near the front of the building.

The bottle stopped an inch from his lips. Vaughn stared at the tubular steel that formed the buggy's frame.

"Son of a bitch," he whispered. Then Vaughn tossed the still full beer aside. It shattered on the pavement.

A smile slowly migrated across his bearded face.

"Vaughn Singleton, you're a goddamned idiot."

CHAPTER 25

Mesmerized, Angela watched Nadine's plump little body kick and swim its way through the module's chilly air. A loud rumble trumpeted from her stomach.

Nadine turned a nervous eye toward her.

Angela looked away self-consciously. The protest of her tortured hollow abdominal cavity went on longer than usual, echoing off of the module's inner walls. When the sound stopped only to resume a short moment later, she realized it wasn't her stomach anymore. A faint voice trickled into the JEM from the direction of the Tranquility module!

Angela's eyes widened. "Vaughn?!"

She pushed off the wall and glided toward the open hatch. She could feel Nadine's babies wriggling in her hair. They had burrowed in there underneath her hoodie. It was one of the few ways they could stay warm in the station's frigid environs. Angela had left the hatches cracked open between Tranquility and the Japanese Experiment Module, overtaxing the JEM's environmental controls. With the reduced electrical supply, the system struggled to keep that much living space above freezing. Fortunately, sunlight warmed the Cupola

209

and its parent Tranquility module for a portion of each orbit. Otherwise, they'd have frozen to death overnight.

Angela's breath fogged as she passed into Tranquility. Now she heard Vaughn's voice clearly.

"Commander Brown! Are you there?" The man's voice sounded as if he was in near panic.

"Oh, thank God," Angela whispered. "Thank you, thank you."

She clamped the headset over her cold ears. "I'm here, Vaughn." A hacking cough racked her body. Then she said, "What happened? Are you okay? Where are you?"

"There you are," Vaughn said with evident relief. "Don't worry about me. Are you okay?"

"I'm all right, still here … Not like I'm going anywhere." Angela winced. "Sorry, I didn't mean it that way … Anyway! How'd the landing go?"

"Uh … Not good. I … I botched it. The plane is toast."

Angela's stomach cramped. Feeling as though she might become ill, she placed a hand over her abdomen—not that there was anything to throw up. All of her earlier doubts suddenly burned with renewed fuel. The man had already told her that this was the only spaceplane.

That was it.

Nothing else existed, nothing that could be fueled and operated by one man, anyway.

Angela would die up here.

"Don't give up on me, Commander."

She shook her head. "It's okay, Vaughn. You did your—"

"I have another plan!"

Angela closed her eyes and released a long sigh. Then she pressed the transmit button and tried to sound enthusiastic. "What is it? Something else there in Area Fifty-One?"

"Well … I didn't actually make it all the way back to Groom Lake."

This time, Angela couldn't keep the disappointment from her voice. "Where are you?"

"I'm in Cabo San Lucas."

"Okay," Angela said, drawing out the word. On the verge of tears, she added, "Glad one of us is getting to enjoy a little vacation."

"I'm not kidding, Angela. I think I really have a way to get up there."

Angela closed her eyes again. A wave of guilt washed over her. This man had risked everything to try to save her, and now she was chewing on his ear. She took a deep breath and then let it out in another long exhalation. Finally, she smiled weakly. "I'm all ears, Vaughn. Talk to me," she said, sounding more optimistic than she felt.

After a long pause, the captain continued. "Listen, Angela. Remember that thruster module I told you about?"

"Yeah, the experimental prototype you and Mark hovered in the vacuum chamber."

"Yes, that." The man's voice took on an annoyingly confident tone. "I'm going to fly it to you."

Angela's brows knitted. She frowned. It took all her will not to yell at the man. After counting to ten, she took a calming breath and then said, "It's a rather big step to go from a thirty-foot hover to making orbit, don't you think, Captain?"

"I don't know ... maybe. But they did say it had crossed the threshold."

"What threshold?"

"Mark said that the power it hovered with proved that the module could reach space."

"As is?"

Suddenly, Vaughn's voice sounded less sure. "Well, not like it currently is." After a pause, he added, "I'd have to make some modifications. Most of them aren't that big of a deal, but there is one that I'm not sure about."

When Angela refused to play along, Vaughn drove on.

"It's the power. Right now, it just has a bank of batteries, probably like you'd see in an electric car, just bigger. I need something that can supply that much electricity continuously and work in a vacuum."

Angela's eyes widened. "An RTG!"

"A what?"

"A radioisotope thermoelectric generator!" she said excitedly. "Like the one on the Curiosity rover."

"Yeah, that," Vaughn said. "But it would probably need to be more powerful than even that one."

Suddenly animated, Angela pulled herself closer to the radio. "Can you get to Houston, Vaughn?"

"Uh ... Yeah, I think so. Why?"

"There's something there that might work!"

Angela spent the next ten minutes describing the device and where he could find it.

"Okay," Vaughn said excitedly. "That sounds perfect! I'm at a small airport now. When I was looking for this radio, I saw an aircraft that can get me there. Ellington Field has a bunch of runways. I'm sure at least one of them will be clear enough to land on."

Angela nodded. "Ellington's close to JSC, too. Did you write down the directions I gave you?"

"Yes, ma'am." After a pause, he said, "It's good to have you back, Angela." The smile had returned to his voice. "Don't give up on me, Commander."

Angela smiled. "Hurry to me, Obi-Wan."

"I'll call you from Cleveland."

"Please do." Angela paused and then added, "Fly safely, Vaughn. You're still my hero."

After a long silence, the man's voice returned choked with emotion. "I'll do my best to live up to that, Angela."

The radio fell silent. Angela removed her headset. For a moment, she watched the planet scroll beneath the station. Finally, she rested a hand on the Cupola's main window.

"You already have, Captain Singleton."

A couple of minutes later, she drifted back into the JEM. Upon seeing her, Nadine emitted a single squeak and started swimming toward Angela and her little rat's nest.

Angela slowly plucked the baby mice from her hair and gently nudged them toward their mother.

Entranced, Angela silently watched Nadine's fat little body as it wriggled through the air.

Then the animals flinched as another stomach growl drowned out the squeak-filled reunion.

CHAPTER 26

A n open operator's manual jittered and danced on the airplane's copilot seat. Before take off, Vaughn had studied the plane's normal procedures checklist and even familiarized himself with the King Air's laundry list of emergency procedures. He had no wish to repeat the spaceplane disaster. Vaughn smiled inwardly. Mark would have called it progress.

A beautiful sunrise greeted the plane as it flew out over the western Gulf of Mexico, crossing the beach just south of the US border. Vaughn guided the airplane northeast, toward Houston. Fifty minutes later, he glimpsed land again. After a moment, he recognized it as Freeport, Texas. Massive uncontrolled fires had reduced its large industrial complexes into twisted masses of melted metal and charred pavement. Beneath the plane, dark, curling waves rolled across Surfside Beach. Back in his high school days, Vaughn had spent many an afternoon surfing those rollers, but now a ruptured and badly listing supertanker blocked much of the town's beach. The ship's load of crude painted the waves black for the next twenty miles.

As the west end of Galveston Island passed beneath the King Air, Vaughn guided the plane north. Ahead, Houston's iconic skyline now looked like a jagged line of burned, fractured giant crystals. Visible beyond his destination, the Houston ship channel painted a black scar across the land. Almost all of its industrial complexes appeared to have fallen to the massive post-apocalyptic fires. The hellish trail of destruction led all the way to downtown's decimated skyscrapers.

Vaughn turned from the disturbing image and focused on his destination. Firestorms had destroyed the hometown of his youth, but fortunately, Ellington Field stood relatively unscathed.

He lined up the plane with the airport's clearest runway. After completing a landing that had required one hop and two quick lateral jaunts to avoid debris, Vaughn taxied the King Air up to the terminal and shut down the engines. Then he searched the parking lot until he found a suitable vehicle. After loading the Mexican ham radio, Vaughn jumped into the truck and exited the field.

He didn't need maps for this part of the voyage. Vaughn had grown up here, knew the roads like the back of his hand. And with the area's flat terrain, he'd have no problem circumnavigating any blocked streets.

Vaughn soon arrived at the entrance to NASA's Johnson Space Center. No guards challenged him at its gate. He passed through the security checkpoint unmolested. A few minutes later, Vaughn parked the truck in front of the facility that Angela had specified.

As he stepped from the truck, Vaughn recalled their brief conversation with Director McCree. He looked northeast. Gazing into the cloudless sky, he tried to envision the rapidly approaching wall of light. In his mind's eye, he watched it expand, swallowing an ever-increasing portion of the visible sky.

A shudder ran down Vaughn's spine. He turned back to the large, white building. Its power had failed, so the electronic locks offered no resistance. He walked straight through the front door and all the way into the main service bay. The sign above its entrance read:

BRUIE ASSEMBLY ROOM
EUROPA BUOYANT ROVER FOR UNDER-ICE EXPLORATION

Vaughn stepped into the bay. A car-sized rover with only two wheels hung from a ceiling hoist. The barbell-shaped device looked like a giant Segway. Thick, hollow metal wheels with four-foot diameters adorned each end of its ten-foot-long cylindrical body. NASA had designed this rover to explore the ice-covered ocean of Europa, one of Jupiter's moons. They had planned for it to melt through the mile-thick sheet of ice that covered the Jovian moon. Once it had penetrated into Europa's ocean, its buoyancy would pin those large wheels to the bottom of the ice. Then it would navigate the sheet's underside, driving around like an upside-down Segway.

According to Angela, the BRUIE rover required a very large and energetic power source to melt through that much ice and then explore the underlying ocean. The Department of Energy had delivered the vehicle's nuclear-powered electrical generator only a few days before the Disappearance. She had told him that it was the largest radioisotope thermoelectric generator, or RTG, ever created for the space agency.

Vaughn scanned the room. His eyes lit upon a large green box. A smile blossomed on his face.

"This is going to be easier than I thought."

Next to its radiation warnings, the green case sported a big red RTG label.

Vaughn smiled and jogged to the generator case.

"Angela, you rock!"

He started unhooking its numerous latches. Multiple labels warned of the dire consequences of screwing with this package. They promised everything from imprisonment to loss of hair and child-spawning capabilities. However, Angela had assured him that it would be safe … as long as he didn't screw up.

A moment later, he slowly lifted its hinged lid, cupping his balls … just in case. The tight piano hinge creaked like a door in a haunted house.

The damn thing was empty!

Dropping the lid—and releasing the family jewels—Vaughn scanned the room but saw no other place where the RTG could be, save one.

"Son of a bitch!"

Vaughn shook his head. He walked to the buoyant rover and scanned its surface. He soon found a compartment decorated with a yellow radioactive warning label and its trio of black triangles. A quick glance told him that roughly a million screws and two miles of arcane plumbing and wiring attached the damn thing to the rover.

Vaughn pursed his lips. "Why did I expect anything less?"

Nearby, he found a very high-tech toolbox filled with expensive-looking wrenches and drivers. Vaughn reached inside of it and retrieved a screw gun that looked as if it should fit the million-odd socket head bolts that affixed the RTG to the rover.

He trotted back to the BRUIE and jammed the Allen wrench bit into the first bolt. Then he froze. A frown spread across his face as he ground his teeth together. Mark's words rang in his ears. *You never applied yourself. You just cruised through life, winging it.*

Vaughn shook his head again and set the tool down on the nearest bench. Several minutes later, he walked back into the room, a thick, three-ring binder under arm. It had taken a little searching, but he'd known the manual had to be there somewhere.

The government wrote instructions for everything. Vaughn had often joked that they not only told you how to wipe your ass, they even specified the number of squares.

After a lot of searching within the binder's three-inch-thick stack of pages, he finally found a section labeled:

RTG INSTALLATION AND REMOVAL

Vaughn leafed through its pages and finally found the instructions for removing the device. After thumbing through the legalese, he started reading. A large warning preceded step one. It warned of dire consequences, up to and including a thermonuclear runaway—the described effects of which elicited visions of Fukushima—should one fail to properly power down and safe the device.

As with most government manuals, this one featured plenty of diagrams and drawings. So Vaughn soon had the RTG shut down and safed.

"Thanks, Mark."

After an hour's worth of toiling, Vaughn finally lifted the outer cover away from the RTG and released a long sigh. The inner capsule appeared to be intact. Not that he'd had cause to think it damaged, but according to the manual's multiple warnings, had it been cracked or otherwise compromised, his remaining days would have been few and rather unpleasant.

"Thank you," he whispered.

Looking down, he pulled his left hand away from his apparently safe testicles.

Several screws later, the last piece of hardware fell away. Vaughn grunted as he gently lifted the heavy power supply from the rover. Turning, he gingerly lowered it onto the cart that he'd brought for the purpose. Then he turned back to the BRUIE and began scavenging anything that looked like it might be part of the RTG's cooling system.

Finally, Vaughn emerged into the sunlight pushing a large cart. Atop its flat surface, the green box jittered with the passage of each crack and expansion joint in the concrete. Vaughn winced at every jolt. He parked it behind the truck. Grunting with exertion, he slid the heavy, lead-lined canister and its nuclear cargo into the back of the vehicle. Then he added the scavenged hardware and plumbing.

An hour later, the fully loaded and refueled twin-engined airplane roared up one of Ellington Field's northbound runways. Finally, the King Air rotated and lifted skyward under a midday sun.

As broken bits of downtown's shattered skyline scrolled past Vaughn's left shoulder, the airplane turned north by northeast, toward distant Cleveland, Ohio.

Vaughn flew the King Air parallel to Cleveland Airport's longest runway. Faded and dust-covered airplane shards protruded from the remnants of the Boeing-fed bonfire. He could still see long scars etched into the concrete. They led from the point where each of the planes had belly-landed all the way to their final resting place. However, green grass had already reclaimed the adjacent scoured earth. Vaughn couldn't see Mark's final resting place. In the late-afternoon sun, the tall grass waved in the wind that streamed in from Lake Erie.

Debris rendered the main landing strip unusable, so Vaughn throttled back the plane's engines and then landed it on the airport's shorter but relatively clear parallel runway. Then he taxied the King Air up to the gate in the NASA perimeter.

Vaughn shut down the airplane. He climbed over the fence and jogged toward the hangar. The old tug he'd left on the corner of the tarmac now looked ancient. It sat on four flat tires. Around it, weeds protruded from the ramp's multiple cracks and expansion joints.

A few minutes after entering the building, Vaughn guided a forklift through its still-open doors. It made short work of the gate, ripping it from its track. He drove it over to the side and deposited the long chain-link panel onto the grass. Then he went to work on the opposite gate, the one that opened to the rest of the NASA facility. Half an hour later, and after a lot of grunting and struggling, Vaughn had the large RTG canister removed from the airplane and loaded onto the forklift's metal tines. He secured the cooling hardware and plumbing to the top of the container using straps he'd borrowed from Houston.

Finally, he jumped back into the forklift. Mindful of the container's dire warnings, Vaughn took his time. He placed the forklift in gear and slowly drove it through the aviation ramp's opposite gate and into the NASA compound, not stopping until he reached the Space Power Annex.

Except for overgrown landscaping and pavement cracks now choked with weeds, everything looked as he and Mark had left it. He guided the forklift through the still-open overhead doors and into the large bay. He parked the vehicle just outside of the vacuum chamber and then killed its engine.

Vaughn was exhausted and starving. He checked his watch.

"Still one more thing to do, Captain."

He jogged back toward the airplane. Arriving at the King Air, he set up the generator and ham radio. Vaughn soon had the system up and running. After a final glance at his watch, he pressed the transmit button.

～

Mixed sounds of wet smacking interrupted by agonized wails echoed through the station's reduced confines.

Suddenly, the radio in the distant Cupola crackled to life.

"Commander Brown? This is Glenn Control. Come in, Angela."

Through watery eyes, Angela looked at her watch. "Oh shit …" Then she gazed self-consciously at her greasy fingers.

It wasn't her fault.

"Come in, Commander."

In spite of her revulsion, Angela hungrily licked the fat from the outside of her fingers.

Another wail escaped her lips.

"Where ya at?"

Angela stuffed the last bone into the bag with the others.

She'd had to do it.

"I made it, Angela!"

After sealing the plastic bag and its gruesome cargo in an airtight container, Angela deposited it inside a hidden niche. Then she pushed off the wall.

A moment later, she drifted into the Cupola, joining the quartet of mice. Not wanting them to watch her eat their mother, she had stuffed the mice inside their vented plastic box and stashed them in the sun-warmed observatory. Now their beady little eyes seemed to stare accusingly.

"I had to," Angela said plaintively. "She was dead. I couldn't … I couldn't …" A sharp sob broke through her defenses. "I couldn't let her just … go to waste."

"Come in, Angela!" Vaughn said, worry now creeping into his words.

Angela wiped the tears from her eyes and then slipped the headset over her matted hair.

"Hey, Vaughn," she said, unable to keep her boiled-over emotions from her voice.

"What's wrong?" Vaughn said, suddenly on edge.

Angela shook her head vigorously. She'd rather die than share this part of her story with the man. Hell no!

She swallowed hard and then said, "N-Nothing."

"I'm so sorry, Angela. It's my fault."

Her eyes widened. "What?! Wasn't it there?"

"Huh? … Oh, the RTG! No, I found it right where you said." His voice softened, suddenly sounding thick with guilt. "No, I'm sorry that you're still up there, Angela, that you're still stuck in that damned station." After a long pause, he said, "It's my fault."

Angela blinked and then understood. "Oh shit. No, Vaughn. It's not you. It's me." A short, self-conscious laugh burst through her lips.

"Oh, so we're going there already, are we?" Vaughn said, the imagined smile back in his words. "My ex never saw it that way. As far as she was concerned, it was definitely *all* me." Then his humor evaporated. "But these days, I'm inclined to think she was right."

After another cough, Angela shook her head. "No, Vaughn. This time it really is me. Just been feeling a little weepy. Guess I'm hormonal today," she lied.

"Now there's a condition no man is *ever* allowed to diagnose."

Angela smiled, but then she saw eight accusing eyes staring at her from the plastic box, and the grin fell from her lips.

Finally, she said, "So you're back in Cleveland, Captain?"

Her use of his rank had its usual effect.

His tone became serious. "Uh … yes. I just placed the RTG in the bay outside the chamber."

Angela's eyes kept returning to the little box-o-mice.

"This will work, Angela," Vaughn said. "I'll make it. I promise."

A long stretch of dead air followed his proclamation. Finally, she keyed the mic. "I know you will, Captain. I trust you, Vaughn."

Apparently placated, the man spent the next several minutes

telling her of his plans, laying out what he'd need to do to get the thruster module ready for trans-atmospheric flight.

Finally, they set a time for their next radio call and terminated this one.

As Angela pulled off the headset, a fresh spasm of coughs racked her body. Each hack felt as if it were breaking off chunks of her lungs.

When the spasms finally subsided, she looked at the scrolling planet visible through the Cupola's main port.

"Hurry, Vaughn."

CHAPTER 27

Even two months after the Disappearance, the break room still smelled of burned eggs and scorched popcorn. Vaughn dropped a thick, three-ring binder onto one of its tables. The report of its impact echoed down the facility's empty hallways. As he walked back to the vending machine, pebble-sized shards of its broken glass crunched under foot. In the otherwise dark room, the light from his Coleman lantern reflected off of them as if the kitchen now floated on a sea of yellow stars.

Vaughn reached into the large hole that the thick book had left in the front of the vending machine and grabbed his dinner. Then he dropped down onto the booth's laminated bench, depositing his ill-gotten booty onto the table between the sputtering gas-fed lamp and the binder.

He shoved aside a pile of pretzels and tore into a bag of Funyuns. After a long day without food, he savored every crumb. The crunchy yellow rings had never tasted so good.

Vaughn drank from a water bottle that he'd liberated from the room's pantry—the damn soda machine had proven stubbornly resistant to his efforts to gain access.

He checked his wrist: 2:00 AM. He opened the three-ring binder.

"I'll sleep when I'm dead."

The exhausted man looked down and read the book's title. "Sigma Reactionless Thruster SSTO."

Contrary to Mark's protestations, Vaughn had paid attention to some of the original briefings. For instance, he remembered that SSTO stood for Single-Stage-To-Orbit. Theoretically, the module was capable of space flight. However, this one was far from complete, and its power source was nowhere near up to the task. But that was about as far as his knowledge went.

"You win, Mark."

Vaughn opened the binder and leafed through the Foreword and Table of Contents until he found the desired page. For a pilot to be master of his domain, to know how to properly respond to any in-flight emergency, he must have intimate knowledge of his aircraft's systems. With the spaceplane, Vaughn hadn't paid heed to that basic tenet, and it had nearly killed him, and it had jeopardized Angela, too.

He wouldn't make that mistake twice.

Vaughn placed his hand on the open page and read its title. "Systems Descriptions."

He took a long drink from the water bottle and then started reading.

Vaughn's eyes opened. He tried to blink the clouds from his mind.

Where in the hell am I?

In the corner of his vision, a horizontal rectangle of soft white light refused to resolve. For some reason, the side of his face hurt. He lifted his head, and something fell away from it. He looked down and watched a pretzel bounce off the open rear cover of a three-ring binder. Vaughn tried to sweep away the crumbs, but his hand just smeared them into a puddle of drool.

He looked back toward the white rectangle. Now that he was sitting up, it resolved as a hallway. Indirect sunlight lit its far end. It was the sole source of light in Vaughn's universe. He didn't remember extinguishing the lantern. It must've run out of fuel.

Rubbing his eyes, Vaughn slid to the edge of the booth. When he turned his head toward the dark lantern, his neck seized.

"Son of a bitch!"

Vaughn tried to massage the knots out of his neck as he exited the break room.

Stepping into the diffuse radiance of an early morning cloudy day, he looked around the courtyard. Even after months of the experience, the world's utter and complete silence still seemed odd. It had been that way since the Disappearance. No birds chirped, no crickets … cricketed, no cicadas pitched their bitch, just the occasional rustle of leaves. With the subsequent failure of the electrical grid, the silence had taken on an ominous depth.

A chill ran down Vaughn's spine.

Shaking his head, he jogged toward the vacuum chamber. He had a lot of work to do and not much time in which to do it. Now that he'd read the manual cover to cover, Vaughn had a good idea of exactly what the module needed to function.

He hopped into the forklift and fired up its engine. Then Vaughn *gently* deposited its precious cargo on the bay's concrete floor, well clear of the vacuum chamber's massive hatch.

The large door still sat partially open, just as he and Mark had left it. After a little coaxing—or in this case, bashing with the assistance of a forklift—Vaughn had the twenty-foot-wide door fully open.

Inside the vacuum chamber, he looked over the module. Everything appeared unchanged. Finally, he nodded and walked back outside.

"Time to go on a scavenger hunt."

An hour later, a white Home Depot truck with a scissor lift hooked to its bumper wheeled into the courtyard outside of the chamber's bay. Hardware and supplies filled the truck's flatbed.

After disconnecting the lift, Vaughn backed the truck up to the vacuum chamber door. He placed the vehicle in park and killed its engine.

The wannabe astronaut stepped out of the truck and walked over to the forklift. Pulling a brand new tape measure from his belt, he checked the width of its tines and the distance between the two steel planks. Then he turned and gave the bottom of the module an appraising look. The thruster still sat atop its scaffolding. After some mental calculations, Vaughn nodded.

Hitching a thumb over his shoulder, he pointed at the back of the loaded truck. "Did a little shopping in Home Depot's aviation aisle," Vaughn said with a crooked grin.

The thruster module had three major limitations, electrical supply primary among them. However, the RTG should take care of that problem. The other two biggies were weight and life support. He couldn't add much to one part of that equation without negatively impacting the other.

In regard to overall weight, the manual had confirmed what Mark had said. The Sigma Module's fifty percent hover power signaled its ability to climb continuously, both inside and outside the atmosphere. The thruster didn't need to be very aerodynamic. That continuous climb capability meant that the vehicle could stay at an aerodynamically sustainable speed until clear of the atmosphere. Once air resistance fell off, it could accelerate to orbital velocity. However, he didn't have unlimited time to reach orbit. The module was completely open. Vaughn had neither the time nor the resources nor knowledge to build a pressurized cabin. And even if he had, he doubted the module could handle the extra weight. So that meant he'd have to make the trip in a spacesuit. But if it took days to catch up to the ISS, Vaughn would run out of air and be dead on arrival. So he had to maximize the module's acceleration capability: he needed to lose all unnecessary weight and affect some aerodynamic improvements to permit moderate in-atmosphere speeds followed by significant exoatmospheric acceleration.

An hour later and covered in sweat, Vaughn climbed behind the controls of the forklift. He'd already repositioned it so that the tongs now supported the bottom of the module. A web of Home Depot-supplied cargo straps secured it to the frame of the forklift.

He fired up the machine's propane-powered engine. Vaughn placed his hand on the lift control lever.

"Here goes nothing."

He eased the lever back and the hydraulic motor whined as it tried to lift the Sigma Module. It didn't budge, but as Vaughn began to release the control lever, the module raised an inch above the platform. The sudden release rocked both the thruster and the forklift. Vaughn froze, chewing his lip as he stared at the slowly swaying machines. A moment later, the rocking subsided. He let out a long sigh. "Son of a bitch, that was close."

Gingerly, he actuated the forklift, raising the module another inch. Suddenly, the vehicle tilted forward, and the module's landing gear dropped back onto the scaffolding. The impact sent a massive bang echoing through the hot chamber. The forklift teetered on its front wheels. The scaffolding creaked and groaned as if it might collapse.

"Shit, shit, *shit* ..." Vaughn whispered, afraid that louder sound waves might bring the whole damn thing crashing down.

Gingerly, he lowered the module back onto the top of the scaffolding. It creaked but held as the lift's rear wheels returned to the floor.

Vaughn released the breath he'd been holding.

"Son of a bitch!"

After a moment's consideration, he nodded and climbed down from the vehicle. He unloaded the materials from the back of the truck and then drove it out of the facility. An hour later he returned with a fresh supply of building materials.

Vaughn heaved bags of concrete onto the back of the forklift. After securing the piled sacks with several cargo straps, he stood back and gave the entire jury-rigged setup an appraising look.

"That dog'll hunt ... I hope."

Vaughn climbed back behind the controls of the lift and started it. He wiped the sweat from his brow and then extended a trembling hand toward the lever.

"Please, God, please, let this work."

He eased back on the stick and the hydraulic motor whined under the load. But this time, it lifted the module straight up. All four wheels of the forklift maintained full contact with the ground.

Vaughn backed up the lift. As the thruster cleared its support structure, he gently lowered the module until it hovered a few inches above the floor. Vaughn breathed a sigh of relief and then guided the vehicle out of the vacuum chamber. When he finally reached the center of the Space Power Annex's large courtyard, he lowered the Sigma SSTO Module onto the pavement next to the stack of hardware.

After parking the forklift off to one side, Vaughn climbed down and wiped sweat from his forehead. Early morning clouds had given way to bright sunlight, turning it into a warm Cleveland day.

Another series of beeps echoed off of the side of the large facility. With Vaughn atop its rectangular metal deck, the scissor lift inched its way up to the fifteen-foot-tall module. Then he donned a stuffed tool belt.

Vaughn started removing equipment and hardware. Using the scissor lift, he worked his way from the top to the bottom of the module. Unnecessary or redundant electronics and fasteners soon littered the ground. Twice Vaughn had fired up the generator and taken a reciprocating saw to a particularly stubborn piece of hardware. He could almost see the vehicle's long-missing engineers cringing.

Vaughn hurled another arcane piece of unnecessary hardware.

"A man's got to do what a man's got to do."

Several potentiometers and other extraneous measuring devices cluttered the now mangled chunk of metal. Like everything else that Vaughn had removed, its loss would not negatively impact the thruster's abilities.

He kept the three-ring binder open on the top of the scissor lift. Vaughn referred to its diagrams on several occasions. The reactionless thruster was a pretty straightforward self-contained assembly. Mounted to a directional gimbal that was, in turn, mounted to the bottom of the module, it had two primary requirements. The drive needed modulated power and a way to cool its electrical components.

During his early morning studies, Vaughn had learned that the thruster's cooling system was integral to the module's chassis. It had been specifically designed to work in a vacuum, to dissipate heat even when there was no air to which to transfer it. So Vaughn was careful not to disturb any of those connections or cooling fins.

Finally, he couldn't find any additional hardware or systems to remove.

It was time to install the RTG.

The thruster module had a large bank of batteries under the crew deck. Those had provided sufficient power for the hover test in the vacuum chamber. However, out here, if Vaughn tried to launch without a recharging source, the electrical supply would soon deplete, sending the module earthward like a homesick rock.

He removed the battery bank and then turned to the RTG's green container. After he released its final fastener, Vaughn reached for the upper handle. He hesitated for a moment. Not all of yesterday's movements had been exactly smooth. There had been a few hard knocks between Houston and Cleveland.

Vaughn placed a protective hand over his genitals and turned his head to one side, closing an eye. Slowly, he lifted the heavy, lead-lined lid. Again its hinges squeaked their protest.

Through a slitted eye, Vaughn studied the RTG.

All looked well.

Vaughn released his gonads and held breath as he fully opened the creaking lid. He soon had the device mounted to the deck of the module. An hour after that, he finished plumbing its cooling system as well.

Covered in sweat and breathing heavily, Vaughn stood back, admiring his work, and then nodded.

"Moment of truth, Captain."

Chewing his lip, Vaughn extended a hesitant index finger toward the module's power switch and then pressed it.

He flinched as a series of loud clicks emanated from beneath him.

Then the thruster's instrument panel came to life.

Vaughn pumped his fist in the air.

"Yes!"

He danced around the cockpit, laughing and shouting like an NFL player celebrating a game-winning touchdown.

Finally, Vaughn powered down the RTG and began preparations for the next task. He raised the scissor lift up to the upper reaches of the module, stopping when it drew even with the base of the cone-shaped collection of tubes that formed the top of the chassis.

Vaughn hung two new tools from his belt. Then he stepped up to a stack of square sheet metal panels and grabbed the top one. Working his way up from the bottom of the cone, he began to drill and rivet the thin, light metal squares to the angled tubes on top of the module.

He lapped them like shingles on a roof. This would leave no edge exposed to the prying fingers of air that would stream across the surface of the makeshift cone. Using tinsnips and a rubber mallet, he molded the panels into shape, trimming edges and rounding corners.

Finally, he riveted a large, orange funnel over the top edge of the uppermost sheets. To save weight, he'd decided not to cover the horizontal walls. During the ascent, it would get drafty inside, but the spacesuit would protect him. Besides, the module wouldn't need to go that fast in the atmosphere. He would save the majority of his acceleration for the exoatmospheric portion of the flight.

Vaughn lowered the scissor lift to the ground and climbed out. He stood back and studied his work. He laughed and shook his head.

His little spaceship looked like something straight out of a steampunk graphic novel.

The aeronautical handyman checked his watch.

"Oh shit! Almost time to call Angela!"

He ran to the truck and grabbed the ham radio set. After a few starts and stops, he finished installing it in the Sigma Thruster. By the time Vaughn powered it up, he was five minutes late for his check-in.

He depressed the transmit trigger on the module's control stick. "Angela, you there?"

"Well, it's about time, Captain. I was starting to get—" A series of hacking coughs cut the sentence short.

"That doesn't sound good."

"It doesn't feel very good either," she whispered. "How did it—" more coughing, "—go this morning?"

After a silent moment staring at the radio with a concerned look, Vaughn pressed the transmit key. "So far, so good. I have a couple of items left to do, but they won't take long. I should be flight-ready in an hour or two."

"That's great news, Vaughn!"

He looked at his watch. "Is that departure time still good?"

"Yeah, then or ninety minutes later will work, too. After that, the next few orbital passes will have me too far south—"

Her words dissolved into another spasm of coughs and she broke the transmission.

"Angela? Are you okay?"

After a worrying silence, she returned. "I'm a long way from okay. Hurry to me, Vaughn."

Looking overhead, he warily eyed the tin roof of his glorified silo. "Okay, Angela. I'll call you back when I clear the atmosphere."

"Good luck, Vaughn, and … thank you for working so hard … Thank you … for everything. You really are my hero."

CHAPTER 28

V aughn gave the cargo strap one final ratchet and then tugged at the modified nozzle of each oxygen bottle. They didn't budge. He'd scavenged them from all over the research center. Their sizes varied from long, thin tanks to short, fat ones. Each of them connected to a long pipe that served as an oxygen distribution manifold. He'd found most of the necessary hardware in the Space Power Annex. However, finishing the project had required another trip to Home Depot, so the first launch window had already passed and the second one was nearing.

Jumping down from the module, Vaughn ran into the facility. A few minutes later, he returned garbed in a new spacesuit. His original one no longer fit. When Vaughn had tried it on, he'd been swimming in its expansive interior. Before donning this one, he had wired a three-lug audio jack into its communication system. It was the same type of socket you would see on an MP3 player or iPhone.

In preparation for liftoff, the astronaut-to-be circumnavigated his unlikely chariot. Everything looked flight-ready, or at least, as much as it ever would.

Vaughn climbed onto the module's flight deck. With trepidation, he eyed the array of oxygen bottles. Lined up like a row of dead soldiers of varying body types, they filled the available floor space between the back side of the foot pedals and the module's outer edge. He would have preferred to bring more oxygen. However, the collection of tanks already amassed significant weight. Vaughn had rigged each with a quick disconnect like those that carpenters use to connect pneumatic tools to their compressed air source. To lighten the load, he planned to remove and discard the tanks as they emptied.

Vaughn connected the O2 supply to his suit. He left the valve closed and his visor open. No sense using his limited oxygen supply while still in an ocean of the stuff. Finally, he plugged the suit's modified communications cable into the module.

After strapping in, Vaughn looked at the copilot seat. He had occupied that one the last time this thing had flown. Back then, he had been a virtual sandbag, just dead weight to prove that the module could hover with two people aboard. He had wondered if Mark had picked him more because of his weight than for the stated reason of his competency.

Vaughn shook his head. None of that mattered now. Only one purpose remained for that seat. And it was time to put it to use.

With hard-learned diligence, he worked methodically through the pre-flight checks. A few minutes later, he had all systems online.

Vaughn's heart raced as his finger traced over the last checklist item. He gave the parachute strapped to his chest an appraising tug. Still secure. He had belted another one into the copilot seat. They served an obvious function. However, until the module was above 1000 feet, a parachute wasn't likely to do him any good.

The panting he heard in his ears reminded Vaughn of his first trip into the vacuum chamber. As he had done that day, he swallowed hard and took a deep breath, willing himself to calm down.

Finally reining in the emotions, Vaughn began to lift the stick in his left hand. It worked like a helicopter's collective control. Pull it up to increase thrust and vice versa.

Unlike his vacuum chamber experience, Vaughn could hear the thruster's hum this time. It began as a murmuring vibration that radiated through the floor and seat, but it escalated into a tooth-rattling drone as he continued to lift the stick and increase power.

Suddenly, the module began to dance and skitter on its landing gear. Then it slid left several feet. Vaughn increased power, and the thruster leaped into the air, and its lateral drift accelerated.

"Son of a bitch!"

His eyes widened as the Sigma Module sped toward the scissor lift. Shoving the center stick to the right, he arrested the drift just as the module bumped the side of the lift. Finally gaining control of the beast, Vaughn haltingly flew the module back into position.

After a few seconds of unsteady hovering and some pilot-induced oscillations, Vaughn got a feel for the flight controls. He soon had the thrumming beast in a stable hover.

The space-rated GPS that he had strapped into the instrument panel showed a ground speed of zero and a digital altitude of ten feet. Earlier, Vaughn had been right not to trust the navigation system's position information. When he had arrived in Houston, the center of the airport's location had been off by more than a mile. However, the error drift was minuscule. It would work just fine for speed and general location data.

Vaughn looked up.

"It's time to get busy living, Captain!"

He raised the collective control, and the ship began to climb. It rose slowly at first. But as he increased power, it began to accelerate. Soon he felt turbulence buffeting the outside of his spacesuit. The wind whipped through his open helmet. Water streamed from his squinted eyes. Keeping his right hand on the center stick or cyclic, Vaughn released the collective and slid the visor down enough to shield his eyes. It worked. He blinked the tears from his vision and the horizon resolved. The trees and then the buildings of the NASA facility dropped out of view beneath him.

Grabbing the collective again, Vaughn added more power. Like a helicopter climbing straight up, the SSTO Module ascended through five hundred feet.

The turbulence under the thruster's makeshift nose cone

increased. It now buffeted Vaughn left and right. A moment later, the altimeter crested one thousand feet.

"Hell yeah! I'm on my way, Angela!"

Vaughn added more power, and the vertical speed increased to 1500 feet per minute. A quick check of the GPS display showed that he'd picked up some unwanted ground speed. Cross-referencing the ground track with his magnetic heading, Vaughn saw that he was drifting left. He applied right cyclic.

Having reined in the drift, the helicopter pilot applied more power. The vertical speed needle crept up to 2000 feet per minute, but the leftward drift returned. His lateral velocity soon exceeded twenty knots and building. He tried to apply additional right cyclic, but it hit the stop.

He couldn't arrest the drift!

Vaughn didn't know if this was upper-level winds or something else. He reduced the power, and the climb rate fell back to 1500 feet per minute. Vaughn applied left pedal, and the module pivoted a quarter turn. Lake Erie rotated into view. Even though he now faced north, the ship continued to drift left. Apparently, it wasn't caused by the wind. The cone must be creating some asymmetrical lateral thrust.

The module climbed through 3000 feet of altitude. Beneath him, most of the airport was no longer visible. However, Vaughn could now see the entire city of Cleveland. Ahead of him and to his left and right, Lake Erie stretched to the horizon. At the reduced climb speed, he was able to zero out the lateral drift again. Vaughn checked the power level. So far, it had not exceeded seventy percent. There was plenty more available, but he'd have to wait for thinner air before he could apply it.

A few minutes later he crossed 10,000 feet. He continued to play with the power setting. Presently, seventy-two percent left sufficient lateral thrust to keep the drift in check.

When the module climbed through 12,000 feet, Vaughn lowered his visor and cracked open the first oxygen bottle. The suit had enough on-board for a couple of hours, but he wanted to save that for later.

An hour into the vertical flight, the Sigma Thruster crested 100,000 feet. The sky had turned indigo blue. From this altitude, Vaughn could clearly see the planet's curvature. A grin spread across his face as he looked down on the Great Lakes and much of the Northeast.

"It's beautiful." Vaughn raised his eyebrows. "Scary as shit, but beautiful."

The ever-thinning atmosphere had permitted incremental power increases. He had decided to cap it at an arbitrary value of ninety percent. However, as atmospheric drag declined, the module's vertical speed continued to increase.

Vaughn turned the vessel so that he faced east. Now that it was clear of the atmosphere's worst effects, it was time to start building lateral velocity. Applying forward cyclic, he tilted the module a few degrees toward the eastern horizon. His ground speed began to grow as the module's vertical velocity decreased. He experimented with varying levels of pitch until he found the ideal combination of vertical climb and lateral acceleration.

Two oxygen bottles later, Vaughn saw that it was time to discard another one. He had fashioned a tether for the purpose. Parachute or no, a misstep at this altitude would be catastrophic, not only for Angela but likely for him as well. He was quickly approaching 200,000 feet. No one had ever done a free fall from anywhere close to this altitude. He would likely spin out of control and lose consciousness. The parachute he had was of the dumb variety; it had no auto deploy system.

Vaughn climbed from the seat and then crawled on hands and knees toward the empty tank. He soon had it disconnected from the supply manifold. He released the cargo strap that held the tanks together and began shoving the empty cylinder out of the row. However, before he could get it clear, the tether pulled up short.

Without looking, Vaughn grabbed the strap with his left hand and yanked.

Suddenly, the ship spun, tossing out Vaughn and the loose bottle.

"Oh shit!"

He grasped desperately, but his hands closed on nothing but empty space. His arms and legs flailed violently as he reached the end of the ten-foot-long tether. His head snapped back in a painful whiplashing motion.

As he'd flown out of the cockpit, Vaughn had glimpsed the tether drifting away from the left pedal. The strap must have snagged that yaw control when he had yanked it. Thankfully, the tether had come clear of the pedal, but, even though the controls had returned to neutral, the module continued to rotate about its long axis.

Hanging from the end of the thin strap, the panicked flailing man now orbited the slowly turning module. Centrifugal force kept the line taut, but acceleration and minor atmospheric drag pulled his body aft, causing him to spin around the thruster like the world's highest swing ride.

Fortunately, he had made the air supply line a bit longer than the tether. Just as he had the thought, something cylindrical flew from the module, and a faint hiss joined the sound of his heavy breathing.

"Damn it!"

Wide-eyed, Vaughn watched the oxygen bottle fly earthward as he desperately grasped the tether. Working hand-over-hand, he began to climb it. Thankfully, the pedals had neutralized. Otherwise, the centrifugal G-forces would have been too strong to overcome. At some point, they would have overloaded the tether and thrown him clear of the module.

No time to think about that right now.

Vaughn grunted as he lunged another hand higher up the tether.

Halfway there!

Two other bottles oscillated at the ends of their hoses.

"Shit, shit, *shit!*"

Vaughn reached for the closest structural member. Then his hand slipped, and he lost a yard of progress before his other hand rejoined the effort.

"Son of a bitch!" he growled through a grunt. "Really?!"

Shaking his head, he shimmied hand-over-hand back toward the structural member. This time, he wrapped the tether around one glove. Just as he grabbed onto the module, a second bottle broke free and floated away.

"Fuck!"

Still holding onto the cross-beam, Vaughn snaked his leg into the cockpit and pressed the right pedal. The module, as well as the horizon, finally ceased its spinning. Fortunately, the ship's angle hadn't changed. It was still climbing.

But Vaughn had bigger problems. His ears popped as the suit continued to lose pressure. A moment later, he identified the problem. When the tanks had broken off, they had left their nozzles in the quick disconnects. Vaughn ejected them, and the hiss stopped. A few seconds later, his ears quit popping as pressure equalized and then rebuilt to pre-leak levels.

On hands and knees, Vaughn crawled to the remaining tanks, mindful of the tether this time. After inventorying the remaining bottles and checking their condition, he strapped them back to the deck.

He'd lost one medium and one large tank. The loss eliminated any margin he may have had.

Vaughn crawled back into the pilot seat. Panting breaths and pounding pulse echoed in his helmet.

He closed his eyes, trying to will himself to relax. Vaughn had to pull it together! If he kept breathing this heavily, burning through his oxygen supply, he wouldn't even make it to the station.

Instead of slowing, his respiration rate worsened. He couldn't seem to get enough air. He felt like a fish out of water.

Vaughn activated the ham radio. "Angela, are … you … there?"

"Vaughn? Are you okay? What happened? Why are you panting?"

"Had an accident … lost a … couple of … oxygen bottles."

"Vaughn, are you breathing pure oxygen?"

He nodded. "I … Y-Yes."

"You're hyperventilating. Cut off the oxygen. Shut it down!"

Vaughn blinked and looked around, his addled brain unable to comprehend the woman's words.

The periphery of his vision began to fade.

Deeper and deeper breaths didn't help.

"Vaughn!" screamed a female voice. "Close the oxygen val—!" Suddenly the sound of hacking coughs filled his ears.

Woman, coughing? A woman coughing! Angela!

The coughs stopped, and her voice returned. "Shut it down, Vaughn!"

Blinking, struggling to breathe, Vaughn groped for the long-handled tool that he'd been using to close the valves.

It was gone! Must have flown off with the bottles!

His vision shrank down to a pinhole universe.

The oxygen supply shut-off valve looked impossibly far away, as if seen at the end of a long tube.

His hands and feet tingled like they had fallen asleep.

Vaughn's eyes widened with sudden realization. His hands groped madly at his chest. A moment later, they closed on a lever. On the third try, his clumsy fingers managed to turn it. The hiss of flowing air died.

His chest heaved up and down as he continued to struggle for breath.

It wasn't working!

Icy panic gripped his heart.

He was going to fail!

No, he was going to die, and his fuck-up was going to cost Angela her life as well.

His mouth guppied as he fought to draw sufficient air. Wide-eyed, Vaughn shook his head.

She was wrong!

He reached for the valve, intent on restarting the O2, but then color and peripheral vision flooded back into his world.

His respiratory needs and rate dwindled precipitously.

"Captain!" The sobs had died. Instead, Angela's command voice reasserted itself. "Turn off your oxygen supply!"

"Thank you," Vaughn whispered. "You were right."

"Oh, thank goodness. I was starting to think I'd lost you." She coughed. "There must be something wrong with your suit. It should have kept your carbon monoxide levels in check."

"I had to make some … modifications, but I don't think this suit was designed for the kind of EVA I just did."

Vaughn's wry smile dissolved as his eyes fell on the shortened line of oxygen tanks. He shook his head. "But we have a bigger problem. I'm down a couple of O2 bottles."

"Oh, no! Do you have enough to get here?"

"I think so, but it's the return trip that I'm concerned about."

"Okay. Concentrate on what you're doing. I'll work on a solution."

Vaughn nodded as he scanned the module's instruments. "I just crossed three hundred thousand feet."

"Great! Less than a million to go."

"A million?!"

"It's not as bad as it sounds," Angela said. "You're about to climb through sixty miles. Only a hundred and sixty to go. What's your current velocity?"

Vaughn looked down. His eyes widened. "Shit! I'm going more than ten thousand miles an hour!"

"Okay," Angela said. "You've already gained more than half of the speed you'll need, but only about a quarter of the altitude. Increase your climb speed." After another spasm of coughs, she added, "Once you've got it stable, let me know your rate of climb and ground speed along with your current position and heading. Then I can calculate an intercept vector for you."

Vaughn nodded. "Okay, I'll call you right back."

He eased back on the cyclic. The makeshift nose cone tilted up. Vaughn monitored the GPS's position and velocity. His speed leveled off just above ten thousand miles per hour. However, the module's rate of climb increased significantly. The last four digits of the altitude changed so fast that they looked like blurred eights.

The GPS's displayed vertical speed had long ago pegged out at its max value of six thousand feet per minute. The actual number was well above that. Vaughn noted the current altitude and started his watch's sixty-second timer. A minute later, he mentally noted the new altitude. After some rough calculations, he whistled.

Vaughn smiled but then remembered the need to keep his emotions in check. He concentrated on sipping the now restored flow of oxygen. Closing his eyes, he took a calming breath and then squeezed the radio transmit trigger. "Okay," Vaughn said in a soft, level tone, almost whispering. "According to my calculations, my vertical speed is now ninety miles per hour."

"Good! What's your current ground speed and heading?"

"Ten thousand two hundred and thirty-eight miles an hour and increasing slowly." Before she could ask, he called out his current coordinates. They'd be off by more than a mile, but at this scale, he didn't think it mattered.

"Okay, good. Hold that speed until you reach an altitude of two hundred nineteen miles, the ISS's current altitude. Once you're there, adjust your pitch to maintain it, but don't change your power setting until you get a ten percent Delta-v."

Vaughn's eyebrows knitted. "Delta-Vee?" He'd heard the term before but had no clue what it meant.

"Sorry—" Angela coughed and then continued. "I mean your change in velocity. In other words, how long it takes you to get from ten thousand miles an hour to eleven thousand. It is a crucial calculation. But once you reach eleven thousand miles an hour, hold that speed and call me right away."

"Hold that speed? Why? I thought the idea was for me to catch up with you."

"If you match my speed too quickly, we'll never merge."

Vaughn nodded. "Okay, got you. Do you have a heading for me yet?"

"Yeah, just got it. Turn right to zero-niner-eight."

"Roger, turning right to heading zero-niner-eight, adjusting rate of climb to maintain a ground speed of ten thousand miles per hour."

"Perfect!" After a brief coughing spasm, she added, "Once you hit eleven thousand miles an hour, call and let me know how long it took to gain that ten percent increase in velocity!"

Vaughn nodded. "Will do, Commander. Talk to you then."

Her voice softened. "You're really doing it, Vaughn ... I'm so proud of you."

He blinked, confused as a new, unfamiliar emotion swelled within him. Pride? Yeah, although not for what he'd done, but for how Angela saw it, how she felt ... about him. He'd never cared about that before.

Vaughn smiled. "Th-Thank you, Commander."

"I told you to make it Angela, Vaughn."

"Okay, thank you, Angela-Vaughn."

She laughed and then signed off with a snort.

Still smiling, Vaughn fine-tuned the module's pitch. As the speed reduced to ten thousand miles per hour, he adjusted the controls to keep it there. The reduced speed bumped up his rate of climb. A minute later, he calculated his new climb rate at roughly a hundred miles an hour.

Vaughn's smile faltered as he saw the current oxygen bottle's dwindling pressure.

"Stay calm, Captain," he whispered. "Just sip the air."

Vaughn cast a nervous glance at the planet's tilted and curved horizon.

Yeah, good luck with that!

CHAPTER 29

"Don't look at me like that, Nate Junior," Angela said. "Nadine was an old mouse. It's not my fault she died."

The rest of Nate's siblings continued to crawl around in Angela's literal rat's nest of greasy hair. As she floated down the tube that connected the Cupola to the JEM, the three of them moved restlessly in her tangled locks. Their faded red and blue oft-washed diapers skittered through her peripheral vision.

Having pushed off the Cupola bulkhead, Nate Jr. paced her down the passageway. Tiny swimming motions kept the adroit little space-walker on a parallel course with her. As he drifted along about a foot right of her head, his left eye seemed to gaze accusingly.

Angela looked away from the flying mouse. "Jesus, Vaughn, you better hurry and get here before I totally lose my shit."

As she drifted into the slightly warmer environs of the Japanese Experiment Module, Angela plucked the mice from her hair. She stuffed all four of them into their vented box and then headed toward O2 control.

The space station stored oxygen in a liquid state. Liquid O2 or LOX took up significantly less space than it did in its gaseous form.

However, you can't just release LOX into the atmosphere. You have to run it through a vaporizer.

Apparently, Vaughn's suit had some but not all of those features. Spacesuits made for extended spacewalks sipped from a vaporizer attached to a LOX bottle while a CO_2 scrubber kept the air breathable. She had previously scavenged parts from her only spare, so Vaughn was stuck with his jury-rigged configuration, and it needed compressed oxygen, not LOX. She could get all the O_2 she needed from the JEM's environmental control, but she had no way of compressing it.

Or did she? As she stared at the various controls and connectors, Angela felt an idea beginning to form. She sensed it as a flurry of activity in her cerebral cortex, something there like a forgotten name, not quite percolating to the surface. She scanned the wall adjacent to the O_2 controls, and her eyes fell upon the long-dormant zero-G crystal experiment.

Angela's eyes widened. She kicked off the wall and drifted toward the tool locker. A moment later she returned with a roll of tape clenched in her teeth and various implements in each hand. Soon the experiment's discarded stainless steel, laser-etched faceplate floated away and drifted behind Angela. Arcane piping, valves, and pumps protruded from the module's dedicated slot.

Angela launched into a flurry of activity. She vented the experiment's nitrogen inerting tank to space. By disconnecting and reconnecting various tubes to the tank and pump, she MacGyvered an oxygen compression system. A few minutes later, she had it connected to the oxygen vaporizer's output coupling. Using a trick she'd seen on TV, Angela rubbed spit across each of the threaded connections. She studied the globules intently. In a couple of places, the spit bubbled. A tweak and a twist fixed each.

After actuating the vaporizer, Angela opened the valve that fed the pneumatic pump. In a series of burps and farts that sounded more like the air brakes of a large eighteen-wheeler than something that belonged on the International Space Station, the pump went about its work. After verifying a gradual rise on the repurposed nitrogen bottle's pressure gauge, Angela kicked off the wall and drifted across the JEM.

As she sailed past the box and its octuplet of accusing eyes, Angela hitched a thumb over her shoulder, gesturing toward the belching and farting pump. "Keep an eye on that for me." She coughed and then added, "I have to find more tanks."

Vaughn pushed the stick forward. The numbers on the altimeter gradually slowed. A moment later, he remembered to reduce power. However, his speed had already increased precipitously. After a few minutes, the module stabilized at 219 miles above the planet.

Vaughn pumped his fist in the vacuum.

"Hell, yeah! Space station altitude, baby!"

The smiling man slowed the module to 10,000 miles per hour. Even going that fast, Vaughn was still well below orbital velocity, but his arms and legs already felt significantly lighter.

He noted the time and then increased the power to ninety percent. Vaughn held the altitude level at 219 miles. The craft rapidly accelerated. When it reached eleven thousand miles per hour, he noted the elapsed time and then reduced power, adjusting pitch until the altitude and speed stabilized.

Vaughn turned the module perpendicular to its path across the planet's surface. With it pointed straight up, he applied just enough power to maintain altitude. Then he toggled the radio.

"Angela, this is Vaughn. Are you there?"

Nothing.

"Angela! Come in!"

A few moments later, a staticky crackle issued from his helmet's speakers.

"Vaughn! Sorry, I've been working on a project. I think I have your oxygen bottle problem solved."

He smiled. "Great job!"

The grin faded when he saw the pressure on his last O2 bottle. If he saw tank pressure that low while scuba-diving, he'd be headed for the surface. After this one, he'd be down to his suit's two-hour supply and its limited-use CO_2 scrubber.

"Okay, Angela. It took seven minutes and thirty-eight seconds to get a Delta-v of ten percent."

"Good! At that rate of change, it should take you ... ninety-three minutes to match my speed. Have you maintained the heading I gave you?"

Vaughn nodded. Remembering that she couldn't see him, he squeezed the transmit trigger. "Yes. Still heading zero-nine-five."

"Good! What is your current position?"

He read off the numbers.

"Stand by." A flurry of keystrokes filled the silence. Then she continued. "That's good! You're close. Turn slightly right to a new heading of zero-niner-eight, and in exactly ten minutes and ... eleven seconds from ... *now*, apply the same power."

Vaughn started his timer. "Roger. Right three degrees to heading zero-niner-eight, and begin my acceleration in nine minutes and," he read from the timer, "fifty-eight, fifty-seven, fifty-six seconds."

"Okay, Captain Singleton," Angela said. Vaughn heard his smile reflected in her tone. "Is there anything else Brown can do for you?"

"No, ma'am," Vaughn said. After a slight pause, he smirked and added, "I'm looking forward to meeting you, Angela-Vaughn."

"Me, t—" A series of hacking coughs cut her words. Then in a hoarse whisper, she said, "Me, too, Vaughn."

CHAPTER 30

Eighty-five minutes into the burn, Vaughn realized something was wrong. He still had another eight minutes until intercept. However, he was already approaching seventeen thousand miles per hour. Over the last twenty minutes, his angle of thrust had gradually flattened out. At the beginning of the scheduled ninety-three-minute burn, it had taken a forty-five-degree angle of attack to counteract Earth's gravity. However, the vertical component had gradually diminished as speed increased. As a result, more of the drive's thrust component went to accelerating the vehicle with every passing minute.

He toggled the radio. "Angela, this is Vaughn, come in."

"Go ahead, Vaughn. What's up?!"

She'd obviously picked up on his tone. He heard his concern reflected in her voice.

"I think something's wrong. Did you include a diminishing lift vector in your calculations?"

"Oh shit," Angela said with a cough. "No, I didn't. What's your current speed?"

Vaughn looked down. "I just crossed sixteen thousand five

hundred miles per hour." He shifted his gaze to his watch. "And I still have six more minutes of thrusting."

"Oh, no! ... Cut it. Cut it now!"

Without bothering to reply, Vaughn cut the thruster to zero. His stomach clenched as he got his second taste of free fall. Through a force of will, he held his concentration and focused on the instrumentation. He was losing altitude. The module wasn't yet at orbital velocity. Vaughn tilted the thruster back to vertical and increased power. Gravity reasserted itself but at a fraction of its normal level. Two percent power was all it took to maintain altitude.

"Vaughn?"

"I'm here. Not accelerating anymore. What do we do now?"

"Okay," Angela said.

Vaughn envisioned her beautiful face nodding as she spoke. "We don't have much time to work with here. I'm closing on you pretty quickly. Give me your exact speed position and course."

Vaughn read off the numbers.

"Okay ..." Another flurry of keystrokes filled the open line. "Turn to heading zero-nine-nine and apply seventy-five percent of the thrust you were previously using."

Vaughn did a quick mental calculation and came up with sixty-eight percent. "When do you want me to apply it?"

"Five seconds ago! Now!"

Startled into action, Vaughn began to apply the stated power, but only the module's altitude changed.

"Shit, shit, shit!"

Shaking his head, Vaughn adjusted the controls, tilting the thruster.

"What?!"

"Nothing. I'm fixing it."

A minute later, he had the module stabilized back on the correct altitude and power setting.

"Okay," Angela said. "We're two minutes from intercept. I should be ... Hey! I see you!"

Vaughn looked left and right. "Where?"

248

"You're at my ten o'clock."

He looked over his right shoulder. "I don't see you." Then one of the background stars appeared to move. It also grew in apparent size. "Well, I'll be a son of a bitch!"

The flying star continued to grow. Soon it took on a cruciform shape as the tattered remnants of the solar panels came into view. During one of their earlier conversations, Angela had told him about their destruction. Looking at it, Vaughn shook his head. The station looked like an ancient relic.

"I love what you've done with the place."

"Just remember those cables, Captain. They're still out there."

Vaughn nodded. The station appeared to float at the center of a hazy halo. "Looks like there's still a lot of debris left, too."

The ISS closed to within a mile, but then it began to pull away from him!

"Hey! Where are you going?"

"I'm just along for the ride, Vaughn. I've done all I can for you. The ball is in your court now. You'll have to wing it from there."

Vaughn nodded and cast a weary eye at his suit's dwindling O2 supply. It was all that remained.

"Okay, I'm on it!" He adjusted the module's heading and power for intercept. Soon the ISS stopped shrinking, but he had to change the ship's angle several times.

"Angela, I keep having to adjust my intercept course."

"Welcome to orbital mechanics one-oh-one. Every time you change one variable, it affects the other. Usually, we have computers to compensate for that. But, like I said, you're just going to have to wing it."

Vaughn nodded. "Okay, but I'm getting low on oxygen. Be ready at the airlock."

"I'll head there now. But I won't be able to talk to you. This radio isn't portable."

"Wait!" Vaughn said. "Where is the airlock?"

Angela described its location. Vaughn could now make out enough of the station to pick out the indicated spot. "I got it."

"Okay, Vaughn. I'll see you there."

"See you there," he agreed. He cast another nervous look at his suit's oxygen supply. A series of zeroes now flashed across its display.

"Shit," Vaughn whispered, careful not to transmit this time.

Ahead, the station grew to its largest yet. He cut the thrust. Weightless again, Vaughn rotated the module one hundred and eighty degrees. With the station now beneath him and closing quickly, he began to increase power.

Suddenly, the red CO_2 warning light started flashing in the upper corner of Vaughn's visor.

He shook his head. "Wonderful."

The module's closing rate slowed. However, he kept having to make slight lateral course changes, but each correction brought him a little closer to the ISS.

A few minutes later, the station's silver white and gold surfaces and similarly colored flakes of debris filled Vaughn's universe. Arcane equipment scattered across multiple trusses surrounded him. After a couple of additional module flips and turns, he zeroed out all velocities.

The thruster now flew in formation with the ISS. Only ten feet of space separated it from the specified airlock.

Vaughn started to have difficulty with concentration. He was breathing heavily again, but this time it had nothing to do with excess oxygen.

He was drowning in CO_2.

Unbuckling his seat belt and careful not to disturb the controls, Vaughn disconnected the tether from the waistline of his spacesuit but kept its free end in his gloved hand. Next, he gently pushed off of the module and began drifting toward the airlock.

As he floated across the ten-foot gap, Vaughn spotted Angela's shockingly gaunt face in the window adjacent to the open hatch. A weary smile hung beneath sallow cheeks and dark, sunken eyes.

"Oh shit, Angela," he whispered between gasping breaths. Vaughn waved, hoping his shock hadn't shown.

Her despairing smile brightened.

Vaughn shifted his eyes to the grab bar that ran the length of the airlock housing. As it drifted into range, he grasped it. Just as he did, the tether tried to yank out of his other hand. Grunting with exertion, he just managed to hold onto both. However, his right hand began to slide down the grab bar.

Like a prisoner being tortured on the rack, Vaughn felt the station and the module trying to pull his arms out of socket. He grunted again as he struggled to rein in the velocity his departure had apparently imparted on the thruster. His sliding hand reached the end of the bar.

Vaughn's shoulders creaked under the strain.

Stars flared in his vision.

Just as he thought he could no longer hold on, the pressure eased.

Fighting for breath, Vaughn hung suspended between the two vessels for a long moment.

His visor had fogged. He could barely see.

Panting, Vaughn eased the tether toward the grab bar.

His moisture-occluded vision narrowed.

As he continued to fight for air, Vaughn watched the hook draw closer to the rod. It was all he could see. Blackness had already swallowed the rest of his universe.

Finally, the hook clicked home, and he latched the module to the station.

Vaughn moved hand over shaking hand to the airlock opening. As he slid in head first, he saw the thruster drifting toward his feet, heading for a slow-motion crash with the airlock door!

Struggling for a breath that wouldn't come, Vaughn braced his arms against the inside of the airlock. As his vision faded to black, he felt the module hit his feet.

He gave a final grunting shove.

Then blackness swallowed the rest of him.

"Vaughn!" Angela pounded on the small window. "Watch out for the module!"

It was a futile effort. He was still in hard vacuum. There was no way the man could hear her, but he must've seen the approaching thruster. His boots suddenly emerged from the airlock and stopped the drifting vehicle.

"Great job, Vaughn!"

Another lung-shredding cough racked her body.

"Now, close the door!"

Nothing happened.

Angela shifted to the airlock window. Peering inside, she saw Vaughn's motionless figure floating within.

"Oh, no!"

The external door was still open!

Angela toggled the manual override, and the hatch began to close. Then it hit the captain's foot and reversed direction.

"Damn it!"

She cycled the switch again. The door stopped and then resumed its agonizingly slow closing sequence. It hit Vaughn's boot. The previous contact had nudged the man deeper into the airlock. This time, Singleton's foot bounced off, and the door finally closed.

"Yes!"

Angela activated the airlock's emergency atmosphere cycle, rapidly flooding its interior with air. Then she threw open the inner hatch and dragged Vaughn's limp body into the station.

She unlocked the man's helmet and pulled it off. His sweaty odor was the most wonderful thing Angela had ever smelled. She patted his face and got no response.

"Vaughn!"

Still nothing.

She pinched his nose and placed her lips over his beard-covered mouth, breathing fresh, oxygen-filled air into his lungs. After a few respirations, she checked his neck for a pulse. It was there: weak, but there.

Angela tried to breathe for him again, but another spasm of coughs racked her body. As they subsided, she looked down.

Vaughn had opened confused eyes.

Oh shit. Does he have brain damage?

Then his eyes focused, and he grinned sheepishly. "Hello, Commander Brown."

"Oh, thank you!" Angela said, hugging the man fiercely.

Vaughn returned the hug just as vigorously.

"Thank you, thank you, thank you," she whispered as tears muddled her vision.

The captain leaned back and shook his head. He studied her face for a long, silent moment. "I'm sorry, Angela." Then his voice became choked as he, too, shed tears. "So goddamned sorry."

Angela shook her head. "I told you to stop apologizing, Captain."

She wiped the moisture from her lids.

After doing the same, Vaughn gazed at her with his warm, green-flecked brown eyes, then looked away with an embarrassed smile.

Angela decided that she liked those eyes.

"I should have figured this out a long—" He turned toward her and stopped mid-sentence, a confused look now on his face.

Angela's eyes widened as a squirming white furball cocooned in a loose clump of matted brown hair drifted between them.

CHAPTER 31

Vaughn tried to keep the shock from his face. Angela was truly emaciated. Above hollow cheeks, sunken eyes stared from a face straight out of a World War II concentration camp image. The sight of her condition deepened his self-loathing.

This was his fault.

He looked away. "I should have figured this out a long—"

Suddenly, something wriggled under the cotton cloth of her hoodie. Then a tiny mouse wrapped in strands of Angela's greasy hair popped out.

"What in the hell is in your hair?" Vaughn blurted and instantly regretted it. "I'm sorry."

Color erupted across Angela's cheeks. She shook her head. "Don't worry about it. Things can get pretty cold in here." Splotchy red starburst criss-crossed her sallow face as she dug in her matted hair. "So these little guys have taken to camping out under my hoodie."

Vaughn watched in amazement as four mice swam in the air around them. Each had a small, tattered diaper that might have once been red or blue, but now the frayed cloths looked like pink and almost white.

Then he noticed the smell. The place stank. Overriding the hot, dank fumes rising from inside his suit, a mix of ammonia, stale air, and perfumed body odor assaulted his olfactory senses. He smiled and swallowed back the bile that threatened to trigger a series of retches.

Apparently seeing something in Vaughn's face, Angela blushed anew. She nodded. "Bad, huh?" Floating in front of him, she continued to try to push her matted puffball of tangled hair back into the hoodie. "Environmental control's been running on reduced power since the flare fried the solar panels."

Vaughn shook his head. "Nah, it's not that bad," he lied.

He fished down the neck of his spacesuit, producing several small packages.

"I brought you some fresh water and a couple of protein bars along with vitamins and antibiotics for that cough."

Vaughn released the bag of pills and pulled out the last item.

Angela's eyes widened, and she released the protein bar she'd grabbed.

He held out the yellow pouch. "Thought you might enjoy th—"

Angela snatched the item and tore it open. "Oh, God bless you!"

A moment later, shattered Funyuns floated out of the bag. Apparently, they didn't fare too well when stuffed inside a spacesuit. This fact didn't seem to deter Angela or the mice. Within seconds, they had sucked or snatched every crumb out of the air.

Seeing Vaughn's interest in the mice, Angela pointed at each in turn. "Vaughn, meet Nate, Natalie, Nancy, and Nadia." Then she gestured to him. "Kids, meet Vaughn."

Vaughn touched two fingers to his brow. "Pleased to make your acquaintance."

He looked at Angela. "They're only a few weeks old."

Her face flushed red again. She looked down. "Their parents … died."

Angela's emotion-filled, choked words drove home to Vaughn just how much his failures had cost this woman. He felt his face flush, too.

She looked up and smiled self-consciously. "Sorry, I was starved for conversation up here. These little guys are all the company I've had for the last two months."

It was Vaughn's turn to hang his head. "I'm sorry, Angela. I should've—"

Suddenly, her arms were around him.

"Shut it, Captain," Angela cooed into his ear. She squeezed him. "Thank you, Vaughn. Thank you for coming for me."

A lump formed in his throat. Overcome by the emotions that rampaged through his mind, Vaughn didn't trust himself to speak, so he just returned the hug.

After a long moment, Angela leaned back. The two spacesuited figures exchanged self-conscious smiles as they wiped moisture from their eyes, both chuckling nervously.

Finally, Vaughn gave her a meaningful look and said, "What do you say we blow this popsicle stand?"

Angela nodded vigorously. "Oh, hell yeah!"

As Angela guided Vaughn toward the JEM, she shook her head. *Way to go, Angela. You greet, literally, the last man on Earth with a head full of mice?! Couldn't you have just left them in their box?* She laughed and shook her head again.

The two of them floated into the Japanese Experiment Module. The mechanical pump's train-like choo-choo sound greeted their arrival. With a final swoosh, it finished pressurizing the last oxygen bottle. Eight tanks of varying sizes floated inside the JEM.

Vaughn pointed at the complex arrangement of repurposed tubing. "You did all this?"

Angela smiled. "Yep."

The man's bearded face nodded appreciably. "Strong work, Commander."

She had envisioned him as smoothly shaven, but Angela decided he looked good nonetheless. Vaughn's salt-and-pepper beard gave him a rugged outdoorsy look that she found surprisingly attractive.

Angela pointed at the bottles. "These are just for you. My suit has liquid oxygen and a CO2 scrubber. It should be good for eight hours, more if I don't exert myself."

Vaughn studied the tanks and their pressure gauges and then nodded. "That should be more than enough time."

She pointed at his chest. "Is that a parachute?"

Vaughn nodded again. "Yep, got one just like it for you back in the module."

Angela felt her pulse quicken. She'd never skydived. "Do you think we'll need them?" she said, unable to keep the fear out of her words.

Vaughn smiled. "Better to have it and not need it than …" He shrugged and left the rest unsaid.

"Oh … Okay." She nudged two of the O2 bottles toward him. "Let's start moving these to the airlock."

A few minutes later, two humans, four mice, and eight oxygen tanks floated in front of the airlock's inner hatch. En route to the location, Angela had grabbed a ninth bottle, this one covered with foil insulation and fitted with a strap.

Vaughn pointed at it. "What's that for?"

Angela grabbed the tank and twisted its cap. "This is for my little friends."

The man looked at her dubiously. "I'm not sure that's a good idea, Angela."

Her eyes narrowed. "Listen, Captain! I'll be damned if I'm going to leave them!"

Vaughn held up his hands. "I just meant there might not be enough air for all of them."

Angela blinked. "Oh … Sorry." Her cheeks warmed. She grabbed the nearest mouse and pulled the cap away long enough to slip the squirming white ball through the opening. "I gave them a little something. They'll be out soon. Should make them sleep for the first part of the trip. Plus, I pumped pure O2 into this before I capped it. They'll be alright." She finally looked back into his eyes. "Thanks for thinking about that, though."

Vaughn gently wrapped a hand around Nate's fleeing form and

then handed him to her. He smiled. "Teamwork, *Commander*," he said, playfully mimicking her use of his rank.

Angela laughed. "Guess I had that coming." She stuffed the last two mice into the tank and then strapped it to the side of her suit. With raised eyebrows, she looked at the man. "What do you think? Will it interfere with the parachute harness?"

Vaughn shook his head. "No. Should be fine."

Angela grabbed her helmet. Holding it above her head, she looked at Vaughn. "Ready?"

He nodded. "Yep."

She looked at him for a long moment. Then Angela leaned forward and kissed his cheek. Grinning at the shocked look on his face, she slid the helmet over her head.

"See you on the other side, *Captain*."

Two airlock cycles later, the pair of unlikely astronauts floated outside of the station with their collection of bottles.

"How's the new headset working?"

Vaughn's face bobbed up and down behind his visor. "Got you loud and clear."

Angela clipped the bottles to her spacesuit and then pointed to the exterior grab bar. "Hold onto that. I don't want you getting blown around by the exhaust."

"What exhaust?"

Not answering, she just smiled and aimed herself toward the drifting module. Then she activated her jet pack.

Vaughn grunted as the blast of compressed air hit him. "Holy shit."

Angela laughed. "Told you to hold on."

"Thanks," Vaughn said wryly.

Her eyes widened as she got her first unobstructed view of the thruster.

"You rode this thing into orbit?"

"Yep."

The nose of the slowly tumbling module rotated into view, and Angela stared in open-mouthed amazement. "Are those …? Are they g-garage …?" Unable to finish the question, she dissolved into laughing hysterics.

"Yes. Garage Sale signs. And there are a few For Sale and For Rent ones in there, too. It's all I could find." Vaughn paused. "Did you just snort?!"

Angela had, several times.

Signs with various messages covered the entire nose of the thruster. Between her laughs and coughs, Angela could barely breathe. She hovered there for a moment, trying to blink the tears out of her eyes. Then she pointed at an orange cone that sported familiar white lettering. "Oh, my God. Is that a Home Depot funnel?"

"Don't make fun! Ole Betsy served me pretty well. And if we're going to survive this, she's gonna have to hold on a bit longer."

Angela stopped laughing. She turned toward Vaughn. "Thank you for coming to get me. I know it wasn't easy. This must've taken an incredible amount of work and … and signage … just to make it all come together."

After a pause, Vaughn spoke in a tone she hadn't heard before. "I definitely applied myself to this one."

She found the wording odd but nodded. "Yes you did, Vaughn."

Half an hour later, they had all the bottles secured and connected. Angela had strapped herself into the left seat while the captain buckled into the right.

He held up a thumb. "Ready?"

Angela scanned the wrecked home she'd occupied these last few months. After a moment, she extended her own thumb. "Oh, hell yeah. I'm ready."

Vaughn grabbed the flight controls.

A moment later the seat bottom bumped Angela's backside. She felt a high-frequency vibration coming through it. For the first time in three months, she also felt gravity. It wasn't the real thing, of course, just acceleration. Initially, the G-force was light, probably less than a tenth of what she would feel on the surface. However, her arms already felt like they weighed a ton.

Then gravity increased, and the station began to recede behind them. It looked like they were speeding away from the ISS, but they were actually slowing down.

Vaughn patted the side of the module. "This thing doesn't have a heat shield. I'll have to hold us above the atmosphere until we've decelerated enough to enter it without burning up."

Angela laughed and looked up. "What? You mean we can't just dive in behind your tin roof?"

Vaughn shook his head. "I think I liked it better when you were coughing more and talking less."

Over the next three and a half hours, the pilot gradually changed the angle of the thruster. Initially, the western horizon had been in line with the center of Vaughn's makeshift nose cone. However, as they slowed, the nose gradually pitched higher. Vaughn had to direct an ever-increasing portion of the vehicle's thrust downward to counteract the planet's relentless efforts to draw them into its gravity well. They were high above the atmosphere, so he didn't try to maintain the original altitude. The decelerating and descending burn soon had them less than a hundred miles above the planet.

"What's our ground speed now?" Angela said.

Vaughn pointed to the GPS strapped to the instrument panel. "We're still going four thousand miles an hour."

Angela held up a thumb. "That's great! You've already bled off thirteen thousand."

Vaughn shook his head. "We were slowing pretty quickly at first, but now I'm having to use more thrust to keep us out of the atmosphere. Our rate of deceleration is falling off."

Angela's eyes widened. "But we've already used half your air." She paused and checked her gauges. "And half mine as well."

"Yeah, this is taking longer than I expected."

"Okay. Let's increase power."

Vaughn nodded hesitantly. "It's already running at ninety percent. I'm not sure what that'll do to the RTG."

Angela pointed to their current ground speed. "If we enter the atmosphere at Mach 6, we'll burn up."

"I know that, Angela!" Vaughn stopped, then shook his head. "Sorry."

Before she could respond, he raised the stick in his left hand. The vehicle's vibrations increased as did the G-force.

Between the ship's thrust and Earth's gravity, they'd been at slightly more than one G for the last few hours. Initially, Angela had almost blacked out. However, after an hour, her circulatory system had finally remembered how to deal with gravity and had redistributed her blood appropriately. Now she could feel her face sagging under the increased Gs, and as it had earlier, her peripheral vision began to gray out.

Afraid that turning her head might cause it to topple from her body, Angela spoke without looking at Vaughn. "What power setting is that?"

"One hundred percent, but that's the module's limit. I have no idea what the RTG's limit is." Vaughn said all of this while moving his hands about, pointing at knobs and twisting dials, as if they were under normal gravity.

Angela supposed that, to him, the current G-load wasn't a big deal.

He looked at her, and his eyes widened. "Oh shit! I didn't think your face could get any whiter. Are you okay?"

"You really know how to charm a girl, Captain Singleton." Angela started to shake her head, but the threat of toppling became very real. With a mighty effort, she pinned it to the back of her helmet. "I'll be fine," she whispered, feeling anything but.

Over the next few hours, Angela fell in and out of sleep. Vaughn kept waking her, afraid she'd passed out. Each time, she assured him that she was fine, just exhausted.

A much younger version of Angela woke in the passenger seat of her daddy's car. It was old and smelled of mildew, but she'd loved riding in it. Later, when it took him from her, the little girl had grown to hate that vehicle. Presently, they were racing down an old country road.

"Go faster, Daddy," the younger version of her urged.

The washboard road made the car vibrate as if it had broken an axle.

Suddenly her daddy grabbed her shoulder. "Wake up, pumpkin!"

"No," Angela whispered as the road worsened. "I'm tired."

The hand became more insistent. "Wake up, Commander!"

Angela's eyes blinked and fluttered and finally opened on a slowly spinning horizon.

The seat beneath her still vibrated viciously.

"We have to jump!"

Angela blinked her confusion.

Vaughn pointed to something. "It's running away!"

Disoriented, she followed the gesture. An object on the floor glowed red-hot. Her eyes widened.

"The RTG?!"

Vaughn nodded. "Yes! We have to jump!"

Angela felt buffeting. Then she saw the surface of her suit ripple.

They had entered the atmosphere!

The captain disconnected his oxygen bottle from the rack and then clipped it to his parachute harness.

The vehicle's slow rotation was speeding up. If they didn't jump soon, Angela would lose consciousness.

He pointed to the GPS. "Still above a hundred thousand feet, but I think we're safe to jump."

Vaughn placed his left hand on his seat belt disconnect. "Are you ready?"

She swallowed and then nodded.

"We have to release at the same time." He pointed toward a tan-colored land mass. "Any difference up here will just get worse down there."

Angela nodded again. "Same time. Got it."

"Alright. Release your harness on one."

Vaughn counted down.

"Three, two, *one!*"

Angela released her belt and immediately flew out of the spinning module. Her mind cleared, as her body welcomed the sudden weightlessness like an old friend. She fell backward initially, but a slow tumble turned her earthward.

She looked around but couldn't see the captain.

"Vaughn! Where are you?"

"Shit! I got hung up for a second. I'm over here."

"Where? I don't see you."

"Look toward the water."

Vast oceans of sand and water met beneath her, desert on her right, ocean to the left. After months in space, Angela instantly recognized it as North Africa. She looked left, toward the Mediterranean.

"I see you!"

Vaughn waved. "I'm drifting away ... you. ... Bluetooth range ..." Then his voice cut out completely.

The rotating module had tossed them in opposite directions. Now they were outside of the range of their Bluetooth headsets.

"Vaughn!"

No reply.

His retreating white spacesuit shrank out of sight.

"Damn it!"

Angela felt gravity reasserting itself. Atmospheric drag ramped up. That same resistance also arrested her sideward drift, causing her to fall straight down. However, the heavier module continued to bore through the atmosphere on its angular dissent. Its apparent size quickly shrank as it raced toward the eastern horizon. Then it disappeared in a brilliant flash.

The thruster had exploded!

Captain Singleton got them out just in time. Any later, and they would've still been too close.

"Thank you, Vaughn."

Over the next several minutes, the initially tranquil atmospheric buffeting increased. Its barely audible whisper soon roared in her ears.

Angela's slow tumble morphed into a flat spin that quickly accelerated. It felt as if the building blood pressure would soon crack open her head.

Her arms flailed wildly as she tried to arrest the spin. She held them at various angles. The first attempts only exacerbated the situation, accelerating the spin. Finally, Angela tilted her hands the other way, and the rotation slowed and then stopped.

Now at terminal velocity, she fell through the atmosphere like a novice skydiver, wobbling through the air with arms splayed and knees bent.

Angela searched the sky for Vaughn, but still couldn't see him.

She peered down. The world looked as it would from a cruising jetliner. On her left, glistening blue sea stretched to the horizon. The dunes of the Sahara desert filled the other half of the world visible through the visor. Beneath Angela, a city that she recognized as Tripoli cut a silver and gray pit into the sandy shoreline. Arterial black highways flowed from the mass and disappeared into the surrounding desert. In the months since Day Zero, the wasteland had reclaimed many of those roads. Ever-advancing dunes now covered vast sections of the highways.

Tripoli looked like an island in a bifurcated sea of sand and water. Angela spotted its airport. As much as she could in a spacesuit, she tried to guide her free fall toward it.

A minute later, Angela yanked the ripcord. The drogue flew out in front of her face and then disappeared above her as it pulled the parachute from the pouch mounted on her chest. Then her feet snapped earthward, and the beautiful vision of a fully inflated canopy blossomed overhead.

"Oh, thank God," Angela whispered.

She scanned the skies, searching for Vaughn. The desert was still on her right, ocean to her left. She did a double take in that direction.

A small white dome hung in the air, just visible against the deep blue horizon.

The captain's parachute!

It looked like he might come down in the ocean.

"Oh, no!"

Angela opened her visor.

"Vaughn!"

If he replied, she couldn't hear him above the hot, dry air blowing through her helmet.

The man was a tiny white dot beneath the parachute. From this distance, she couldn't even tell if he was moving. Vaughn was definitely lower than her. He'd opened his parachute later than her.

As Angela descended below skyscraper height, she saw Vaughn splash down. His canopy went slack, but the point of impact disappeared behind the cityscape before she could judge his distance from shore.

Angela looked down to see that she was descending toward a parking lot full of vehicles. She tugged on the right riser, desperately trying to steer toward a clear patch of pavement, but the unwieldy, round parachute responded slowly. The odd collection of cars rushed up toward her ill-prepared feet.

"Not good!"

She was going to come down hard on weak legs and crash into a bunch of strange-looking vehicles.

"No, no, *no!*" Angela shouted as the mass of metal and concrete rushed toward her.

CHAPTER 32

Angela cringed in anticipation of the coming agony.
"Shit!"
Suddenly, just as she was about to slam into a dusty car, her feet yanked up and shot skyward.

Angela started swinging like a pendulum.

The canopy had snagged on one of the parking lot's light towers.

"Oh, thank you."

A moment later, Angela convinced the parachute harness to release. It dropped her unceremoniously onto the ground. She collapsed into a pile and then lay there, struggling to catch her breath.

After climbing to a seated position, Angela removed her helmet and gloves. Breathless, she leaned against a hot car. Then she removed the lid from the makeshift mice habitat and fished out her little stow-aways. She gently placed the lethargic, gravity newbies inside the rocking helmet. Then she unlocked the top half of her spacesuit.

Dizzying minutes of struggle later, Angela freed herself from the suit's plastic and metal confines and stripped down to a t-shirt and a pair of shorts.

Sitting in the shade of the car, she pulled the water bladder from the discarded suit and drained it in long, slurping draws.

Angela tried the car's door. Mercifully, it opened. Oven-like heat poured from its interior. From the dusty ground, the driver's seat looked impossibly high. She craned her neck around to check the ignition.

Empty.

She reached through the open door and raised the near corner of the mat.

"Thank you!"

Angela grabbed the hidden key and wormed her way onto the hot driver's seat. It felt as if the back of her thighs would melt into its vinyl surface. She set the helmet on the passenger side and belted it into place.

A wave of nausea washed over Angela. Each step exhausted her, every exertion threatening to rob her of consciousness. She could feel her eyes trying to roll back.

Angela leaned into the headrest, breathing heavily. Finally, color returned to her grayed-out world.

"Move it, Commander Brown!" she said, with a growl that launched a fresh spasm of coughs.

It took both of her hands to raise a key that felt as if it weighed twenty pounds. Once she had it in the ignition, it also took both of them to twist it to the start position. The engine lugged, turning over slowly. On the third try, it fired to life.

"Woo ... hoo!" she said through a cough.

Angela leaned back and stared at the dusty headliner. She looked over to the passenger seat.

One of the mice had wakened. Nate Junior's pink nose and white whiskers were twitching above the rim of the upturned helmet. He regarded her with his little eyes.

Angela nodded and sighed. "Yeah, yeah, we're going."

By the time she maneuvered the car out of the parking lot, she was out of breath and soaked with sweat. Angela grabbed the crank. After a brief struggle, she managed to crack open her window. Relatively cool air flowed through the gap.

As she guided the car out of the parking lot and turned toward the ocean, Angela looked at Nate and tilted her head toward the opposite window. "Sorry, buddy. You're on your own with that one."

The road's northerly path took her through a burned-out section of the city. Melted asphalt and shattered glass crunched beneath the car's tires. Mid-rises had lined both sides of the two-lane road. Now only their heat-distorted metal frames stood.

A block later, Angela came upon an intersection choked with burned-out husks of vehicles. She turned down a side street. As the car rounded a bend in the road, she glimpsed sparkling blue water through a gap in the carnage. Angela resisted the urge to speed up. She'd be no good to Vaughn if the car plowed into some unseen obstacle or careened off a washed-out road.

A few minutes later, driving as quickly as she dared, Angela rounded the last corner. A broad swath of the Port of Tripoli scrolled into view, revealing an apocalyptic panorama.

The same thing that had happened to the road vehicles had also afflicted the shipping industry. Having followed their autopilots to this location, several unmanned supertankers had run aground. The tremendous inertia of the massive ships had wrought incredible damage. Four of their towering command decks protruded from the mangled wreckage at varying angles. Beneath their crumpled bows, broken concrete slabs pointed skyward like questing skeletal fingers.

A burned-out oil refinery sat to the car's front left, framing that side of the hellish milieu. Beyond the facility, an expansive tank farm covered a finger of land that extended into the bay. The burned and distorted walls of the massive storage vessels leaned inward like collapsed soufflés.

Angela scanned the water. Small, multicolored bits of debris littered its glinting, choppy surface. However, she soon spotted a white patch that she thought must be Vaughn's parachute, but it was too far away to make out any other details.

To the right, beyond the grounded tankers, a long, floating dock extended perpendicularly from the waterfront. Fishing boats of varying sizes lined its gently undulating length.

Angela struggled with the wheel, trying to guide the car toward the pier and its water access. It felt like the power steering had failed. After a moment of breathless struggle, she managed to point the vehicle toward her destination. Breathing heavily, she relaxed her grip. Color flooded back into her grayed-out vision.

The car quickly closed on the pier.

The water's edge rushed toward her.

Angela mashed the brake, but the pedal barely budged.

"Damn it!"

She threw her other foot into the effort, now stomping the pedal with both feet. For good measure, she yanked up on the handbrake as well.

The brake pedal dropped to the floor.

The car didn't slow!

"Really?!"

The subcompact was about to become a submarine!

Large, metal poles bracketed the imminent point of departure.

Using both hands, Angela pulled down on the left side of the steering wheel, leaning her body into the effort. With all the enthusiasm of the Titanic dodging an iceberg, the car grudgingly heaved to port.

As if welcoming an end to its pathetic existence, the vehicle finally accepted the new course and tracked unerringly toward its demise. The car struck the foot-thick post dead center. The obstacle proved as formidable as Angela had hoped. Black car met white pole with an explosion of glass, metal, airbags, and mice. The front bumper wrapped around the pipe, welcoming the bollard into its warm embrace like the returning prodigal son.

In Angela's expanded perception of time, the helmet floated up from the seat belt's loose confines. A leisure somersault tossed out its furry occupants, briefly reintroducing them to weightlessness. Their legs splayed wide as did their eyes. The mice appeared to stare at her accusingly until they bounced off the already inflated airbag.

Then the normal flow of time reasserted itself with extreme prejudice. The shoulder harness captured Angela, snapping her head forward. Her eyes began to burn as acrid smoke billowed from the airbags.

She released the seat belt and fell out of a door that she couldn't remember opening. She clambered back into the car and found the mice lying on the rear floorboard. They seemed lethargic but otherwise unfazed.

Angela deposited Nate Jr. and his siblings back in the now-abraded helmet.

Finally, she backed out of the vehicle.

Angela pushed off of the car and stumbled to the edge of the floating pier. Up close, its undulations looked anything but placid. There was a fair bit of chop churning the nearby waters. Sounds of slapping waves and bouncing hardware filled the air. The dock's heaving deck drew even with the top of the waterfront's concrete bulkhead. Angela's eyes widened as she watched it drop six feet.

Her shoulders slumped.

"Oh, come on! Give me a break!"

Angela scanned the water, but still didn't see any sign of the man. She shook her head and then cupped hands around her mouth.

"Vaughn!" The yell came out as a weak croak, barely audible above the din of the waterfront.

She inched up to the edge and set the helmet on a shaded patch of concrete. A twitching pink nose regarded her over its chrome ring. She held up a finger.

"Don't worry, Nate. I'm taking you with me."

Angela turned toward the pier and swung her legs over. The second time it came up and touched the bottom of her feet, Angela pushed herself over the precipice.

Unfortunately, her timing sucked.

The dock fell away almost as fast as she did.

"Crap!"

Angela floated weightlessly above the descending deck.

Then the dock reversed course.

Angela didn't.

She crumpled face first into the wood planks.

Stars burst into her vision.

A blast of thermonuclear pain burned through her skull as a loud crack emanated from the region of her nose.

Angela moaned loudly and rolled onto her side. Hot liquid drizzled down her upper lip and across her cheek. The coppery taste of blood filled her mouth. The darkness tried to pull her all the way under this time. Angela fought it off.

After a few moments of panting groans, Angela struggled to her hands and knees. She crawled back to the concrete bulkhead. Timing it right this time, she snagged the helmet on her first try.

It was empty!

With wide eyes, Angela scanned the waterfront. There was no sign of the mice.

She called for them, her voice now nasal and weak. "Nate!"

Nothing, only the sound of the waves and the rocking boats.

Coughs racked her body. Angela collapsed into a sobbing mass. Lying on her side and curled up into a ball, she wept uncontrollably.

"Oh, God … No, no, no—"

Something touched her cheek.

Angela's eyes snapped open.

Four little pink noses twitched not three inches from her own. Their owners paced awkwardly on the wet boards of the rising and falling pier. Nate squeaked and climbed into her hair. Then his siblings followed him.

Stunned, Angela lay there for a long moment. Finally, she rolled onto her back and dissolved into laughing sobs.

A male voice came from below her. "I'm glad you're having such a good time."

Angela's eyes flew wide open.

"Vaughn!"

"A little help here?"

She rolled toward his voice and then burst into a fresh round of laughter.

Still in his spacesuit, visor open, Vaughn floated on his back, bobbing like a cork.

He saw her face and his smile vanished.

"Oh shit! What happened?"

Angela ran a hand across her upper lip. The fingers came away covered with blood. "It probably looks worse than it is," she said nasally. "You should see the other guy."

"I'll bet."

Vaughn pointed at his spacesuit. "Think you can drop me a line? Something that'll stop me from sinking while I pull this off? Drowning seems like a rather silly way to end the day." He paused and momentarily closed his visor as a bigger wave splashed over him. He opened it and then chuckled. "I learned that lesson the hard way. My ass cheeks probably look like a pair of wrinkled prunes by now."

Angela laughed again, but another wave of nausea swept over her, and suddenly, nothing seemed at all funny. She nodded and then clambered to her feet. Walking unsteadily on the pitching pier, she stumbled toward a nearby fishing trawler. It had a hoist that should work. After crossing the boat's oily bulkhead, she dropped clumsily onto its rust-covered deck.

"Paddle over here, Vaughn."

"On my way."

Vaughn's arms stroked back and forth. A moment later, he pulled alongside the boat and squinted up at her with worried eyes. Then he guffawed. "I see our four little friends have returned to their rat's nest."

Angela felt her face flush.

Vaughn waved. "Sorry, not making fun." His eyes softened. "I know you grew close to the little tykes."

She nodded self-consciously.

The man pointed to his waistline. "What do you say you lower that hook down here?"

Angela nodded. After a little coaxing, she swung out the hoist's small three-foot-long boom. Every movement took incredible effort. She had to stop between each and catch her breath.

The worried look had returned to Vaughn's face. "I don't know, Angela. This is too much. Maybe I should look for another way—"

"Shut it, Captain." Angela grunted as she turned the hoist's handle, playing out the cable. She cocked an eyebrow. "Just grab the damned cable, mister."

Vaughn smiled and nodded. "Yes, ma'am."

He grabbed the end of the line and then squinted, blinking as a large wave cast its salty spray into his face. Finally, he attached the hook to the suit.

The Army captain held up a thumb. "Take up the slack, and I'll do the rest."

Angela flipped a lever on the side of the crank. She turned it clockwise this time. It ratcheted loudly, and the line went taut. The crane's mast creaked under the surging loads generated as the waterlogged astronaut bobbed in the waves.

Vaughn held up a thumb. "That's perf—!"

The boom snapped with a sharp crack. The man's spacesuited figure flailed as the next wave swamped his helmet.

Then Vaughn disappeared, sinking out of sight.

"No!" Angela screamed. She tried to crank him back up, but the handle wouldn't budge.

"Vaughn!"

A mass of bubbles boiled to the surface. The dangling hoist cable snapped taut as the now water-filled suit tried to sink to the bottom of the harbor.

Angela reached over the bulkhead and grabbed the writhing cable.

She couldn't move it!

Angela heaved and yanked on the line, screaming his name again and again.

Then it stopped vibrating.

"Vaughn? Oh God, no!"

Through flowing tears, Angela stared into the water.

"Vaughn!"

CHAPTER 33

Cold, briny liquid flooded into Vaughn's nostrils. Before he could close the visor, the last of the suit's trapped air exploded through the opening.

The world darkened as he rapidly sank into the murk.

Vaughn's hands grasped at the hook with panicked desperation.

He closed his eyes. Through a force of will, he stopped thrashing.

The last thing he should do was disconnect the hook. It was the only thing stopping him from sinking all the way to the bottom.

Vaughn purposefully and methodically searched the suit's waistline for its interface, the point that locked the two halves together. A moment later, he found the lever and actuated it. Vaughn felt the lower half of the spacesuit begin to drift away. He kicked it off and then threw his arms over his head as if shrugging out of a turtleneck.

It wouldn't budge!

Panic gripped him as he began to sink.

Vaughn couldn't break free of the suit's upper half!

His lungs burned!

Then it slipped away, and Vaughn swam free of the spacesuit.

Kicking his feet, he followed his bubbles up. A moment later he broke the surface.

Blinking burning eyes, Vaughn stared up at the back of the boat. He couldn't see Angela.

Just as he was about to call to her name, Vaughn heard her say something.

A knotted length of rope hung from the back of the fishing vessel. He grabbed it and started pulling himself from the water.

"Angela!"

Another shout from her drowned out the call.

Vaughn couldn't see her or discern the words.

Then a long, keening wail ended with a single clear word: "Vaughn!"

He grabbed the ledge and pulled himself up.

"Over here, Angela."

The commander's head snapped up. She looked at him from the trawler's deck with wide, scared eyes.

"Vaughn?"

"None other."

He grunted as he crested the transom and swung his legs into the back of the boat.

Angela stood shakily.

"I thought you were … I thought I killed you!"

She stumbled toward Vaughn as he stood. Her ghostly white face smiled up at him. Then her eyes rolled back, and she collapsed, falling forward.

"Oh shit!"

Vaughn threw out his arms, catching her just before she could fall all the way to the deck. He easily arrested her momentum. The waif-thin woman felt as tenuous as midsummer Las Vegas fog.

This was the first time he'd seen Angela outside of her spacesuit. Vaughn had been shocked by her hollow cheeks and sallow skin on the space station, but her condition was worse than he'd imagined.

Vaughn carried her to the trawler's cabin. Inside, he found a bunk that looked relatively clean. A window had been left open, so it wasn't as hot as he'd feared.

He laid her gently onto the bed's wrinkled wool blanket. After running his fingers across her clammy forehead and brushing hair from her face, he stood and began searching the vessel.

Vaughn soon located a closet-sized room that appeared to serve as the boat's galley. Inside, he found several bottled waters along with some canned meat and a sealed bag of crackers. He scooped all of it into his arms and ran back to her cabin.

Seeing her lying there, so insubstantial, Vaughn shook his head.

You're an idiot, Singleton! Should've figured this out months ago!

He knelt beside her and draped a wetted washcloth across her forehead.

"Hang in there, Angela."

Her eyes fluttered and then opened. "Vaughn?" she said weakly.

"I'm here." He held the open water bottle to her lips. "Drink this."

She took a couple of sips and then shook her head.

Vaughn tore open the bag of crackers. He held one of the Saltines to her mouth.

She took a tentative nibble and then shook her head again.

"Can't, nauseous …"

A shiver followed by a coughing spell shook her body.

"So cold," she whispered through now-chattering teeth.

Vaughn pulled another wool blanket from a nearby shelf and wrapped it around her, tucking the olive drab cloth snugly under her chin.

He didn't like that cough. It sounded like bronchitis. If the antibiotics didn't kick in soon, it would probably progress into pneumonia —if it hadn't already.

He held the water to her lips again. "You need to drink this, Angela."

She shook her head.

"Just a little," he insisted.

Angela relented and took a couple of sips. A fresh wave of coughs racked her body.

Small squeaking sounds came through the room's open door.

Angela's eyes widened. "The mice!"

Vaughn looked over and smiled. All four of the little guys were standing in the opening. He retrieved her helmet from the dock and then placed some crackers and a small cup of water on a table adjacent to the bed. He deposited the mice next to the stash and set the dome over them.

Angela watched the foursome through the clear visor. Then she smiled up at him.

"Thank you—" Another coughing spasm cut off her words.

Vaughn gently caressed her cloth-covered temple with his thumb. "Angela, listen to me."

Her lids raised to half-mast. Then she focused on his face.

"Where are the antibiotics?"

After staring at him for a few seconds, understanding dawned in Angela's eyes. She shook her head. "Left them in my suit." The words elicited another string of hacking coughs. "Back at the airport. I'm sorry."

Vaughn nodded. "That's okay. I'll make a quick supply run."

Fear and concern blossomed in Angela's eyes.

He held up both hands. "I'll be right back. I won't be gone long, I promise."

Vaughn gave her another sip of water and was relieved to see her accept it. Then he placed a full water bottle under her right hand.

"Right back," he said with a raised hand. "Scout's honor."

She smiled. "I knew you were a Boy Scout." Fresh coughs followed her short laugh.

Vaughn stood. He snapped to attention and raised two fingers to his brow. "Eagle Scout Vaughn Singleton at your service, ma'am."

Angela giggled.

And Vaughn fell in love.

CHAPTER 34

Awhite minivan with yellow fenders careened down a littered Tripoli street. With a sudden swerve, it narrowly avoided a small dune that had drifted into the road. Vaughn almost hadn't seen it. Everything had a fine coating of the tan powder, providing the mounds with perfect camouflage.

He hadn't spotted a pharmacy in the industrialized area around the port, so he turned the minivan down the next crossroad and headed deeper into the city.

A few blocks later, the urban milieu began to change. Office buildings gave way to storefronts. Fortunately, the fires had spared the area.

Finally, Vaughn spotted his quarry. A green crescent adorned the façade of a white building halfway down the block.

He brought the cab to a skidding stop in front of the pharmacy's glass door. Leaping from the still running minivan, he trotted over to the entrance.

Locked!

A moment later, Vaughn threw a cinder block through the door. The glass shattered and fell away. He stepped through the opening. In the dark interior, he fished out the flashlight he'd brought from the trawler. He flipped it on and followed its circle of light deeper into the shop. Then Vaughn hopped over the counter and into the pharmacy proper. He soon found several huge bottles of antibiotics. Fortunately, most of them had English labels. He wasn't sure which one was appropriate, but he thought Angela might have an idea about that. After all, NASA had trained her to be self-sufficient while stuck on a space station two hundred miles above the closest doctor.

Vaughn began to climb back over the counter, but a sudden epiphany struck him. What if Angela had lost consciousness or couldn't think clearly enough to answer his questions? He nodded and then swung his legs back into the pharmacy. Near the back, he found a book titled *Diagnosis and Dosage*.

"Bingo!"

Under the beam of the flashlight, Vaughn leafed through the three-inch-thick volume. He found the section on bronchitis and was relieved to see that he'd already collected one of the specified antibiotics. Vaughn nodded and tossed the book and his cache of drugs into a bag.

A few minutes later, he hopped down onto the undulating surface of the floating dock and scrambled onto the boat.

"I'm back!"

No response.

He stepped into the warm room.

The commander lay motionlessly on the bed and didn't respond to his arrival.

"Angela?!"

Nothing.

Vaughn dropped the bag and ran to her side. He placed a hand on her shoulder. "Angela, it's me. Wake up."

She still didn't respond, but as he reached to check her pulse, he saw her chest slowly rise and fall.

"Oh, thank you," Vaughn whispered. Then he did a double take.

Four pairs of nervous eyes stared out from Angela's matted hair.

"Hey, guys. How'd you get out?"

Then he saw the upturned helmet. Angela must have freed them.

He shook her shoulder.

"Angela!"

She still didn't respond.

Vaughn had to get water and medicine into Angela. He scooped up the mice and placed them back in their helmet habitat. After raising Angela to an inclined position, he pushed the first of two large antibiotic pills into her mouth. Then he held a bottled water to her lips.

"Drink this, Angela."

He tilted the bottle and allowed some of the water to run into her mouth. Thankfully, she swallowed the pill. Vaughn placed the second one there and repeated the process. Angela coughed twice but soon took that one as well.

Vaughn eased her back down onto the pillow.

Still hot with fever, she began to shiver again.

He wrapped her up in the wool blanket and then added another for good measure.

Over the next two days, Vaughn repeated the procedure twice. On the second day, he packed her and the mice into the minivan and moved the whole family into an opulent suite. There, he finally coaxed Angela into taking some meat and canned potatoes.

Nate and friends had needed no coaxing.

After Angela started eating, color returned to her face. Her cheeks soon lost their hollow, death camp pallor, but she remained bedridden, unable to stand for more than a moment or two without getting dizzy.

They spent their days talking, comparing experiences. The pair discussed their highs and their lows. They laughed together, and they cried together as well. Angela spilled some of those tears when Vaughn related his experience at the Royal Gorge and how it had changed him, focused him.

Angela told him of her struggles with starvation. She broke down while describing the mouth-watering smell generated by the accidental torching of Nadine. The evident guilt dredged up by the memory sent Angela into a fit of tears. There seemed to be something more, but he decided not to push.

Her smile and wonderful laugh returned when Vaughn told her of his presidential lunches and how the nearly disastrous end of the final one had led to his "What can Brown do for you?" epiphany.

The commander improved a little each day.

And each day, Vaughn fell more deeply in love with Angela. However, beyond her gratitude—a thankfulness for which he felt unworthy—Angela hadn't shown any sign that she shared his feelings.

Presently, Vaughn walked down the hotel's long central hall, careful not to trip over the wires that fed electricity from the remote generator. Reaching the end of the hallway, he opened the door and stepped into the suite.

"What's the plan, Stan?" asked a surprisingly strong female voice.

Vaughn looked up to see Angela. She was outside of the bedroom for the first time.

Angela smiled at him from her seated position on the couch. With legs propped up on the coffee table, she regarded him over the rim of the steaming mug of Java clutched in both of her hands.

"You're up!" Vaughn grinned. "It's about time. Thought you'd never get that skinny butt out of bed."

Still sitting, Angela leaned onto one cheek and regarded said posterior. "Hey, my butt's not that skinny. It's starting to fill in."

"Seriously, it's good to see you up." The aroma of garlic and freshly brewed coffee washed across Vaughn. "Smells like you've been getting around pretty well. Any trouble walking?"

Without answering, Angela set the mug on the table and began to stand. Vaughn started to walk to her, but she held up a hand. "I got this." A moment later, she stood fully upright. Then she held her arms out at shoulder level and smiled self-consciously. "Ta-da."

"That's great!"

Angela walked haltingly toward Vaughn. As she drew within a foot, she stumbled toward him.

With panicked urgency, he threw his arms around her waistline, but then her lips were on his.

Shocked, Vaughn froze. Then he returned the kiss, softly pressing his lips to hers.

After a long, wonderful moment, Angela leaned back in his arms and stared at him with her beautiful hazel eyes. "You're my hero, Captain Singleton. You saved me ... Twice!"

Vaughn felt his face flush.

She ran a hand across that now-smooth face. "I like this. You clean up nice, Captain."

He'd shaved off the beard two days earlier. "I thought you hadn't even noticed."

"Oh, I noticed," she said, running her hand along his chin again.

Vaughn's empty stomach suddenly joined the conversation, rumbling loudly.

"I see someone noticed my cooking." She released him and walked toward the kitchenette.

Good thing. Had Angela lingered any longer, she would've known that her cooking wasn't the only thing Vaughn noticed.

He looked toward the bubbling pot. "How could I miss it? That smells delicious. What is it?"

"Chicken stew. I had to scavenge through several bags of the military rations you found before I had enough to make a meal."

"Well, it smells awesome." He gave her a knowing look. "And it can't be any worse than the gruel I've been making."

Angela stepped up to the countertop. "No comment." She grabbed a wooden spoon and began to stir the stew.

Vaughn set bowls and spoons on the table. Then he opened the refrigerator and pulled out two brown bottles. He held up the beers. "Feel up to one?"

Angela nodded enthusiastically.

She had risen another notch in his already high estimation when she'd previously proclaimed her love of all things beer.

Vaughn set the tall bottles next to the bowls.

Angela stepped next to him and ladled generous portions of stew into each bowl. As they sat down, she hoisted questioning eyebrows. "So where have you been for the last couple of hours?"

Vaughn smiled. "I've been working on a little project."

She picked up her spoon and then looked at him with eyebrows that said, "Go ahead."

"Nope, not going to ruin the surprise."

After a long, appraising stare, Angela nodded. "Okay ... for now."

"Is this really necessary?" Angela said as she stumbled over another unseen obstacle. "Wearing a blindfold while walking through post-apocalyptic Tripoli just doesn't seem like a good idea."

"I won't let you fall," Vaughn said. Holding her arm, he steered Angela in a new direction. "Just a few more steps to go."

After dinner, Vaughn had driven her to the port area from their hotel. Before letting Angela out of the car, he had insisted on blind-folding her. From their parking spot, she had only been able to see a very narrow channel of water. However, since donning the blindfold, she estimated they had walked a couple of hundred yards toward the shoreline.

Vaughn released her elbow. She heard him move behind her. Placing both hands on her shoulders, he turned her a few degrees to the right. "That should be perfect."

"Can I look now?"

"Oh! What was I thinking?" Vaughn said with that familiar smile in his voice. He began to fumble with the knots on the blindfold. A moment later, it slipped from her eyes.

Directly across from her lay the most beautiful ship Angela had ever seen. From their observation point behind and right of the ship, she stared, mouth agape, at its eloquent curving lines. They looked almost organic. Windows and hatchways blended so smoothly into its surface that it was difficult to see where one left off and the other began.

"Oh, Vaughn ... It's beautiful."

"It's a mega yacht." He dangled a set of golden keys. "And she's all yours." He pointed at the back of the ship. "See?"

Angela gasped and then laughed. "I can't believe you did that!"

Vaughn moved to stand next to her. His smooth, handsome face sported a huge smile.

On the back of the boat, a squared-off area of slightly different color made it apparent that its original name had been painted over. A new epithet scribed in broad, flowing letters now adorned the ship's aft bulkhead:

Angela's Dream

"I spent the last week cleaning and stocking it." Vaughn pried open her right hand and dropped the keys into it.

Angela just stared at them mutely.

He grabbed her elbow and urged her along. "Come see."

They spent the next hour touring the ship's labyrinthine halls and passageways. Its opulence left her speechless. Angela had no doubt that all of the gold trimmings were exactly that, pure gold.

Vaughn beamed as he guided her into the galley. Judging by its overstocked pantry, he had raided all of the kitchens within twenty miles of the port.

Angela smiled. "Show me the bridge."

Vaughn's grin broadened. "This way, ma'am."

A few minutes later, they emerged from a passageway and stepped onto a high-tech control deck.

"This looks more like the bridge of the Starship Enterprise," Angela said. "How can just the two of us control all this?"

"We don't have to. It's all state-of-the-art. I read an article about this ship a few months ago. Some sheik had commissioned it out of a shipyard in Virginia. It can practically run itself."

Angela nodded appreciably. "I don't see any dinghies. Not every place has a port like this. How are we going to get to shore?"

"We have several boats on-board. They're hidden behind retractable watertight bulkheads." Vaughn held up a finger and then walked toward one of the forward panels. "However, there's an easier way." With an exaggerated flourish, he pressed a big red button.

She felt a clunk through her shoes. Something moved beyond

Vaughn. Outside, below the bridge's front window, a panel had started retracting.

Vaughn pointed at the revealed machine and then held out his hands just as Angela had after she'd stood in the suite. "Ta-da!"

A sleek, gold, twin-engine four-bladed helicopter with retractable landing gear sat on the ship's green and yellow helideck.

Angela clapped and giggled. "I believe I know someone who can fly that thing."

Vaughn laughed and then turned toward the exit. "Follow me. There's one more thing I want to show you."

Several passages and hatches later, they stood before a large, ornately trimmed door. Like a game show model presenting the next big gift, Vaughn held both hands toward the door. "Your quarters, ma'am."

When the doors didn't open, Angela took a tentative step forward. With silent solidity, the large doors parted, sliding left and right.

Vaughn nodded. "Every door in the living quarters is actuated by an RFID tag." He pointed down. "I took the liberty of installing one in each of your shoes."

Testing it, Angela took a backward step. The door silently closed. She stepped forward and they reopened. This time she noticed the interior. It was incredible. A huge chandelier hung from the center of a twenty-foot-high ceiling.

"Are you sure this wasn't a ballroom?"

Vaughn shook his head. "Actually, I think you could play basketball in here. But no, this was the main quarters for the previous owners, although I've added a few personal touches just for you."

"Really? Like what?"

"I modified one of your five walk-in closets."

"Five?!"

Vaughn laughed and walked into the room.

Angela followed him toward one of the closets. There was something odd about its interior. The room beyond the gaping frame had an amber glow.

Vaughn arrived at the doorway first. He turned and looked at her with an expectant gaze. The man looked like he was ready to burst.

Angela gave him a questioning look. "What?"

He waved her over. "Come see."

Angela stepped to the doorway.

She stared in shocked silence, unable to speak. Finally, her voice returned. She turned to Vaughn and pointed into the room. "You did this." It was a statement, not a question. She snickered. "I can't believe you did this!" Then the giggle dissolved into one of her snort storms. "Oh, my God … Where did you find …" She paused and then swept a hand across the entire scene. "… All of it?"

Vaughn was laughing too hard to talk.

Still snorting, Angela stepped through the open door. From floor to ceiling and wall to wall, a maze of yellow plastic hamster tubes filled the garage-sized closet. Within its expansive confines, she eventually spotted all four of the mice. Angela smiled at the largest of the foursome. "Are you having a good time in there, Nate Junior?"

Nate stood rocking in his now stationary exercise wheel, regarding her over twitching whiskers.

Angela turned to Vaughn.

He suddenly looked uncomfortable under the intensity of her stare.

After a moment, she bent over and pulled off one of her shoes. Standing, she held it out to him. With a devilish grin, she said, "Here's your key, Captain. What do you say you bring over a toothbrush, and we call this *our* quarters?"

CHAPTER 35

Vaughn stared at the ornate ceiling. Why had it taken the end of the world for him to find this level of happiness?

Angela's head lay on his chest. Her rhythmic breathing told him she'd fallen asleep.

After she had handed him the shoe, they had walked to the room's massive, satin-clad bed. Their slow, tentative kisses had turned passionate. At first, Vaughn had feared he would hurt her, that she might still be so frail that if he gripped her too tightly, she might break. However, Angela had kissed him hard, had clutched the back of his salt-and-pepper hair with a strength and passion he wouldn't have thought she could muster.

Soon they'd been pawing off clothes, and the room's temperature had seemed to rise by several degrees. Slow, passionate lovemaking had crescendoed into sweaty, fervent thrusting. Finally, they had collapsed into one another.

Presently, Angela began to snore lightly.

Vaughn dragged a violet satin sheet across her. As he stared at Angela's sleeping form, he traced the lines of her face with the fingers of his left hand. They glided frictionlessly across her sweat-glistened skin.

"Where do we go from here?"

Angela's eyes fluttered open. She looked at him for a long moment. Then she gave him a wry smile. "Switzerland."

Vaughn blinked his confusion. Through stitched eyebrows, he said, "What?"

"We need to go to Switzerland. And thanks to you, the first part of that journey will be oh so comfortable." She finished the sentence with a long, contented sigh.

"Switzerland?" He smiled. "Got a hankering for some good chocolate?"

Angela shook her head, and her look suddenly turned serious. "No, that's not it."

"What, then? What's in Switzerland?"

"The center."

"The center of what?"

Angela swept an arm across the sheets in a long, broad arc. "Everything, I think."

"You're not making any sense. Are you still asleep?"

She stared into his eyes intently. "No, Vaughn. Thanks to you, I'm thinking clearer than I have in months." She looked around the room. "And for the first time in a long while, I don't have to worry about how I'm going to live through another day. I can concentrate on tomorrow, but more importantly on what happened two months ago."

A measure of understanding dawned across Vaughn's face. "Okay, but what does Switzerland have to do with the Disappearance?"

Angela sat up and stared at him with her deep, penetrating eyes. "It's the epicenter."

Vaughn shook his head. "I'm sorry, you lost—"

"I saw it," Angela said, cutting him off. Before he could speak, she continued. "I saw the energy wave."

Vaughn nodded. "Yeah. Told me that before."

Angela returned his nod. "Yes, but there are some things I haven't mentioned."

Vaughn raised questioning eyebrows.

"When we passed over the Alps, I couldn't see the wave anymore.

When I reported that to McCree in Mission Control, he told me that we were over the epicenter."

Vaughn nodded again. "So what makes you think it's Switzerland? Why not France?"

"Actually, Captain." She paused and then gave him a meaningful look. "It's *under* both."

Vaughn's eyes widened. "CERN?"

Angela smiled. "Bingo! The fact that the world's largest supercollider just happens to lie at the epicenter of this shit storm strikes me as a little more than coincidence."

Vaughn stared at her for a long moment, mouth agape. Finally, he closed it and then whispered, "Holy shit."

"But there's more." Angela's face darkened. Then she told Vaughn an incredible story about disappearing nukes, gravity wave anomalies, and overflowing lakes and rivers.

Vaughn shook his head. "A gravity flower?"

Angela's eyes cleared, and she focused on him. "Yeah. Looked like a daisy. Big center, long, thin petals."

Vaughn chewed on his cheek for a moment. Finally, he said, "Why didn't you tell me this before?"

Angela pursed her lips. "I thought about it, but you had so many other things going on, I didn't want to add anything else to your plate."

Vaughn nodded thoughtfully and then grinned self-consciously. "Yeah, probably not a bad idea."

"But now that you've nursed me back to health, it's time to find out what happened."

"Okay," Vaughn said. "What do you think we'll find? I mean, what in the hell could they have done at CERN to cause this?"

Angela shook her head. "That's the thing I've been trying to wrap my head around. We weren't doing anything with our supercollider that nature hasn't done millions of times. Cosmic rays regularly collide with far greater energies than we can produce. Then there are the gravity waves. *We* don't even know how to generate them."

The way she emphasized 'we' made Vaughn pause. Then his eyes widened. "You think there's someone else involved!"

Angela nodded and then looked down. "The way the gravity lines matched those rivers …" she said, suddenly sounding defensive. Her eyes raised to meet Vaughn's. "They almost looked like … I don't know … tentacles reaching out for something."

"Reaching out for what?"

"I don't know!" Angela said. Her gaze fell back to the floor.

Vaughn placed a finger under her chin and tilted her head up. "I believe you, Angela."

"Do you, really?"

He nodded. "Yes, of course, I do."

She visibly relaxed. "Thank you."

Vaughn kissed her and then leaned back. "So what do we do next?"

Angela smiled. "Let's go sailing, Captain, get a closer—"

Suddenly, the entire ship rocked as if struck by a huge wave. Then a shadow darkened the room's windows. After exchanging startled glances, Vaughn and Angela ran to the nearest port and threw open its curtains. A torrential downpour fell from a blue sky. Then the strangely confined column of rain moved out to sea, and the sun returned.

Standing naked at the window, the couple exchanged another confused glance. Then a metallic wedge appeared in the sky. As they watched in open-mouthed amazement, an entire supertanker slid into view as it glided northward a thousand feet in the air.

At the image of a million tons of steel flying over their heads, the two of them stepped back from the port.

"What the hell?"

"*Who* the hell?" Angela corrected, but then the floor rocked, and another burst of rain fell across the yacht as the sky darkened again.

They inched back toward the window. Looking up, the couple watched torrents of water pour from the bottom of another tanker as it passed over their new home.

Vaughn pulled away from the porthole and dashed across the room to the other side of the yacht.

Angela followed him.

Reaching the far wall, they eased open the curtain on an opposite-facing window. Three of the crashed supertankers still sat where they had run aground. However, as they watched, first one and then the other two slowly lifted out of the water. Each departure sent another wave racing across the bay. When it reached them, it rocked the yacht just as the first two had.

Vaughn glanced down at the floor of their ship. Then he cast a horrified look at Angela. "We have to get out of here!" He pointed at the deck. "This ship could be next!"

Angela shook her head and pointed through the open curtains. "Whatever or whoever is moving those ships is being very selective. Look, the wooden boats haven't budged."

She was right. Several other vessels remained. Some were splintered wrecks, but others bobbed in the turbulent wake of the departed tankers.

Vaughn was suddenly thankful for their ship's fiberglass hull. There had been another luxury liner in the harbor, a steel-hulled monstrosity. Just as he had the thought, the other mega yacht launched skyward.

Suddenly, at the far side of the bay, the northmost burned-out and warped petroleum reservoir began to rise from the tank farm. Then its neighbors began to ascend as well.

Vaughn and Angela exchanged frightened glances as they stepped onto the room's balcony. Peering naked from beneath its overhanging awning, they watched in shocked silence as the surreal fleet of flying steel ships and twisted tanks sped toward the northern horizon.

"Oh shit!" Vaughn pointed at the line. "It's one of the petals."

Angela nodded. "The gravity flower." Goosebumps rose on her skin.

Vaughn felt a shiver run down her body. He squeezed her tightly and then tilted his head toward the surreal line.

"That shouldn't be too hard to follow."

Angela looked at him and then grinned. "What are you waiting for, Captain?"

Find Out What Happens Next!

Multitude: Dimension Space Book Two
Now Available!

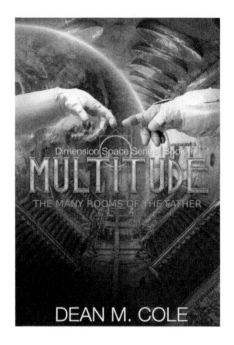

Get Multitude Now!
deanmcole.com/multitude

Multitude: Dimension Space Book Two
Now Available!

**Find the links to Multitude on your favorite bookseller site by
visiting:
deanmcole.com/multitude**

When an alien attack rips a hole in spacetime, can humanity's last two navigate looping dimensions to reverse the event and return life to the planet? Following the incredible events of *Solitude*, Vaughn and Angela must probe the depths of space and time to unravel and perhaps even reverse the enigma of humanity's disappearance. But first, they must get past themselves. If you enjoyed *Solitude*, you'll love the action and plot twists in this apocalyptic epic.

Vaughn had visions of plying the seven seas with Angela at his side. Then she and fate crapped all over his plans. Bent on discovering the truth about what happened to humanity and the rest of the world's life, Angela drags a less than willing Vaughn across the Mediterranean and into central Europe. However, even the overhead presence of a line of levitating steel structures and ships couldn't prepare them for what lied ahead. The size and scale of what they find in Geneva rocks them to their cores.

Angela and Vaughn fall into the center of a world-consuming machine. While struggling to survive, they wander through a looping chain of utterly alien lands. When they finally deduce the true nature of their situation, Angela discovers a potential way out, not just for her and Vaughn but all of Earth's life.

Angela can bring back the whole of the human race!

But only if she and Vaughn can survive the journey home.

Find Out What Happens. Scroll Up, And Order Your Copy Today!

Visit deanmcole.com/multitude to Order Your Copy Today!

Thank you for reading Solitude: Dimension Space Book One!

Dear Reader,

I hope you enjoyed *Solitude*. Thanks for riding along with me on this journey.

I appreciate your feedback. Actually, you are the reason I develop these apocalyptic tales. While I work on my next novel, I'd love to hear from you. Tell me what you liked, what you loved, even what you hated. You can email me at dean@deanmcole.com and visit me on the web at www.deanmcole.com.

Finally, I need to ask a favor. If you're so inclined, I'd truly appreciate a review of *Solitude*. In this day of e-marketing, you have the power to make or break a book. Please post a review for *Solitude* to its page on your favorite book retailer's website.

Thank you so much for reading *Solitude: Dimension Space Book One* and for being my copilot on this adventure. Don't forget to follow me on your favorite site by clicking the appropriate links on the About the Author page.

Fly safe!

Dean M. Cole

Sector 64: Sneak Peek
The *Sector 64* Timeline
1947 - *First Contact a Sector 64 Prequel Novella*
Today - *Ambush* - Book One of the *Sector 64* Duology
Tomorrow - *Retribution* - Book Two of the *Sector 64* Duology

Find links to all the Sector 64 books on your favorite bookseller's
site by visiting:
deanmcole.com/sector 64

Seventy years after the events of *First Contact*, most of humanity is completely unaware of the coming changes. We live and die believing we are alone. In 2017, Air Force fighter pilots Jake Giard and Sandra Fitzpatrick discover the decades-old secret project to integrate Earth into a galactic government, but then the plot renders our world a disposable pawn. An interstellar war spills onto our shores, plunging the planet into an otherworldly post-apocalyptic hell. Can Jake and Sandy save humanity from extinction? If you like action-packed, page-turning novels, then you'll love the electrifying action in this apocalyptic thriller.

SECTOR 64: AMBUSH SNEAK PEEK

Captain Sandra Fitzpatrick's steady rhythmic breathing, a technique born through years of cardio training, belied the horror gripping her soul. The teddy bear, oh God, the teddy bear. An image she couldn't shake, the vision would haunt her for the rest of her days.

Earlier, while jogging toward the distant terminal building, Sandy came across a still idling airport transfer bus. Hoping to use it to expedite the crossing, she peered into its closed glass doors. In spite of the eastern glow of the coming sunrise, she couldn't discern details through its dirty windows. However, the bus looked empty.

Jamming her fingers into the rubber gap between the panels, Sandy tried to pry the split glass doors apart. After a fruitless, half-minute struggle, she finally noticed a backlit, recessed emergency-release button left of the door. Activating it, Sandy heard a short blast of compressed air. She jumped as the doors popped two inches out of their opening and then parted, each sliding in opposite directions.

"Hello?"

No reply rose above the bus's droning diesel engine.

She took a tentative step into the opening. "Is anybody in here?"

Standing half in the doorway, Sandy screamed as two strong hands, squeezing from both sides, grasped her shoulders. Another blast of compressed air burped from under the bus, and the door trying to close on her retracted.

"Shit!" Sandy kicked the right panel of the retreating glass door and shook her head. Keep it together, Captain Fitzpatrick. She stepped all the way into the bus, and its doors slid closed. Air-conditioner blower noise replaced the engine's. Getting over her skittishness, she stepped into the driver's compartment. In the dawn's wan light, the seat looked empty. Groping in the darkness, Sandy worked her way closer. A few awkward seconds later, she finally dropped into it.

Something was wrong with the seat. It felt like someone had left a towel or cloth on it. Running her fingers across the material's loose, rippled surface, Sandy froze, remembering what she saw while peering down into the empty F-18's cockpit. An uncomfortable hard object dug into her right thigh. Wide-eyed in the dark, she leaned left and pulled it out from under her leg. Breathlessly holding the object up, she studied its angular silhouette against the deep turquoise hue of the early morning sky. A round ball on one end and a long rod on the other, it felt metallic. With her opposite hand, she blindly searched the instrument panel for a light switch. A huge windshield wiper arm sparked to life, its dry, rubber blade chattering against the dirty glass. Another switch later, the bus's cabin lit up like an exam room. Sandy blinked and squinted as the sudden blast of light burned her dark adapted eyes.

Finally able to see, she squinted at the device in her hand. Struggling not to scream, Sandy dropped the artificial hip. Jumping to her feet, she looked down to see a bus driver's uniform strewn across the compartment. While the driver's shirt was on the floor, the pants, belt still buckled, lay in the seat. She saw several shiny objects littering the interior of the pants. Bending, she looked closer. In a sudden epiphany, she recognized the parts as titanium screws.

What the hell could do that? She looked from the strewn articles, to the screws, and finally to the artificial hip where it had landed next to her right foot. Why isn't there any blood?

Backing away in shocked dismay, Sandy stumbled. Regaining her footing in the bus's central corridor, she looked aft and froze. Visible in the cabin's stark, white light, emptied articles of clothing littered the entire bus.

A glint of light drew her attention to one of the front left seats. A teddy bear's half-open, glass-bead eyes peered from under a vacated toddler's outfit. On the narrow bench, a little girl's tiny white and yellow dress sat between piled clothes of an apparent mother and father. Worn in anticipation of an early morning departure to some exciting destination, the tiny girl's yellow ribbons and pink bows now lay strewn about her emptied clothes.

Sandy had a mental image of the parents casting horrified glances at the monstrosity hovering overhead while they tried to calm their frightened little girl. But in Sandy's vision, she and Jake were the anxious couple. The child between them was the little girl with golden locks that she'd often imagined would grace their future. Unconsciously, her hand drifted to the point where the baby bump would soon show.

As a tear threatened to breach the levee of her lower eyelid, Sandy extended a trembling hand toward the stuffed animal. After a short hesitation, she caressed its furry belly.

The teddy bear's lifeless, doll-like eyes snapped wide open. "Are you my mommy?"

Find out why this happened and what's next!

Find links to all the Sector 64 books on your favorite bookseller's site by visiting:
deanmcole.com/sector 64

ABOUT THE AUTHOR

Amazon Top 20 and Audible Top 10 Author Dean M. Cole, a retired combat helicopter pilot and airline pilot, has penned multiple award-winning apocalyptic tales. Solitude, book one of Dimension Space, won the 2018 ABR Listeners Choice Award for Best Science Fiction. Previously, IndieReader named Dean's first full-length novel, Sector 64: Ambush, to their Best of 2014 list. His sixth book, Amplitude, the third Dimension Space novel, is now available.

Follow Dean on BookBub!
bookbub.com/authors/dean-m-cole

For More Information:
www.deanmcole.com
dean@deanmcole.com

facebook.com/authordeanmcole
twitter.com/deanmcole
instagram.com/deanmcole

Printed in Great Britain
by Amazon

78196477R00181